UNINTENDED TARGET

A Novel

BOOK ONE OF THE UNINTENDED SERIES

D.L. Wood

UNINTENDED TARGET
Book One of the Unintended Series

ISBN-13: 978-1-5171-7097-4
ISBN-10: 1-5171-7097-4

Library of Congress Control Number: 2015915884
CreateSpace Independent Publishing Platform, North Charleston, SC
First Edition
Printed in the U.S.A.

D.L. Wood
dlwoodonline.com
Huntsville, Alabama

FOR

Ron, Caroline, and Kathleen,
And my parents—
for making me believe I could do anything I put my mind to.
Thank you Lord, for allowing me to do this.
To you be the glory.

ONE

"He's done it again," groaned Chloe McConnaughey, her cell held to ear by her shoulder as she pulled one final pair of shorts out of her dresser. "Tate knew that I had to leave by 3:30 at the latest. I sent him a text. I know he got it," she said, crossing her bedroom to the duffel bag sitting on her four-poster bed and tossing in the shorts.

Her best friend's voice rang sympathetically out of the phone. "There's another flight out tomorrow," offered Izzie Morales hesitantly.

Chloe zipped up the bag. "I know," she said sadly. "But, that isn't the point. As usual, it's all about Tate. It doesn't matter to him that I'm supposed to be landing on St. Gideon in six hours. What does an assignment in the Caribbean matter when your estranged brother decides it's time to finally get together?"

"Estranged is a bit of a stretch, don't you think?" Izzie asked.

"It's been three months. No texts. No calls. Nothing," Chloe replied, turning to sit on the bed.

"You know Tate. He gets like this. He doesn't mean anything by it. He just got . . . distracted," Izzie offered.

"For three months?"

Izzie changed gears. "Well, it's only 3:00—maybe he'll show."

"And we'll have, what, like thirty minutes before I have to go?" Chloe grunted in frustration. "What's the point?"

"Come on," Izzie said, "The point is, maybe this gets repaired."

Chloe sighed. "I know. I know," she said resignedly. "That's why I'm waiting it out." She paused. "He said he had news he didn't want to share over the phone. Seriously, what kind of news can't you share over the phone?"

"Maybe it's so good that he just has to tell you in person," Izzie suggested hopefully.

"Or maybe it's—'I've been fired again, and I need a place to crash.'"

"Think positively," Izzie encouraged, and Chloe heard a faint tap-tapping in the receiver. She pictured her friend on the other side of Atlanta, drumming a perfectly manicured, red-tipped finger on a nearby surface, her long, pitch-colored hair hanging in straight, silky swaths on either side of her face.

"He'll probably pull up any minute, dying to see you," Izzie urged. "And if he's late, you can reschedule your flight for tomorrow. Perk of having your boss as your best friend. I'll authorize the magazine to pay for the ticket change. Unavoidable family emergency, right?"

Chloe sighed again, picked up the duffel bag and started down the hall of her two-bedroom rental. "I just wish it wasn't this hard." The distance between them hadn't been her choice and she hated it. "Ten to one he calls to say he's had a change of plans, too busy with work, can't make it."

"He won't," replied Izzie.

With a thud, Chloe dropped the bag onto the kitchen floor by the door to the garage, trading it for half a glass of merlot perched on the counter. She took a small sip. "Don't underestimate him. His over-achievement extends to every part of his life, including his ability to disappoint."

"Ouch." Izzie paused. "You know, Chlo, it's just the job."

"I have a job. And somehow I manage to answer my calls."

"But your schedule's a little more your own, right? Pressure-wise I think he's got a little bit more to worry about."

Chloe rolled her eyes. "Nice try. But he manages tech security at an investment firm, not the White House. It's the same thing every time. He's totally consumed."

"Well, speaking as your editor, being a *little* consumed by your job is not always a bad thing."

"Ha-ha."

"What's important is that he's trying to reconnect now."

Chloe brushed at a dust bunny clinging to her white tee shirt, flicking it to the floor. "What if he really has lost this job? It took him two years after the lawsuit to find this one."

"Look, maybe it's a promotion. Maybe he got a bonus, and he's finally setting you up. Hey, maybe he's already bought you that mansion in Ansley Park . . ."

"I don't *need* him to set me up—I'm not eight years old anymore. I'm fine now. I wish he'd just drop the 'big-brother-takes-care-of-wounded-little-sister' thing. He's the wounded one."

"You know, if you don't lighten up a bit, it may be another three months before he comes back to see you."

"One more day and he wouldn't have caught me at all."

Izzie groaned jealously. "It's not fair that you get to go and I have to stay. It's supposed to be thirty-nine and rainy in Atlanta for, like, the next month."

"So come along."

"If only. You know I can't. Zach's got his school play next weekend. And Dan would kill me if I left him with Anna for more than a couple days right now." A squeal sounded on Izzie's end. "Uggggh. I think Anna just bit Zach again. I've gotta go. Don't forget to call me tomorrow and let me know how it went with big brother."

"Bigger by just three minutes," she quickly pointed out. "And I'll try to text you between massages in the beach-side cabana."

Izzie groaned again, drowning out another squeal in the background. "You're sick."

"It's a gift," Chloe retorted impishly before hanging up.

Chloe stared down at the duffel and, next to it, the special backpack holding her photography equipment. She double-checked the *Terra Traveler* I.D. tags on both and found all her information still legible and secure. "Now what?" she muttered.

Her stomach rumbled, reminding her that, with all the packing and preparation for leaving the house for two weeks, she had forgotten to eat. Rummaging through the fridge, she found a two-day old container of Chinese take-out. Tate absolutely hated Chinese food. She loved it. Her mouth curved at the edges as she shut the refrigerator door. *And that's the least of our differences.*

Leaning against the counter, she cracked open the container and used her chopsticks to pluck julienne carrots out of her sweet and sour chicken. *Too bad Jonah's not here,* she thought, dropping the orange slivers distastefully into the sink. *Crazy dog eats anything. Would've scarfed them down in half a second.* But the golden retriever that was her only roommate was bunking at the kennel now. She missed him already.

She felt bad about leaving him for two whole weeks. Usually her trips as a travel journalist for *Terra Traveler* were much shorter, but she'd tacked on some vacation time to this one in order to do some work on her personal book project. She wished she had someone she could leave him with, but Izzie was her only close friend, and she had her hands full with her kids.

Jonah would definitely be easier than those two, she thought with a smile. He definitely had been the easiest and most dependable roommate she'd ever had—and the only male that had never let her down. A loyal friend through a bad patch of three lousy boyfriends. The last of them consumed twelve months of her life before taking her "ring-shopping," only to announce the next day that he was leaving her for his ex. It had taken six months, dozens of amateur therapy sessions with Izzie and exceeding the limit on her VISA more than once to get over that one. After that she'd sworn off men for the foreseeable future, except for Jonah of course, which, actually, he seemed quite pleased about.

She shoveled in the last few bites of fried rice, then tossed the box into the trash. *Come to think of it*, she considered as she headed for the living room, *Tate'll be the first man to step inside this house in almost a year*. She wasn't sure whether that was empowering or pathetic.

"Not going there," she told herself, forcing her train of thought instead to the sunny beaches of St. Gideon. The all-expenses paid jaunts were the only real perks of her job as a staff journalist with *Terra Traveler*, an online travel magazine based out of Atlanta. They were also the only reason she'd stayed on for the last four years despite her abysmal pay. Photography, her real passion, had never even paid the grocery bill, much less the rent. Often times the trips offered some truly unique spots to shoot in. Odd little places like the "World's Largest Tree House," tucked away in the Smoky Mountains, or the home of the largest outdoor collection of ice sculptures in a tiny town in Iceland. And sometimes she caught a real gem, like this trip to the Caribbean. Sun, sand, and separation from everything stressful. For two whole weeks.

The thought of being stress-free reminded her that at this particular moment, she wasn't. Frustration flared as she thought of Tate's text just an hour before:

Flying in tonite. Ur place @ 2. Big news. See u then.

Typical Tate. No advance warning. No, *"I'm sorry I haven't returned a single call in three months"* or *"Surprise, I haven't fallen off the face of the earth. Wanna get together?"* Just a demand.

A familiar knot of resentment tightened in her chest as she took her wine into the living room, turned up Adele on the stereo and plopped onto a slipcovered couch facing the fire. Several dog-eared books were stacked near the armrest, and she pushed them aside to make room as she sank into the loosely stuffed cushions. She drew her favorite quilt around her, a mismatched pink and beige patchwork that melded perfectly with the hodgepodge of antique and shabby chic furnishings that filled the room.

What do you say to a brother who by all appearances has intentionally ignored you for months? It's one thing for two friends to become engrossed in their own lives and lose track of each other for a while. It's something else altogether when your twin brother doesn't return your calls. He hadn't been ill, although that had been her first thought. After the first few weeks she got a text from him saying, *sorry, so busy, talk to u ltr.* So she had called his office just to make sure he was still going in. He was. He didn't take her call that day either.

She tried to remember how many times she'd heard "big news" from Tate before, but quickly realized she'd lost count years ago. A pang of pity slipped in beside the frustration, wearing away at its edges.

She set her goblet down on the end table beside a framed picture of Tate. In many respects it might as well have been a mirror. They shared the same large amber eyes and tawny hair, though she let her loose curls grow to just below her narrow shoulders. Their oval faces and fair skin could've been photocopied they were so similar. But he was taller and stockier, significantly out-sizing her petite, five foot four frame. She ran a finger along the faint, half-inch scar just below her chin that also differentiated them. He'd given her that in a particularly fierce game of keep-away when they were six. Later, disappointed that she had an identifying mark he didn't, he had unsuccessfully tried duplicating the scar by giving himself a nasty paper cut. In her teenage years she'd detested the thin, raised line, but now she rubbed it fondly, feeling that in some small, strange way it linked her to him.

He had broken her heart more than a little, the way he'd shut her out since taking the position at Inverse Financial nearly a year ago. He'd always been the type to throw himself completely into what he was doing, but this time he'd taken his devotion to a new high, allowing it to alienate everyone and everything in his life.

It hadn't always been that way. At least not with her. They'd grown up close, always each other's best friend and champion. Each other's only champion, really. It was how they survived the day after their eighth birthday when their father, a small-time attorney, ran off to North Carolina with the office copy lady. That was when Tate had snuck into their mother's bedroom, found a half-used box of Kleenex and brought it to Chloe as she hid behind the winter clothes in her closet. *I'll always take care of you, Chlo. Don't cry. I'm big enough to take care of both of us.* He'd said it with so much conviction that she'd believed him.

Together they'd gotten through the day nine months after that when the divorce settlement forced them out of their two-story Colonial into an orange rancher in the projects. Together they weathered their mother's alcoholism that didn't make her mean, just tragic, and finally, just dead, forcing them into foster homes. And though they didn't find any love there, they did manage to stay together for the year and a half till they turned eighteen.

Then he went to Georgia Tech on a scholarship and she, still at a loss for what she wanted to do in life, took odd jobs in the city. The teeny one bedroom apartment they shared seemed like their very own castle. After a couple of years, he convinced her she was going nowhere without a degree, so she started at the University of Georgia. For the first time they were separated. But Athens was only a couple hours away and he visited when he could and still paid for everything financial aid didn't. She'd tried to convince him she could make it on her own, but he never listened, still determined to be the provider their father had never been.

When she graduated, she moved back to Atlanta with her journalism degree under her belt and started out as a copy editor for a local events magazine. Tate got his masters in computer engineering at the same time and snagged a highly competitive job as a software designer for an up-and-coming software development company. It didn't take long for them to recognize Tate's brilliance at anything with code, and the promotions seemed to come one after the other.

Things had been so good then. They were both happy, both

making money, though she was only making a little and he, more and more as time went by. The photo in her hands had been taken back then, when the world was his for the taking. Before it all fell apart for him with that one twist of fate that had ruined everything—

Stop, she told herself, shaking off the unpleasant memory. The whole episode had nearly killed Tate, and she didn't like to dwell on it. It had left him practically suicidal until, finally, this Inverse job came along. When it did, she thought that everything would get better, that things would just go back to normal. But they didn't. Instead Tate had just slowly disappeared from her life, consumed by making his career work . . .

She brushed his frozen smile with her fingers. Affection and pity and a need for the only person who had ever made her feel like she was a part of something special swelled, finally beating out the aggravation she had been indulging. As she set the frame back on the table, her phone rang.

Speak of the devil, she thought, smiling as she reached for her cell. "Hello?"

A deep, tentative voice that did not belong to her brother answered.

* * * * *

It never ceased to amaze him how death could be so close to a person without them sensing it at all. Four hours had passed and she hadn't noticed a thing. It was dark now, and rain that was turning to sleet ticked steadily on the car, draping him in a curtain of sound as he watched her vague grey shadow float back and forth against the glow of her drawn Roman blinds. He was invisible here, hunkered down across the street behind the tinted windows of his dark Chevy Impala, swathed in the added darkness of the thick oaks lining the neighbor's yard.

Invisible eyes watching. Waiting.

Watch. Wait. Simple enough instructions. But more were coming. Out of habit he felt the Glock cradled in his jacket and fleetingly wondered *why* he was watching her, before quickly realizing he didn't care. He wasn't paid to wonder.

He was just a hired gun. A temporary fix until the big guns arrived. But, even so . . .

He scanned the yard. The dog was gone. She was completely

alone. *It would be, oh, so easy.*

But he was being paid to watch. Nothing more.

Her shadow danced incessantly from one end of the room to the other. Apparently the news had her pacing.

What would she do if she knew she was one phone call away from never making a shadow dance again?

TWO

One hundred and two miles an hour. 102. It was how fast the trooper that called her that night estimated Tate had been driving. One hundred and two, flying down Miami's I-95, when he plowed into a divider, nearly splitting the car in two. Chloe couldn't rid herself of that image. It crept into every part of her life—her dreams, while she ate, in the shower. Now it tortured her here, as she stared into the gray, slushy streets of Atlanta from the window of Izzie's twenty-first floor office. She hadn't wanted to know the details of the crash that had killed Tate, hadn't looked at any pictures of the wreckage. But the scene her imagination conjured haunted her just the same, rolling around in her head relentlessly since she got the call two weeks ago.

In these moments she tried to follow Izzie's advice and think on the things that were good and whole about Tate. But things that started out good and whole in her life had always ended up bad and broken, and so it was with her remembering. When she drifted to the happiest time in their lives, when his programming career was at its height, it inevitably led her to what had come next.

It had started with an argument with the software company he was working for about the rights to a product design and ended in his being fired. For four months Tate laid around his apartment in his underwear, barking at lawyers and fixating on his million-dollar lawsuit that was ultimately dismissed before it even got started, but not before eating up most of his savings. Then the depression set in. One day she went to his place, and he was just gone. No note, no call, nothing. She panicked for a good month before finally accepting he just didn't want to be found. It was the first time in her life she'd ever felt completely alone. Alone and as if half of her was missing.

Then one day nearly eight months later, he just showed up. For a week he camped out on her sofa, going on and on about how he'd been living in Silicon Valley picking up odd programming jobs, and how he was worth so much more than they were paying him. Just glad to have him back, she eagerly chalked his heartless disappearance up to stress and let herself just be happy that things were going to be normal again. But then he left again, just as suddenly as before, that time for a whole year. The next time she saw him he was curled up in a ball, asleep on her front step one chilly October night, completely wasted and shaking in his own sweat. She took him in, held his head over the toilet, forced him into rehab, and brought him back from the dead. But depression still loomed, and they had both been one frayed strand away from the end of their ropes when Inverse called and changed everything.

A friend of a friend who had once worked with Tate knew he was exceptional and put the head of the Miami investment firm onto him. They had flown Tate down for a couple of interviews and even brought Chloe down in the private jet for wining and dining one weekend. She'd been as impressed as Tate. The offer for the position as the firm's technology security director was a godsend, and Tate swore it was the lottery ticket he had been waiting for. Even as she'd protested, he'd promised that within a couple of years he would have her so "set up" that she would be able to do her own photography full time or maybe just retire. Whatever she wanted.

But after he moved, he evaporated from her life again. He had only flown back to Atlanta once, and even then he spent the entire weekend on the phone and computer, unable to make the only dinner out they'd planned. That was the last time she'd seen him. She had tried flying to him, but he was always too busy to play host. The gulf between them hurt, and she had routinely waffled between missing him and being furious with him. But the eight-year-old in her had concluded that if her brother had finally found a place to use his amazing talents and achieve the success he'd always craved, she should be happy for him—even if he handled it badly. But now there was no one to be angry with, or to miss. Like everyone else, he was just gone.

Behind her, Izzie ended the heated discussion she had been carrying on by slapping the phone down and promptly lighting a cigarette. "That kid's the laziest fact-checker I've ever seen. He's going to get me sued if I'm not careful. Caught him quoting a movie star about some resort his agent says he's never laid eyes on. Third unfounded attribution from this guy in . . ." She stopped, taking in the far-away quality of Chloe's gaze. "Hey, hon', you okay?"

Massaging her temples as if erasing the thoughts, Chloe turned from the window. "How many times do I have to tell you those things will kill you?" she nagged, nodding at the cigarette.

Izzie blew out a curl of smoke and shrugged. "It's my one vice. Besides, you've got to go some . . . how." She stumbled over the last bit, apparently regretting her words. She wrinkled her nose apologetically. "Sorry."

Chloe dropped onto the black leather couch, drew her knees to her chest and waved off the comment. "It's okay."

Izzie ran her manicured fingers along the smoothed hair gathered in a tight bun at the base of her neck. Narrow black glasses stylishly accented her heart-shaped face. Olive-skinned hands stretched from her shirt cuffs, one of which brought the slender cigarette to her mouth again. She exhaled thoughtfully. "So you really think you're ready to come back to work?"

Chloe nodded. "It's too hard being in this city when he's gone. Too many memories. I actually drove by our old house. The one we lived in with . . . well, the one we lived in before our father left." With obvious strain she slid her hands over her head, pulled her hair back in a knot and held it there. "I just need to not be here."

Izzie leaned over her glass desk and crossed her arms. "Come stay with me. You don't have to be alone. The kids would love it. A perpetual sleepover with Aunt Chloe."

Chloe smiled and shook her head. "I can't. But thanks. Really. It just wouldn't change anything."

It wouldn't stop the memories from coming. Not the memories of Tate. Not of her dead mother. Not of her father who, after nearly twenty-five years of silence, would be more difficult to connect with than the other two. Tears pooled in Chloe's well-worn eyes. *Every person who was supposed to give me something to belong to in this world has left me. And all this city does is remind me of that.* She swallowed hard and kept talking. "Besides, I have to get back to my life. The world doesn't stop turning because of my personal tragedy."

"You know," Izzie started, toying distractedly with a pencil, "you could come with me tonight. Might be good for you to be around other people. You'd know some of them. They came to your house—"

"Look, your friends were great, really," Chloe interrupted gently, "and I appreciate everything your church did—my fridge has never had this much food in it—but, honestly, if God wanted to help me out, it would've been great if he'd jumped in before now." She stopped, hoping she hadn't insulted her friend. "The best thing for me right now is to get to St. Gideon. It's only for a couple of weeks," Chloe continued. "If I'm wrong about needing to be away, there's no harm done. Either way, the magazine gets its article."

"I don't care about the article, Chloe."

She smiled wistfully at her friend. "I know. But I *really* need you to let me do this. It's time. I want to go."

Several moments passed as Izzie absentmindedly tapped ashes into a tray beside her phone while staring into Chloe's gaze, appraising her. In the end she just nodded.

Ten minutes later, zipping down Peachtree Avenue, Chloe fumbled with the presets on her radio until hitting a Maroon Five tune mid-stream. She turned it up and eased back into her seat. The music eased her tension, and she began making mental preparations for the trip and work ahead of her. Halfway home she realized that for the first time in weeks she had gone almost five minutes without the car crash playing out in her head. And for that small span of time, it had been just the tiniest bit easier to breathe.

* * * * *

Five cars back a beige rental discreetly followed Chloe's white Honda Civic. The dark-haired driver stared intently at the tail of her car, shuffling between lanes to keep up without being noticed. When his cell rang, he answered, never slowing down as he followed her onto the side street leading home.

THREE

Three thousand feet above the earth, Chloe peered out one side of the plane carrying her and two dozen others to the only airport on St. Gideon. From that height, the island resembled aerial photos of the slightly larger St. Lucia or Barbados that one might find plastered on a travel agency's wall. Like many of the Caribbean islands, St. Gideon was nearly a continent unto itself, managing to squeeze almost every kind of terrain into its mere one hundred twenty square miles. Dark green, rain-forested mountains towered in its center, sloping into lighter green hills and then into the lowlands that stretched into sandy beaches dipping beneath the water's surface. On one side a large rocky plateau dropped hard and steep, straight into the waiting sea.

Countless inlets made for a jagged natural coastline marked by fishing docks, marinas, and ports. Villages and tourist resorts dotted the entire landscape. The bustling hub of it all was Binghamton, the island capital on the south shore. Though a metropolis by island standards, it boasted a population of a mere twelve thousand.

The moment Chloe stepped out of the plane and onto the tarmac she knew two weeks on St. Gideon wouldn't be enough. Sizzling sunlight engulfed her. A cool, salty breeze whipped her hair around her face, leaving her both warmed and invigorated after the lengthy flight. She easily navigated the airport's single terminal and within twenty minutes was in the back of a white-and-black checkered cab driving down Binghamton's main thoroughfare. The cab had none of the stale, sweaty smells commonly found in its large city counterparts, but instead smelled only of salt and sea and faintly of citrus, owing to the wisps of scented smoke rising from an incense stick balanced on the dash beside Tomas, the cab's balding, dark-skinned driver. He grinned at her with a large smile that showcased his crooked teeth and, upon learning it was her first trip to the island, enthusiastically became her own private tour guide, pointing out shops, landmarks, restaurants, and must-sees as they bounced down the potholed two-lane road that coursed along the coast.

On her right, Binghamton's modest skyline scrolled by, primarily consisting of one and two story buildings offering flashes of vibrant pink, yellow, and blue cleanly outlined in stark white trim. The tallest structures were the hotels, a few of them uninteresting copies of sister hotels in every other part of the world, but many designed with a tropical flair. Grand arches. Stucco. Palms lining cobblestone drives. Sea grass and thatch. Tiki-torches. One had attendants in red-and-green tropical print shirts with spotless white pants and spotless white leather shoes to match. Another piped jovial steel-drum calypso over its courtyard that drifted into the street and right into Chloe's cab.

Pedestrians of all colors, shapes and sizes piddled toward their destinations. Some toted chunky shopping bags; others towed children who were laughing and darting around one another. Chloe thought she could make out the locals: those wearing loose, airy cotton clothing, and leather-strapped sandals, flip-flops, or no shoes at all. She put her money on the tourists being the ones sporting plaid shorts and caps, cameras and tennis shoes. Regardless, they all seemed to be smiling, all seemingly content going about their business, satisfied with where they found themselves in the world. *Why can't that be me?* she wondered. It was more a hope than a lament, and Chloe realized that somehow she was strangely reassured by the sight, by the notion that somewhere, in some person, contentment existed.

Through the opposite windows she gazed on miles of outstretched ocean. Crystalline swells bashed rocky outcroppings and lapped up on brown sugar sand, foamy and wet, delighting the toes of beach-walkers and evoking happy shouts from youngsters filling their plastic pails. At the wide expanse of New Compton Bay, home to several marinas, sails flapped and horns sounded across the slips. Somewhere in the sky above her, gulls squawked.

She pushed her face through the open window to take in the

rushing wind. She tasted brine. *Brine laced with freedom*, she thought. This place was everything Atlanta was not. No Tate. No ghosts of a mother beaten down by life or a father who didn't care enough to try to love her. No well-intentioned friends. No pressure. No nothing. Just . . . new.

"I've changed my mind," she blurted, leaning over the front seat. "Do you know a rental office we could run by?"

He did, and at Ocean Cap Realty, Anna Baptiste, a woman with flawless umber skin and hip-length braided hair helped her cancel her hotel reservation. In English seasoned with more than a little Island Creole, she described Chloe's rental options. Her mellow words rolled off her tongue, in almost hypnotic fashion.

"Dis one is available for two weeks."

"Do you have anything that's available indefinitely?"

She tapped on the computer keyboard. "Well now," she said, almost surprised, "seems tha' we do."

Half an hour later, Chloe left Ocean Cap Realty the proud month-to-month lessee of a seaside cottage just outside Binghamton. It was impulsive. Fiscally irresponsible. A career killer. An impractical departure from the life she owned. And it was perfect.

Not once as she congratulated herself on her perfectly courageous break from reality did she happen to notice the vehicle tailing her three cars back.

FOUR

126 Edwards Street. The address echoed in Korrigan's mind as he pulled onto the quiet drive nestled in the heart of one of Atlanta's tucked away downtown neighborhoods. At six at night it was already dark, the blackness cut only by pockets of light from street lamps sparsely lining the road. Ancient oaks towered above even the tallest of the ivy draped brick homes, most of which were red, although several had been painted white or some other classic shade as part of the area's restoration.

He slowed to a crawl as he came upon it, the white one-story with green shutters. The long porch displayed concrete planters, filled with struggling yellow and purple pansies. Burgeoning hollies threatened to overtake the windows, already partially obscuring the sills. A stone path led through the brown Bermuda grass to the front steps. A wrought iron fence encircled the backyard and served as a trellis for the dormant rose bushes along its length.

It was charming, but had an unmistakable sense of neglect about it. Baseball sized patches in the paint showed through to raw wood. Two ugly cracks snaked across the panes of the front bay window. At one corner, a section of gutter sagged sadly below the roofline. Ms. McConnaughey's landlord was apparently too busy or too cheap to be diligent about upkeep.

Korrigan turned into the pebbled driveway, followed it to its end behind the house and parked. A quick glance in the rear view mirror confirmed his cap was on straight, his dark hair tucked neatly beneath it. Out of habit, he felt for the weapon beneath his grey coveralls, then grabbed the air-pump insecticide dispenser off the passenger seat and tucked it under his arm. He stepped out, confident that the combination of a uniform, equipment and a magnetic "T&B Exterminators, Inc." sign slapped on the SUV's side would lead nosy neighbors to believe he was simply a bug-man finishing up a late afternoon appointment.

Ten quick strides and he was at the back door. Kneeling down, he retrieved a small black case from his jacket pocket, opened it, and selected the middle of five short-handled, metal picks. He inserted the tiny tool into the keyhole and maneuvered it expertly back and forth until he heard a click, then slipped inside.

The house was quiet and dark. Korrigan slipped a pencil flashlight from his back pocket and, after drawing the blinds, flicked it on. He stood just inside a buttery-yellow kitchen that was no doubt obnoxiously cheery in daylight. A weathered French country dining set was centered in front of the window overlooking the backyard. A ceramic bowl on the floor cradled several nuggets of old dog food.

He set to work immediately, searching drawers, cabinets, and anything else that seemed a plausible hiding place. He pulled the backs off of framed photographs and checked behind artwork on the walls. He removed cushions, then replaced them; unscrewed the bottoms of lamps, then re-tightened them. Nothing. No hard paperwork or documentation of any kind. Her laptop was gone, presumably with her. He found a few random memory cards and flash drives in a desk drawer and scooped them up. He doubted they were what he wanted, though, left out like this, unhidden. Probably just more of her regular photography.

Under the four-poster bed in the master bedroom he found tattered pillows, outdated magazines, and lots of dust. The closet contained more than a dozen shoeboxes. In one he found a single strand of pearls and two hundred dollars in bills of various denominations, possibly hidden for safekeeping by McConnaughey before her flight to St. Gideon earlier that day. He replaced the box, then checked the chest at the foot of the bed. The pine armoire. The dresser. Still nothing.

He checked his watch. Nearly seven. Staying more than an hour was imprudent. Leaving the house looking no worse for his having been there, he locked up behind him and headed back to his SUV. As he started to slide into the driver's seat, he heard someone call out, "Excuse me . . . young man?"

Korrigan whipped around to see an elderly woman in a pink-flowered housedress and well-worn slippers padding over to him from the house across the street. She waved weakly at him as she started up McConnaughey's short driveway and called out again. "Young man?"

He stepped away from the truck and, keeping his face tilted low, plastered on a smile. "Yes?"

She stopped about halfway, apparently unwilling to get any closer, which was fine by him. All the more difficult for her to make him out.

"I've got an ant problem on my back porch and wondered if you might come take a look at it. I was going to call someone, but I saw your truck and thought maybe you could do it while you're here. I could pay you."

He could have snuffed her out in about ten seconds' time and even made it look like an accident. An unfortunate tumble down her own stairs. But given that she hadn't seen him close up, that would be an unnecessary complication that would likely lead to more questions than his mere presence at McConnaughey's home. It wouldn't be clean, and he was all about clean. All about *precise*.

Effecting a strong country accent, he replied, "Sorry, ma'am. Can't now. Full load and I'm already late—the boss'll kill me. I could come back later tho'. It'd be one hundred for the initial visit and then three–fifty for the treatment. That okay?"

Her eyes widened at the mention of the pricing, apparently too high for her liking. Which was exactly what Korrigan had been counting on.

"Oh, well, no. No, that's all right. I'll just . . . call someone else if it . . . can't be now. Thank you," she stammered, and turned back towards her house, padding away.

"Suit yourself, ma'am," he mumbled, starting up the truck and backing down the drive. He rolled down the street, watching in the rear view mirror as she went through her own screen door. Satisfied he had neutralized the situation, he turned his gaze back to the road and took stock of his search.

Not a surprise, really. McConnaughey's apartment in Miami had been the same. Completely clean. And every contact Tate McConnaughey had there and here and everywhere in between had also turned up absolutely nothing. Which meant the girl really was their only link. But her place was squeaky clean, too.

18

The side trip to Atlanta had represented a substantial delay, but he didn't trust the job to anyone else. He had needed to know for certain and the only way he could have any real confidence in the results was if he handled the job himself. *Purposeful. Pitiless. Precision. Leads to perfection.* It was his mantra, one that had been beaten into him by his stepfather, and one that had made him very, very good at his job. The best.

Now that he was confident the answer wasn't in Atlanta, there was only one trail left to follow. And it led straight to St. Gideon.

FIVE

Whistling. Cheerful, melodic whistling. Chloe yawned and opened her eyes, squinting at the sunlight streaming through the ocean view window beside the bed. A soft breeze darted between the sill and sash, rippling the gauzy white sheers. She spotted the happy culprit; a tiny green parakeet perched on a palm branch outside. Chloe glanced at the clock. It was nine in the morning.

She padded through the cottage, the tile cool on her bare feet. The first order of business was coffee, brewed strong and sweetened with French vanilla creamer. Chloe carried the ceramic mug back to her room and pulled on a white tee shirt and running shorts. After downing what was left in the cup, she left it in the sink and headed out the front door.

The cottage was one of two dozen in a development ensconced at various altitudes of a steep but narrow hill overlooking the shore. Chloe's was one of three perched on its minimal top, offering her a glorious panoramic view of the uncompromised beach and the gentle tide beyond. The pebbles of her front walk crunched beneath her feet as she made her way to the gravel road that spiraled down the hill to the highway seventy yards below. The wood siding cottages were small but inviting variations on the same basic floor plan, each crisply painted some neutral, earthy shade and trimmed in stark white, fronted by stained timber doors. Chloe's brisk stride quickly took her past the house next door where, as usual, its silver haired, muumuu wearing occupant was fixed firmly in her front porch swing, hard at work on what was, no doubt, the *Sun Times* crossword puzzle.

"Hey Ruby," Chloe called, waving without stopping.

Sixty-two-year-old Ruby Kreinberg, with her outdated beehive hairdo and kind eyes, looked up and smiled genuinely. "Hi sweetie," she yelled back. "Want some coffee? It's 'Snickerdoodle' something or other. My daughter sent it." The widow's husband had made the down payment on the little beach house with their retirement savings, then died of a heart attack before they could move there. Ruby had honored their plans, following through by herself, hoping to find a little peace in the change. Chloe could relate.

"Thanks, but no. I've already had a cup today."

"Well, maybe later, then. After your morning walk. You're so good to do that every day." She patted her swollen hips. "Putting on a few pounds too many myself. Maybe I should start. Never really wanted to take long walks back in Chicago, but this place is different."

"Well, you're welcome to tag along anytime."

"You're so sweet to this old widow. Promise you'll come by later, doll. I'm baking brownies."

Chloe nodded as she waved goodbye. "Promise."

Past Ruby's house the road steepened sharply, and Chloe's footsteps quickened as she descended around the bend. She breathed in deeply, taking in the salt air and feeling the muscles stretch in her legs. Ruby was right; it was good exercise. And not just for her body. Her mind got a workout, too.

She'd been on the island for three weeks now. She couldn't decide if it seemed like an eternity or no time at all. For the most part it depended on her mood, and whether she had been reminiscing. She had been disappointed to find that even on the island she couldn't avoid the spells of remembering, which on these morning walks occurred frequently. But it was part of the process, or so Izzie assured her. At least she wasn't crying as much anymore. *Maybe that's progress*, she hoped. But she still missed Tate with an acute ache that, had she not known better, she would have sworn ebbed from an actual, physical hole in heart where he'd been cut out.

Chloe reached the end of the street and crossed the highway that ran parallel to the beach. She headed to the shore by way of the small gravel lot occupied by a few cars and one Jeep. At the edge of the gravel she picked up the pace and started down the sand.

* * * * *

21

She didn't even look at him as she passed by his door. He was just another tourist, spending one precious vacation morning out for a look at the sea before the sharp heat of noon.

His cell phone vibrated in his shirt pocket, sending an unpleasant sensation through his chest. Keeping Chloe McConnaughey in his sights, he answered.

"Yeah."

"I just got word from Miami," reported a clipped voice on the other end. "They've got a lead they're working on. We should know something soon."

"What does he want me to do?" he asked, shifting a bit to maintain his view of the woman.

"Stick to the plan for now and stay as close as you can."

* * * * *

Chloe figured she'd do her standard two miles, one mile one way, then back up. Though early by island standards, a few people had already staked claims along the beachfront. The waves were lazy, likely a letdown for surfers paddling their boards near the sandbar. She passed several sunbathers and children building lopsided castles in the sand. A couple strolled by in the other direction, their feet toying with the water's edge.

As her feet pummeled the sand in a steady jog, she considered her time on the island. It had been a good decision to stay here, even if it did qualify as running away. She could breathe and she could think and she could pretend she wasn't the product of the tragic life that she'd had no choice in. And though she missed Izzie and Jonah, they were the only parts of her life in Atlanta that she missed.

Her creative juices were flowing here, too. The island had proven to be a treasure trove of interesting, culturally distinct locales. She'd spent the first week, which was the only one on *Terra Traveler's* tab, exploring as much of the British sugar-cane-colony-turned-vacation-hot-spot as she could. She'd hit the artsy town on the western tip near the hundred-foot cliffs where divers risked their lives with every leap. The rustic fishing villages that still used centuries-old methods. The beach clubs nestled amongst ocean front resorts on the flat stretches of sand to the south. And Binghamton's market quarter, where locals hawked spiced meats, local produce and handmade clothing. The praise-filled article highlighting the island for potential vacationers had come easily, and she'd emailed that to Izzie last week. Now she was on her time.

She passed a young, alabaster-skinned family of four, all tow-headed and all painfully red on nearly every place not covered by a swimsuit. Their crisp clip of an accent gave them away as British, and they bustled about, setting up chairs and umbrellas. Despite their sunburns they all sported happy faces and bright eyes. It struck her that they were terribly out of place and exactly where they should be all at the same time, and she wished she had her camera to capture it. It would make a great addition to the hundreds of photos she'd already taken. In her heart she was convinced that the best ones would make a great compilation for a coffee table book. If *Terra Traveler* wasn't interested, maybe Izzie could help her shop it around.

She was moving at a good pace, swift but relaxed, when a muscular, tawny boxer raced out in front of her in hard chase after a lime green tennis ball. Cornering it, he chomped down, then sped back down the beach. Longing welled up as she thought of Jonah. Izzie had graciously agreed to take him in until she came back, but Chloe wasn't sure just how long that might be. *Maybe I could fly him down—*

Her train of thought derailed as something powerful slammed into the back of her head.

"Ow!" she yelled and, grabbing her head, spun in the direction of the blow. A few feet away a brown football rolled sluggishly in the sand. She marched over, still rubbing the sore spot, and scooped up the ball.

"Are you okay?"

Shielding her eyes from the sun with her free hand, Chloe looked up to see a tall man, cotton tee shirt billowing in the wind, racing towards her. "Hey, are you okay?" he repeated, coming up short and spraying a cloud of sand over her feet. He ran a well-tanned hand through chestnut hair that spiked a little at the crown. "I told him," he spluttered, nodding back up the beach towards a man behind him, "to wait till you'd gone a little farther."

Chloe shook her head. "No worries," she said casually, tossing him the football. It did sting, though, and she involuntarily scratched at the sore spot again. His eyes narrowed and his mouth tightened doubtfully.

"You sure?" he asked. Strong jaw line. Pronounced cheekbones.

Mid-thirties looked good on him.

"It's a football, not a baseball bat. I'm fine."

From behind him the boxer cantered up, tail wagging furiously, and dropped the tennis ball at his feet. The man reached down to pat the dog's flank, snatched up the ball and with a snap sent it hurtling back up the beach. The dog darted after it, chomping on it when it landed several feet away from the man's friend. "Missed him," he apologized, turning back to Chloe with an impish smile. "But I tried."

"Is he yours?" Chloe said, nodding at the dog pounding down the sand.

"Nah. Zeus belongs to Mike."

"He makes me miss mine back home." She wasn't sure why she said it. She wasn't typically chatty with strangers, and it surprised her that she'd offered this up. But then again, it had been weeks since she had a conversation with anyone other than Ruby.

He hesitated a second, then thrust out his hand. "I'm Jack. Jack Collings."

She was equally hesitant, slowly extending her own arm. "Chloe. McConnaughey."

"Hey, you're welcome to join us. Toss the ball to Zeus. Whack Mike in the head once or twice." He spun the football in his hands and grinned. "It'll make me feel better."

She stopped feeling for a rising knot on her head, pursed her lips and raised her eyebrows. "Join you, huh?" She eyed him suspiciously.

He cocked his head. "What?" he asked uncertainly, still smiling but eyebrows narrowing slightly, confusion clouding his face as she continued staring him down.

"You know you could have just asked and saved me the migraine."

Understanding flashed across his face. "Oh, hey, wait," he laughed, holding his hands up in mock surrender. "That is not my style. And I can't imagine that would be an effective pick-up method."

"No," Chloe retorted, unable to keep her own smile from creeping outward. "I wouldn't think so," she finished, staring into the spirited green eyes that met an angular nose and thin lips reminiscent of that actor in *Sweet Home Alabama*.

Walk away, a warning sang in her head. *Walk awaaaay*.

"So, you're, uh, a tourist?" he asked, apparently interpreting

Chloe's smile as an invitation to stick around.

"Sort of. Long term tourist, I guess you could say."

"Me too. I'm going on six months. You?"

Why are you still standing here? The voice asked. She ignored it.

"Three weeks."

"Well," he said, flipping the football again. "If you're gonna take off from home for a while, this is the perfect place to land. It's a great place to escape from reality."

Her stomach tightened. "Why do you say that?"

He shrugged. "Has been for me."

The boxer loped up to her and dropped the ball on her shoe. "So," he ventured, as she picked up the ball and fired it down the beach, "are you a professional beach bum or is there some job you're playing hooky from?"

"I work for an online travel magazine," she answered.

"You're a writer." He smiled appreciatively.

"Photographer. The writing's just a necessary evil."

"You know, this place has some of the best sunsets I've ever seen—" He stopped when she wrinkled her nose ever so slightly at the suggestion. "What? Sunsets too pedestrian?"

"What? No," she started, a little embarrassed. But when his eyebrows shot up doubtfully, she continued, "It's just that . . . it's been done."

"Well, if sunsets aren't your thing, I might still have a few ideas. The local guys I know have shown me just about every inch of this island. If you wanted somebody to take you around . . ." His voice trailed off hopefully.

"Hey, are we done here?" bellowed Mike from down the beach.

"Hold up," Jack barked back, turning his head to direct the sound, but never taking his gaze off Chloe.

"Sounds like you're needed," she said, gesturing toward Mike.

Jack shrugged. "He can wait. So what do you think?"

Say yes. Say no. "Look, thanks, really, but . . . I don't even know you, and besides . . ."

His smile turned up at the corners. It made him even cuter. *Darn it.*

"Name's Jack Collings—"

"So you said," she interrupted good-naturedly.

"I'm a beach concierge over at the Southern Star Resort—that's not my career by the way, it just pays the bills while I'm here. My friend is an idiot, and I have terrible ideas about how to pick up women." His green eyes twinkled. "What else is there to know?"

She felt herself smiling and realized she had started leaning into his personal space without knowing it. *This is ridiculous,* she thought, straightening up. *First guy that hits on you in months and you're going all teenager.* She knew it was stupid. So why was she still there?

"Jack, man, let's go! Work—half an hour!" Mike hollered, motioning for Jack to come back as he moved towards the Jeep in the parking lot.

"I think your ride is leaving," Chloe said, nodding in the friend's direction.

With an aggravated swipe, Jack motioned for Mike to wait a minute. "How about it? Dinner? One drink? Just one. If you decide I'm creepy you can pretend you got an emergency text and bail, no questions asked."

She'd sworn off men. She was still dealing with Tate. And this guy *lived* here for Pete's sake. The island was only temporary for her. *But still . . .* In the next five seconds she carried out an entire argument with herself from start to finish.

No way, you don't know him.

But he's . . . interesting. It's just one drink.

Serial killers can be interesting, too.

If he's creepy, I'll leave.

They aren't creepy until it's too late. Besides you don't want anybody around. That's why you're here.

But . . . I'm lonely.

And you're even lonelier after they leave.

He's cute.

Cute only means they leave sooner.

She cleared her throat. "Maybe some other time."

"Yeah. Well, okay," he said, sounding disappointed, then continued, "probably a smart move." He winked and a butterfly or two actually took off in her stomach. "I guess that's my cue. Sorry again about the football."

"Forget the football—next time just ask a girl already," she quipped lightly, unable to help herself. *Stop talking, you idiot, and let him walk away.*

He grinned. "Anyway," he said sucking in a breath, "nice to meet you, Chloe McConnaughey. Guess I'll see you around."

"You too," she said as he turned and jogged off, football in hand.

She watched him fly down the golden stretch. *Good decision, McConnaughey. Would have been a total waste of time. This would have gone nowhere. Absolutely nowhere.*

Then a burst of something that felt like recklessness propelled her down the beach after him.

"Jack!"

He turned, then stopped to wait for her to catch up.

"Okay," she stammered as she drew close, "so . . . how about tonight?"

Tonight? What are you doing? The warning bells in her head were deafening.

"Oh," he said, clearly trying to hide his genuine surprise. "You serious?"

She wrinkled her nose warily. "Apparently."

"Okay, then. Well, tonight's great," he said, taken aback but obviously pleased.

There was a lull as each waited for the other to speak. Finally Jack jumped in. "So, should I pick you up or . . ."

"Why don't we meet somewhere?"

"How about Mendoza's on Pebble Avenue, the one by the—"

"I know it," she interrupted a little brusquely, and tried to recover. "I did a shoot near there."

"Good, so, say . . . seven?"

Chloe nodded. "Seven," she answered, then turned and jogged away before he could see the panic start to set in.

* * * * *

Jack waited till she'd run back down the beach, then headed to the Jeep.

"So?" Mike asked, patting Zeus and tossing him half an uncooked hot dog.

Jack hopped in and threw the football in the back. "Knew I shouldn't have listened to you," he griped.

"What?"

Jack shook his head. "I looked like an idiot."

"Well, it worked didn't it? Now you're in."

Jack leaned back as they pulled out onto the road. "We'll see," he said skeptically, running a hand through his hair. "We'll see."

SIX

With tired eyes, Herb Rohrstadt, Esquire, peered over the papers heaped on his chiseled oak desk and wondered what had become of his little Miami law practice. The steady stream of work spawned by his ever-expanding client list had ballooned to a nearly unmanageable size for a solo practitioner. Years ago he had craved this kind of personal success after resigning his junior partnership at Hearns, Bates and Hughes. But in the end all he had really done was trade eighteen-hour workdays as slave for the law firm for eighteen-hour workdays as a slave to the rent, electric bill and staff salaries—and without the benefit of the firm's expense account. He was making money, but he was working too hard for it. And with a fiftieth birthday around the corner and two ex-wives to support, that was not a good thing.

Venice had only made things worse. He'd tacked the weeklong holiday onto the end of two solid workweeks in Rome assisting in closing the sale of a leather handbag factory to one of his clients with European holdings. He had come home to find the place drowning in a deluge of files and folders, messages and manila envelopes, each one screaming for attention.

A week later he was still struggling to surface and, sensing the ocean of paper rising over his head, wondered what was slipping through the cracks. *Or rather,* he corrected broodingly, *what else was slipping through.* He was still frustrated with Elena over that one. His secretary should have noticed the first time Tate McConnaughey failed to call the office to check in, but she didn't. His subsequent failures to check in over the next weeks went unnoticed by her, too. It wasn't until Rohrstadt returned to the States and McConnaughey missed the call scheduled for *that* week that Rohrstadt realized something might be wrong. When his phone calls to Tate McConnaughey went unanswered, a quick check of the Internet confirmed his death in a crash on I-95 weeks before.

At least it was a dead client and not a living one he'd failed. It wasn't likely anybody was going to complain. Besides, technically he'd followed McConnaughey's instructions, albeit a little late. He'd express-mailed the package yesterday. Hopefully whatever was in there wouldn't be compromised by a couple weeks delay.

Truth was, he was glad to be rid of it. The whole undertaking had made him uncomfortable from the beginning. He'd been paid a lot of money to simply accept the client's weekly calls, safeguard the package and promise to deliver it in the event of the client's death. He wasn't stupid. No doubt something wasn't quite on the up and up about this one. But his role was definitely legal, and, after all, when your first kid from your first marriage is starting Brown University in the fall, you don't turn down easy money. Even when the clients are a little weird, or a little paranoid, insisting that their file be locked in your very own *personal* safe. In the end he just hadn't been able to come up with a good reason not to take the money.

Click-click. The office was so quiet it wasn't hard to hear Elena's key turning in the front door. She had been coming in the last few Saturdays to help him get caught up. He'd offered her double-time, and with kids of her own in college, she was happy to do it.

"Elena, I'm back here," he called out. "Hey, have you seen that Braxton contract? They called about it last night." When silence followed, he frowned, then moved down the paneled hall into the outer office, talking as he went. "Don't tell me you sent that out, because—"

He sucked back the rest of the sentence, startled to find himself squared off against two hulking men, their arms crossed resolutely.

"Um, I'm sorry. The office is closed now. Come back—"

"Herb Rohrstadt?" interrupted the particularly barrel-chested of the two.

Herb nodded. "Yeah, but I'm not technically working today. You'll have to come back—"

"Tate McConnaughey says hello."

They moved so swiftly that Herb didn't even have time to react.

As the butt of the man's gun struck him, so did the panicked realization that there had been a very good reason not to take McConnaughey's money after all.

SEVEN

The place looked like any number of seafood dives she'd scouted along the Florida panhandle. Plank floors grayed and worn from years of foot traffic. Fishnets and mounted swordfish, grouper and marlin dotted the dark paneled walls. The bar along one wall was completely packed, barstools squished together elbow to elbow. A steady buzz of chatter filled the room, interrupted by a whirring blender mixing up a batch of margaritas. The entire rear wall consisted of large rectangular windows, which presently had their shades rolled up and panes propped open, so that a warm, slightly sticky breeze rolled through. From where she stood, Chloe had a perfect view of the outdoor patio which sat on a short pier that ran along the back of the building, and beyond that, the cobalt water of New Compton Bay. And there on the patio sat Jack Collings.

He was staring out at the sea and hadn't seen her yet. *There's still time to chicken out,* she told herself. And she had come close several times already, vacillating between reminding herself that she'd sworn off men because her life was just too complicated right now, and countering with the argument that it would be refreshing to have a little non-committal companionship and a few hours of intelligent conversation with someone who didn't know her baggage. As lovely as Ruby was, well . . . it just wasn't enough.

She'd waffled for a good thirty minutes, even driving back to the cottage once after reaching the bottom of the hill. That last bit had made her late. *He probably already thinks I've stood him up.* But when he turned, and those green eyes lit up at the sight of her, Chloe suddenly knew she wasn't going anywhere except out onto that patio.

She waved hello and walked through the little restaurant, the mouth-watering smells of cheeseburgers, grilled fish and everything fried floating around her. As she stepped through the screen door, the breeze caught the hem of her black sundress, twirling it in a little tarantella. She quickly grabbed it, hoping to avoid a Marilyn Monroe situation, and smiled sheepishly as she walked to the table where he had stood to meet her, his chair grating loudly against the floor.

"Hey, there," he greeted, stepping to one side of the weathered table for two and pulling out her chair.

"Hey." She said, taking a seat. She waited for him to sit, then said, "Sorry I'm a little late. Time just got away from me."

He pushed the small hurricane lamp housing a single candle to one side of the table, then leaned forward on his arms. "Only by ten minutes." He cocked his head to the side and looked at her appraisingly. "I'd say ... second thoughts? Considered standing me up?"

Chloe's eyes widened with embarrassment. A few awkward seconds passed before she managed a non-committal, "Ummm . . ."

A look of uncomfortable realization blossomed on Jack's face. "Oh," he said through a half-grimace. "Sorry, I was just . . ." His words trailed off, then, recovering, he brushed off the discomfort with a shake of his head and leaned back.

"Well," he started, "if you *weren't* thinking of standing me up before, I'll bet you are now." A subtle grin replaced the grimace, and Chloe felt the corner of her own mouth twitch. "You know, actually I can't hold it against you. Give any sensible girl an entire afternoon to rethink a blind date with a perfect stranger, and she's bound to have her doubts." He glanced down at his fork, feigning distraction, and began twiddling with it. "I'd say it's pretty much a fifty-fifty proposition even on the best day." He looked up at her again, an impish glint in his eye. "But we know that going in."

"*We* who?" she asked, playing along.

"Those of us brave enough to risk getting shot down."

"So you'd call what you did out there today, brave?"

"Absolutely," he said, then leaned in a bit closer. Something that smelled like sandalwood drifted across the table. "Given today's odds."

Chloe grinned amusedly. "You gave me odds?"

Jack nodded. "Eleven to one. Would've been twelve but you

seemed to warm up to Zeus, so I had that going for me."

She actually laughed out loud before asking, "So if I was such a long shot, why risk it?"

"The long shots are the only ones worth it." He let that sit for a second before nonchalantly taking a sip of water.

"I'll bet that line works better than the football every time."

He snorted, half choking on the water just as the waiter approached the table.

They ordered calamari for an appetizer and, for dinner, grilled grouper and twice-baked potatoes. Out in the harbor, waves rippled away from the hazy horizon, where half a dozen sailboats outlined in festive strands of white lights bobbed towards the rosy sunset. Squawking gulls sounded their evening cries, and a nervous fish leapt and spun once before plunging again. As she took it in, Chloe unconsciously wrapped and re-wrapped a stray curl around her finger, the last of the sun streaming through her hair and turning the chestnut strands golden.

"This place is really beautiful," she offered.

"Well, I'm glad it's okay. I was trying for comfortable casual, but obviously I screwed up the 'comfortable' part in the first five minutes."

Chloe reached for her water glass. "Well, here's to second chances."

His eyes met hers as their glasses clinked. "I really am glad you decided to come tonight."

The comment was genuine, without a trace of flirtation. It caught her off guard, and she wondered, just as the waiter returned with their drinks, whether she was blushing.

"So aren't you curious?" he asked.

Chloe eyed him with uncertainty. "About?"

"This absolute stranger you had the poor judgment to go to dinner with despite knowing nothing about him."

"Not *nothing*," Chloe protested and swallowed a bite of warm bread drenched in butter. "I know you're Jack Collings. You're a beach concierge, whatever that is. And your friend is an idiot."

He chuckled. "So far, so good. What else."

"Hmmm." Chloe thought for a moment, looking him up and down for telltale clues. "Can't place the accent. Sounds a little southern, with something else thrown in."

"Not bad. Not bad. Born in Birmingham, bounced around,

finally ended up in Manhattan when I got my first real job."

"Which was?"

"College professor."

Chloe sat back in her chair and cocked her head in surprise. "You're kidding."

"That's not interesting enough to joke about."

"It's just," she hesitated, "well, it's not what I'd have guessed. You don't look like any college professor I ever had."

Instead of being deterred, he seemed amused. "Really? And what would you have guessed?"

She offered him the breadbasket and he took it. "Let's just say not a professor and leave it at that," she said, skirting the issue. "So where did you teach? What subject?"

"NYU. English," he answered, buttering a roll.

"NYU. Impressive."

"Stifling, more like."

"So is tonight going to end with you quoting some fancy British poet, or whatever?"

"Absolutely not," he said determinedly, pulling off a piece of bread.

"Why not?"

"Because," he started, popping the bread in his mouth and swallowing, "that would be cheesy and stupid and worse than throwing a football at a girl's head to get her attention."

"*Almost* as bad," she chuckled. "I was never very good in English class," Chloe continued, jabbing her fork into her salad. "At least not the literature part—all the old writings, British Lit, Early American Lit, you know? Kind of funny that half my job is writing for a living." She paused for a moment, waiting for him to offer something more, but he didn't. "So how does an NYU professor end up a beach concierge on St. Gideon?"

"Well, frankly, I don't like to talk about the professor thing because it doesn't jive with the whole beach bum vibe I've got going on here which, by the way, really impresses the ladies."

"Mmmm."

"Plus, once I spill the beans women usually run as fast as they can the other way." He said it lightheartedly, but a little too rehearsed, as if maybe there was more truth than joke to it.

"Try me. I promise not to get any emergency texts when you're done."

The corner of his mouth turned up, and he held his hands out in surrender. "I got divorced," he said, and despite the smile, Chloe thought his voice sounded pinched.

"Sorry, Jack. I . . . I didn't mean to pry."

"It's a fair question. It's just that I like to get to know a woman a little better, say through dessert, before laying that out there." He grinned. "Gives me better odds. I mean, it's been two years since Lila and I were together, but women still see a big, red warning sign on my head, 'Divorcee seeking rebound girl. BEWARE! BEWARE! BAGGAGE!'"

Wonder what you'd think of the Samsonite I'm lugging around, Chloe thought sympathetically. "Well, I'm not going anywhere," she replied encouragingly. "At least not till after dessert, anyway."

He chuckled and after a few bites of salad, continued. "You know we weren't together that long, Lila and me. We dated and got married in just eight weeks." He noted Chloe's skeptical expression. "Yeah, I know. Should've been my first clue. Eighteen months later she left me for her 'soul mate,'" he said, rolling his eyes, "who turned out to be some artist in the Village. The decent thing would've been for her to just walk out, but she was greedy, and the thing's been in court for the last two years. When the judge finally signed off six months ago I'd had enough of the real world. Hopped right on a plane and came here."

"Well, I can definitely appreciate the benefits of a break from reality."

"Good," he said resolutely. "We're off me and on to you. So what would have someone like you wanting a break from reality?"

Chloe's heart skipped at the thought of talking about herself. Scrambling mentally, she started back in on him. "No, no, no. You can't change the subject that easily. You've still got work to do. Jury's still out on whether you're creepy or not." She winked, hoping it would help. "So, what do you do when you're not trolling for women on the beaches of St. Gideon?"

He smiled as if he knew exactly what she was doing. But he answered anyway. "Mostly diving. Sailing. Sometimes taking the tourists out for a spin." His eyes sparkled. "Still trolling, just a different venue." He leaned forward and tilted his beer mug toward her. "But you're not getting off that easy either. What should I know about you besides the fact that you struggle with punctuality?"

So there it was. She wasn't going to get around it. She was either going to have to answer, or she would have to leave. And, really, what had she expected? Who goes to dinner thinking that they won't have to talk about themselves? *I could lie. Make it all up. I could be Izzie. He'd never know. Then I could stay. Then I could . . . what exactly? Enjoy the night as someone else—be free to leave with no strings attached?* And then it hit her. She didn't want to leave.

So she started with the harmless subject of work and the book of photographs she was doing on the island, hoping she'd get by without delving into her demons. But by the time dinner arrived, his follow-up questions took a more personal turn, and there was no avoiding it. So she told him about the bad break-ups, about Tate, about dropping everything to stay on St. Gideon indefinitely while she tried to run away from life and figure it out all at the same time.

"So," she said smiling faintly, "the way I see it, my baggage trumps yours any day."

"Chloe, I am so sorry. If I'd known . . ."

"Hey. It's a fair question," she said, parroting his earlier reply as she smiled warmly, hoping to put him at ease. But he looked sad, and pity was the last thing she'd come there for. She breathed in deeply, exhaling a tired sigh. "The thing is, Jack, I can tell by the look on your face that it wasn't fair of me to come. Cocktails with someone drowning in her own sorrows isn't exactly what you were expecting."

"And you were expecting a recently divorced Manhattan escapee?"

"Still, I'd totally understand if you'd rather just call it a night."

Jack sighed melodramatically. "Well," he said, his gaze locking onto hers as he swirled the liquid gold in his glass, "first of all, we've ordered key lime pie, and we are not letting it go to waste. And secondly," he said, unleashing another smile, "I look too good to go home early. So you're stuck with me—at least through dessert anyway."

The rest of their conversation pointedly avoided the personal, and they bounced seamlessly from painless topic to painless topic, interrupted only by their laughter and the waiter tending to their table. By the time coffee came, darkness engulfed them, and the stars had spilled gloriously onto the pitch of sky. As Chloe leaned over her steaming cup, blowing into it, Jack tapped the handle of his black coffee and eyed the silver bauble dangling from Chloe's neck that she fingered mindlessly.

"Habit of yours?" he said, nodding at the necklace.

She looked down, almost as if surprised to find herself holding the pendant, and pulled it away from her neck to see it better. "Apparently. I catch myself hanging onto it a lot. Subconsciously sentimental, I guess. Tate sent it to me for my birthday last year. When he stopped calling—I was so mad I shoved it in a drawer. Refused to wear it. But for the funeral . . . I haven't been able to bring myself to take it off since." She pulled it out from her neck, turning over the front side with its intricate, latticework-like etching, to reveal an inscription on the back.

"Always?" Jack asked, squinting to make out the words in the candlelight.

Chloe nodded. "He used to say he'd always be there for me."

"Whatever happened, he must have really loved you," he said gently, leaning back into the chair.

"I would've rather had phone calls than the necklace."

Jack nodded, and she turned to face the water, trying, without succeeding, to stop tears from forming in the corners of her eyes. The moment hung over the table, the sound of waves lapping against the pier accompanied by the clinking of glasses from the bar and nearby tables. Jack watched her intently, silently, as she pulled windblown strands of sun-highlighted hair from her face. Chloe waited for the awkwardness to set in, but instead the air between them remained comfortable, almost strangely . . . familiar. They let it be until, as if some green light somewhere had flashed, he said something charming that made her laugh gently, and conversation slowly began to flow again. And so they sat on the moonlit pier, neither one in a hurry to leave, drinking their coffees long into the dark Caribbean night.

* * * * *

Fifty yards away, on the edge of a long pier perpendicular to the terrace, he refocused his binoculars. He could barely make out their figures now, huddled over the candlelight. The last of the daylight had vanished an hour ago, making surveillance all the more difficult. Equally frustrating was the fact that he couldn't hear a word they were saying. He considered moving closer, but decided against it, fearing a nosy passerby might give him away.

He had followed her to the restaurant on his rented moped, indistinct among the hundreds like it on the island. Dressed in khaki shorts and a golf shirt, he easily passed for a tourist scanning the night horizon for ships. So far, no one had taken an interest in him. And so far he had learned nothing of interest. But knowing Korrigan would expect a full report, he remained alert.

Finally they stood up from their table and turned to leave. He followed them with the binoculars until losing sight of them in the interior dining room. Then he walked briskly off the pier to a spot with a clear view of the building's entrance. They exited almost immediately, then walked through the parking lot towards her car. He leaned against the side of the building, trying to look like he was waiting for someone, and watched.

* * * * *

"This is me," Chloe said, leading Jack to her rented convertible, a somewhat worn Volkswagen Cabriolet. They stopped beside the driver's door. "I guess I should head home. It's getting late."

Jack looked past her towards the ground. "I don't think so."

Chloe's eyes narrowed. "Excuse me?"

Jack nodded towards the ground. Turning around, Chloe saw that her left front tire was completely flat. "Oh, you've got to be kidding me," she exclaimed in frustration.

"Just pop the trunk," he told her, moving towards the car's rear, "and I'll put your spare on."

"I hate for you to have to do that, Jack."

"It's really not a problem."

"Are you sure?"

"Chloe," he said looking determinedly at her, "I'm sure. Now pop the trunk."

She did and walked over to where he stood behind the car.

"Um, Chloe?"

"Yeah?"

"There's no spare in here."

"What?"

"There's no spare," he repeated, holding up the mat on the trunk floor to reveal an empty hole where the spare should have been.

Chloe sighed. "I guess I'll just call a tow."

"Don't do that, it's a waste of money. Look, I'll take you home and tomorrow we'll go get a tire, come back and change it."

It was a little too convenient. "I don't know, Jack . . . "

"Look, if you're worried about me, don't be. I promise to be the good little Methodist boy my mother raised me to be." He put his hands in his pockets. "These will stay right here. Promise. Nothing funny. Just a nice guy trying to give a girl in trouble a ride home. That's all."

Chloe squinted, judging his intentions.

"I mean it. Right here," he said, jiggling his hands in his pockets.

She laughed out loud. "Okay, okay. You win."

* * * * *

He watched as they moved away from her car and got into the Jeep. Throwing caution aside, he bolted across the open parking lot, reaching his moped just as they pulled onto the main road.

EIGHT

As they motored down the stretch of coastal highway that led to her cottage, Chloe sank into the leather seat and listened to the engine's steady growl. The wind whipped through her hair relentlessly, forcing her to hold it ponytail-like at the side of her neck. She gazed upward into the clear night sky and a fat, glowing moon. To her left was the ocean, its rolling waves tumbling onto the shore rising up in a choral roar, and Jack, silhouetted against the passing scenery.

During the last three hours her heavy heart had seemed to grow measurably lighter, and frankly, she just didn't get it. She didn't know this man. Aside from being privy to a few facts about his life, Jack was a complete stranger. But for some reason he had snapped her out of her funk like nothing else had been able to. Izzie would say she was compensating. That it wasn't really this *particular* man, it was just that he was someone new and different. That she had conjured the connection out of sheer loneliness. *Maybe I'm just latching onto the first person to come along,* she thought.

In that case, she should definitely steer clear. *Definitely.* That kind of attachment couldn't be healthy. *And,* she pointed out to herself, *it isn't fair to start something I'm not prepared to finish. AND this has no potential beyond St. Gideon, anyway. Talk about a doomed relationship.*

Relationship? How had that word even entered her mind? Now was the time for her to learn how to be strong on her own. Alone.

"You know," Jack started, interrupting her internal dialogue, "I've got access to the catamarans at the resort. I don't suppose you'd want to try one out tomorrow after we get your tire changed?"

He's getting the wrong idea. Chloe sighed. "I don't know, Jack. I mean . . . well—"

"Hey, it's okay," he offered quickly, "Don't worry about it. I didn't mean to push."

"Jack, I'd like to go. It's just . . ." Seconds of silence added up as her common sense and her heart argued back and forth like an emotional see-saw. Finally a compromise surfaced. *Friendship. How dangerous could friendship be?* "It's just that I can't tomorrow. I really need to get some work done," she fumbled. "If you're free the next day, though—"

"Chloe, really. I don't want to push you. Don't feel like you have to."

"I don't. I want to. It sounds like fun."

He eyed her suspiciously. "If you're sure. But just so you know, there's no pressure. Besides," he said, a teasing lilt to his voice, "it wouldn't be the first time I've been turned down. I'm pretty sure I'd survive."

He grinned cheekily, disarming her completely. "I don't know," she drawled, unable to keep from adopting the same teasing tone. "You've never been turned down by me."

His grin grew wider as he shot back, "Wonder what that says about you?"

A few minutes later, as they neared Chloe's development, Jack cleared his throat cautiously. "Look, Chloe, I know you're not sure about me." He paused, but when she didn't argue with him, kept going. "You've got a lot going on that I can't even begin to understand. But this is weird for me too. The fact is, I'm not the kind of guy that asks perfect strangers out to dinner. But something made me do it this morning, and I can't just dismiss that." He paused to cross into the oncoming lane, zip past a slow car and shift back into his lane.

"I understand your situation. I know you feel like, now that Tate's gone, you're all alone in this world and that you've got to figure out what living like that looks like, but," he hesitated, "the thing is, you're not alone. Not unless you want to be. And I don't think you'd have come tonight if you really just wanted to be alone. And that's okay because we're designed to need other people, you know? God didn't make us to be islands unto ourselves." He turned for a quick look at her. "Am I making you uncomfortable?"

Chloe shook her head. "No," she lied.

"Look, I enjoyed tonight. I think maybe you did too. But I'm worried you're going to get nervous or feel smothered or something, and disappear on me. So can I just say up front that I don't want you to do that? I think you're too lonely for your own good. I don't think it's a coincidence I stumbled onto you this morning." He took a deep breath. "I guess what I'm trying to say is that—I'm not expecting anything from you. Except maybe," he said, his gaze warm and sincere, "that dinner's on you next time."

Chloe sat frozen, with no idea of what to say to this kind of, well . . . honesty. Was it honesty? *Because either he's the most skilled charmer I've ever met, or I've actually stumbled onto a guy who isn't afraid to share his feelings. And on a first date no less.*

When she didn't say anything, he pushed ahead, "So, how 'bout it?" he asked, staring at the black roadway ahead. "Think we can just be friends and leave the complicated stuff out of it for now?"

Friends. Friends would work. She extended a hand towards him.

He slipped his right hand off the wheel and shook hers. "Good enough."

And as Jack drove silently the rest of the short distance through Chloe's development, she couldn't help but wonder how she'd found herself here, with this person, feeling better than she had in a long time.

* * * * *

At the top of Chloe's driveway, Jack turned off the engine and stepped out, heading to her side to open her door for her. But by the time he got there, she was already standing on the pavement, so instead he leaned casually against the Jeep, facing her.

"Thanks again for the dinner invitation," she said.

"Thank *you* for not standing me up."

Chloe shrugged playfully. "It's the least I could do."

"The very least," he grinned.

"So tomorrow then, right? You'll pick me up to go get that tire?"

"How about nine-thirty?"

"Sounds good," she told him.

He nodded. "Okay then," he said, spinning off the hood and sliding around the car in one fluid movement. "See you tomorrow."

From the driver's seat, he watched her enter the house and close the door. As he turned the key in the ignition, he hoped that he had put to rest any need she felt to run headlong in the opposite direction *and* that he really was as good a liar as everyone said he was.

* * * * *

Chloe closed the front door behind her and leaned heavily against it, realizing for the first time how tired she was. She reached for the light switch, when suddenly something rammed her in the chest, forcing all the breath out of her body. A second blow to the stomach sent her to her knees, gasping for air. She craned her head up for a look at her attacker, but all she could make out was a black figure hovering over her. He kicked her hard in the side and pulled back to kick again, but she rolled away, slamming her head into a table and sending the vase atop it crashing to the floor.

* * * * *

Jack's Jeep had just crossed the end of Chloe's driveway when he heard the shattering ceramic, followed by Chloe's shrill scream. Jamming his foot down, he gunned it forward.

* * * * *

Dazed, Chloe shook her head back and forth, trying to clear the fog, but it only made her head hurt more. Out of the corner of her eye, she saw a fist raised above her, ready to strike. She clawed at it, catching her hand in what must've been a jacket pocket, followed by the sound of ripping and jangling as something dropped to the floor. Her attacker roared and she cringed, throwing her arm up over her head and turning her face protectively towards the floor. She caught a shadowy glimpse of something familiar, but out of place, lying near her head just before squeezing her eyes shut in anticipation of the impending blow.

The front door flew open, slamming into the wall with an almighty thud as Jack burst through it. Suddenly Chloe was no longer beneath her attacker, and she scooted over to the wall as Jack and the intruder smashed around her living room. With a tremendous roar they fell backwards, crashing down onto the glass coffee table, pulverizing it into a million pieces.

Mustering herself, Chloe hobbled to the coat closet. Jack yelled out in pain as a shard of glass from the decimated table slashed into his thigh. Undeterred, he rolled over on top of the intruder and pounded him with his fists. Despite Jack's barrage, the intruder managed to swing his right arm around, slamming it into the left side of Jack's head. The blow sent Jack sprawling across the floor. The intruder rose to his feet and swung a leg back to kick, when Jack swept his other leg out from under him, flipping him onto the floor with a heavy thud. Jack scanned the room, but there was nothing useful within reach. As the intruder got up, Jack readied to charge again, then froze. The intruder had a gun in his outstretched hand.

A loud crack echoed through the room, and the intruder dropped like deadweight to the floor. Jack looked up to see Chloe standing behind the intruder, wielding a massive golf driver. Jack quickly scrambled over and snatched the man's gun away. Stepping back, he aimed it at the intruder and prodded him with his foot. There was no movement. Jack reached for the intruder's wrist.

"He's alive," Jack said, dropping the hand and turning to look at Chloe. "But I think he'll be out for a while." Jack spotted the light switch on the wall and flipped it on. The man at their feet was dressed all in black. A ski mask covered his face. Jack quickly patted him down for weapons, but found nothing. Then he pulled off the mask.

"You know him?" he asked Chloe.

Wrapping her arms around herself, she shook her head, no.

"Come on," Jack said, moving to her. "You got knocked around pretty good. I think you'd better sit down." All Chloe could manage was a nod. Putting his arm around her to steady her, he walked her into the kitchen and sat her in a chair. "Where's your phone?"

"Over there on the wall," she replied weakly, nodding towards it.

Jack quickly strode over and dialed the operator. Chloe sat silently in the chair, while Jack asked for emergency services and moved to the doorway leading to the front room. He watched the unconscious intruder intently as he stayed on the line. Within half a minute he was off. "They're on their way," he announced walking back to her. "They're sending an ambulance, too."

Chloe lifted her eyes to meet his. "He jumped me as soon as I walked in. I think I surprised him. I didn't even see him," she said, her voice trembling and anxious. She looked down at the weapon in

Jack's waistband. "He had a gun, Jack. If you hadn't been here . . ."

Jack knelt down in front of her and took her hands in his. "Hey, I *was* here. And it's over now. You're okay. Besides, you did a pretty good job taking care of yourself. Of the both of us for that matter." He walked back to the doorway, eyeing the intruder again, still out cold. He turned back to Chloe. "It's a good thing you had that driver," he said, nodding towards the front room and delivering a small smile.

"It's not mine. Somebody left a few odd clubs in the closet."

"Do you have any duct tape—anything I can tie him up with?"

He could tell from her twisted expression that it hurt her just to think. "No . . . I don't know. There might be some in that drawer by the sink."

Jack rummaged through the drawer. "Nothing," he said, letting the drawer roll shut. "He's bleeding a lot," he said, moving to stand where he could watch both the intruder and Chloe. "I hope they get here soon, or else—"

At the sight of Chloe's whitened complexion, Jack cut himself off. "Chloe, you don't look so good—"

"Jack, I'm fine. Really. You're the one who looks hurt," she said, gesturing towards a large, bloody gash on his shirtsleeve.

"Nah. Just a scrape or tw—Chloe?" he asked in concern, as her eyes glazed over and she tilted to one side. "Chloe!" he shouted, diving for her as she slumped out of the chair onto the floor.

Jack pulled her onto his lap and nervously checked for a pulse. "Thank God," he muttered when he found it, and tried to adjust her into a less awkward position. When he removed his hand from behind her head, it was covered in bright red. Fear filled his eyes as, turning her gently, he found a two-inch wound on her scalp that had turned much of the back of her head into a matted, bloody mess.

He held her, whispering to her to wake, to stay, until finally, sirens screamed up Chloe's driveway. "In the kitchen!" Jack yelled as he heard the front door open.

Two uniformed officers strode into the room, followed moments later by a medic.

"She's hurt," Jack told them, as the medic moved to Chloe's side and began working. "What about him?" Jack asked, tilting his head towards the front room.

"Who?" asked a burly, dark-skinned officer.

"The guy on the floor in there," Jack replied, clearly annoyed.

"He's the one who attacked her."

The officers looked at each other, then at Jack. "Sir, there's no one in there," the burly one said in a thick island accent.

"Yeah there is. I just left him," Jack replied impatiently. "She whacked him in the head with a golf club. He's out cold."

"He's right," the burly officer's partner replied insistently. "There's no one in there. What happened here?"

Jack's eyes narrowed and he eased himself out from under Chloe as they took her. He sprinted into the next room and stared at the floor in disbelief. There, at the spot where only minutes ago the intruder had laid unconscious, was nothing except a dark red pool of blood.

NINE

Parker stumbled back as Korrigan's fist unexpectedly launched into his cheek, the blow echoing around the room. Parker clutched his face, bracing for more as Korrigan stepped closer. But Korrigan only looked at him, his black eyes narrowed to slits. Another man in the room stood silent in the shadows, well out of Korrigan's way.

"How stupid are you?" he spat at Parker, pacing a circle around the man like an animal studying his prey. Weak rays of the cloudy St. Gideon dawn slipped through narrow gaps in the rusted aluminum siding of the abandoned storehouse, situated forty yards behind a closed cannery. It was exactly the opposite of the suite Korrigan had rented indefinitely in the posh hotel in downtown Binghamton.

Parker struggled to remain composed, despite the waves of pain coursing through his head. "Mr. Korrigan, I—"

"Shut up," Korrigan grunted, as he walked to a table on the far side of the dimly lit room. He reached for a towel bunched up on its top, wiped Parker's blood from his hand and exhaled a deep, menacing breath.

"Purposeful. Pitiless. Precision. Pre. Ci. Sion." He growled each syllable slowly. "How did you let this happen? They were tailed! You were in contact! But somehow, you still managed to be there when she got home. Were you deliberately trying to screw this up or are you really that stupid? Because honestly, I'm not sure which is a better answer."

Parker said nothing, but the fear in his eyes suggested he was too frightened of making things worse to respond.

Suddenly a disconcerting, altogether too easy calm came over Korrigan. "Well," he continued, reaching into his pocket and extracting a cigarette case. "I am at a complete loss." He took his time choosing a cigarette, then lit it and inhaled several deliberate puffs, as if drawing power from them.

"Let me fix it," Parker muttered.

"Fix it?" Korrigan asked snarkily. "Fix it? I don't think so. Too late for that."

Parker's eyes widened. "Wait. What . . . what are you going to do?"

Korrigan's eyes raked over the man, his brows arching with understanding. He snorted, shaking his head in disbelief. "See, that's what I'm talking about. *Precision*, man, *Pre. Ci. Sion.*" Again he growled each syllable at Parker. "You think I'd take you out over this? No. That would be messy. That would not be precise. That would not make the situation cleaner. It would create more problems than it would solve. So, no, I'm not going to do that. I am, however, going to send you packing."

Parker's shoulders visibly relaxed at the pronouncement, though his nervous gaze never wavered from Korrigan.

"And," Korrigan tagged on, causing Parker to clench again, "since we didn't bring you down here to make stupid mistakes, you're going to leave twenty with us when you go."

"Wait . . .what? Twenty grand!" Parker squawked. "That's more than you've paid me for this job! And I earned that fair and square! I've already been here three weeks, doing the job. One mistake doesn't wipe all that out! Just don't pay me for this last week, call it even, and I'll walk."

"You can't do the job so we have to bring someone else in. And we've got to clean up your little mess. So you *are* going to walk, and you *are* going to pay us back what we've paid you plus a little more to cover our expenses in bringing someone else in," Korrigan said, a thin curl of smoke escaping from his lips.

Parker squared himself off against Korrigan, the threat of losing twenty thousand dollars apparently steeling him with courage he hadn't had before Korrigan took bodily harm off the table.

"I'll give you the five for this week and that's it."

Korrigan leaned in until Parker's face was only inches from his own. Lifting the hand that held his burning cigarette, he jabbed his first and middle fingers at Parker's nose in sync with his words. "Or what?"

Parker inhaled resolutely but nervously, taking in some of Korrigan's expelled smoke. "Or you don't take the five, you insist on the twenty, and maybe the next time I get picked up, I have something more interesting to trade than the name of the dope dealer on the corner."

Korrigan stood, his expression unchanged, taking in Parker's threat. Then Korrigan walked three brisk paces from him and rotated swiftly, his Walther extended in his right hand. He fired once, instantly dropping Parker to the floor.

"Congratulations," he said to the corpse. "You just made your elimination the least messy option." Korrigan turned, unaffected, and strode out of the room. The other man darted out of the shadows and hustled after him.

"Get that cleaned up, Vargas," Korrigan barked.

"Yes, sir," the follower answered, turning on his heel and striding back towards Parker.

Korrigan slid his cell from his pocket and dialed. After a few seconds, he spoke.

"Yeah. It's me. I need to speak with him. Tell him I've got an update."

TEN

The rain pelted on the window in a steady cadence that guided Chloe back to consciousness. She stirred slowly, her clouded mind registering one sense, and then another. The thick smell of chemical sanitization. A quiet clinking of metal on metal somewhere not too far away, in concert with a timid repetitive beeping somewhere close by. In the background, voices spoke words she could not quite make out. She blinked. Once at first, then several times, willing herself into a clearer state of mind. Hazy shapes slowly resolved into recognizable objects. One of them turned.

"Chloe?" it said, moving to her bedside. "Can you hear me?"

She tried to answer, but the words wouldn't come at first. Finally, she managed a raspy, disoriented whisper. "Tate's dead."

The shape took Chloe's hand and sat down in a chair at her bedside. "It's all right, Chloe. You're safe now," it whispered back.

"Ruby?" Chloe asked weakly, very confused.

"Yes, dear," she replied softly, patting Chloe's arm.

Chloe squinted, taking in her surroundings. "I'm in the hospital?"

Her neighbor nodded. "Since last night. You're going to be fine. Just a concussion."

"How did you—"

"The police came over last night asking me about the break-in. Wanted to know if I'd heard anything. They told me you were here."

"Where's Jack?" she asked, concern evident in her voice. She started to push up into a sitting position, but the dizziness set in immediately.

"Don't try that just yet," Ruby said, gently easing her back down onto the bed. "He was here until a few hours ago. The police wanted him to come down this morning. Wouldn't leave until I promised to stay with you." A wry smile spread across her face. "I think he's a little taken with you. He was really worried."

"How is he? Is he hurt?" Chloe asked.

"He's fine. A few cuts and bruises, but nothing serious." Ruby nodded at the bandage wrapped around Chloe's head. "Nothing quite like your bump there."

Instinctively, Chloe reached up to finger the bandage, cringing when she touched the area over the wound on the back of her head.

"Eight stitches," Ruby offered.

"Ouch," Chloe whimpered, running her hand over the gauze again.

"You shouldn't touch that," fussed a nurse in a starchy, white uniform as she stepped into the room. She smiled perfunctorily. "Good to see you're awake. I'll let the doctor know."

For the next few minutes, the nurse went about her tasks, taking Chloe's blood pressure and temperature, checking the monitors and such. After scribbling a few notes on her chart and informing them the doctor would be in shortly, she marched out.

"What time is it?" Chloe asked.

"Noon." Ruby smiled, then hesitated. "You know, I don't want to pry, but several times when you were asleep you mumbled something about a 'Tate' and that he was dead. Was someone else hurt over there?"

Chloe shook her head. "He's . . . he was . . . someone close to me that died recently."

"Oh, hon', I'm sorry. We'll, I'm sure what happened last night didn't help," Ruby said sympathetically. "Speaking of which, a Detective Sampson came by." Ruby fished his card from her pocket and handed it to Chloe. "Asked that you come see him after you leave here. I told him I'd bring you if you were up to it."

"You don't have to do that. Honestly, Ruby, I hate that you even had to come here."

"Don't be ridiculous. If my daughter were hurt I would hope someone would look after her. But I tell you what," she said, picking up her bag, "if you think you'll be all right for a few minutes, I'd like to go down and get a cup of coffee."

"Of course."

"All right then. You rest while I'm gone."

Chloe watched Ruby slip through the door, then obediently closed her eyes, drifting into a light sleep as she listened to the rain fall.

* * * * *

Two hours later the doctor released Chloe with strict instructions to take it easy for a few days. Over Chloe's objections, Ruby promised him she would keep an eye on her and insisted on driving Chloe home, by way of a short detour to see Detective Sampson.

The unremarkable one-story building that served as St. Gideon's main precinct was located in the center of Binghamton proper. Several marked police vehicles were parked in the front lot. Two officers leaned against one near the door, smoking and talking. There was no sign of any other activity.

Chloe and Ruby walked through a glass door etched with the words "Binghamton Police Department," into an unassuming lobby that smelled of stale coffee. Behind the laminated front counter sat one plump, uniformed officer, and behind him stretched two rows of unoccupied desks. Everything appeared orderly, with papers stacked neatly, coffee cups lined up beside the coffee maker, and chairs pushed under their desks. There was no clutter anywhere. Even the bulletin boards appeared thoughtfully organized. It seemed uncharacteristically neat for a police station, giving the impression that nothing much ever happened there.

As they neared the counter, Chloe turned her attention to the officer behind it, who was absorbed in whatever was displayed on his computer screen.

"Excuse me?" Chloe said.

The officer twitched, seemingly startled by the interruption, then busily shuffled nearby papers about, as though he had been in the thick of department business.

"Sorry, yes. What can I do for you?" he fumbled.

"My name is Chloe McConnaughey. I'm here about a break-in at my house last night. Detective Sampson asked me to come by."

"Yeah, okay. Hold on." The officer turned away, picked up a handset and dialed. A muffled ring sounded from a private office at the rear of the room. Someone must have picked up because the desk officer mumbled something into the receiver, then hung up.

His eyes flitted back to Chloe. "He'll be right—"

"Hello, Ms. McConnaughey," a voice from the back of the room interrupted. A tall, lanky man in his forties had stepped out of the private office and was walking towards them. He was dressed casually in a white, button-down shirt, navy tie and dark slacks.

"I'm Detective Pete Sampson," he said in a heavy, New York accent, shaking Chloe's hand. "I'm sorry about what happened to you last night. We don't get too much of that here." His gaze fell on Ruby. "Nice to see you again."

"And you."

"Well, thank you for coming so soon," he said, motioning them behind the counter and to one of the desks. "Please, sit," he invited, gesturing to two metal chairs in front of the desk as he pulled out the chair behind it and plopped down. He eyed the bandage on Chloe's head and a concerned look crossed his face. "You know, we can do this later if you're not up to it."

"No, this is fine," Chloe assured him "I feel okay right now. Besides, I'd rather just get it over with." Already more tired than she would like to admit, she pushed her hair back off her face and leaned into the chair as much as she comfortably could.

"Well then," he said, shifting in his seat and uncapping a pen, "let's get started so you can get home."

He began by having her relate what had happened, then had her go through it again, pinning down as many details as possible. Then he asked her about Jack, other witnesses, potential motives and anything else remotely relevant. When he ran out of questions, he dropped eight mug books in front of her. After an hour, she had examined hundreds of photographs. Not one resembled the man who had bled all over her living room floor.

"I'm not surprised," he told her. "You were under a lot of stress when you got a look at him. I'm not sure I would have done much better, Ms. McConnaughey."

"Please, it's Chloe."

"Well, Chloe, we had Mr. Collings stop by earlier, and he didn't recognize anyone either." He smiled thinly and ran a hand through his wavy, brown hair, a thick, gold-crusted ring on his right hand glinting in the light. He wasn't bad looking, but had a certain slickness about him. And, given the premature lines on his face, the years were showing. "Based on what we've got, I'd have to say that this seems like a run of the mill break-in. Fact is, rental properties are more prone to this kind of thing than hotels since they generally don't have any security. Normally, these guys aren't violent. If you hadn't walked in on him, I suspect none of this," he said, gesturing towards her bandage, "would've happened."

"But do you think it's safe for her to stay there?" Ruby asked.

"I don't see why not. I really don't think you'll be seeing him again." He flipped a report over and scanned some handwritten notations on its backside. "From what we could tell, it didn't look like anything was missing from the cottage. But you obviously would know better. When you get back, take an inventory, check to see if anything's gone. If you realize something's missing, or if anything else seems strange, let me know. Is someone staying with you?"

"Well, I'm right next door," Ruby volunteered. "I'll be checking on her."

"Good," he said approvingly, then was quiet for a moment, as if considering something. "I know you're ready to go, but do you think you could hold on one second? I'll be right back and then I think we'll be done."

"Sure," Chloe said.

He disappeared down a hallway at the back of the room and Chloe returned to flipping through the mug shots absentmindedly. Something bothered her about the identification issue. She had looked right at her assailant's face and, concussion or not, she was sure she had never seen him before. But there was still something familiar about him. The thought nagged at her desperately, but she couldn't make any sense of it. By the time Sampson returned, she was no closer to it.

The chair behind the desk creaked unforgivingly as he sat down in it. "If you don't mind," he said, looking at Ruby, "I'd like to talk to Chloe alone for a minute."

Ruby glanced at Chloe, who nodded. "Okay, then," she said. "I'll be outside in the car if you need me."

Sampson waited until Ruby was out the front door, then leaned towards Chloe.

"There you go," he said, sliding a small pistol across the desk. She looked at him, unsure of what she was supposed to do.

"A gun?" she asked.

"It's already loaded. Just a spare I keep around. You can return it when things seem back to normal. Just turn off the safety if you need to use it. You have any experience with guns?"

"A little," she answered, thinking of her third to last boyfriend, a gun enthusiast who frequently took her on dates to the Atlanta Gun Club.

"Well, this one is really simple." He ran through the mechanics of it quickly.

"You really want me to take this?"

Sampson nodded. "I thought it might make you feel more safe when you're alone."

"I thought you said I had nothing to worry about."

"I don't think you do," he confirmed confidently. "But it never hurts to be prepared."

Chloe slid the weapon off the desk and placed it in her purse. "Are you sure this is okay?"

He nodded and slid a piece of paper towards her.

"Just fill this out—it's a license application and gun registration. I've already filled out the weapon information. It gives you a temporary license till it goes through, which should be later this week."

She nodded and scribbled out her information.

"Just be careful with it, and don't go waving it around unless you have to," he warned, taking the completed form back.

"Don't worry, I won't," Chloe replied. "Anything else?"

He shook his head. "Nah. Go home and sleep it off."

Chloe shook his hand, then headed towards the lobby. She had only gone a few steps when Sampson called her back. "You know, this isn't exactly encouraged, if you know what I mean," he said in a hushed tone. "They probably wouldn't appreciate me arming a civilian, so, maybe it'd be best if you kept it to yourself."

Chloe smiled appreciatively. "No problem," she said, and headed out to join Ruby.

ELEVEN

Twenty minutes later, standing in the front room of her cottage, Chloe felt like bursting into tears. It was an unqualified disaster. With the exception of a desk in the corner, all of the furniture had been flipped, shoved or broken. Directly in front of her, the remnants of the coffee table lay on its side, shards of glass from its center littering the jute rug, now folded over itself and covered in soil from an overturned planter. The couch was turned sideways, its creamy cushions marred with ugly streaks of dirt. A toppled shelf unit leaned precariously against the back of a side chair, the knick-knacks that had adorned it all tossed or smashed.

But the worst was the blood. Dried rusty drops of it were spattered haphazardly on the furniture and floor. A softball sized brown circle covered the spot where Chloe had fallen after being tossed aside like a rag doll. An even larger circle, smears stretching out from its center, marked the place where the intruder had fallen.

"Oh, dear," Ruby murmured, swiveling her gaze from the debris to her ward's ashen face. "Are you all right?"

Chloe nodded. "I just wasn't expecting it to be this bad."

She reached down for a broken piece of pottery and Ruby grabbed her hand. "It'll keep until tomorrow. You need your rest."

Chloe shook her head. "I'll never sleep knowing this is out here waiting for me. Besides, what if there's something, some detail I'm forgetting. Maybe sifting through this mess will drag it out of me."

Ruby stared at her, hands on her hips. "Thirty minutes, Chloe. That's all. I mean it, too."

"Thirty minutes," Chloe agreed.

They started by filling a trash bag with the unsalvageable remains. Then, with Chloe still busy scooping dirt off the tile, Ruby carried the empty coffee table frame to the street. When she returned, Chloe was preparing to vacuum the rug.

"Don't even think about it," Ruby ordered. "I'll do it. Same goes for moving the furniture back. Just leave it where it is."

"Ruby—"

"Why don't you start looking around, see if anything is missing like Detective Sampson told you to?"

Chloe sat down as Ruby set to work. She rubbed her forehead, recognizing the mild throbbing that was always a precursor to a major migraine. As much as she didn't want to admit it, the activity was a little much for her.

Following Ruby's suggestion, she started going through the cottage, looking for anything that was missing or wrong. But nothing caught her eye, and everything that mattered was exactly as it ought to be. Her laptop was in the kitchen drawer where she usually hid it. Her passport and other important documents were still in her nightstand drawer, concealed under a few books. Even the bag of camera equipment she had dropped beside her bed the day before seemed undisturbed. She fingered the pieces of jewelry she kept on a small, silver-colored tray on the dresser. *It's all here,* she mused, surprised that nothing in the house had been taken. *Either I walked in on him right after he got here, or he wasn't interested in robbing me in the first place.*

"Time's up," Ruby chided, her round face appearing in the bedroom doorway.

"I'm done anyway," Chloe said, tucking a renegade strand of curled hair behind her ear and exhaling deeply. "I think you were right about me getting worn out. I should probably lie down for a while."

"Good. Now go," Ruby directed, pointing at the bed. "I'll wake you in a couple of hours when dinner is ready—"

"But you don't—"

"And I'm not taking no for an answer."

Chloe didn't argue any further. As exhausted as she was, she expected she would be asleep as soon as her head hit the pillow. But minutes later, snuggled under her duvet, she found herself completely preoccupied by that stubbornly elusive detail about the attack. When replaying the incident over and over failed her, she tried to think about something else. The first thing that came to mind was Jack.

Poor guy, she thought. *He got a lot more than he bargained for. And then to stay all night at the hospital* . . . Chloe glanced at the clock. It was still early. She picked up her cell and dialed the number Jack had left with Ruby.

"Hello?" a strong voice answered.

"Jack?"

"Yeah." He paused for a moment. "Chloe?"

"Now what would you have done if it had been one of your other girlfriends?"

"How are you?" he asked urgently, ignoring her teasing.

"Fine, thanks to you. I never got a chance to say thank you last night."

"For what?" He asked, his tone lightening. "I just distracted him. You're the one that took him out."

"Seriously, Jack. I don't know what would've happened if you hadn't shown up."

"Well, you're welcome. What did the doctor say? I'm sorry I had to go. Some stuff came up and I wanted to get—"

"Don't apologize. Ruby told me you stayed all night." Something unexpectedly caught in her throat. "Thanks."

His tone softened to match hers. "Like I said. You're welcome. So, really, what did he say?"

"I just need some rest. But only two hours at a time. I ended up with a concussion," Chloe said, rubbing her forehead.

"Been there, done that."

Chloe's eyes narrowed. "What do you mean? Ruby said you weren't hurt."

"I wasn't. But I've had a concussion before. That getting up every two hours is miserable."

"Yeah, I'm not looking forward to it." She closed her eyes for a moment, trying to ward off the threatening headache, and changed subjects. "So, I was surprised to see my car in the driveway. Ruby said that was your doing."

"I had a friend help me. It was nothing. Couldn't have you stranded, could I?"

"Well, I'll pay you back for the tire."

"I'll just add it to your tab. You can owe me." Chloe could almost see his impish grin. "So is somebody with you?"

"Ruby. She's staying the night."

"Good. You don't need to be by yourself. If you need somebody tomorrow night, I'll be glad to hang out. Probably don't cook as well as she does, though."

Chloe sighed, feeling guilty. "You really don't have to go out of your way like that for me, Jack. I hardly know you."

"This again? Okay—my name is Jack Collings, I'm a concierge at the Southern Star, my friend is an idiot—"

"And you are terrible at picking up women." Chloe finished playfully.

"Well, if you're talking about the football to the head thing, after last night I'd have to say things are even on that score. You took a bump on the head from my football, and I've got ten stitches thanks to your coffee table."

"Ten stitches? Oh, Jack. I'm so, so sorry," she apologized, her voice full of regret. "Ruby didn't tell me. She said you were fine."

"Hey, stop," he said reassuringly. "It's no big deal. And I shed more of his blood then he shed of mine. I just got banged up a little. Nothing a few days of rest and relaxation won't cure. Besides, a trip to the ER is the perfect excuse for some time off work."

"The *ER*, Jack? That's more than 'a little banged up.'"

"Stop worrying, will you? Come see me at the club tomorrow and I'll prove to you that I'm fine."

"But I thought you weren't working."

"I'm not, Sherlock. I told Mike he could use some scuba gear I've got stored there. Just come meet me for lunch, and I promise you a relaxing afternoon with no worries."

It wasn't a bad idea, really. *The last thing I need is to spend tomorrow alone with my imagination,* she told herself. Besides, it was only lunch. And he did save her life. If he was crazy enough to want to see her again . . .

"Okay, then, lunch. Say, noon?"

"Noon, it is," he echoed triumphantly. "Meet me at the beachside bar."

"Okay."

"And Chloe," he said, his voice turning tender. "Feel better."

Two minutes later Chloe was snoring.

TWELVE

Chloe slept so deeply that she was only vaguely aware of Ruby waking her every two hours to make sure she wasn't comatose. In the morning, she rolled out of bed to the beckoning smell of sizzling eggs and bacon.

"Good morning," Ruby sang as Chloe padded into the kitchen. She had on a bright floral housedress that made her short, rounded body look even more so. Fluffy blue slippers covered her feet and her graying hair was piled on top of her head in a loose bun.

"I heard you coming and fixed a plate," Ruby said, nodding to a solitary dish on the table.

"You're not staying?"

"I've got some things to take care of at the house." An afterthought of concern flashed across Ruby's face. "You will be all right for a few hours won't you?"

"Of course I will. You go ahead. Actually, I feel a lot better this morning."

"I'll come by a little later to check on you."

"You don't have to do that. Why don't you just call—"

"I'm coming by, Chloe," she said adamantly. "So stop arguing."

Chloe held up her hands in surrender. "Are you always this pushy?"

Ruby slung her bag over her shoulder. "Three daughters, remember?" she asked, grinning. "Pushy comes with the territory." Ruby hugged her, then left Chloe to her breakfast. It was the first real meal she'd had since the attack, and she downed it in minutes. Not yet ready to begin the day, she made a cup of Chamomile tea and settled into the front porch swing where her thoughts drifted to Tate.

She had dreamed incessantly about him the night before, although, thankfully, there had been no nightmares this time. Just memories. One in particular had repeatedly visited her, of a time at UGA when Tate had come to her rescue. Or at least tried to. They'd been playing pool at this dingy student bar, when a redneck twice Tate's size started hitting on her. She'd blown him off and wanted to leave, but Tate's testosterone got the better of him and he took the guy on. He'd been beaten senseless and ended up making his own trip to the emergency room that night.

It hadn't mattered that he was obviously outmatched. Tate had it in his head that it was his responsibility to deal with the guy, and there was no dissuading him. Once he got his teeth into something, there was no shaking him loose. The same bullheaded attitude had nearly ended his career. Did end it, until this last job rescued him.

She smiled warmly at the thought and sipped her tea. They'd had so much fun in Miami on the weekend the company had insisted she come down to join them. On their final night, when the execs had wooed Tate on a private dinner cruise down the canals of Fort Lauderdale, she'd had her last truly good moment with him. Leaning against the deck rail, he had hugged her excitedly, his eyes brimming with possibility.

"This is it, Chlo. I know it. All the disappointments. All the dead ends. They were all moving me—us—to this." His wavy hair had hardly moved in the wind, and his amber eyes focused intently on hers. *"Six figures, Chlo. Three plus—and that's just to start. And significant profit sharing, not just some mere token percentage of a percentage because I happened to be employed by the company when I developed the software."*

She had put aside her selfish sadness over the distance the job would put between them and enthusiastically encouraged him. This was the opportunity he'd been seeking his whole life, and she wouldn't dare dampen it in the slightest. All she had ever wanted was for him to be happy and content. All he'd ever wanted was for the two of them to be set, taken care of, so they'd never have to rely on anyone or anything again. This job promised to do both.

But as the months cranked by, it became obvious to Chloe that, though the position provided plenty of money, it offered little contentment. When she did manage to get him on the phone he was tired and grumpy, admittedly work-obsessed and dismissive of any notion of breaking away for even a day or two to see her. He'd never not had time for her before. She tried to talk to him about it, to tell him that he needed to get his priorities straight, but he didn't want to listen. The last time she'd brought it up, during their last conversation a few months before he died, he'd exploded. The echoes of their angry voices still sounded in her head.

"You're ignoring me, Tate. I can hardly get you on the phone anymore. I'm not some friend you can just blow off! I'm family. Your only family—"

"Ignore you?" he bellowed back. "I'm working, Chloe! Killing myself down here. And not just for me. For you too. Don't you get that? So you never have to—"

"What, work again? Tate, will you just listen to yourself? I'm fine. I'm making good money. I can take care of myself. I'm not eight anymore. I don't need you to set me up in some mansion on a hill somewhere. I just need you to be around."

"It's never good enough. I'm never good enough. You're never satisfied with what I do—"

"What are you talking about?" she had shrieked. "You're the one who's never satisfied. I'm perfectly happy in my life. I don't need all the money and the fancy clothes and dinners and cars! That's your dream, not mine."

"I don't know how you got so naive, but I haven't forgotten that the one thing you can count on in life is that life will turn on you in a second. This is our insurance against pain, Chloe. Our insurance that no one and nothing can ever really touch us. I still see that, even if you don't, and I'm going take care of you whether you like it or not." He paused, taking a deep breath. "Come on, Chlo. I don't want to fight." The edgy anger in his voice was gone, replaced by imploring tenderness. "Don't you get it? I have to do this. I'm your big brother."

His soft tone kneaded her heart as seconds of silence passed. "Bigger by only three minutes," she finally offered up as a white flag.

She could almost see his toothy grin. "Three very long, very important minutes."

"Yeah, yeah."

"Truce?"

"Truce."

That was the last thing she remembered ever saying to him. Had she known it would be their parting words, she would have said so much more. He really was the only thing she had ever been able to count on in this life. Her best friend. Her safety net. She wished she could have told him that. Chloe slid a finger beneath a gathering tear and flicked it away. *At least we ended the conversation well,* she consoled herself, raising her gaze to the swelling ocean. *At least I can be grateful for that.*

It was then that she noticed a taupe four-door parked on the opposite side of the street a couple of houses down from hers. The driver, alone in the car, sat stoically behind the wheel, his eyes hidden behind aviator glasses. And he seemed to be watching her.

Chloe's radar tingled nervously. *Was he there when I first came out?* She didn't remember him being there, but she didn't remember seeing him drive up the street either. Two days ago she wouldn't have given it a second thought, but now . . . She stared at him, feeling stupid, but unable to quell her concern. As her imagination churned with thoughts of her attacker coming to finish what he had started, the driver leaned over the passenger seat. After fumbling around, he sat back up holding a camera, turned away from her and starting clicking off shots of the ocean.

"Paranoid," Chloe muttered, exasperated by her runaway imagination. "Totally paranoid."

* * * * *

"What's she doing?"

The voice in his earpiece boomed and he cringed.

"Going inside," Vargas reported, reaching up to lower the volume. The cottage door closed behind her, but he continued holding up the camera for appearance's sake.

"Did she see you?"

"Yeah, but I took care of it."

"I told you not to park so close."

"I can't get a good visual any further away."

"I think you'd better leave."

"And what about her?"

"We'll send somebody else over. We can't risk her spotting you again."

"Okay, okay," he said, dropping the camera into the seat beside him and cranking the car. "I'm headed out now." After turning around at the end of the street, he cruised past McConnaughey's cottage, down the hillside, and onto the beach highway towards Binghamton proper.

* * * * *

Chloe piddled with work for most of the morning, playing with the computer layout of the photos she might use for her book before getting ready for lunch with Jack. She chose a white cotton sundress and strappy leather sandals and pulled her hair back in a loose ponytail, trying her best to cover the bald spot where the stitches were. As she grabbed her keys to go, she had a thought and stopped to call Ruby. After thanking her again for breakfast, she filled her in on her plans.

"Do you really think that's a good idea?" Ruby chided. "I mean, should you drive? Can I take you?"

"No, no. It's not far. Just lunch with Jack at the resort where he works."

"Well, I suppose that's all right. I've got a feeling he'll look after you. But you make him bring you right home if you start feeling poorly."

"I will."

"By the way," Ruby continued, "I just made some banana bread. Thought you might like some. It's warm, just out of the oven."

Chloe looked at her watch. "You know that normally I'd run right over to take you up on that, but if I wait any longer I'll be late."

"Well, you should come by later, then. Or I could bring it by when you get home."

"That would be great."

"And I almost forgot, I have some of your mail here. I don't know why that blessed mailman can't get the houses straight. I've had it about a week now, dear. I'm sorry I held it so long. Senioritis, I guess," she said, chuckling.

"Don't worry about it. I'll get it when I see you later."

"It's a date."

Chloe hung up and started for the door, but guilt slowed her steps. Ruby had been so good to her and all the woman wanted was a little companionship. *I'm already going to be late,* she thought. *Ruby did go to all that trouble. I suppose five more minutes won't make that much difference.*

Chloe stepped out the door and down the white wooden steps leading into her backyard. Shielded from the view of the street by their privacy fences, she crossed into Ruby's yard and knocked on her back door. Ruby timidly peeked through the window as if expecting to see a burglar, complete with black ski mask and leather gloves, standing on her steps in broad daylight. Her apprehensive stare quickly morphed into a cheery smile upon spotting Chloe.

"Well, hello dear," she said, unlocking the door and swinging it open for Chloe. "Did your plans change?" Ruby asked hopefully.

"No," she answered, "I just kept thinking about how good that bread sounded and thought I would take some for Jack. If that's okay?"

"Well, of course, dear," Ruby said, beaming. "Come on in." Chloe obediently followed behind her as she waddled into the bright white kitchen.

"Ruby, what if we got together later tonight for coffee and banana bread? How does that sound?"

Ruby smiled, handed Chloe a banana bread loaf wrapped in tight plastic, and brushed breadcrumbs from the front of her dress. "Sounds good to me, dear." Ruby paused, tapping a nail on a tooth while she thought. "I know there was something else . . . oh!" she exclaimed. "Your mail. I nearly forgot again." She reached for a stack of papers by the phone and shuffled through them, pulling out a padded manila envelope with Izzie's return address on it.

"Here you go," she said, a sheepish expression on her face. "Sorry it took so long."

"Not a problem," Chloe told her, immediately stuffing the envelope inside her cavernous straw bag. "It's just mail forwarded by my friend. I'm sure it's mostly junk mail and stuff from the office, anyway. So, I'll see you tonight at my house at . . . well, is eight o'clock too late?"

"Perfect. I'll be there with bells on," Ruby promised, patting Chloe's shoulder as she left through the back door.

Chloe waved goodbye then walked through Ruby's fenced backyard into her own, locked up behind herself, and sprinted out the front door.

THIRTEEN

The moment Chloe stepped out Ruby's back door, Ruby locked it behind her. After what had happened to Chloe, she wasn't taking any chances. A life-long resident of Chicago, Ruby was no stranger to the dangers of unlocked doors. At least a dozen friends in her old neighborhood had been the victims of burglary at one time or another. Her husband, Mort, God rest his soul, had even had an alarm system installed when the Dooley's house three doors down had been broken into.

Ruby puttered back to the kitchen to pour herself another cup of coffee. *What a nice girl, making a detour for this old lady. You just don't see that in young people these days.* Ruby decided that to show her appreciation she would bring Chloe some of the fancy French coffee her daughter had given her for Christmas. It would be the perfect complement to the banana bread.

Ruby spent the morning working a puzzle her daughter had sent and watching a broadcast of *Wheel of Fortune*. Right in the middle of Pete from Detroit choosing "A" for his vowel, her doorbell rang. Suspicious in light of recent events, Ruby went to her bedroom down the hall and clandestinely peeked out from behind the curtains to see who was calling. A clean-cut young man, dressed in a white golf shirt and khaki pants, stood waiting on the front porch. He wore dark sunglasses and carried a clipboard in his right hand. *He doesn't look like a thief,* Ruby thought. *More like a salesman, or maybe,* she thought, suddenly intrigued, *a plainclothes detective investigating Chloe's break-in.* Her interest piqued, she quickly made her way to the front room.

"Yes?" she asked, opening the door just a crack.

"Hello, ma'am. How are you today?"

"Fine, thank you. Are you from the police department?"

Looking slightly amused, the man cocked his head. "No, I'm not. May I ask if you're the lady of the house?"

"Well, yes, I am. And you are?"

The man smiled large and purposefully, clearly attempting to disarm her. "I'm sorry. Didn't I say who I was?" Ruby shook her head, no. He held the clipboard out so that she could see it and pointed to the logo on top. "Sea and Shell Realty, ma'am." He thrust out his free hand and Ruby shook it. "I understand you're the owner?"

"Why do you need to know that?"

"I'm sorry. Let me explain myself. We're speaking with the owners of properties in the area to determine if they have any interest in selling. We have a buyer interested in acquiring numerous properties to rent out. Based on real estate records it appears you own this house?"

"That's right."

"If you have a moment, I'd like to tell you about my client's proposition." He leaned toward the open door and sniffed the air. "Is that . . . banana bread I smell?" As Ruby nodded, he smiled warmly. "My mother used to bake that for me. Haven't had it in years."

Ruby wasn't keen on salesmen in general and normally her reaction would have been to politely dismiss him, but he seemed like a nice man, and, after all, he appreciated a good banana bread. She had not been looking forward to spending the morning alone anyway, and chatting with him for a little while seemed a good alternative. Truth was, for weeks she had been considering finally heading back to the States to be closer to her daughter and grandchildren. Without Mort, St. Gideon hadn't been the retirement paradise she'd dreamed of. And with the cottage being worth what it was, she might even get enough to move into her daughter's fancy golf course neighborhood. *It's at least worth talking about,* she convinced herself.

"Come on in," she said, stepping aside to let him enter. He did, and she closed and locked the door behind him. "Would you care for some banana bread and coffee while we talk?"

He stood by the coffee table and grinned. "You read my mind."

Ruby grinned back at him. "Well, you sit," she told him,

gesturing towards the couch. "I'll be just a minute."

Ruby hurried off to the kitchen, excited about the prospect of companionship and conversation. "You know," she called out, "I always thought it was crazy to buy this place instead of rent. But on a wild hair, Mort bought it to surprise me on the day he retired. Couldn't exactly fuss at him for that, could I?" She carefully arranged a plate of banana bread slices and two cups of coffee on a tray and scurried back to the front room.

She was disappointed to find him still standing. "Well, here we are," she said, moving past him to set the tray down on the coffee table. As she turned around to face him, her eyes scrolled down to his hands, which were no longer holding the clipboard. Puzzled, she looked up at him. "Isn't it a little hot outside to be wearing gloves?" she asked.

"Yes," Korrigan replied evenly. "It is."

FOURTEEN

Chloe found Jack nursing a beer by the largest of the club's three kidney-shaped pools, all overlooking the beach. He looked very relaxed, kicked back in khaki pants and a lightweight grey button-down, rolled up to the elbows.

"You made it," he said, rising to pull a striped canvas chair out for her.

"Just following orders," she quipped good-naturedly, scooting up to the white metal table. A waiter appeared nearly instantaneously and set a Perrier with a lemon wedge in front of her.

"Figured I couldn't go wrong with water," Jack explained.

Chloe smiled. "Thanks. So what's good?"

On Jack's recommendation, they ordered a light lunch of shrimp and cold salads. As soon as the waiter left, Chloe eyed a padded area around Jack's bicep that looked to be a bandage hidden beneath his sleeve. She raised her eyebrows. "Not hurt bad, huh? Let's see it then."

Rolling his eyes, Jack proceeded to show her his trophies from the attack, consisting of nearly half a dozen stitched lacerations and twice as many lesser cuts. But like he had said, none seemed very serious, although when she gently prodded the stitchwork on his collarbone he winced noticeably. While they ate, Chloe brought Jack up to speed on her diagnosis and her visit to the police station, but not wanting to worry him, didn't mention Detective Sampson's gun.

"Just a regular break-in, then. That's their take on it?"

Chloe's brow furrowed. "You sound skeptical."

"No, no. It's . . . well, what else would it be, right?"

"Jack." Her tone demanded elaboration.

"Well, it's just that the guy seemed to know what he was doing. He was really tough to put down."

"Well, that makes sense doesn't it? He doesn't want to go jail, maybe he's even high, too. It's amazing you weren't the one who ended up knocked out on the floor." Her brow rippled with curiosity. "Come to think of it, how did you manage that?"

Jack's eyes flicked up to hers. "Just lucky I guess. He was pretty busy with you when I came in the door. And, as I recall, laid out on the floor was exactly where I *did* end up by the time you came in with that club."

"Not bad for a girl who always got picked last for softball."

"I find that hard to believe."

"Sports were never my strong suit," she said.

"Well, how about *water*sports?" Jack asked. "See that catamaran over there?" Chloe's eyes followed his pointed fingers to a large, red-sailed catamaran parked on the shoreline.

"Yours?"

Jack shook his head, no. "Resort's. I don't know if you remember me asking you after dinner the other night—"

"I remember," Chloe interrupted.

"So then, I thought maybe now would be a good time for you and I to go for that spin. Get you some fresh air."

Chloe raised her hand to her forehead to block the sun from her view. "I don't know. You think an afternoon in the sun is the healthiest way for a recently comatose individual to spend the day?"

"Yeah I do. The sunshine won't hurt you, and the fresh air would probably do you good."

She paused momentarily to consider it. "Well, how can I argue with a medical opinion from a beach concierge?"

He shook his head. "You can't."

After lingering over lunch, Chloe picked up a swimsuit at the club shop, which Jack insisted on springing for. By two-thirty they were headed out with Jack capably steering the craft beyond the breaking waves into the smooth water beyond. He let her try her hand at sailing the catamaran, and, surprisingly, she wasn't half bad. A little jerky perhaps, but Jack assured her that would change with a few more lessons. After a couple of hours, they headed back to the club. By the time they were changed and ready to go, it was nearly five o'clock.

"You hungry?" Chloe asked as they made their way to the parking lot.

"I guess I could eat. What'd you have in mind?"

"Well seeing as how I owe you dinner, I was thinking we could hit this little Italian place on the east shore."

"You're not tired of me yet?"

"To death. But I can't stand knowing I owe you."

The two hopped in Jack's Jeep and started around the coast. By the time they reached the little trattoria Chloe had discovered during her first week on the island, both were starving. As they filled up on lasagna, spaghetti Bolognese, and cannoli, Chloe marveled at how comfortable and easy it was just sitting there with Jack. So different from the others somehow. *It's probably not smart,* she thought, watching him lasso noodles with his fork. *Probably setting myself up. But,* she argued with herself, *we're just friends, so there's no risk. I'm just having dinner with a friend. Just friends.*

The dinner and conversation stretched smoothly until nearly seven-thirty, when Chloe proudly claimed the check. After she paid, they stepped out of the lobby to an exquisite display of radiant color on the horizon.

"Jack, if you're not tired of *me* yet, I have an idea."

He leaned on the hood of his Jeep. "Shoot."

She laughed.

"What?" he asked, bemused.

She chuckled and dug a camera out of her enormous bag and held it up. "It's just . . . that was kind of the idea. If you're game, we could get some terrific photos of that sunset. If we hurry."

"I thought sunsets were too pedestrian," he reminded her.

"So maybe I'm reconsidering."

He eyed her thoughtfully. "I know a place," he told her, already sliding in behind the wheel. "Hop in." She apparently wasn't moving fast enough because he chided, "Seriously, come on or we'll miss it."

Chloe stepped lively around the front of the Jeep and swung her legs inside. She had barely closed the door when Jack zipped backwards out of the parking space. "Buckle up," he warned before peeling brazenly out of the lot and rocketing down the highway.

* * * * *

A few parking spaces over a driver fumbled in his seat, reacting to the quickly departing Jeep by cranking his engine and stepping on the gas. His sedan shot forward, nearly taking out an older couple just leaving the restaurant. The driver jammed his foot on the brake, stopping just inches from the would-be victims who remained frozen in place. Swearing, he backed up, pulled around them, and gunned it to the bottom of the road, where the Jeep had disappeared from sight. Swearing again, he pulled onto the main road, headed in the direction of the resort.

* * * * *

After a ten-minute drive, Jack turned off the main road onto a sharply inclined driveway that ended half a mile later at a circular gravel lot near the top of a hill.

"This is absolutely gorgeous," Chloe said, admiring the thousands of tiny red and pink flowers covering the thick foliage at the lot's edges. She hopped out, retrieving her camera before tossing her bag into the Jeep's large, rear security compartment for safekeeping.

"If you think this is good, wait till you get to the top," Jack told her as he pointed her toward a set of narrow stone steps.

"How high does it go?" she asked.

"All the way," he answered, stepping over a tangle of leafy vines that had grown across the path.

After what seemed like three stories worth of climbing, Chloe pushed through bushes that served as a natural gate onto a towering stone cliff rising straight out of the water's edge. It was nothing more than a deep ledge really, room for four or five people at most. She toed out to the edge and took in the panoramic view of the southern coastline. The fiery sun bronzed the sky, its pink and red streaked clouds mirroring the flowers on the bushes behind her as frothy waves broke on the rocks below.

"Wow."

"God certainly knows how to put on a show, doesn't he?"

"Hmmm," she said as she adjusted the dials on her camera.

"Makes it hard to believe all this just popped here."

"What?" she asked, peering through the viewfinder.

Jack shrugged. "You know, order out of chaos? The Big Bang?" He kicked a lone pebble over the edge of the cliff. "I've seen a lot of chaos. Never saw it turn into order. What about you?"

"I don't know," she shrugged, staring out at the sea. "I've never really thought much about it. I'm not exactly from a—what did you say the other night—a 'good little Methodist' upbringing." She changed positions and clicked off a few more shots. "My mom wasn't religious, and my dad's only god was himself." *Click. Click.* "I've always been more of a do-it-yourself kind of girl. I don't like the thought of not being in control of what happens to me."

"Control's a slippery snake. Hard to hold onto."

"Don't I know it." She turned to smile at him. "You this deep on all your second dates?"

He squinted at her. "Hey, this is no date. Just two friends hanging," he corrected.

"Right," Chloe said, her insides blushing as she turned back to the view and raised the camera. "So, are you this deep with all your *friends?*"

"This isn't deep. This is just making conversation."

She chuckled as the shutter clicked. "By asking my theory on the beginnings of the universe?"

"Well," he surrendered, "when you put it that way."

"My theory is that all you've got is now. Enjoy it while you can." She stopped and pulled the camera down thoughtfully. "It's like photos. You capture the moment when it's good. Doesn't matter what was there before or what's coming after. You better get the shot when it's there, or you never will."

"Okay, so now who's being deep?"

"Shut up and stand behind me," she said with an exasperated grin. "You're throwing shadows across my frame."

"Oh, so sorry," he drawled and moved to stand behind her as she stared out into the grand expanse. He leaned in. "You'd better hurry," he urged, his breath warm on her neck as he nodded toward the horizon. "It'll set soon."

Ignoring the dizzy heat spreading from the spot where his words had touched her, Chloe refocused and continued shooting.

* * * * *

"Sorry I kept you so late," Jack apologized as he pulled into the parking lot of the club.

"Don't be. This was great. And I've still got time to see Ruby."

She lifted her camera from her neck as she twisted to open the door. "Oh, my bag," she said, turning back to him.

He nodded and slipped out, moving around to the rear of the Jeep. "Call if you need anything," he said as he unlocked the security compartment.

"I will," Chloe replied, glancing at her watch to confirm the time as she grabbed her bag from where it had slid amongst the pile of diving equipment, tools, magazines and other random junk strewn inside.

"You want me to follow you home?" he asked.

"No, I'll be fine. Ruby's got my back." She smiled wryly and so did he.

He ran a hand through his hair. "Well, I'll check in with you later. Okay?"

"Okay." She paused. "And thanks again for today."

"Anytime," he replied and nodded toward the road. "Now go keep your hot date."

Jack watched until her taillights disappeared in the distance, then rolled towards the exit, intending to turn in for the night. But as he waited for an opening in traffic, he changed his mind and swung the car around. *Maybe just one drink,* he promised himself, *while I figure out how to handle that girl.*

FIFTEEN

Chloe unlocked the front door tentatively, poked her head inside, then went quietly from room to room, flipping on lights, confirming that she was alone. Finally satisfied, she set her bag on the kitchen counter and dug her cell out to call Ruby.

The phone rang several times with no answer. Chloe hung up and dialed again. Still nothing. *Her car is outside. She's definitely home.* Worry prickled the back of her mind. *She's fine. I'm sure she's fine. She's probably just asleep.* Another prickle. *But it's not like her to miss a chance to have somebody's ear for an hour.*

Deciding a quick check was warranted, Chloe headed out her backdoor and crossed through to Ruby's backyard. A faint light bled through the drawn kitchen curtains. She marched up the back steps and knocked on the door. Once. Twice.

"Ruby?" she called out. Pushing away visions of the man that attacked her, Chloe opened the screen door and knocked harder on the inner door. It swung inward, the latch making a popping sound as it moved away from the door frame.

This isn't right.

"Ruby?" Chloe called timidly. "Are you in there?" She poked her head inside. The darkness was cut only by a small lamp casting heavy shadows around the kitchen. Summoning her courage, Chloe pushed the door open and stepped through.

"Ruby?"

Chloe stood very still and listened. The only sound seemed to be that of a television located somewhere down the adjacent hallway that ran the length of the small house. Stepping tentatively into it, she looked to her right and saw a flickering glare emanating from Ruby's bedroom at the far end of the hall.

She fell asleep with the television on and doesn't hear me. That's all.

"Ruby please answer if you're—"

Something moved against her leg. She screamed, jumped to the side, and kicked furiously at what she imagined was a hand trying to grab her ankle. Her second kick made contact.

"Mmmeooooooowwww!"

At the ear-piercing screech, Chloe's hand flew to her chest, clutching at her pounding heart. "Rummy," she panted, staring at Ruby's pet tabby. The cat measured her with its golden eyes, then, decidedly unconcerned, slinked off into the kitchen. Her pulse still racing, Chloe picked her way down the hall and looked in the bedroom. But Ruby wasn't there, or in the bathroom either.

An uneasy sense of foreboding swelled. Chloe took a few controlled breaths, still pushing aside images of stumbling onto the intruder from her cottage. Going back up the hall she went into the living room, felt the wall for a light switch, and flicked it on.

Ruby's purse sat on the entry table by the front door. *She wouldn't leave this. No way.*

The images of the black clad intruder came furiously now, and, reversing directions, she ran headlong to the back door, flinging it open and catapulting through it. She stumbled down the steps, tripping on the last one and barely catching herself before face planting onto the grass. After sprinting through the two yards, she ripped her back door open, locking it behind her before dashing to the kitchen, where she snatched her cell off the counter. Frantically, she scrolled through her contacts and pressed "call."

"Hello?"

"Detective Sampson?" she asked, her voice high.

"Who is this?"

"Chloe, Chloe McConnaughey," she answered between heaving breaths. "I'm sorry to bother you, but, you said to call if . . . well, if anything happened and . . . it's my neighbor. She's not home, but her bag's there and her car's there, and something just isn't right."

"You were right to call, Chloe. Where are you?"

"In my house."

"I'll be right there. Just stay put," he instructed authoritatively. "She's probably just been picked up by a friend, or took a cab."

76

Chloe shook her head. "No, she wouldn't leave her bag. Please just hurry," she urged.

"Ten minutes, I promise. You have your gun?"

"Under my pillow." Rising anxiety cut her voice to nearly a whisper.

"Go get it. Then lock yourself in your bedroom."

"Okay."

"I'm gonna hang up now. I'll be there in just a few minutes."

She nodded as he disconnected. Clutching the phone, wishing he had stayed on the line, she headed to the bedroom.

Jack. I could call Jack. No, I couldn't involve—

A noise from somewhere else in the house snapped her to attention.

Her first thought was the overhead light in the kitchen. She reached up and flicked it off. *The gun. Under my pillow. All the way down the hall.*

I need a weapon. She went to pull the butcher knife from the block on the counter, but it wasn't there. Snatching up a smaller blade, she reached into the hallway and flicked off the light. Brandishing the knife in front of her, she started down the hall toward her bedroom. Halfway down she stretched out a quivering hand to push open her bedroom door. One second too late she sensed the presence behind her.

A cord yanked hard against her neck, cutting off her oxygen. She pulled against it with her free hand, but her attacker was much stronger. Chloe swung the knife behind her in a downward arc, but struck the wall instead of her attacker, the impact forcing the knife out of her hand.

Chloe bucked wildly as her attacker dragged her backwards into her bedroom, yelling at her to stop moving. When she didn't, he tightened the cord until black started to creep in at the edges of her vision. *I'm going to pass out and then he's going to kill me.* He leaned in and over the ringing in her ears whispered with hot, stale breath into her ear.

"Just sit down and shut up." He shoved her hard in the middle of her back, sending her flying onto the bed where she landed face down on the mattress. She flipped over quickly, grabbing at her neck and massaging the welt left by the cord. She forced herself to control her breathing. *Can't hyperventilate. Can't.*

Still watching her, he pulled out a cell and dialed. Chloe kept her eyes on his, surreptitiously sliding her hand beneath her pillow. In a burst of motion, Chloe yanked the gun out and released the safety, looking up just in time to see him lunging at her, arms outstretched. She leveled the barrel at him and fired.

Thunder exploded in the tiny room. Chloe watched in horror, expecting him to drop. The terror in his eyes told her he expected the same. But when he clutched his torso, searching for the wound, there wasn't one.

"You didn't miss," growled a voice in the doorway.

Chloe turned, her stomach plummeting at what she saw.

"I knew we couldn't risk you picking up your own piece," Detective Sampson crooned as he walked over to Chloe and lifted the .22 from her trembling hand. "Somebody," he said, emptying the remaining blanks from the gun, "could have gotten hurt." He cavalierly tossed the weapon to the other man, then sat down in a wicker chair by the dresser. As if taking a cue, Sampson's associate moved to stand protectively in the doorway.

Bewildered, Chloe gasped, "Detective . . . what—"

"I was a little closer than ten minutes away. Look, I've got a job to do," he said, ignoring her gaping expression that begged for an explanation. "So what do you say we get started and have a little talk?"

Shock, disbelief, and nausea churned within her. *Betrayed again.* And she was alone. No one was coming.

"Talk?" she stammered. "What—about what?" Horror struck her heart again as she thought of Ruby. "Tell me what's happened to Ruby," she said, almost in a whisper.

Sampson sighed in exasperation. "You really want to do it this way?"

"Do what this way? I have no idea what you're talking about." Her voice trembled and she struggled to rein in the tears.

His eyes narrowed. "The way I see it, you can drag this out if you want, but one way or another we'll get what we're after. How painful a process that has to be is entirely up to you."

"I *swear* I don't know what you're talking about!" she protested vehemently. "You're making a huge mistake."

Sampson scooted forward to the edge of the chair, leaned his elbows on his knees, and squinted up at Chloe. "If you make me spell it out for you, it's just going to make me more frustrated than I already am."

"But I don't—"

She was cut short by a hard backhand to her left cheek. Sampson stood and began pacing in front of the chair.

"See, I knew it'd be like this. I told him she'd be stubborn. Could have been real simple, but noooo. Gotta be just like a woman and go and make things difficult." He took a couple more calm steps, then, in one swift movement angrily yanked up the wicker chair and slammed it down backwards in front of Chloe, making her jump. He threw a leg over the chair and straddled it, resting his arms on the back.

"I am gonna get tired of this real fast, Chloe. I want that flash drive and I want it now."

Chloe's mind raced. "What flash drive? What, for my photos? I've got two or three in the desk dra—"

She was interrupted by another swift slap. Her hand moved to cradle her tender jaw as she turned to face him again.

"We already found those," he snarled. "Where's your purse?" he demanded.

"It's . . . it's in the kitchen," she offered, her voice shaky.

Sampson nodded at the other man, who headed in that direction. "Check it," he called out. "Bring me any memory cards or flash drives, or any data storage devices you find."

He turned back to her. "We know you have it. We know you got it today. If you continue this, it's going to get real ugly, real fast."

Chloe answered him in a steely voice. "I didn't get any flash drive today. I can't give you what *I don't have*."

After about half a minute, the other man reappeared in the doorway, shaking his head at Sampson. "Nothing," he reported.

Sampson cursed resignedly. "All right then. If that's how you want it." Taking her right hand, he yanked it towards him. "But ten-to-one you tell us before I get to the second finger."

"Please, don't," she begged, choking back a sob, "I promise, I *really* don't know what you're talking about!"

Sampson shrugged, grasped her pinky finger with both hands and started to twist. Her scream sounded just as Sampson's cell phone rang. He dropped her hand. "You've got to the end of this call, honey," he threatened, pulling out his cell.

He stood up and turned towards the wall. "Sampson, here." Silence followed for several seconds while he listened and paced.

"You've got to be kidding me. I'm kinda in the middle of

something, and I—" Sampson exhaled in defeat. "Okay . . . *Okay*. I'll be there in twenty minutes." He shoved the phone in his pocket and swiveled back around.

"Something's come up. I've got to go to the station," he announced, turning to face Chloe. He jabbed a finger in her face. "You should've talked. My boss isn't as nice as I am." He pushed past his associate into the hallway. "Go on and take her to him. He can do this there. We don't need somebody showing up here, anyway. Give me a minute's head start, then you go."

"Yeah, okay," the man answered, eyeing Chloe with interest.

"And don't screw this up," Sampson barked, then interpreting his associate's gaze, added, "and don't touch her. Got it?"

"Hey, I don't work for you," he grunted back. "Take care of your business and I'll take care of mine. And if I were you I'd be more concerned about how unhappy he's gonna be that you left."

Sampson glared at the man, but instead of sparring with him, turned and strode out of the house. The man in the doorway grinned cruelly at Chloe, obviously enjoying the power he had over her. He motioned with the gun in his right hand for her to move to the door. "Let's go. And this one ain't full of blanks, just in case you were wondering."

Her panicked nerves screaming, she rose off the bed and moved slowly towards him.

"Pick up the pace, McConnaughey," the man grumbled, prodding Chloe out of the room. "And don't get any ideas. I can cause a whole lot of damage without actually killing you, understand?"

"Where are we going?"

"Just shut up and move. I'm in no mood."

When they reached the front door, he spun her around to face him.

"All right. Now, like he said, you can make this easy, or you can make this hard. My car is parked about halfway down the hill. You are not gonna make a sound." He waved his silencer-equipped gun in front of her face. "You so much as sneeze, and I will shoot you. Got it?"

Chloe nodded affirmatively.

"Good." He slipped his right hand, still holding the gun, into the right pocket of his nylon windbreaker. He grabbed her by the shoulders and turned her around again. She could feel the silencer pressing against the left side of her back.

"Let's go."

He opened the door, and they stepped out into the dark. At the bottom of the walk they turned left, down the slope of the street towards his car. No one was out. The moon was just a sliver at best. Even if someone happened to look out, they'd never notice anything strange about the pair of them. She was on her own.

With only twenty yards to go, they walked with her left side overlapping his right just enough for the concealed gun to be jammed into her back. Closer to the car, she recognized it as the same one she had seen from her porch that morning. *So I wasn't crazy after all,* she thought. *Small consolation now.*

Clutching her left arm, he pulled her closer, pressing the gun harder into her side. They were just ten yards away now, and Chloe could almost hear the countdown clock ticking in her head. She knew if she got in the car, it was over. Nobody would know where she'd gone. No one would know how to find her. *I'm the only chance I've got.* She swallowed her panic and forged a steely ball of determination in the pit of her stomach.

Swiveling her gaze in search of the one chance she needed, she spotted a huge grey rock that marked the top of a rough hiking path that led down the hillside on the right side of the street. 'Path' was really too generous a word for the series of sharp boulders and steep grooved ruts that descended dangerously to the beach highway below. But if she could navigate it, maybe she could flag down a car. Maybe he wouldn't follow her. *Or maybe he shoots me.*

They reached the passenger door.

"Move over against the car."

Chloe stepped aside, pressing her back against the rear passenger door. With his right hand still wrapped around the gun in his pocket, he reached forward and opened the passenger door. "Get in," he barked.

The open door blocked just enough of his right side to temporarily shield her from the concealed gun. Taking a step forward, Chloe put one hand on the open door and one on the roof, as if preparing to lower herself inside. But instead, she brought her right leg up and kicked him unmercifully in the groin. When he doubled over, she slammed the door into his head twice, then sprinted down the street, crossed to the opposite side and all but threw herself over the hillside.

Groaning, he straightened up just in time to see her head disappear over the cliff. Yanking the .38 out of his jacket, he clambered after her.

Pebbles and dirt shot out beneath her feet as she scrambled and slid her way to the bottom. She slipped several times, slashing herself on jagged edges and tearing a long gash in the skirt of her dress. She looked up just as he came over the top of the cliff.

She was completely unprotected. There was nothing to hide behind. No rocky outcropping, no trees, not even a street sign. She looked back at her pursuer, now slipping and sliding down the incline just thirty yards away. He would be at the bottom in less than a minute.

With the beach her only avenue of escape, she sprinted across the two-lane highway. Her pace slowed instantly when her feet hit the sand. *I'll never outrun him in this stuff,* she thought, snapping her head back around to check his position. Just a yard from the foot of the hill, he slid the rest of the way down and bounded out into the road.

He was less than twenty yards away now, and there was nothing between them. He had a direct shot if he wanted it; if he didn't, he would definitely be able to catch up to her. It seemed futile to run, and Chloe was considering surrendering to avoid being shot, when a large delivery truck rounded a bend in the road and slammed into her pursuer with a sickening thump. He flew backwards, hit the pavement, then flipped into a deep gully of weeds on the shoulder as the truck screeched to a halt.

Shock riveted Chloe to the spot. She dropped down and waited, expecting the truck driver to get out to check on his victim. Instead he revved his engine and shot forward, barreling away from the scene. In seconds, its taillights had disappeared around the next bend, and she was alone again.

Running on pure survival instinct, Chloe scrambled back up the hillside and raced to her cottage. She charged into the kitchen for her bag, which sat on the counter, its contents dumped beside it. She scooped them up, then dashed to the bedroom, popped open the nightstand drawer and fished out her passport from its hiding spot. She started to leave, then as an afterthought grabbed the old tee shirt, shorts, and canvas shoes she'd worn that morning and shoved them in the bag too. She ran back to the front room and pushed the curtains aside just enough to peer out. Seeing no one, she darted out the front door and dove into her car.

At the highway she turned south, speeding towards Binghamton with no particular destination in mind. Sobs came uncontrollably as she let herself melt. *None of it made any sense! What were they after? What flash drive was Sampson talking about?* He'd been ready to torture her, probably kill her for it, and she knew absolutely nothing about it. And Ruby—where was she? And then there was the man in the gully. Nausea set in once more.

Once downtown she turned off the main road onto dark back streets, making quick turns from the wrong lanes and running red lights, trying to lose anyone that might be following her. But when she passed a patrol car, she slowed down, realizing that erratic driving might get her pulled over, which would likely land her right back with Sampson.

And that's when it hit her. There was no one to help her. She couldn't go to the police for obvious reasons. She couldn't go to Jack—not after Ruby. Her trembling hands gripped the steering wheel harder.

What flash drive? Sampson's words replayed in her mind, scrolling along with the black pavement. Her heart fluttered frantically, and she breathed deeply, unsuccessfully trying to force herself to be calm. *Why was he so sure I was playing games with him? Why involve Ruby—*

Suddenly, comprehension struck and she swerved to the curb, screeching to a halt and causing the car behind her to honk in frustration. *The envelope Ruby had given her!* Whirling towards the passenger seat, she grabbed her bag and raked through it, finally dumping its contents out.

But the envelope wasn't there. Chloe threw the bag aside and banged hard on the wheel a couple of times before seizing it, her knuckles white, eyes fixed forward. She closed them and breathed in deeply. *Had Sampson or his man found it?* She considered this. *No. If they had found it they'd have said something.*

She strained, trying to remember. *Ruby gave me envelope and I threw it in my bag. I drove to the resort. We ate and then went to the resort shop. Did it fall out in the dressing room?* But Chloe didn't remember ever opening her bag in the shop. She hadn't even needed her wallet because Jack had paid . . .

My receipts, she thought. *Where are my receipts?* She always kept a paper-clipped stack of work receipts in her bag, but she hadn't seen them when she'd rummaged through it just now. Her eyes shot down to the passenger seat and she took a quick inventory of the bag's contents. The receipts and Ruby's envelope weren't all that was missing. A lipstick and brush were gone, too.

Chloe's heart skipped a beat as a wave of understanding passed over her. Cursing herself for not figuring it out sooner, she threw the car into drive, turned it around and zoomed away.

SIXTEEN

Jack stepped into the cabin of the 40-foot yacht that served as his home and froze at the sight of shredded upholstery, scattered papers, and glass littering the teak plank floor. Desk drawers had been dumped out, and books swept off their shelves. Senses on overdrive, he stepped cautiously over the rubble to an open closet at the rear. Sports and boating equipment lay in a jumble at its bottom, topped by suitcases that had the lining cut out and ripped back. The locked box where he kept extra cash had been pried open, the bills left scattered around it. And the small gun rack on the back of the door was empty. Jack fished a golf club out of the pile and, brandishing it like a bat, spun into the sleeping quarters.

No one. But it had been trashed, too. He felt under the mattress. His .45 was gone.

A docile warbling sounded from his pocket. Watching the door intently, he steadied himself and pulled out his cell phone. "This is Jack."

"Oh, thank God you're there," Chloe exclaimed, her breathing heavy and rushed. "Listen, I know why I was attacked. It happened again tonight." The words rushed out without a break between sentences.

"What? Chloe? What happened?"

"Jack, just stop talking and listen. I think you're in danger."

Jack's eyes flitted around the room. "Danger? Look Chloe, what's going on? I came home and found my boat ransacked."

"You've got to get out of there right now!"

"I'm okay. No one's here." He paused, her earlier words finally registering, "What do you mean it happened again?"

"Somebody tried to kidnap me tonight, and I got away but—"

"What!"

"Jack, I know this sounds crazy, just listen. Someone tried to kidnap me tonight after I got home. I think it's the same people who were in my house before, and it's because of some flash drive they're after. I think whoever wrecked your boat was looking for it." She paused. "I think they thought Ruby had it, and now she's gone. You have to get out of there."

"Ruby's gone?" he asked disbelievingly.

"I checked myself. Jack, please, I couldn't live if one more person—"

"Chloe, who's after you?"

"Not on the phone."

"Not on the . . . what, you think they're listening in on cell phones?"

"I don't know," she squeaked desperately. "The cops are involved."

"The cops? How can you—"

"One of them was there tonight. He threatened to torture me for information."

Jack's body tightened. "What?" he growled. "This is crazy. I'm coming to get you."

"No, listen. You know where we took those pictures? You know where I'm talking about? Meet me there."

"Okay," he agreed quickly. "I'll be there in ten minutes."

"Drive your Jeep, Jack, okay? *Your Jeep.*"

"What else would I—"

"Hurry, Jack, please," she begged, then hung up.

He stared at the cell a moment, thrown by the sudden cut off, then set aside his questions and waded through the flood of belongings to the stairs at the front of the cabin, golf club in hand. He had just set his foot on the first step when a gloved fist smashed into his face, sending him stumbling backwards over the piles on the floor. The club flew from his grasp as he landed hard on his back. Shaking it off, he jumped up, instinctively shifting into defense mode.

The intruder, a huge, hulking figure dressed in black, charged towards him, raising a Glock 9mm. Jack executed a sweeping kick, knocking the gun from the intruder's hand to the floor, where it disappeared beneath the clutter. Two more swift kicks to the intruder's head stunned him long enough for Jack to shove past and run up the stairs. As he landed on the top step, the man's hand wrapped around Jack's right ankle, bringing him crashing down on the upper deck. Shaking his leg violently, he freed it from the intruder's grasp, kicked the man square in the face, and scrambled away.

Jack scanned the deck for a weapon. His gaze fell on the cockpit, where a flare gun was strapped to the shelf by the radio. He started towards it and heard a silencer-muffled gunshot. Instantaneously, pain seared across the outside of his calf, and he cried out before forcing himself to continue sprinting down the port side. Clambering up the cockpit steps, he caught a peripheral glimpse of another man in the distance headed for the boat dock, gun in hand. Propelling himself inside the cockpit, Jack unstrapped the flare gun, removed it from its holster, and looked up to see the intruder right behind him on the stairs. He fired.

The flare struck the intruder in the chest, igniting on impact and sending him flying backwards. Jack jumped down to where the man landed. He was unconscious, his Glock resting a few feet away, precariously near the edge of the deck. Jack scooped it up just as he heard footsteps on the opposite side of the yacht.

Jack flattened himself against the cockpit, crouched down, and considered his options. Committing himself to the best of those, he crawled three feet to the edge of the deck and gently lowered himself down the side of the hull. Without a sound, he slipped like a dart into the water and disappeared while the second intruder boarded from the starboard side and started around.

Barely half a minute passed before Jack emerged from the black water on the starboard side of the stern, directly behind where the second man had just boarded. He pressed himself against the hull. Grasping a tethering rope dangling off the side of the boat, he began climbing hand over hand out of the water. When the top of his head was level with the deck, he stopped moving, his fingers on fire as the rope dug deeper into his skin. His biceps bulged as he hung above the water's surface. He craned his neck until he could see over the edge and looked around. The starboard side was clear.

Using the side rails, he pulled himself the rest of the way up, swung his legs over, and dropped quietly onto the deck. He crouched, clothes dripping wet and sagging on his frame. Removing the Glock from his waistband, he crept to the cockpit wall. He inhaled deeply, then scooted to the right and peered around to the port side. The second man had moved past his dead counterpart and now stood fifteen feet away, his attention focused on the bow. Jack stepped out into the open and took a firing stance.

"Turn around slowly," he barked.

The man hesitated, then in a flurry of motion, whirled towards Jack, his semi-automatic poised to fire. Jack dropped to one knee and fired two shots, striking the man in the arm and chest. The impact spun the intruder around in the opposite direction, slamming him into the railing. He bounced off and dropped to the deck.

Neck veins bulging, his face hot from the adrenaline-infused blood pumping angrily through him, Jack strode to the fallen man and kicked his weapon away. He kept his gun trained on the man's chest, where the bullet wound poured red as he struggled for breath against his filling lungs.

"Who sent you?" Jack growled through clenched teeth.

The man's lips moved, but only wet choking noises escaped.

"Talk to me!" Jack bellowed. The man's head rolled to one side and the sounds stopped. Jack hunched down and checked for a pulse, but there wasn't one. A quick search revealed that all that the man carried on him were two ammunition clips. No identification. Jack tucked the clips in his pocket before rolling the corpse into the water. Then Jack moved to check the man's cohort. After finding no pulse or identification on him either, Jack pushed him in the water too.

Jack grabbed the second man's gun off the deck and slipped it into his waistband as he sprinted down the steps into the cabin. Half a minute later he shot back up, stuffing a folded envelope into his waistband and covering it with his shirt as he raced down the dock to his Jeep.

SEVENTEEN

Jack ripped into the cliff's parking lot and headed straight to Chloe's car on the far end, sitting by itself in the dark. Chloe was at his door before he'd even killed the engine.

She threw her arms around his neck and pressed the side of her face against his. "Thank you, thank you," she whispered, and began to shake.

"Hey," he said, wrapping his arms around her. She buried her face in his shoulder, muffling her crying. "Hey, it's okay." He pulled back from her and turned her face towards him. "You hear me?" he asked, smiling reassuringly. "It's going to be okay."

Chloe straightened up. "It's . . . it's just that this is so . . . insane." She felt something trickling down her arm and realized she was wet from hugging him. She scanned his soaked body. "What happened to you?"

"I'll explain later. Now tell me what happened."

The story poured out of her like a verbal deluge, as she told him everything about Ruby and Sampson and her escape. He interrupted only once, when he insisted on examining the vicious red welt on her neck caused by her near strangulation.

". . . And so that's why I needed your Jeep," she finally finished.

"Okay," he said, still confused, as he compliantly unlocked the Jeep's security compartment. "And why is that?"

"Because I tossed my bag into your trunk when we walked up the cliff, and then we drove off with it still in there," she explained, leaning past him to look inside the Jeep. "I think it must've slid around on some of those curves . . . yeah, here's my lipstick," she announced, pulling it out from underneath a pair of running shoes and handing it to Jack. Her hand dove in again, rummaging through the random clothes, tools, and clutter covering the compartment bottom. "And my receipts, and," she said, her voice triumphant as she pulled out the manila envelope from where it had slid down behind a gym bag, "my mail."

"And you think that's what they were after?"

"It's the only thing connected to Ruby," she said, turning it over to open it, and finding that the clear tape covering the flap was loose. "It's loose, but sticky, like someone opened it then sealed it back." She pulled off the tape, opened the metal brad, and pulled back the flap. It came off too easily. "Somebody's been through this. Must've been Ruby," she said wistfully.

She extracted a stack of mail from the envelope and started flipping through it. There was a letter from Tate's insurance company containing papers to sign, correspondence from *Terra Traveler*, a couple of sympathy notes from friends, random bills, and then, in the middle, a lightly padded envelope with a return address of *Herbert K. Rohrstadt, Esquire, Attorney at Law, 1919 Westwood Avenue, Building 3, Suite J, Miami, Florida.*

She tore the end off the envelope and shook it vigorously. The smallest flash drive she'd ever seen fell into her waiting hand.

"What's on that?" Jack remarked, squinting to get a better look.

Chloe shrugged. "No idea," she said, handing the empty envelope to Jack. "For Chloe," was scrawled with a Sharpie on the drive. In Tate's handwriting.

"Chloe," Jack said, pulling a sheet of paper from the envelope and handing it to her. They hovered over it, shoulder to shoulder.

Dear Ms. McConnaughey,

I'm sorry it has taken me so long to get this to you. I've been out of the country for the last month, and only just learned of Tate's passing. I send my deepest sympathies.

Tate left instructions with me to forward the enclosed to you should anything happen to him. As such, I have done so. I was further instructed to tell you that this is for your eyes only and that not even I have reviewed it.

If there is anything I can do to assist you with his affairs here in Miami, please let me know. Again, please accept my deepest condolences.

> *Sincerely,*
> /s/ Herb Rohrstadt
> *Herbert K. Rohrstadt*
> *Attorney at Law*

The letter was dated thirteen days before.

Chloe squeezed her eyes tight and shook her head. "No. No. No." She sucked in a breath. "Please, please don't let Tate be involved in this thing."

"Do you know this Herbert—Herb Rohrstadt?"

She shook her head, choking back the threatening tears.

"You sure this is what they were after?"

"It has to be." She flipped through the remaining envelopes. "There's nothing else here." Pain crossed her face as her thumb ran over her name printed on the flash drive. "They did something to Ruby because of this thing," she said quietly, her voice starting to tremble. "I just know it. She was just trying to be nice. Holding my mail. What if . . . Jack, what if they knew she was a little nosy . . . what if she really did open this and they found out . . ." Eyes filled to the brim with tears met Jack's. "If something's happened to her . . . it's Tate fault!"

Jack bent down so his green eyes were level with hers and covered her hand holding the flash drive with his. "First thing we have to do is get somewhere safe, see what's on this thing," he squeezed her hand, "and figure out our options. You up for that?"

Clamping her lips together determinedly, she nodded.

"You didn't happen to bring a laptop?" he asked hopefully.

Her face fell. "No. I should have. I just didn't think about it. I was in such a hurry to leave. It's at the cottage, but—"

"There's no going back there," Jack interrupted. She nodded her agreement. "Mine's on the boat. Or at least it was. We can't go there either, though. We'll have to try somewhere in the morning. One of those office-type copy shops or maybe a hotel."

"What about Ruby?"

"If you're sure she's not in the house, I don't think there's anything we can do until morning. We'll have to drive to another part of the island. Try to talk to some other authorities—somebody not connected to Sampson."

Chloe started to reach for a curl to twist between her shaking fingers, then realized he still had her hand. She gently drew it from his grip and ran it through her hair. Tears dribbled from the corner of her eye. "Look, I'm really sorry, Jack. I didn't want to involve you. I just wanted to get my stuff out of your trunk. You can go, they don't want you. If I'd known that any of this—"

"I'm already in this. They searched my boat looking for that thing," he said, nodding in the flash drive's direction. "Besides, I couldn't leave you alone now anyway. And you don't have anything to apologize for. It's not your fault."

"No, it's Tate's. Again. Even from the grave he's ruining everything."

"You don't know that. Maybe he was just—"

"He was just being Tate. But it doesn't matter," she interrupted, feeling that familiar, cold knot of exasperation that Tate had so often engendered tightening around her heart. She wasn't willing to hear excuses for him. Not now. Sniffing, she felt her resolve swell, grateful to the anger for that at least. "What do we do now? Where do we go?"

Jack exhaled deeply. "I think I have an idea."

EIGHTEEN

The motel was about half a mile inland in an undeveloped patch of the island, just outside Binghamton. They pulled into the parking lot in Jack's Jeep, having already dumped Chloe's car in a gully down one of the side roads leading into the woods. They'd camouflaged it with brush, hoping to buy a little time.

The long, narrow building hadn't seen a fresh coat of paint in decades, its whitened wood peeling back where water and wind had tortured it regularly. A weathered wooden sign mounted on the roof read "Shores Motel." Painted above the faded, royal blue letters were dancing, happy-faced starfish, one of which was missing from the middle. Two dozen private rooms stretched down the motel, with the lobby at the end closest to the road. Wild foliage, growing as high and as thick as it cared to, separated the edge of the property from the deep woods that stretched behind it.

"A *little* seedy?" Chloe questioned. "You said it was a *little* seedy."

Jack shrugged. "Okay, maybe a lot seedy. But it's clean, and out of the way, *and* the only traffic coming by here is for the motel. And we had to get out of sight. Sampson's bound to be combing the streets for you. For us." He pulled into a spot in front of the lobby. "I'll get us a room."

"You don't think this is exactly the kind of place they'll expect us to go?"

Jack shrugged. "I hope not. But I've got to get cleaned up, and we need to regroup. I'm not ready to drag anybody else into this yet.

Are you?"

Chloe shook her head.

"We're just gonna have to take our chances tonight."

"You need a credit card or something . . . wait, no."

Jack nodded in agreement. "We can't use plastic."

Chloe's face dropped. "I've only got fifty, maybe fifty-five on me."

"It's okay. I've got enough to cover us for a while."

"What about after that?"

He smiled and reached over to squeeze her hand. "We'll drown in that river when we get to it." He opened his door and stepped out. "I'll be right back."

Through the lobby's large window, Chloe watched Jack approach the counter and ring the night bell. Eventually a yawning wide-mouthed teenager stumbled through the doorway behind the counter. It was well after midnight, and from the look of the boy's tousled hair, Jack had woken him from a deep sleep. The two spoke briefly, then the clerk pushed the register to Jack. He signed it, slid the book back to the clerk, and tossed two bills on top of it. The clerk withdrew a key from a drawer and handed it to Jack. As he walked back to the car, the lobby lights flicked off.

"Number twenty-four," he said, sliding into the driver's seat. "Thought it'd be better if we were on the end."

He parked as far around the building as he could to hide the car from the road. Gathering what little they had, they walked the few yards to room twenty-four. The door squeaked noisily on its hinges as Jack swung it open.

Run down was an understatement. A queen-sized bed covered in a thin, flowered spread that had seen too many guests took up much of the room. The rest of the sparse furniture was mismatched and duct-taped together in places, and the standing lamp was missing all its bulbs. But it was clean and, as exhausted as Chloe was, that was good enough for her. She dropped her things on the floor and fell backwards onto the bed. Jack locked the door and latched the chain.

"I'm not moving from this spot," she announced, closing her eyes. Jack sat down beside her.

"Why don't you get some rest?" he urged. "I'll stay up for a while."

"You wouldn't think I'd be able to sleep right now, you know?" she muttered. "But it's all I want to do."

"It's fine."

She breathed in deeply, ignoring the slightly ruined smell of the linens. She just needed to disconnect. To escape. Just . . . for a moment . . .

She didn't realize she had fallen asleep until the sound of running water ushered her back to consciousness. Groggily, she raised her left arm to her face and checked her watch. It was 1:03 in the morning. She had been out less than half an hour, but the heaviness in her limbs made it feel like it had been half the night. She squinted and blinked, trying to moisten her dry eyes.

"Jack?" she called out weakly.

"Yeah?"

"What are you doing?" she asked, sitting up. The room was dark except for the sliver of light emanating from where the bathroom door sat slightly ajar.

"Just cleaning up," he called from behind the door. "Go back to sleep."

A glint of metal on the bedside table caught her eye. The sight of it chilled her.

"Jack," she started nervously, "whose gun is that?"

"Mine," he answered matter-of-factly from behind the door. "Or at least it is now."

"I didn't know you liked guns," she said tentatively, lowering her feet over the bed's edge.

"I wouldn't say *liked*, exactly."

She focused on the gap in the doorway. "So what did happen to you earlier, after I called?" She pushed off the bed and moved to the door, leaning her face into the gap. "You never said how you got all wet—"

The rest of her sentence was choked off by a horrified gasp as she caught a glimpse of Jack through the opening. She swung the door open to him sitting on the closed toilet lid, left leg propped up on the tub. Drops of blood from an ugly gash on his calf peppered the floor. A second gun lay beside him on the edge of the tub.

"What happened to you?" she shrieked, gaping at the wound.

"It's nothing."

"Nothing?" she gasped, pointing at the blood. "How did I not notice that before? Why didn't you tell me?"

"Wasn't important. It's fine. I've pretty much stopped the bleeding."

Her face contorted as she scrutinized the gash. "Is that . . . a gunshot wound?"

"Just grazed."

"*Just grazed?* Are you kidding me? You need a doctor, Jack!" Nausea rolled over her as she pushed away thoughts of what could have happened to him. *All because of her. All her fault.*

He pulled his leg back. "I'll wrap it up and be fine. Besides," he smiled, "it's only a flesh wound," he finished in a poor attempt at a cockney accent.

"That's not funny," she mumbled, as she took the rust-colored washcloth from him. "Here, let me do that." She rinsed the cloth in warm water from the sink and wrung it out, a stream of reddish-brown trickling into the basin. She soaked the cloth again, then wrung it over the wound to irrigate it. After repeating the process several times and being certain the wound was free of debris, she hung the cloth over the edge of the sink and got up off her knees. "Don't move," she ordered and went into the bedroom.

Chloe returned with a long strip of white fabric and knelt down beside him. "Let's just pray they washed the pillowcases sometime in the last decade," she remarked as she wrapped the strip tightly around his leg twice to cover the wound, then secured it with a knot.

Jack checked the bandage for himself. "Not bad," he admitted.

"This is insane," she pronounced in a hollow voice, slumping dejectedly against the bathroom doorframe. Her gaze rolled up and settled randomly on a spot on the wall tile, where it stayed, zombie-like, for several long moments. "What are we gonna do?"

"You," Jack started, peeling her off the doorframe and ushering her back onto the bed, "are going back to sleep. I," he said, sitting down in a rattan chair by the bed, "am taking first watch." He held one of the guns ready in his right hand, as he slid the second gun off the bedside table and held it out to her. "Take it."

"But—"

"You need to be armed, Chloe. Understand? Now take it."

She slipped the gun from his open hand and laid it beside her pillow. Jack eased forward, resting his elbows on his knees as he spoke.

"We're going to do exactly what we planned. Tomorrow we find a computer, take a look at whatever's on that flash drive, and figure out what's going on. Then we'll see about getting off this island and in touch with someone we can trust."

Chloe rolled over to face him. "What happened to you, Jack?"

Ignoring her, he brushed a wisp of hair from her face. "Your forehead's starting to bruise," he said.

She pressed him. "Jack."

He sighed heavily. "I went home and found the boat trashed. Then you called. Right after, two guys came at me, and, long story short, I got the jump on them. This," he said gesturing at his leg with the gun, "is where one of them grazed me, but . . . well, he got it worse. I took the guns off them." He leaned back in the chair. "Nothing else to tell, really."

He made it sound so simple. So normal. As if any of this was normal. As if any of this could even be digested.

"How did you even *do* that?" she asked desperately. "One unarmed guy against two guys with guns? You could have been killed. And that's the second time you've nearly been killed over me."

"But I wasn't."

"You were lucky."

"I prefer to think I was protected."

She squeezed the pillow beneath her head and sighed. She just didn't have the energy to wrap her mind around it. She drew her knees to her chest, wishing she could just go back to sleep. Back into nothingness. But the images lingered.

"He told me he was going to break my fingers one by one," she said quietly, not meeting Jack's gaze, and not knowing quite sure why she was telling him this.

"Who?"

"The detective. Sampson. He was twisting this one," she said, and wiggled her pinky at him weakly. "But then the phone rang and he got called off."

Determination shadowed Jack's face as he turned her face to his. "You're safe here," he promised, certainty casing each word.

Safe, she thought, sinking into his green eyes. She could wrap her head around safe.

"You hear me?" he pressed, his voice low and steady. "*Nothing* will happen to you here."

Her need to believe him battled her fear. "I'm scared, Jack."

He nodded his understanding, but a rock-steadiness emanated from him. "You. Are. Safe. We will work this out in the morning." He gave her hand a small squeeze. "Now go to sleep or I'm going to."

It sounded so good to her—sleep and safety. When she was asleep, none of this was happening. None of this was real, and Jack would be watching over her. Jack, her unexpected savior. This man she barely knew, who had put himself in harm's way for her. Twice. *What would I have done without him?* The universe had sent him to her at exactly the right moment.

The thought momentarily sparked something in her belly that felt almost like . . . doubt. But she let the flash slip away as quickly as it had come. Because she needed to believe in him. There was nothing else. She simply had to.

She closed her eyes. "Jack?" she murmured.

"Yeeessss?" he drawled, feigning exasperation.

"Thanks."

Rocking forward, he bent over her, soothingly tucked a few wisps of hair behind her ear and in a low voice whispered, "You're welcome."

* * * * *

She was snoring. *A good sign.* He relaxed a bit, leaning into the chair as he watched her breathe, in and out, in and out. He ran a tired hand through his hair, resting it on the back of his neck where he could feel the beginnings of a knotted muscle. This was going to be harder than he thought. Much harder.

NINETEEN

When Chloe finally stirred the next morning, she had about ten seconds of blissful forgetfulness before everything came rolling back. A burst of panicky nausea punched her in the gut as she rocketed up, expecting to see Jack asleep in the old rattan chair beside the bed. He wasn't.

"Jack, you in there?" she called out hopefully towards the closed bathroom door. No answer. Throwing herself out of bed, she swept towards the bathroom and swung the door open. Empty. She checked her watch. 7:38 a.m.

Scratching sounded outside the front door. The lock clicked. Someone was turning a key in it.

Chloe dashed to the bed, fumbled amongst the pillows, then snatched up the gun, diving down beside the bed just as the door opened. Peering beneath the bed, she saw a man's leg in the doorway.

She readied herself to swing her arm over the bed and take aim.

"Chloe?" a familiar voice called out.

Her pounding heart slowed as she exhaled in relief. "Really, Jack? Why didn't you say who you were?" she groaned, rising to her feet and brandishing the gun in front of her as he locked the door behind him. "I could have shot you."

"Not with it like that you wouldn't," he quipped, nodding at the gun. "Safety's on."

She rotated the gun to get a look at the safety mechanism, which sure enough, was still engaged. She could feel heat rising in her face. "I . . . I just woke up, you came in . . . I just grabbed the thing. I wasn't thinking."

He raised his eyebrows and smirked. "We'll have to work on that."

She didn't bite. "I woke up alone and thought you . . ." She hesitated, embarrassed now to tell him what her first thought had been.

"You thought I left," he finished for her. He plopped down on the bed, laid his head back and closed his eyes, releasing a satisfied sigh. Moments later he opened his eyes to find her still standing, looking abashed.

"It's okay," he offered. "I would have thought the same thing." Her shoulders sagged, and she sat down beside him. He closed his eyes again. "You looked so peaceful . . . you needed rest. I didn't want to wake you. I stayed right in that chair all night," he said firmly, but reassuringly. "I only left about a half hour ago. Went down to that convenience store off the highway," he said, tossing a paper bag onto the bed, "picked up a couple things."

She snatched up the bag and pulled out a couple of Cokes, some bananas, and a box of Pop-Tarts. Jack held out a hand, and she passed one of each to him.

"Sorry about the breakfast. There wasn't much to choose from."

"It's great," she mumbled, taking a bite of the stale blueberry pastry. "Did you sleep at all?"

"I caught an hour or two." His eyes flicked open. "But I'm a light sleeper. It was perfectly safe."

"It's fine, really. I'm glad you slept. I'm not complaining," she offered. "Thanks for letting me rest."

He nodded and pushed himself up, leaning against the rattan headboard. "So, I think we're okay for now. No traffic. Only a few cars here."

She popped open the Coke can, took a sip, and set it on the nightstand. She lifted the bag again. "What else is in here?" she asked, rummaging through it. "Tylenol. And bandages, bottled water, and . . ." She stopped short, pulling her hand from the bag to reveal a cheap, flip-style cell phone. "For me?"

Jack nodded, extracting a matching one from his front pocket and wiggling it. "I took the batteries and SIM cards out of ours last night while you were out. On the off chance that Sampson might try to use them to find us."

She nodded, then pulled from the bag an old box of hair dye so dusty, it must've been on the shelf for years. A raven-haired woman sporting a very nineties hairstyle graced the front. Chloe eyed Jack suspiciously. "Really?"

Jack shrugged. "It's a small island. It can't hurt. There's another one in there. Blond. I'll let you pick—ladies first."

Her gaze drifted back to the soiled box for a moment, then, very reluctantly, she sighed and nodded.

"There's some scissors down in there, too."

Chloe squeezed her eyes, as if shutting out the idea, but after a moment nodded again. "So what next?"

"I did some thinking while you were getting your beauty sleep," he said, "and I think our best bet is to get in touch with the U.S. authorities. We can't trust anybody down here."

"That, I totally agree with," Chloe said without hesitation.

"Well, don't get too excited. I'm not sure it'll do much good. There's no U.S. presence here. No embassy. So the best we can do is a phone call to the closest one. We'll have to check that when we get to a computer. And even if we get through to someone who matters, I'm not sure what they'll be able to do down here. But we've got to get help from somewhere. Maybe they can smooth our way out of here and back home."

"Sampson will be watching the airports."

He nodded. "That's why we need the help," he said, pushing out of the chair. "But we've got to be able to back up what we're saying. Before we do anything, we've got to get a look at that flash drive and figure out what and who we're dealing with. I checked up front. They've got nothing we can borrow. Just an ancient desktop—doesn't even have a USB port. Anyway, they'd be standing over us the whole time." Jack checked his watch.

"So, what, we head to, some place with public access to computers? Like a copy shop or library . . . or, hey, there's a cyber café near the airport."

He shook his head. "Too obvious. I think we have to assume they knew the flash drive was in the envelope and that they might be expecting us to try to get a look at what's on it. This isn't New York. There's only a couple of 'office away from the office' shops here. They'd be watching them. The library too. And I don't think we should get anywhere near the airport." He paused. "I tried calling a guy earlier—"

"I thought we agreed not to involve any more friends," she interrupted, looking surprised.

"Well, he's not a friend, exactly. He's, well, it's sort of hard to explain, but trust me, he wouldn't mind. And he owes me a favor." He held up a hand to hold her off when it looked like she was going to protest again. "It doesn't matter anyway. He didn't answer. And we can't wait on him. Sometimes he's out of pocket for a while."

"Okay, so what else?"

"We could try picking one up at a pawn shop, but I don't think we should chance running a credit card. I've got about two hundred cash, but we're gonna need that—"

"Hotels."

His eyes flicked to hers and doubt creased his mouth. "Hotels?"

"We just worm our way into one of those complimentary business offices at the hotels. Most of the larger ones have them now, or at least a couple of computers available for airline bookings. There are dozens and dozens of hotels just on this side of the island alone. They can't possibly watch them all."

He nodded. "Okay. Yeah, that could work. We'd have to snag a room key."

"Not necessarily. When I first got here I toured dozens of hotels as part of researching my article. Some of them had business centers just off the lobby, no room key needed."

Jack considered that. "Sampson might have notified the hotels to watch for us. We still might be spotted."

"Well," she said, tapping the box of darker dye, "we won't look the same, and if we do it right, they won't even notice us. But if you've got a better idea . . ."

Jack inhaled deeply and shook his head. "No. But if we do this, we wait a couple hours. It's still too early. We need lots of people out and about. It'll make it easier to blend in." He glanced at the bathroom. "I'm gonna shower, try to re-energize and," he said snatching the blond hair dye out of the bag, "give this stuff a shot. Meanwhile, why don't you try to come up with a couple of good hotel options?"

Minutes later, with the sound of steady streams of water in the background, Chloe flipped through the ragged phone book, checking it against her memory of the hotels with computer access. Using the dingy hotel notepad to make a list, she finally settled on the LeClaire Resort, a hotel complex on the opposite side of the island from

Binghamton, on a strip of beach with several other resorts. She'd checked it out soon after arriving on St. Gideon and remembered the lobby being pretty busy. You didn't need a room key to get in the "business office," which was really just one computer in a room off the lobby. And one computer meant no one would be looking over their shoulders. Satisfied, she set down the pen, and more out of habit than anything, flipped on the television.

A minute later Jack stepped back into the room. "So apparently I've got to leave this stuff in for—" He stopped short, her ashen face and gaping mouth cutting off the rest of his sentence. "Chloe?"

She sat on the edge of the bed, tears filling her eyes, staring at the television. "I can't believe it," she said quietly.

"What?" he asked, moving to where he could see. A photograph of each of them was displayed in the top right of the screen, while the main view was of a rocky beach and a body bag being loaded into an ambulance.

" . . . *According to police sources, Kreinberg's body shows unmistakable signs of foul play. Police would not speculate on motive, but did confirm that nearly $8,000 U.S. dollars' worth of jewelry and cash was missing from Kreinberg's residence, suggesting a robbery gone wrong. McConnaughey, Kreinberg's neighbor, and her companion, Collings, are wanted for questioning. Police would not comment on whether there is evidence linking the two to Kreinberg's death, but did insist that the two should not be approached. Rather, anyone with information should contact the Binghamton police immediately. Now, turning to the weather . . .*"

"Chloe," Jack started gently, putting his hand on her shoulder as he sat down beside her. "I'm so sorry."

She stared straight ahead, tears now trickling down. "She didn't deserve this," she said swiping roughly at the wetness. "She just made the wrong friend." She swallowed, sniffing back more threatening tears, an angry determination clouding her face. "He didn't have to kill her. She's not part of this."

"He must have thought she knew something. You thought she'd read the mail too."

Chloe squeezed her eyes shut, forcing more tears down her cheeks, and in condemnation whispered harshly, "Tate."

Jack rose, and slowly began pacing. "This changes things. Now the whole island will be looking for us. And there'll be no flying out of here. We'll definitely be on some kind of no-exit list. Probably at the ports, too. And making us out to be involved, but not necessarily suspects, was a great move on his part. Since we're only wanted for questioning Sampson can blow it off once he gets his hands on us. He doesn't have to hold us. So—"

"So nobody's going to be looking too closely. If he brings us in, he can say we didn't have any information after all and that he let us go—"

"But he won't. He'll hand us straight up to his boss. Not to mention that he just undercut our credibility with the U.S. authorities. Now it just looks like we're running from potential charges here. And if it comes to it, he can probably stick us with the murder charge just to keep us here."

Chloe's voice trembled. "I was all over her house, Jack. My fingerprints will be everywhere." Her eyes widened even more. "A knife was missing at my house—" She gasped. "You don't think . . . they used it to . . . " She let the sentence hang, unable to finish.

Jack grimaced. "I don't know. Maybe. And I wouldn't be surprised if that cash and jewelry conveniently turned up somewhere incriminating—my boat, my work locker, your house . . ."

It was all too much. She buried her face in her hands, then ran them over her head, as if to clear it. If she could just crawl back in the bed, close her eyes . . . it already felt like she'd been up for hours. She dragged her gaze up to Jack's. "So . . . what now?"

He sat back down beside her. "I think that we still have to know what's on that flash drive before we do anything. But after that—"

"There's no way we can just call a nearby embassy, or whatever, now," she parried, taking a few strained steps from the bed, turning to face him as she moved. Her tightly drawn expression was fearful. "Jack, come on. I watch the movies. You know what happens when a 'wanted' person goes to the authorities for help?" She waved him in animatedly, as if directing him to come closer. "They say 'sure, come on in,' then they turn you over to whoever you were running from in the first place. Or they tell you to 'come in and we'll protect you,' and somebody on the bad guys' payroll blows your head off on the way to the courthouse."

"Chloe—"

"We can't call anybody now, Jack." She dropped onto the bed. "We've got no proof that our story is true, and they'll have every reason to believe Sampson. It's just his word against mine."

"And my word—"

"Yeah, your word—the word of a guy with two dead bodies

floating under his boat."

"You know, maybe that'll actually help us. A planned assault by trained men? Come on. That doesn't just happen. It supports our side of things. They can't just dismiss that. Somebody will have to listen. We just have to get to the right people."

"How do we do that? And who knows how far Sampson's reach is down here? And what if we go ahead and call the embassy or the C.I.A. or whatever? Can you promise me that they won't make us go through the process here? Can you promise me they won't turn us over to Sampson? That whatever laws apply don't *require* them to?"

Jack pursed his lips, then swallowed. "No."

They stared at each other, desperation hanging between them. Finally, Jack spoke. "So we get home. We get off this island, away from whatever influence Sampson has in the area, and we take whatever is on that flash drive to somebody that can help us in the States, face to face. It'll be much harder for Sampson to pull strings there, and we'll have rights."

She looked at him with a pained, hopeless expression. "You should leave now, Jack. Get as far away from me as you can. They've got nothing on you, nothing linking you to Ruby, except me. Just tell them we went out a couple of times till you realized I was nuts."

"You're forgetting about the two dead bodies feeding the fish under my boat."

Her shoulders caved a little more, and she closed her eyes, sighing.

"Why is this happening, Jack?" she whispered beseechingly. "*How* is this happening? And how are we going to get back to the States with that," she said, pointing to the television, "going on?"

He eyed her carefully, then spoke, his words cautious and slow. "I don't know why this is happening, Chloe. I wish I could tell you. Sometimes bad stuff happens to good people." He paused, as if paying homage to some memory. "Believe me, I know that better than anyone. But, I have to believe there's a reason. That it's not pointless—"

"A reason for Ruby? Really?"

He didn't respond, but instead inhaled deeply and clasped his hands together. "Look, first things first. Let's get a look at that flash drive, okay? Let's just concentrate on that. One thing at a time. As for getting back to the States, well . . . we'll figure that out. I've got some ideas, but right now we've got to get out of here. That clerk up front—if he watches the news . . ."

She gave a quick nod, and he squeezed her shoulder. As they moved around collecting the few things in the room, a lump rose in her throat, and Chloe swallowed hard to keep it down. She'd been afraid that he'd tell her she was crazy, that her ranting about not calling the authorities was the result of an overactive imagination. She'd been afraid he wouldn't listen, that he'd dismiss her fears. But he hadn't. He had agreed with her. And that scared her even more.

TWENTY

"O, dear Lord, what have I done?"

Black curls littered the floorboards of Jack's Jeep, as he stared, disgusted, at the scissors in his hands.

With big eyes, Chloe peered into the vanity mirror. "It's okay. It had to be done. I couldn't get the back by myself. And, it could be worse."

His eyebrows shot up, his expression doubtful.

She met his gaze with a sad, conciliatory look. "Well, it'll grow back, anyway. Just give me these," she said, reaching for the scissors, "so I can even it out."

The Jeep was parked deep in the woods, in a small clearing they'd found after driving inland from the Shores Motel and taking as many back roads as they could find until one finally dead-ended. A yellow-tufted bird called cheerfully, against the mood, as Chloe trimmed and snipped uneven hairs. They'd stayed in the room just long enough for her to get the dye in her hair and wash it out, then drove to this spot to finish the job. She glanced sideways to see Jack staring forlornly at her.

"Hey, I'm pretty sure I got the better end of this deal," she said, nodding at his newly platinum head. The bleached blond look just didn't suit him at all. The tone was all wrong for his skin. Anybody taking a hard look would see that. But from a distance, or to people just passing by, he wouldn't be remarkable at all. And that would probably be good enough.

Hers looked less forced. The black color actually was sort of striking against her complexion. But the cut wasn't her style at all. It resembled Emma Watson's when she cut her long hair off in favor of a pixie cut.

If Emma Watson's stylist had been blind and using garden shears, she thought dully.

"Okay, I think I've done what I can here," she capitulated, tossing the scissors in the baseboard and turning towards Jack, who had moved to the back of the Jeep and was working on removing the license plate.

"Okay," he grunted, twisting off the last screw. He tossed the plate in the back seat. "It's better than it being on there, but no license plate will draw attention, too. We'll have to swap it out. Actually," he offered, running a hand along the vehicle's side, "it'd be better if we dumped it and got another."

"We can't even get a computer. How are we going to get another car?"

Jack gently bumped his fist on the door. "We could borrow one—"

"Borrow?"

"Well it's not stealing if you leave it for them somewhere else." Chloe raised her eyebrows skeptically. He shrugged shyly. "At least that's what I'd tell myself. But a stolen car would draw Sampson's attention faster than anything. We'll just have to pray he's not on the road when we are. Maybe park a decent hike from the hotel and walk in." He focused on her. "You ready?"

She nodded.

The path out of the deep woods was rough. In order to avoid the main roads and, hopefully, being spotted by Sampson, they'd had to cut through some pretty obscure areas in the heart of the island. The Jeep jarred them violently as it bounced in and out of deep cavities that marked what was really little more than a wide dirt trail.

"Hold on," Jack warned just as the Jeep lurched and a heavy smattering of what resembled brown cake batter smacked his side of the Jeep, leaving a trail all the way up his window. "Sorry about that. I'd try to avoid them, but there's more pothole than road out here," he said, half grinning at her. She knew he was trying to make her feel better, and she tried to smile back, but all she managed was a grimace.

He squeezed her shoulder and turned back to the road. She, however, kept her eyes on him, watching him as he drove, completely composed. If any of this had shaken him at all, he wasn't showing it. Square jaw set. Eyes riveted forward. Smooth, even breaths taken with quiet confidence. He was not the least bit rattled.

She, on the other hand, was completely in knots and not hiding it very well. One look at her greenish face in the side view mirror had proved that. Their situation already had her stomach on the spin cycle, and now this roller coaster ride wasn't helping. She hadn't thrown up yet, but was pretty sure that was only a couple potholes away. *How to be more like Jack?* she wondered, eyeing him. Was that even possible for her in this insanity? Gunmen chasing her, torturing her. Shooting Jack. A mysterious flash drive. Literally running for her life. Tate at the heart of it.

And there was the answer. Tate at the heart of it. Yes, this whole thing was crazy, but she had no doubt that Tate's ambition could have driven him to do something stupid enough to land them in a mess like this. She wished she felt differently. She wished she had faith that Tate had cared more about her safety than his greed. But Tate had proven time after time that putting faith in him just left you disappointed. Just like everyone else.

She eyed Jack warily. When would it be his turn? Something like courage flickered as she realized that it was probably inevitable. Given that, she had to accept once and for all that this was her reality, as insane as it seemed. If she didn't own that soon, things were not going to get easier. Helplessness and fear were not her friends here. They led to dependence. And when you become dependent on someone, anyone—even a good guy like Jack—you eventually get hurt. *I've got to pull it together,* she ordered herself. *He's here now, but he might not always be. Won't always be.* She took a deep breath, stared down the scared, queasy-faced girl in the mirror, and resolved to be tough. It was time to get control of this thing.

It was a half hour before they reached what you could technically call a road. At least it was covered with gravel and the potholes were fewer and farther between. Another ten minutes landed them on an actual paved road that Jack said would take them to the beach on the northern shore and the LeClaire. Sure enough, little shacks and sheds began sporadically popping up on the roadside, then more modern structures, until finally they reached the town of Tasso. The town had existed since long before the English settlers had arrived and had managed to retain its native name despite the influx of western influence. Like Binghamton, it was set on a bay, with wharfs and all matter of sailing vessels dotting its shores. However, unlike the island's capital city, it was more serene, less a victim of the invasive tourist industry that had transformed the rest of the island. The locals outnumbered the tourists here, with the majority still engaged in the fishing industry that had supported the island for centuries. Tourists wanting a slice of the old island came here for the day; most fled back to Binghamton or the nearby resort strip for their creature comforts before nightfall. The LeClaire was part of that small, developed resort strip just on the other side of Tasso proper.

After rehearsing the plan to the point of redundancy, they grew quiet. As they rolled towards the LeClaire, Chloe kept an eye out for Sampson, or any police for that matter. But they saw nothing even remotely suspicious. What they did see were cars carrying tourists off for their day in paradise. Locals working in the fish and craft markets lining the roadside. Brightly colored fabric hanging from racks just outside shop doors, twirling in the breezy sunshine.

A family of six seemed to be picking their way from one of the dives serving breakfast towards a row of outdoor markets. The frazzled mother darted after a small boy as he charged out ahead of the group. She scooped him up, and he giggled so enthusiastically that Chloe could have sworn she heard him as their Jeep zipped past.

Why couldn't that have been her? Mother, wife . . . part of a family. The same old thing she'd been wanting her whole sad life. A life apparently destined to forever move from bad to worse based, not on her own choices, but on the selfish, miserable choices of other people.

But not Jack, said a little voice in the back of her head. *He was a bright spot in your bad, before it turned to worse—through no fault of his own, by the way.* The thought challenged her need to protect herself, pitting it against her need to hope that maybe, just maybe, something good could happen to her. The internal debate raged.

If she let him, maybe Jack could be part of something good in her life. After all, he'd never done anything but look out for her. Was it fair to assume that, sooner or later, Jack would hurt her? Where was the proof of that?

Where was the proof he wouldn't?

But she wanted to trust him.

But trust is dangerous.

Okay, so forget trust. What about just enjoying the moment—

110

the uncomplicated . . . *goodness* . . . they'd shared before everything fell apart. Why couldn't they just go back there? Where might they have been right now if Sampson had never entered her life?

Maybe they'd be in Tasso, combing the market for some trinket to send to Izzie. Or maybe they'd be taking that catamaran out for another afternoon of sailing, golden rays beaming down, Jack's warm hand on her shoulder, steadying her—

"You okay?"

Jack's voice jerked her back, and visions of the catamaran receded. She blinked, taking in reality again. "Yeah, fine."

"You just . . . I thought maybe your head . . ."

"No. I'm fine," she said, reaching to gather her curls in one hand, then realizing there weren't any curls left to gather. Her hand dropped limply to her lap. A moment passed, and then he gently laid his arm across her shoulders and pulled her towards him. It surprised her, and she hesitated. But then, the lure of comfort beckoned her, and she caved, leaning into him.

"What are you thinking?" he asked.

She shrugged, hesitating to answer. "It's stupid."

"Come on."

She sniffed, using the moment to decide whether it was worth it to say anything. "I was thinking about where we'd be right now if all this wasn't happening." She immediately regretted sharing and, embarrassed, looked out towards the sea.

"Not stupid. So what do you think we'd be doing?" he asked, playing along as the Jeep bounced, speeding ever closer to whatever awaited them at the LeClaire.

"Jack, I don't want to do this."

"Come on. What do you think we'd be doing?" he pressed.

"I don't know. Eating somewhere? Sitting on the beach?" she offered lamely.

"Pathetic. Isn't writing part of your job description? I would have expected better."

She hated and loved that he could joke at a time like this. *How does he do it?* "Well, what do you think we'd be doing?"

"Hmmm." His eyes settled on the distance where they stayed for several silent seconds.

"Well?" she egged, turning to look at him.

"Shhh. Hold on, I'm thinking."

Despite herself, the corner of her mouth turned up slightly, which she realized had been his goal. She lightly swiped his arm. "Come on—"

"Okay, okay," he mock-whined. "Forget morning. It'd be night. A thousand stars out. And you'd be in that dress, you know, the black one you wore that first night . . ."

It tumbled out, complete and serious, belying any suggestion that he'd made it up on the spot or that he was playing. It wasn't the answer she expected. It was far more personal. And it drew her in, pulling her focus to him even more as he stared straight ahead, eyes unwavering from the road.

". . . And we'd walk down that pier, right by Mendoza's. Right to the edge. And I'd make you close your eyes. Really tight. And then I'd tell you to listen very closely, to see if you could hear the change in the water hitting the pilings as the next boat came in. And then . . ." He trailed off and her eyebrows arched, begging the answer. He cut his green eyes at her, flashing with amusement. ". . . being the wonderful, uncomplicated, no-strings attached friend that I am, I'd shake your hand, just to let you know how I feel."

She let loose a full-on grin, shaking her head as she turned away and rolled her eyes. "You're impossible," she muttered.

"Then we'd walk back inside, open a bottle of the most expensive red wine in the house, and I'd make you tell me how you got that little scar on your chin," he finished, running a finger along his own chin in the same spot where her scar was, "just there."

"Well then, I guess after that I'd make you tell me how you got that huge scar on your back, right over your left shoulder."

He cut his eyes at her again, seeming surprised. "Noticed that did you?"

"Mmm-hmm."

Then the Jeep rounded a bend in the road, bringing up the resort stretch of beach, with its large communes of buildings and palm-dotted drives. The LeClaire's entrance sign rolled into view a few hundred yards away, and all thoughts of night stars and red wine and trading stories of scars evaporated, as if they'd never been.

TWENTY-ONE

The telephones at the station had been ringing off and on since the first story aired around seven-thirty that morning. Sampson sat at his desk, twirling a pen, while beat officers fielded the phones. Despite getting several dozen calls, few had provided even remotely relevant tips and, of those, none had panned out. *Nine-fifteen already and no sign of them,* Sampson recounted, watching the clock as he took another swig of Pepto, his third that morning.

The call he had gotten at McConnaughey's the night before was about a burglary at a downtown duty-free jewelry shop. He had gone straight there after leaving her cottage and was still there at eleven when Korrigan's people called him asking where McConnaughey was. Dover, the man Korrigan had sent to McConnaughey's house, was supposed to have made it back to the hotel with her by then. But he hadn't shown.

They knew why once Sampson found Dover's corpse in the gully at the bottom of the hillside. Worse, McConnaughey's car was gone and there was no sign of her. As expected, the call to Korrigan had not gone well.

"*You understand that this is your problem, Detective Sampson?*" Korrigan barked.

"*And I'll rectify it,*" Sampson growled back.

"*I certainly hope so, because the last thing I want to do is call him and tell him that she has disappeared with that flash drive.*"

"*No, no. We'll have her in eight hours or less. I promise you.*"

"*Detective, I hope for your sake you're correct. I paid good money for your services, and I can't have a reputation of accepting less than satisfactory results. You can see how that would negatively affect the success of my projects. You can see how I would be forced to . . . respond negatively."*

"I said eight hours."

"I'll be counting the minutes," Korrigan spat. "Literally."

Sampson had come up with the idea to frame McConnaughey and Collings in the hope that it would bring them back to him, and he, in turn, could deliver them to Korrigan as soon as possible. It wouldn't be hard to come up with a convincing story that they had simply escaped. The island's sad excuse for a police force was a bumbling circus, anyway. That development wouldn't exactly seem far-fetched.

And so, at five-thirty that morning, he had placed the anonymous call to the department about a problem at Kreinberg's the night before involving "her neighbor." When the third shift officer finally found Ruby's body down the beach from her house where Korrigan had dumped it, Sampson was assigned to the case, just as he knew he would be. Between the knife they'd taken from McConnaughey's, and a tip from the "anonymous caller" that McConnaughey had been seen leaving Ruby's house late in the night, she was now the prime suspect. Hopefully, the public would unwittingly assist him in getting her back.

Until then his neck was on the line. For the first time since he took the payoff from Korrigan, he wondered if he had made a mistake. It wasn't the illegality that bothered him; it was the question of whether he had chosen to go to work for the wrong man. Sampson had been a cop for nearly fifteen years. Early in his career, he had learned two truths: one, being on the right side of the law was not profitable; and, two, if something wasn't profitable it was a waste of time. So he manipulated the job to make some extra cash, though it was never enough to give him more than a better apartment and a snappier wardrobe than the rest of his brethren-in-blue. It worked for years until Internal Affairs accused him of confiscating narcotics evidence for resale. They hadn't been able to prove anything, but he had left the force just to put some distance between him and that possibility.

He figured his career in law enforcement was over for good, until a couple of years later a bar buddy mentioned that the Caribbean took med students nobody else wanted. Wondering if the same might be true of cops, he applied to a dozen departments, including St. Gideon's. Chief Hunt must not have even checked beyond his phony references, because he gave Sampson a job as soon as he got the application and never looked back.

As it turned out, though, neither the job nor the island lived up to Sampson's expectations. St. Gideon may have been a vacationer's paradise, but for a guy used to the fast lane, it was a wasteland. And his time on the job was a nightmare. He was surrounded by fools and a boss who was more interested in becoming governor than being chief. Worst of all, there was no extracurricular business of any significance to be had. He had arrived on the island with plans to make a fortune as a player in the drug trade he was certain flourished in every Caribbean locale. But the best he had been able to do was cut deals with the small timers on the island. After two years, he had finally had enough. He was in the middle of planning his return to the States when he had gotten the call from Korrigan.

He wasn't sure how Korrigan had known he was dirty in the first place. But when he called three weeks ago, Korrigan made him the kind of proposition he had been craving for two years. Fifty thousand up front and the promise of a real job in Miami when it was all over. Sampson couldn't say yes fast enough.

"Pete!"

A couple of desks over, a young officer in his late twenties held a telephone receiver against his chest.

"What?" Sampson scowled.

"I got a guy on the phone I think maybe you should talk to."

"Yeah, why's that?"

"Just seems different. Keeps ranting about how it's his civic duty to report this."

Sampson glared in exasperation. "How many times did he ask about a reward?"

"Twice already."

"Just screen it, take the information and check it out. You know, *police work*," he barked, waving him off and swiveling his chair away. Sampson snatched a chipped mug off his desk and chugged a hefty swig of black coffee, chasing it with another dose of Pepto. Behind him he heard the officer muttering.

"Yeah, okay. Shores Motel . . . Yeah, yeah. So no girl, but . . . what . . . wait, what makes you think he might have been shot—"

"Wait a minute!" Sampson bellowed, lurching for the officer's desk. "Gimme that phone!"

* * * * *

Twenty minutes later Sampson was standing in room twenty-four of the Shores Motel. The flowered spread lay crumpled in a pile on the floor where he'd thrown it with the sheets and pillows after tearing apart the bed. Every drawer had been opened and left there. The sad, faded picture of a palm tree had been removed from the wall, its back ripped off. Nothing.

"So, um, you guys are gonna fix this back up, right?"

Sampson ignored the ratty clerk and stood in the center of the room, his head swiveling back and forth as he surveyed the space for anything they might have missed.

An officer exited the bathroom. "Anything?" Sampson growled at him.

"No," answered the officer, shaking his head. "Nothing."

Sampson pushed him out of the way and stepped inside the tiny room. Shower, sink, cabinet—all clean. He strode stiffly back to the clerk.

"And you've got nothing from him?"

"Just a signature—"

"Yeah, the fake name."

"Well, he paid in cash, man, you know? And look, we aren't the kind of place that cares about names so much. Hey listen, what about the reward? I told you what I know and . . ."

But Sampson wasn't listening anymore. He resumed scanning the room, revolving on the spot to look at the television, the door, the window, the bed, the nightstand . . . He stopped, studying the nightstand again. They'd already checked the phone book and the worn-edged hotel notepad beside it. But the pen beside that . . . It hadn't registered earlier. The pen with the cap off, as if someone had just used it.

Stepping desperately to the nightstand, he took the pad and held it up to eye level, flat to the light spilling in through the open curtains. Tiny shadows betrayed indentions on the page. Indentions that formed a list of things, one of which was circled.

"You," he snapped at the clerk, "get me a pencil!"

TWENTY-TWO

The LeClaire Resort, a sprawling property surrounded by a four-foot-high plaster fence and even taller bushes, sat on the right side of the road. In the far distance behind it, the ocean glistened in the mid-morning light. On the left, the land sloped gradually upward, until reaching the base of what seemed to be a series of steep hills leading into a forested area. As they neared the gated entrance to the LeClaire, Chloe readied herself. But to her surprise, they rolled right past.

"What are you doing?" Chloe asked in surprise, as Jack kept going.

"I need to get a sense of what we're dealing with here," he answered as he turned left into the parking lot of a collection of buildings that housed a crafts shop, market, and some kind of chicken restaurant. "Just pull out your cell phone—act like you're taking some shots."

Because of the slope of the land, they had a decent view overlooking the resort property. The main building at the center was the original hotel, containing hundreds of standard rooms. Surrounding that were a dozen stand-alone units that resembled large private homes. These upscale buildings had their own pools and hot tubs, as well as tall, bushy landscaping to seclude those areas from the view of other guests. The communal property at the front entrance of the resort contained a large fountain and several rows of high hedges. Traffic was minimal. Visible security consisted of a single guard posted in the shed by the gate.

"All right," Jack said, starting up the car and pulling back onto the road. "We can't park here. The Jeep might be noticed. Let's see if there's a turn off or something up ahead between here and the next place. We really need the Jeep to be within short walking distance of either place, in case we've got to make a run for it."

The FountainSea was the next resort down, about a quarter mile from the LeClaire. They decided to walk through the FountainSea to the beach, then head down to the LeClaire. The hope was that, by coming in from the beach entrance, they would appear to belong at the hotel and draw less attention when they went to the business office. Unfortunately, there weren't many good parking options to choose from. Their best one turned out to be an area behind a vacant shop on the left, about halfway between the two resorts. Jack followed its gravel parking lot around to the back where it ended in a short, wide, dirt driveway leading to a rusted-out shed. Most of the dirt driveway was completely grown over by the forest.

"I wish we had time to circle around, come in from another direction and park somewhere up in the forest. We'd have a longer walk, but it'd be safer."

"We don't have more time."

"Yeah, I know," he responded, regret in his voice as he stepped on the gas again, inching as far into the forest as the dense vegetation would allow. They got out and worked together, breaking off vines and branches and laying them over the Jeep in an attempt to camouflage it from view. Though not completely hidden, by the time they were finished it was at least very hard to see the Jeep unless you went to the trouble of actually coming around the building and going down the dirt driveway.

From there it was a five-minute walk down the road's pebble-strewn shoulder to the beginning of the FountainSea property. To avoid unnecessary contact with the gate guard, in between passing cars they pushed through the tall hedges that created a natural fence around the resort. Brushing themselves off and straightening up, they joined hands and gave every impression of a happy couple embarking on their day together.

"You really think this'll work?" Chloe asked, doubt burgeoning now that they were actually here, following a long sidewalk into the heart of the property.

"Absolutely. We'll be fine."

"What about you, with your leg? That's got to be killing you.

You're hardly showing it."

"It's not that bad. Tylenol's helping." He'd been popping them like candy every hour.

He steered them towards the lobby, staying on the concrete paths generously lined with oversized ferns and lanky palms. This resort was smaller than the LeClaire, consisting solely of three adjoining buildings located close to the ocean. As they went, they did their best to avoid eye contact with anyone. It wasn't hard. The few people they passed weren't interested in them in the least. Chloe's heart raced as they turned onto the last path and neared the lobby doors.

"Here we go," Jack muttered, as he pushed one open and held it for her.

The lobby was bright and clean, dotted with people milling about, slowly getting started on another day in paradise. A desk clerk glanced over as they walked in, then, unimpressed, turned back to his computer to finish whatever he was doing for the impatient guest gesturing animatedly on the other side of the counter. A few groups were scattered here and there, some checking in for sightseeing tours, others getting breakfast at the hotel café. A couple of people sat in overstuffed chairs facing the water, drinking coffee and perusing copies of USA Today. Jack slipped his arm around Chloe's waist as they passed through the heart of the community area and headed to the outside deck.

"John said to wait for them out by the pool, that they were running late," Jack offered, starting in on the script they'd come up with to make it seem like they belonged there. He spoke in a slightly louder than normal tone, one that wouldn't draw attention, but would be casually overheard by anyone that might be listening.

"Okay, but ten more minutes and I'm ordering. I'm starving," Chloe answered back, leaning into him in a friendly way as they walked purposefully towards the rear of the room. It had seemed a silly ruse to Chloe, but Jack hoped it would throw off anyone who might notice that they looked a little like the photos from the broadcast that morning. As it was, no one seemed to care.

Jack squeezed her waist reassuringly as they pushed through richly stained teak doors to the ocean-side pool and grille deck. There was more activity here; mostly young families getting an early start before the heat of the day set in. Several young children dashed around the pool's edge, screaming in delight. Chloe nearly tripped over a girl with jet-black pigtails and neon pink arm floaties, who came out of nowhere to jump bravely into the three-foot end of the pool. The pure joy in the little girl's laughter filled Chloe's heart with longing for her camera and what she knew would have been a wonderful shot.

They left the pool area by way of a meandering concrete path through lush, tropical landscaping that ultimately ended in the gritty sand of a long stretch of beach.

Jack eyed her questioningly. "You good?"

Chloe nodded, pulling off her shoes. "Let's go." He removed his Docksides as well, but tied the laces together and hung them on his shoulder. She looked at him quizzically.

"Need free hands. Just in case," he explained with a grimace, patting one of the guns in his waistband.

"Right," she mumbled, her stomach starting to churn again.

Though the two resorts were a few football fields apart by road, their respective properties dovetailed towards the ocean, putting their beachfront entrances only half that distance apart. Chloe and Jack moved down the beach as quickly as they could without jogging—not wanting to do anything that might appear odd. They weren't exactly dressed for running.

Chloe's bare feet gummed through the grainy shoreline. It was such a contradiction, walking here, down this beautiful expanse, with its salt and pepper sand, emerald waters and open sky, but having intentions like theirs. It only exaggerated the otherworldliness of their situation. This was not the place for such things. Here, with her back to the strong sea wind and gurgling waves breathing their last on the shore—this was the place for that life she longed for. The one she'd perpetually been denied.

She glanced down at their intertwined hands. He had taken hers in his once they had started walking on the beach. She still felt warm from it. She wondered if he'd noticed. At the thought, pinpricks of frustration needled her gut as she tried to reconcile two irreconcilable things—a burning desperation to be anywhere but here, doing what they were about to do, risking what they were about to risk . . . and the maddening truth that some part of her relished being here, with him. With Jack. Whatever the circumstances. It was crazy. *She* was crazy.

They'd managed about thirty yards when her gaze flitted to his face. *Was it the same for him?* But his eyes were glued to the horizon, distant and unfixed. He didn't seem present. That was, Chloe thought, a first for Jack. He was always so *in* the moment. And it unnerved her.

"Are you . . . okay?" she asked tentatively.

"Mmmm. Fine."

They kept moving, closing on the LeClaire, now less than eighty yards away. His gaze remained trained on something beyond the hazy line where the water met the sky. "I was just . . . well . . . asking for help."

It took her a second to understand. "Oh."

He blinked, his eyes moving to hers, his amusement clear on his face. "You think I'm crazy."

"No, no . . . I don't . . ."

Jack's eyebrows drew into doubtful arches as she stumbled over her words.

Chloe gathered herself and sighed. "No. Of course not. I . . . I think it's great that you believe in something out there bigger than yourself. We can use all the help we can get." Fifty-five yards. Fifty-four. A jogger loped by, an iPod clipped to his side. "I really didn't mean anything by it, Jack. It's not for me, but if it helps you, I get it," she offered apologetically. "I think it's nice. Izzie's the same way. It works for her, too."

A couple of sea gulls duked it out over a stray bit of food. Jack ran a hand through his too-blond hair and smiled. "I don't think of it so much as 'working for me' as I do a connection. A relationship," he said softly, their feet continuing to pound softly into the sand.

Chloe shook her head. "That's a nice idea. Really. And given what we're dealing with, and the fact that Sampson could show up any minute, I wish I could believe it. I truly do. But I have prayed, Jack. More than you could know in my lifetime. And nothing good ever came from it. No one ever rescued me." She abruptly stopped walking and turned towards him. "Except you."

They stood a few feet apart now, hands still together, their arms stretched across the distance between them due to Chloe's unannounced stop. Jack studied her for the briefest moment, then sucked in a steadying breath through his nose. He opened his mouth as if to speak, but quickly shut it, apparently changing his mind. Instead, he pulled her back to him and she moved easily. He stared into Chloe's eyes purposefully, as if trying to decide if something he was looking for was in there. The breeze ruffled her short hair as he sighed and spoke hesitantly.

"Given what we're up against, what we're likely to face, now would be a really good time to consider that maybe not everything is as it seems. Maybe there's a bigger picture. Maybe you've been rescued in other ways—"

"Jack, I know you mean well and all, and maybe sometime later we can discuss this. But *right now*, we need to get inside."

"It can wait. For this."

"Jack, seriously—"

"Seriously."

She inhaled and cleared her throat, buying a few seconds while she decided if he really had finally lost it, getting into this subject at a time like this. But there was a burning in his gaze that told her he knew exactly what he was doing.

"Sometime, ok?" she promised, urgency coating the words. "Sometime *later*."

He hesitated, as something like disappointment flashed briefly in his features, then nodded. Squeezing her hand, he inhaled another large gulp of salty air. "Okay," he conceded. "Okay. You ready, then?"

"Can I say no?"

A tiny smile creased his mouth. "Not really."

"Then let's go."

Together they started again, padding closer to the resort with each step. Thirty yards. Twenty-five. The short, weathered boardwalk stretching into the LeClaire's grounds was a bustling highway filled with beachgoers. Jack and Chloe remained quiet as they started up its steps, but once they reached the pool area and put their shoes back on, they started up their fake conversation again, just to aid in blending in.

Whites and blues bathed everything. Grass mats covered the floors in front of royal blue sofas that filled the common areas leading into the lobby. They walked past these, into a wall of floral-scented air fresheners creating a barricade around the area near the front desk. Without skipping a beat, Chloe led Jack right past the desk to a long hallway off to the right. The desk clerk, busy checking in a very loud family, didn't even look up from his paperwork.

They walked down the hallway, past the elevators and lobby bathrooms. The last door on the left just before the hallway took a ninety degree turn to the left, was labeled, "Business Center." A thrill ran through Chloe as she saw that, as she had thought, no room key was required for entry. Peeking inside, they found the room empty, and Chloe slipped inside.

She turned when she noticed Jack wasn't following. "Wait here," Jack said, as he started to pull the door shut.

"Where are you—"

"I'm just checking out the lay of the land. I'll be right back." He nodded toward the computer. "You go ahead," he said, and closed the door.

The space was tiny, really no more than a glorified closet, with one ancient PC and a printer atop a melamine table pushed against the wall. Half a window, overlooking the front parking lot, made up part of the outside wall, suggesting that maybe the room had been an afterthought, carved off of a part of a larger, adjacent room.

"I can't believe no one was in here," Chloe muttered, taking the rolling chair in front of the computer and reaching into her bag. Terrified of losing the flash drive, she'd been feeling it inside the bag's zippered pocket every five minutes or so since they left the car. Now she extracted it and leaned over the machine to locate the USB port. She found it and inserted the drive.

The machine whirred, working slowly to recognize the flash drive. Chloe sighed impatiently and turned to stare at the door. She didn't like separating.

As if in answer to her thoughts, the door swung open, then closed quickly, as Jack hastened inside then locked it.

"We okay?" Chloe asked.

Jack nodded. "Is it working?" he asked, stepping to the window and drawing the blinds so that he could see out, but making it difficult to see in from the outside.

Chloe shrugged. "It's slow. It's still reading it." She tapped her fingers uselessly on the bottom of the keyboard. "Come on, come on," she softly urged the machine. Jack continued peering through the blinds.

"There!" Chloe exclaimed, grasping the mouse and clicking. "It read it." She paused. "It's a video file," she acknowledged weakly.

Jack slid next to her to look over her shoulder. "Will it play?"

Chloe bit her lip. "We'll see."

But instead of double clicking the file to start it, Chloe just stared at the screen, unmoving. Jack looked from the screen to her face, which had grown pale.

"You can do this," Jack encouraged, squeezing her shoulders gently. "You know you can."

She nodded again and double clicked the file. Another window opened, and the video started to play.

* * * * *

A solitary chair set against a bare, mocha-colored wall flashed onto the screen. The chair was modern, made of black leather stretched over a shiny chrome frame, and Chloe recognized it immediately.

"I think that's in Tate's apartment in Miami," she said hollowly.

The picture jiggled a bit, as if someone was adjusting the camera. Then the frame shifted so that the chair moved to the center of the screen and the jiggling stopped. Shadows fell over the left of the screen. Then suddenly, there was Tate. A long, quiet breath stole slowly from Chloe's lips, and her frame folded inward ever so slightly.

Tate's auburn hair was badly in need of a cut and had started to curl at the ends. Thanks to the broiling Miami sun, his fair skin was darker than she'd ever seen it. His gaze seemed to bore straight through her and for a moment she had the eerie feeling he could actually see her sitting there with Jack. Then he smiled, and the familiarity of it took her breath away.

"*Chloe,*" he said, leaning forward in the chair, propping himself up with his elbows on his knees. How many times had she heard him utter her name in her lifetime? Thousands. Thousands upon thousands. His voice washed over her, taking her instantly through a life's worth of precious moments and memories, wrenching her heart, tearing at the hole where he used to be.

"*Chloe, first you have to know that I did all of this for you. For us. It was my chance and I took it, and, well, I hope you can understand. Even though . . . even though, if you're watching this it probably means that I'm dead.*" He looked down for a moment, summoned his composure, then looked back at the camera. "*It doesn't necessarily mean that, by the way. It's possible I'm hiding out somewhere, waiting for the right opportunity to hook back up with you—*" A brief, ridiculous hope expanded in Chloe like a bubble, then popped instantaneously. She had identified her brother's remains. He was wrong. It wasn't possible.

"*But, if I am, it brings me to the second thing. Which is . . . I'm sorry. I never intended for this to happen. It seemed like the perfect plan, you know, and then, well, things just sort of spiraled out of control. But,"* he quickly pointed out, *"I've still got contingency plans in place and it's looking good, so as I sit here, of course I'm hoping you'll never see this. I'm hoping that everything will work out exactly as I've planned, and pretty soon you and I will have everything we always deserved but never had the luck to get. There's just so much I've— we've—been cheated out of. So,"* he said decidedly, a guilty twitch in his expression suggesting that he was already certain she would disapprove, *"I finally came to the conclusion that if cheating is the only way to get anything in life, then so be it."*

"Oh, Tate," she moaned ruefully. "What did you do?"

"I'm going to tell Rohrstadt to send this to you as soon as he gets word I've disappeared, or . . . been killed. Or whatever. No matter what anyone has told you about how I died, whether it was a drowning, car accident, heart attack, whatever, you need to be very careful. I promise it was no accident. I was murdered. And, well, there's a slight chance . . . although I think I covered my tracks pretty well, and they shouldn't suspect you in the least . . . that the people that killed me are going to be coming after you."

"Idiot," Jack growled, and the tone was so foreign on him that Chloe looked up just to make sure he'd actually said it. "Sorry," he said, but his eyes still flashed.

Tate continued, and she turned her gaze back to the screen.

"So, this is all on you now. And the reward is all yours, too. You'll just need to hold on for a few weeks—and then you're home free. After that, go someplace safe, someplace secret. Somewhere not even I would guess. Buy a house, buy a villa, hey, buy a yacht. You'll be able to afford it. But before then, you're going to have to come to Miami . . . but I'll get to that.

"For now, start using just cash. No credit cards. These people are very powerful. They have fingers everywhere. And don't trust anyone."

Anyone. The word echoed in Chloe's mind as she became acutely aware of Jack's presence behind her. But Jack wasn't just anyone. He was Jack. And she needed him. At least for now.

"I've thought this through a thousand times. I know I've covered all my bases. I don't think I'm going to need this video, but it's kind of like life insurance, you know? Just in case. With this much money at stake, I'd be stupid not to take this precaution."

"Money," Chloe mumbled in a distant, knowing sort of way.

"I guess I should start at the beginning. I'd been in Miami about six weeks when I met this guy in a bar in Bayside. I never caught his name, but he worked for WorldCore Bank's Miami office in some kind of management position.

Anyway, he tosses back one too many and gets loose-lipped. We get to talking about our jobs, and when he finds out I'm in tech security, he launches into this story about how he's in for a conference on system security, and isn't that a coincidence. Tells me how they could really use a guy like me because so far they haven't been able to come up with a reliable gatekeeping system. How they're constantly crashing, getting invaded, hackers playing havoc with accounts. And apparently WorldCore's not the only one with the problem. He even names names for me. He's practically on the verge of tears because he had something to do with buying their current firewall program and his job's on the line. Well, eventually, he wanders off, and starts blubbering to somebody else. But I can't stop thinking about it, and suddenly, I realize that the universe has dropped the perfect opportunity into my lap."

Chloe shook her head side to side, as if trying to convince Tate not to say what she felt sure was coming next.

"Please tell me he didn't," Jack whispered.

"So, I started checking out some of the banks he'd talked about. It's me, so, you know, it wasn't even really that hard to hack in and cover my tracks. But it didn't take long to figure out that I would need someone else, someone on the inside—"

A light flashed from the window, and Jack's head whipped towards the blinds. He squinted through them, and watched as a brown sedan jerked to a stop at the bellhop stand by the lobby. "Stop it!" he barked at Chloe, over Tate's continuing monologue.

"What?" Chloe said, spinning towards him and following his gaze to the window.

"The video, stop it now," he repeated, and moved to stand against the wall to hide his body from view. As two men leapt from the sedan, two patrol cars pulled up right behind it.

"What? What's happening?" Chloe asked, pausing the video.

"Sampson," Jack said turning toward her. "We've got to move. Now."

The color drained from her face as she continued to sit, unmoving.

"Chloe, now!"

The sharpness of his voice jolted her into action. She clicked out of the video window and ripped the flash drive from the back of the PC. Her heart pounded as Jack grabbed her hand and pulled her to the door. He peeked out for a moment and closed the door again.

"They're at the front desk," he said. Chloe felt unsteady on her feet and Jack's voice was starting to sound distant and fuzzy around the edges. She was having trouble focusing.

"Hey," he said, grabbing her face with his hands. "Chloe, you hear me? Chloe. Look at me."

"We're dead, Jack."

"Hey, listen to me. We're not dead. I don't want to hear that again, got it? I don't think they know we're back here or they'd already *be* here, okay? We need to go out this way," he said, tilting his head in the direction that the hallway continued down. "You ready?"

She nodded.

"Come on, then," he urged, pulling her hand to him as he opened the door just enough to slide out. An advantageously placed potted palm blocked them partially from view as they sprinted the short few feet to the end of the hall, where it turned left ninety degrees and out of sight of the front desk.

A resounding crash rang out followed by a chorus of sharp cries, as Jack and Chloe cleared the corner and immediately ran full force into a hotel employee carrying a tray of covered dishes above his shoulder. All three flew backwards from the impact as silver lids and china plates smashed on the blue and white tiles, clattering incessantly as they circled one another amongst splattered food and scattered utensils. Chloe slammed hard against the wall, then ricocheted back, losing her footing in the spilled food and landing spread-eagled on the floor. Jack and the waiter landed on either side of her, their clothes smeared with food.

The waiter, fumbling in the sloppy mess, cursed loudly. Jack, apparently dazed, shook his head as he stood. "Get up, Chloe," he urged, reaching toward her and pulling her to her feet. "We've got to go. Fast. They'll have heard."

As she straightened up, Chloe shook her hand violently to sling off some scrambled eggs, leaving a gushy splatter on the opposite wall. New panic seized her as she stared at her empty hand. The hand that had been squeezing tightly around the flash drive before the crash.

To the bewilderment of both Jack and the waiter, Chloe dropped back to her knees and began frantically groping through the soggy mess of china and glass shards, eggs, juice, and potato hash.

"Hey lady, wait—" started the waiter.

"Chloe, now!" Jack barked, tugging on her arm. "What are you doing?"

"The flash drive!" exclaimed Chloe in a panic, jerking away from

Jack.

"What?"

"The *flash drive*—I had it! I dropped it when I fell!"

Dread washed over Jack's face, his eyes now reflecting Chloe's panic. He moved to crouch beside her, when suddenly a well-muscled man in a dark sports coat stepped briskly around the corner. He stopped mid-stride, his gaze landing first on the mess, then on Chloe. In the same second that recognition flashed across the man's face, Jack was on him.

Jack's first blow broke the arm reaching for his gun. The second to the throat drove the man into the wall and left him gagging. The waiter scrambled crab-like away from the brawl as Jack slammed the man's head into the wall. When he landed in a crumpled heap on the floor, Jack ripped the gun from beneath the man's jacket. Chloe was still fishing through the wreckage from the tray. The waiter practically tripped over himself trying to stand, his eyes wide and hands splayed in front of him as if to wave Jack off. As soon as the waiter got a foothold, he maneuvered clumsily past Chloe while staying as far away from Jack as possible. When he reached the corner, he took off towards the lobby.

"Let's go," Jack growled, grabbing Chloe under the arm and pulling.

"No!" Chloe screamed as she shrugged him off. "I can't. I've got to find it!"

Practically dragging Chloe up off the floor, Jack ordered harshly, "Chloe! They. Are. Coming. Leave it! Come on!"

Her shoulders slumped, and with a forlorn groan she shoved off of the floor and gave in to Jack's pulling, taking his hand as they raced around a quick turn to the right, then ran full speed down a long hallway. They flew past several doors, but Jack didn't slow.

"Where are we going?" Chloe cried in between labored breaths.

"Not sure—wait—right here," Jack grunted as they reached the middle of the hallway and a door marked "Laundry." He ripped it open as footfalls sounded from somewhere behind them. After darting inside, he shut the door quickly, but quietly. Several commercial-sized washers and dryers lined the gray walls. The steady rolling hum of the machines and the swishing of fabric inside the wet drums filled the room, masking their whispers.

"Where now?" she asked as he turned over a heavy table, dumping a stack of folded towels on the floor.

"Just a second," he said, sliding the table over a few feet, then wedging the top diagonally between the knob and the floor. He handed her the pistol he'd taken off the man he disarmed, then pulled a Glock from his waistband.

"That should give us a little time," Jack hissed softly, striding across the room to a set of double doors on the outer wall. "Delivery doors," he told her, his hand grasping the knob. "We go out here."

"To where?" Chloe said in a hushed tone.

"Further down the front of the building. With the maze of hedges out there, we should be able to get close to the road without being spotted. After that we'll have to just see."

Chloe huddled behind him as he opened the door and peeked outside. The service doors and the sidewalk leading away were shielded from the view of the guests by full, green hedges taller than Jack. They slipped out, letting the door close silently behind them. Trying to look natural and invisible at the same time, they followed the walk down the side of the building to where it curved around the back. Here the sidewalk hedges ended, exposing them.

"We've got to head towards the road," Jack said, as another marked car flew into the lot headed towards the others near the lobby. "And we better move fast."

Chloe's pulse raced as they ran to the first long line of tall hedges encircling the closest house unit, just a few yards away. As quick as they could, they pushed their way between the long, flimsy branches, which scratched and pulled at them until they fell through to the other side. They landed in the private courtyard of the house which, fortunately, was completely empty. Picking themselves up, they dashed across the yard and tried to peer through the hedges to the other side.

Chloe rubbed a long welt drawn up on her forearm, left by one of the branches. "What now?" she said, panic rising in her tone. *Everything was closing in. She'd lost the flash drive. Sampson was seconds away . . .*

"Sidewalk. We'll have to book it to the next house. Then we just keep going till we get as close to the road as possible. Then we'll have to see if we can cross to the car."

Grabbing the long, reedy branches, he pushed them aside to create a hole, then stepped through. This time Jack held them for Chloe. They stepped out right in front of a swimsuit-clad guest carrying a tray of to-go coffees.

Jack smiled and shrugged. "Lost," he told the man, offering a guilty chuckle.

The man nodded skeptically and kept walking, glancing back over his shoulder once after he passed.

"We're never gonna make it," Chloe groaned as they hustled towards the next house.

"It's not over yet," he urged, pushing through the next set of bushes into another private courtyard. "It's a lot of property for them to search. We just have to keep moving." This time three people were sunbathing around the pool. All of them looked up as Chloe and Jack broke through the hedge and strode across the lawn.

"Hey, man, what—" one of them started.

"Just a hide-and-seek challenge," Jack interrupted. "Business conference. Sorry," he apologized, giving an awkward little salute as they walked to the front of the house.

They stopped at the corner to survey their options. They had made it close enough to the road that now only an open stretch of lawn stood between them and the tallest hedges lining the plaster wall separating the resort property from the road.

"Now we run across."

"Out in the open?"

"We've got no choice. They'll be crawling all over this place soon. Ready?"

Chloe nodded.

They dashed across the twenty-yard span, nearly tossing themselves head first into the bushes at the four-foot-high wall.

"Stay down," Jack instructed. "I'm going to get our bearings."

Chloe nodded as he rose and peeked over the top. She sat with her back to the wall, her heart pounding and out of breath. Tears started down her cheek. *What have I done?* she thought, desperation clawing at her. *I've lost our only evidence. And now we're trapped.*

Jack sank down beside her. "This guy is fast."

"Why—what's happening?"

"He's got a car on the road already."

"What?"

Jack nodded. "Between us and where we parked. It's possible he's got another one going the other direction," he nodded his head towards the far side of the LeClaire complex, "maybe just around the bend. So even if we manage to get to the car, we may not be able to drive it out of here." He exhaled in frustration. "I should've parked farther down."

"We still couldn't have crossed. I should have picked a different hotel—not one we couldn't run away from."

Jack shook his head. "One closer to town would've had its own risks." His shoulders sagged slightly and he exhaled. "This could've worked. I should've anticipated this. I . . ." He took a good look at her, taking in the tears for the first time. "Hey," he said. "It'll be okay."

Chloe shook her head in disagreement. "No. No, it won't. It can't. Because I lost that flash drive. The only thing we had—"

"That's not your fault," he countered. "It just happened. Look, I really think we're going to have to get out of here on foot," he said resignedly. "We'll still have to get across the road and into the forest, but if we time it right, we might not be spotted." He sighed in frustration. "Thing is we've got no idea where that forest leads. We might just end up lost in there. If they end up using dogs—"

"What about heading back to the FountainSea? If we could get to the edge of that property maybe we could find a way to get across the road unseen."

Jack shook his head. "They'll be at the FountainSea soon, if they aren't already. It's why I didn't park there to start with. And we'd be sitting ducks if we tried walking down the beach. I thought we'd be able to get to the Jeep. I never thought he'd organize a mass effort like this so quickly."

A nervous silence settled between them. "We'll be fine," Jack assured her, though he didn't sound very confident. "We'll just have to try for the forest. We'll stick as close to the perimeter as we can. Maybe find a car we can use. Or bikes or something." He took a deep breath. "Listen, if they see us, if this goes wrong, I'll distract them. You just run—"

They both heard it. A faint rhythmic buzzing. As confusion spread across Chloe's face, Jack fumbled for his pocket, then whipped out the prepaid cell and answered it.

"Yeah?" he asked hopefully, his eyes locked onto Chloe's as she searched him for an explanation.

Seconds passed as Jack listened, his face brightening with relief. "Oh, man," he gushed at the caller. "Am I ever glad to hear your voice."

TWENTY-THREE

Chloe sat quietly, straining to understand who was on the phone as Jack quickly recounted the critical aspects of their situation for the caller.

". . . All that's left is the forest across . . ." He stopped mid-sentence to listen. "The Jeep's over there, but if they see us, we'll never get to it in time . . . Yeah, okay. . . . No, two, three minutes, tops. They'll find us eventually . . . How's he going to . . . okay. Hold on."

Jack met Chloe's gaze, his eyes alight. "Here, hold this," he said, handing her the cell, then ripping a branch from the bush. "I'll explain everything later, but right now, I just need you to trust me. Okay?"

She nodded. Twisting around, he shoved the branch onto the wall ledge, easing it out so it lay across the top and would be noticeable from the other side. He dropped back into a squat and pressed against the plaster.

"In a couple of minutes a car's gonna pull up right here," he told her, taking the phone again. "We've got to hop over the wall and get in. Fast. Okay?"

She nodded her understanding.

He put the cell up to his ear again. "Okay, it's done . . . All right, just let me know."

He turned to Chloe. "He's going to tell me when," he said, and grabbed her hand. "Just go when I go, got it?"

She nodded, her heart racing even faster than before. His hand was steady, but perspiring, suggesting he was nervous, which made her even more nervous. The seconds seem to drag, and she tried to peer through the thick bushes for any sign of Sampson. A couple of times they heard what might've been aggravated voices barking in the distance, but no one had come closer than that.

And then Jack pressed the cell tighter against his ear, his stare still focused on Chloe, as if trying to channel confidence into her. "Okay . . . got it," he told the caller.

"He's through. Almost here," Jack said, apparently relaying whatever the caller was telling him. He rose up as high as he could without putting his head above the wall ledge. She followed him. She heard the sound of a car engine rolling toward them, growing steadily louder.

"And three, two, . . . now!" He pulled her up and pushed her ungracefully onto the ledge, the thick bushes tearing into them as he hoisted himself after her, then rolled off. She was already at the rear door of the grey sedan, yanking it open and diving inside as the car started to roll.

"Go! Go! Go!" Jack yelled as he dove in behind her and slammed the door shut.

Tires squealed as the driver pulled wide and spun into a one-eighty, gunning it back towards the roadblock he'd just come through.

The officer manning the roadblock was yelling into his radio and diving behind the wheel of his patrol car, which was straddled across both lanes of traffic. As the sedan rocketed towards him, the officer revved his engine, but didn't move, apparently unsure of which way to go to best block the sedan. At the last second, the sedan's driver pointed the car towards the front end of the patrol vehicle, aiming for the little bit of open road between the patrol car and the narrow gravel shoulder.

"It's not wide enough!" Chloe screamed as the officer, apparently changing tactics, leveled his weapon through the window and began firing.

"Get down!" Jack bellowed, forcing Chloe's head into the seat as two shots popped off. The sedan's left side collided with the patrol vehicle, metal screaming against metal and glass shattering as the impact spun the patrol car away and they rocketed past.

"Stay down," their driver ordered, pressing the pedal to the floor as the car approached ninety miles per hour. Behind them, sirens sounded. "They'll catch up quickly. Listen—we'll be coming up to a bend soon." A side road flashed past. Then another. Suddenly, the driver began to slow. "Nothing there but trees. You'll have just a few seconds before they can see us." The sirens grew louder. "I'll slow down as much as I can. You roll out—"

"Roll out?" Chloe echoed incredulously.

"Chloe, just listen," Jack said firmly, pressing his hand against her arm.

"Yeah, *roll out*. There's a lot of brush. Get under it. Wait till they've gone by—then walk about twenty yards into the trees. There'll be a car waiting."

"What about you?" Jack asked.

The driver snorted. "Don't worry about me. You got it?"

Jack nodded. "Yeah." He turned towards Chloe. "Jump for the shoulder and roll. Ok?"

She looked at him, petrified.

"Jump and roll," he reiterated and squeezed her hand.

"Here we go," said the driver. With the sirens bearing down on them they rounded a narrow curve in the road. The driver slammed on the brakes, slowing to about twenty miles per hour.

"Now!" yelled the driver.

Jack threw open the door and leapt for the brush, followed by Chloe. She cried out as her knee hit the gravelly shoulder before she tucked and tumbled into the dense underbrush that filled a three-foot-deep gully bordering the shoulder. Copying Jack she pushed through to the gully's bottom, making herself as flat as possible.

As sirens screamed by, she squeezed her eyes tight, hoping against hope.

* * * * *

Korrigan sat alone at a pristine dining table covered in white linen and fine china. The table was strategically positioned in front of the sitting room's large window overlooking the hotel courtyard, and beyond that, the harbor. Korrigan methodically ate his brunch, cutting one piece of poached egg with hollandaise, lifting it to his mouth and swallowing. Then another. And another. He did this until the eggs were gone, then moved on to the sautéed potatoes, following the same ritual.

The door to the enormous suite creaked as Vargas entered.

"I thought you knew better than to disturb me during a meal," Korrigan remarked caustically, never looking up from his plate.

"I assumed you would want an update," the tall, twenty-something offered confidently.

Korrigan stopped slicing. "And?"

"No sign of them since they lost the car an hour ago. They did locate Collings's Jeep near the resort. But there's nothing in it either."

Korrigan laid his gleaming fork on the table and glared at Vargas. "You interrupted me to tell me that there has been no change?"

The rebuke failed to shake Vargas's composure. Unlike most of Korrigan's men, Vargas was not easily unnerved by him. The quality impressed and annoyed Korrigan equally. Korrigan's surly expression remained static, but he pushed back from the table. "Get him on the phone," he barked.

Vargas fluidly retrieved a cell phone from the inside pocket of his dark suit. "He's already on, sir," he said, holding the phone out to Korrigan. "Just unmute it."

Korrigan reached for the phone, mildly pleased by Vargas's forethought, though not completely surprised. Of all his men, Vargas was the most consistently capable. Not perfect, but generally very precise. He nodded sharply at Vargas as he snatched the cell and paced to the expansive window.

"Sampson?" he growled, staring out at the crystal waters but not seeing them.

"You know I'm in the middle of something here Korrigan, so make it quick."

"You should have them by now."

"Well, I don't. And before you start in, it's not for a lack of effort. They could be anywhere by now. This kind of thing takes time."

"Time is something I don't have, Sampson. I paid you a lot of money precisely because I did not have a lot of time. You promised quick results. You promised me positive action. But I am getting neither."

"Hey, this landed in my lap less than forty-eight hours ago," Sampson shot back angrily. "Don't blame me for your people's screw-ups."

"I blame you for your screw-ups. You have an entire department at your disposal. Use it."

Sampson snapped, "You act like I've got an army here. In case you've forgotten, this is a small outfit. And by the way, this is not my first rodeo. I know what I'm doing. Your interference is only causing more delay. Why don't you just kick back in that five-star hotel room of yours, knock back another martini, and let me do my job. Because right now, you're only getting in the way."

Silence thick with loathing followed, until Korrigan said in a low, smooth voice, "I don't know who you think you are, but I'll tell you who I am. I am the man who will take out of your flesh every cent we paid you if you don't have those two here by five o'clock. You've seen what I can do. Have done. *Will* do."

"Look," Sampson started, a slight hesitation suggesting he was rethinking his bravado, "take it easy. All I'm saying is—"

Korrigan groaned in disgust. "Just find them. And while you're out there keep an eye out for your spine. Seems you've lost it."

Sampson's temper flared again. "You pompous—"

"Just do it. And remember what I said. Five o'clock."

Korrigan hung up before Sampson could finish. The familiar rush that always followed the institution of fear in others washed over him. Next to wielding the power of life and death over someone, it was this he enjoyed most. The power to make others *fear.*

He moved back to his food and sat down.

"It's cold," Korrigan groused, pushing the plate away. "Take care of it."

Vargas moved to the suite phone and placed a call to room service while Korrigan extracted a cigarette from a silver-plated case and lit it. Taking a long drag, he eyed Vargas expectantly.

"Where are they on Collings?"

"Still working on it. There's no record of him here or in the States before he first put into the marina about six months ago. The boat's not even registered to him. It's rented out to some law firm in New York. Miami's working on it now. We're still working a connection with the island's passport office to compare photos, but it's slow."

"Stay on it," Korrigan grumbled, crushing his cigarette in a black lacquer ashtray on the coffee table. "If Collings *is* working this, I don't want him finding that money before we do."

TWENTY-FOUR

Sampson cursed angrily and plowed through a red light, nearly causing a delivery truck to collide with him. Over the truck's horn, Sampson cursed again and pressed the gas harder.

After two hours, they'd found no sign of McConnaughey and Collings. Dogs at the hotel had been just as useless, always stopping at the wall where the two had gone over.

Now Korrigan was breathing down his neck and making threats. *That pompous, sanctimonious . . . always treating me like one of those meatheads who goes around breaking necks for him.* "I didn't come down here to put up with this garbage again," Sampson muttered loudly, thinking of the brass in Jersey and the brown-nosing he left behind when he walked away from there.

But the threats . . . they were threats Korrigan would probably make good on. Sampson's stomach dropped a little. He'd seen what happens when Korrigan's guys really screw up—that Parker guy disappeared after getting himself caught at McConnaughey's place. Korrigan *had* paid Sampson a lot, nearly a year's salary for a few weeks' work, and he was obviously expecting a lot. He briefly wondered if he could walk away if he paid Korrigan back, but he doubted it. Besides, a good chunk had gone for a deposit on the boat he'd always wanted. He doubted he could swing a loan to make up for it. Which meant his only option was to show up about five hours from now with two people who had effectively disappeared from the face of the earth.

His phone beeped. Ripping it out of his pocket, he saw it was one of his guys.

"Yeah?"

"We got something, boss. That waiter—the one that ran into McConnaughey—they just got around to re-questioning him, and he said he found something when he cleaned up that mess from the collision. A flash drive. Hid it in his storage locker in case it was valuable. Wanted to get a sense of what was going on before he gave it up. He's got some petty larceny charge and wants to make it go away in trade."

Relief flooded Sampson. "You tell that idiot whatever you have to tell him in order to get that flash drive. You hear me?"

"Sure, yeah—"

"I'm headed back to you. Do *not* let that flash drive out of your sight? Got it?"

"Got it."

Sampson disconnected and tossed the phone on the passenger seat as he lit up his siren and swung the car around.

TWENTY-FIVE

"Can I get you some more water?" asked the woman named Marta, rising from the table. Chloe watched her deep brunette ponytail swing as she collected her empty plate, her handsome bronze skin a severe contrast against the china.

"Um, sure," Chloe said as Marta took her glass to fill it at the sink, "but you really don't have to wait on me."

"It's nothing," said Marta, returning with the glass and setting it before Chloe. "You're a guest in our home." The home was a two-story modern structure that looked like it belonged on a hillside overlooking Los Angeles, not buried deep in the St. Gideon forest at the end of a private, hidden road.

"Thanks," replied Chloe, taking another bite of the chicken salad sandwich Marta had prepared. "This is really delicious."

"I'm glad you like it," Marta said, sitting back down. "Old family recipe."

"So . . . is it just you and your brother here?"

Through the ceiling-high glass panes lining the west side of the house, Marta eyed the two armed men walking the property, and nodded. "Just Manny and I in the house—though we always have a couple of . . . guests on the property." She smiled. "I keep telling him to get a wife, but he says he's too busy."

"And, um," Chloe fumbled, not wanting to pry, "what, do you—"

"I'm actually in school here," Marta interrupted, rescuing Chloe. "At the local college. It's small, but it's just for the first year. Manny says if I do well, he'll pay for me to study in the States. I think he would have done it this year, but he wasn't ready to let me go just yet."

"Well, that's nice that he wants you close."

"I think he wants to keep me close to keep an eye on me."

Chloe smirked thinly. "I've had one of those."

Marta grinned. "So you've got an older brother, too?"

Chloe nodded, yes, not wanting to explain.

"And what does he think of Jack?"

Chloe paused mid-reach for her water. "Umm . . . He hasn't met him." At the uncomfortable look on Marta's face she shook her head. "But . . . it's not like that with Jack and me."

"Really, you and Jack—no?"

"Well, it's not really a . . . good time."

"Hmm. I would have thought . . ." she paused, appraising Chloe. "Well, never mind. When I saw you two earlier . . . well, I just thought that it made sense now."

"What made sense now?"

Marta considered her, then plunged ahead. "Did Jack tell you how he met Manny?"

Chloe shook her head. "He just said he'd explain later. Everything was so . . . so crazy. We didn't get a chance to talk before he went off with your brother," Chloe replied, indicating the back of the well-appointed house where Jack had gone with Manny more than an hour before.

"Well," Marta started, "a few months ago I was at the resort where Jack works. I'd been with friends, but they left early. I'd had a fight with Manny and wasn't ready to go home. So I planted myself at the bar and started my own pity party. I had a bit too much to drink and actually was flirting with Jack, but he wasn't interested. So I started talking to this table of guys—there were three of them—and they kept buying me drinks.

"Of course, all this is what Jack told us later. I barely remember any of it. Anyway, Jack said he was concerned, thought the guys were a little too keen on me drinking. At one point he thought he saw one of them slip something into my drink. But he wasn't sure so he just kept watching." She paused, looking down at her glass sheepishly and running her finger around the rim.

"It was stupid, I know. But not too long after that, Jack said I started sliding out of my chair. The guys had their arms around me, kind of like they were helping me out of the bar, and were still talking to me like I was aware. But Jack said I was basically out of it at that point. The bar was pretty packed, so I guess no one really noticed." She smiled. "Except, Jack. He wouldn't let them leave. Even though it was three to one. When he pushed them back from the doorway, one of them swung at him. That was it. Thirty seconds later it was over. Jack had a split lip and a pretty good cut from a bottle one guy slashed his head with, but the three guys were on the floor. Two of them were out cold.

"What about the third guy?" Chloe asked.

Marta snorted. "He was bawling on the floor. Jack had kicked his knee out or something. Jack found my cell, saw Manny as my last call and told him what happened. Manny was there in ten minutes."

"Nobody called the police?"

"Oh, sure. Somebody did, because by the end they'd showed up. Good thing, too, because if the cops hadn't been there, Manny probably would've k—" She stopped short and paused, as if thinking better of whatever she had been about to say. "Well, it just would've been bad. For them. I've rarely seen Manny that angry."

Her expression lightened. "But he was so grateful to Jack. Manny told him that if he ever needed anything to just ask. But he never did. Until yesterday. He was so excited when he got Jack's message."

"Marta, I'm really grateful that Manny got us out of there. But that was really risky. I don't know what Jack was thinking. We'd decided we wouldn't drag anyone into this."

"Nobody's dragging anybody anywhere," boomed a jovial Manny, walking in with Jack. "After all Jack did for Marta," he said, throwing a brotherly arm around Marta, "it's the least I can do."

"But," Chloe said, flashing a disapproving look at Jack before turning back to Manny, "if you help us, Sampson will be after you too."

Manny worked to repress an amused smile. "Let's just say I . . . well, I'm used to being on the police radar. My business," he paused for emphasis, "sometimes puts me there. But it's an issue I'm equipped to handle and not one you should worry about." Manny was being vague, but the general message was clear. These were people used to being at odds with the law.

"We'll be fine," he continued. "And," he sighed, slapping Jack on the back, "so will you. There's a couple of rooms upstairs. Rest up, change—there's a closet in the one on the left with clothes you can use." He looked at Jack. "I'm working on the things we talked about. They should be here soon. We should be able to leave in about two hours."

Confused, Chloe looked from Manny to Jack.

Manny smiled. "Don't worry, Chloe. I'm sure Jack will explain everything upstairs."

TWENTY-SIX

Sampson pounded on the door to Korrigan's hotel suite until it finally opened a crack.

"What?" Vargas answered, a slice of his face visible behind the door.

"I've got news for him."

"I hope for your sake you've got two warm bodies to go along with that information," Vargas snapped as he swung the door open.

Sampson steamrolled through. "Move out of the way you little—"

Vargas shoved Sampson inside so hard that he tripped, falling to his knees.

Korrigan appeared from the rear of the suite, striding over to Sampson. He looked around expectantly. "I don't see anyone with you."

Sampson rose, clearly angry, his chest shaking as he sucked in air. His eyes locked onto Korrigan.

"Where are they?" Korrigan demanded.

"I'm working on it," Sampson rasped. "If your gorilla'd held off for two seconds I could've given you this," he baited, pulling out the flash drive and twisting it between his fingers.

Korrigan plucked the flash drive from Sampson's grip and examined it. "Where did you get this?"

"She dropped it," Sampson spat. "In the hotel."

"Get me the laptop," Korrigan ordered, tossing the flash drive to Vargas, who disappeared wordlessly through a door at the back of the sitting room.

"That's what you wanted, right? If you've got that, then you don't need those two anymore," Sampson said, as if that decided the matter.

"Wrong, detective," Korrigan said. He looked at his gold watch and raised his eyebrows doubtfully. "Tick-tock," he taunted, and nodded Sampson towards the door.

* * * * *

Five minutes later Korrigan pushed back from the laptop, lighting another cigarette as he stared at the black screen following the end of Tate's video.

"So," he mused, "we were right. She is the key." He took a long puff. "We have to find her."

"What now?" Vargas asked.

Korrigan rubbed his chin thoughtfully. "Stay with Sampson. That idiot will never find them on his own. Make sure he doesn't make things worse than they are." A thin vapor of smoke trailed from his lips. "We need to start moving on, expanding the search. Be sure Sampson has alerted whatever contacts he has on nearby islands. But keep this under the radar. We can't use legitimate law enforcement channels. We don't want any questions being asked once we do find them, given that eventually they'll be disappearing for good. Tell Sampson to spread some cash around. And keep our people on the airport."

Vargas nodded compliantly. "I've got a couple patrols running the ports, but it's a lot of water to cover."

"Double them. Those two are headed off this island. The way I see it, there are two likely possibilities. One—they still don't understand what's happening and are running scared. They'll either try disappearing or getting to someone that can help them, most likely the Feds. If they get as far as the States, this thing becomes a whole lot harder. We can't have the Feds involved. Too many questions, too many checks and balances. We would never be able to make them quietly vanish after that."

"And two?"

Korrigan's eyes flicked up to Vargas. "If she's figured it out, they just got everything they need to finish what Tate McConnaughey started."

"So they'd have to head to Miami."

Korrigan nodded. "Keep an eye on all the likely spots. I'm not sure of the end game yet, but maybe they'll try making a connection with someone linked to her brother. I doubt they'll get there for another day or so, but still—if they arrive first and we miss them . . ." He trailed off ominously, pondering the possibility. "A lot depends on Collings's role in this."

"We're still working that out," Vargas confirmed.

Korrigan exhaled another cloud of smoke. "Well, get it done. Because if we don't—if those two get their hands on that money," he posited, pausing to crush his spent cigarette in a tray, "they may get their happily ever after, but I can promise you, we won't."

TWENTY-SEVEN

A lopsided wave smacked into the hull, sending spray over the railing and generously spritzing Chloe. She licked the salt from her lips and ran a hand over her damp hair, or at least what was left of it. A deck hand moved industriously around her, working the forty-foot trawler, never making eye contact. The captain, presently perched above her in the cockpit, would smile at her occasionally, but that was the extent of their interaction. Jack had instructed them to leave her alone. He trusted Manny, but the men in his employ were a different matter. It seemed to have worked. They were a day into the two-and-a-half-day trip from St. Gideon to Puerto Rico, and not one of them had bothered her in the least.

Jack strode over from a spot on the opposite side of the bow and cupped a hand over her ear. "We're hitting a bit of a rough patch," he said, his shirt flapping wildly in the breeze just as it had on the beach the day they met. The boat listed unpredictably, and Jack steadied himself with a hand on the rail.

"We okay?" Chloe asked, growing concerned about the darkening clouds.

Jack nodded. "We checked the radar. It looks like a tiny system. Shouldn't amount to much, but you'd probably be better off in the cabin."

Despite the looming trouble, she swore he was nearly grinning. He'd spent most of the their time on the craft playing captain to the actual captain, overseeing the cockpit, barking directions to the deck hands, checking and rechecking their plotted course. He was clearly no stranger to extended sailing. Knowing he was on top of things, especially out here on the water, made her feel safer. *I couldn't have picked a better partner in crime if I'd planned it.*

She left him on the deck and moved below to the cabin they occupied at the far aft. It was exceedingly small, with a bed barely larger than a twin and an airplane style bathroom just large enough for her to squeeze into. She had no idea how Jack managed it. A sudden pitch to the left threw her off balance, and she stumbled, landing awkwardly on the bed. Rolling over, she stared at the low ceiling as the rocking picked up, trying to distract herself from the growing storm by making sense of the mildew stains that formed shapes like clouds. Before long her thoughts had drifted again to the journey that lay ahead.

According to Jack, they'd land in San Juan sometime late the next night. They'd chosen Puerto Rico because it was a U.S. territory. If they did run into trouble using their passports, at least they'd be on U.S. soil with a better chance of being heard out and not sent back to St. Gideon. If all went well, the morning after arriving they'd fly out of San Juan to Orlando, rent a car, and head south to Miami, where they'd walk into Herb Rohrstadt's law office and finally get some answers. Or at least that was the plan.

The boat leaned hard to the left, and for the first time since they'd sailed from St. Gideon, Chloe felt nauseated. She closed her eyes. Despite the lurching, it wasn't long before Chloe slipped into a light sleep, hazy and warm. She was aware of nothing else until Jack finally returned to the cabin and clicked on the single-bulb sconce, casting a dim sixty-watt glow about the tiny room.

"What time is it?" she asked, slowly sitting up and rubbing reality back into her eyes.

"Six."

"How's the weather?" she asked groggily.

"Better." As he said it, she noticed that the boat wasn't rocking quite as violently anymore.

Jack sat on the foot of the bed and patted her leg in an 'atta-boy' fashion. "You slept through the worst like a pro. Even snored a bit."

Chloe smiled and caught the scent of something wonderful. Her stomach rumbled. She hadn't eaten since breakfast that morning. "Whatch'ya got there?"

Jack held a plate out to her. "Freshly caught this afternoon. Broiled it myself. Sorry the rice is plain, but we ate the last of the potatoes yesterday."

The grouper, drizzled with butter, melted in her mouth. "This is amazing, Jack." She held the fork out to him.

He shook his head. "Had mine already, thanks."

"Well," she said, her mouth half full, "this could definitely be a second career for you."

He smiled. "I was working on my second when you came along."

She rolled her eyes and favored him with a smile. "At least we know you'll never take a turn as a hairdresser."

He snorted. "You're one to talk," he said, running a hand over his head, reclining on the bed so that he was stretched out on his back beside her.

The hair might be different, but the smile was the same as the one she'd first seen on the beach. And just as endearing.

"Can I ask you something?" she said.

His eyes narrowed quizzically, "Um, sure," he said uncertainly.

She grinned. "How many times before me had you used that 'football to the head' pick-up act?"

He flipped onto his left side and propped his head up on one elbow. "I admit that was *really* bad. And, for the record, I did not tell him to actually hit you with the ball. But," he said, his voice softening, "can you blame me?"

Her heart hummed as his gaze held her, drawing her in. The distance between them seemed to close without either one moving, until, finally, he *was* moving towards her. And then, suddenly, he wasn't.

Pressing his eyes shut, he let out a controlled, exasperated breath and pushed himself up to sit on the edge of the bed. She sat there, unmoved. When he turned back, he gave a sympathetic half-smile. "You said friends, right? You swore off the entire male race. And here I go taking advantage."

Take advantage, already.

"Forgive me?" he asked hopefully, a mischievous glint in his eye. "Wouldn't want to frighten you off now when you need a friend the most." He raised his hand, configured in the Boy Scout's sign of honor. "I promise to remain harmless for the duration." He closed his eyes. "Pooped and harmless."

"Yeah, sure," she eked out, her breath having finally found its way back to her lungs. "No problem. Totally forgiven."

"So," he said, "It's been kind of a long day. Would you mind if I took a quick shower and turned in for the night? Or do you need me to keep you company?"

She shook her head. "Nah. Go on. You've got a long day of playing sailor ahead of you tomorrow."

After a very quick shower in what he described as trying to wash in a shoebox, Jack fell soundly asleep, his chest rising and falling in an even, peaceful pattern. *He really is a good guy,* she thought, watching him intently. *He shouldn't be here. Shouldn't be mixed up in this.* Guilt mingled with anger mounted, with anger steadily overtaking. Some of it was directed at herself for losing the flash drive and for being so gullible when it came to her brother. But the greater share was reserved for Tate.

Tate, the only man she'd ever truly trusted, had let her down in the worst way possible. Jack, a complete stranger, had proven himself to be the closest thing to a savior she'd ever known. The irony pinched her spirit as she reached over to pull the blanket up over Jack's shoulder and waited for morning to come.

TWENTY-EIGHT

Chloe had no idea how long she'd been asleep, but when she woke Jack was asleep next to her, his arm thrown protectively over her. She blinked a few times and yawned drowsily. She was restless, ready to stretch her legs, but she quashed the instinct, afraid that the slightest movement would wake him. And he was so tired. She forced herself to relax and simply wait for him to stir so she could slip out from under him, unnoticed. But he slept like the dead, and, ten minutes later, he hadn't even twitched.

I have got to get up. But despite what her brain said, another part of her had to admit it did feel nice. Very nice. And safe. *But I would get up if I could. Did almost. Will get up, as soon as he moves.* But it was so warm. And comforting. She sighed contentedly, and he grunted, then rocked away from her. Chloe hesitated, momentarily considering not moving at all, then slid off the lumpy mattress and tip-toed to the bathroom a few feet away.

Calling it closet-sized would be too generous. When she drew shut the accordion panel that served as a door, she had only enough room to stand in that spot, or to sit, but nothing else. The tiny shower by the toilet was just a two-foot square shower pan surrounded by a worn navy curtain on an angled rod.

"How did you even fit in there, Jack?" she mumbled, eyeing the shower before leaning over the narrow metal sink and peering into the mirror. She placed her hands on either side of her face and pulled her cheeks taut, then released them. Her skin seemed limp, worn out. Why shouldn't it be? Every other part of her was. Grey circles underscored her eyes, the whites feathered with strands of red. And then there was the hair. *Hopeless.*

"I thought short styles were supposed to be low maintenance," she grumbled, turning on the chrome-plated faucet and wetting her fingers. She ran them through the matted mess, taming the worst of the stragglers. *Not much better.* Deciding she might feel better after washing her face, she grabbed what used to be a white bar of soap in a cup attached to the wall. She went to wet it, but smacked her elbow on the countertop. Her funny bone zinging, she dropped the soap, which rolled under the metal sink unit. She gritted her teeth, waiting out the pain and trying not to groan, afraid she'd wake Jack. Once the pain subsided, she got down on her knees and peered under the sink, looking for the soap. It had rolled as far back as possible, stopping against a wrinkled envelope that was folded in half. *Must've slid under there during one of the boat's constant lurches,* she thought, grabbing them both. She stood back up, replaced the soap and unfolded the envelope.

The first thing she pulled out of it was a passport. She flipped it open to the inside cover and chuckled. "Nice beard, Jack," she said, eyeing a photo of him that must've been taken a while back, judging by the facial hair and the little bit of extra weight he was carrying. *Gotta be more careful with your things, though,* she thought, realizing he must have somehow lost the envelope when he showered earlier. Then she noticed the name typed below his picture.

Michael Jonathon Bartholomew.

Nails fired in her stomach in all directions, her heart galloping in her chest as she stood there, shaking. Staring at those words. *No. It can't be,* she told herself. *But then . . . what is this?*

The truth was, she knew. Deep down inside, she knew. She flipped through the other things. A New York driver's license for Michael J. Bartholomew. A couple of credit cards in that name. A checkbook.

It can't be. It just can't be. Her knees buckled and she dropped to sit on the toilet lid, competing voices screaming in her head.

This doesn't make any sense.

Another voice countered. *Oh, yes it does. It makes horrible, awful, perfect sense.*

All the little things that had given her pause about Jack at one time or another, all the things she had dismissed because she had wanted to, needed to, started to add up. Why would anyone care about a stranger as much as he seemed to care about her? Why would anyone follow her this far, put themselves in this kind of danger? They wouldn't. Not unless they had a reason to. And then there were the other things. Like how he had bested the intruder in her cottage. Overpowering two armed assailants on his boat. His relationship with a drug dealer. Not to mention his familiarity with guns—

The guns. They were both in the bedroom with him. She returned the items to the envelope and tucked it in her back pocket. After flicking off the overhead light, she gingerly pulled the door open. It squeaked, but Jack's form remained motionless on the bed. She tiptoed over to a low shelf built into the wall beside it. Traces of moonlight filtering through the porthole outlined a spare blanket stuffed into the shelf. She reached a timid hand up, groped beneath the blanket, and felt the gun she knew was hidden there. Gently, she slid it off the ledge. Jack didn't budge.

She didn't have to look for the second gun. The night before he'd slept with it under his pillow, easily within his reach. She wouldn't give him the chance to get to it. Moving to the foot of the bed, she aimed the gun at Jack's chest, then released the safety.

TWENTY-NINE

Korrigan sat rigidly in his seat on the private jet, just an hour out from the Miami Regional Airport. His head was slightly tilted back, his eyes shut as if resting, though in actuality he was fully alert. Across the aisle from him, Vargas finished tapping on his phone and set it down.

"Sir?"

"Yes?" Korrigan answered, his thin lips barely moving.

"You said you wanted an update if anything changed."

Korrigan's eyes flicked open. "And?"

"We've got him."

"Collings? Where?"

"No, sir, not physically. I mean we've identified him."

Korrigan raised his eyebrows expectantly.

"It's what we thought. He's ex-military. The dangerous kind."

* * * * *

Jack's eyes flew open when he heard the click of the safety.

"Chloe, what—"

"Who are you," she interrupted in a steady, firm voice. Her stare was riveted on him, her amber eyes narrow and dark.

"What are you talking about?" he asked, pushing himself up.

"Don't!" Chloe shouted, jabbing the gun in his direction.

"Chloe, don't point that thing at me!"

"I mean it, Jack! I found the passport. *Michael Bartholomew's* passport."

His face dropped tellingly. "Look," he cautioned, motioning downward, "just be careful."

"Start explaining or I'll shoot just to be on the safe side."

"It's not what you think."

"And what do I think, Jack? That you're a liar? That you aren't who you say you are? What part of that isn't true?"

Jack spoke slowly. "You have to know I wasn't—I'm not—"

"You've got ten seconds."

He sighed in surrender. "Michael Bartholomew is me. Michael *Jonathon* Bartholomew. Jack is short for Jonathon."

"Then who's Jack Collings?" she demanded.

"That's me, too." He watched her closely. She hadn't moved but the gun had begun shaking. "It's just an alias. A name I've been using to avoid . . . people."

"You're *in* on this aren't you?"

"No! See that's exactly—"

"You're working for them!"

"Working for them? They *shot* me, Chloe!"

"I don't know who shot you! For all I know you shot yourself to make it look good," she stammered. "You set me up on the beach didn't you? It was all just a ploy to get close."

"Meeting you on the beach was a total fluke, Chloe. I did *not* set that up," he countered emphatically. "And I am not working for anybody! I tripped into this thing just like you."

She ignored him and barreled on. "Maybe you're working for yourself. Maybe you knew Tate from Miami. Did he tell you about this, this, scheme, or whatever it is? Did you decide to go after the money yourself—"

"Chloe, will you shut up and listen to me? I don't know anything about the money and I'm not out to get it or you."

"Who recruited you?" she persisted.

"Are you listening to me? It's just a coincidence."

"You want me to believe that right before this insanity starts I coincidentally meet the one person who *happens* to perfectly fit the bill for the position of white knight? Your average unarmed person can't hold off two armed men, Jack—no wonder you've been so rock steady. And, let's not forget," she added, her voice bordering on hysterical as she gestured with her free hand at the boat, "who also happens to have *access to the perfect getaway vehicle!*"

"I know how it looks, but you have to believe me." His voice leveled and his eyes took her in as if trying to will her into believing him. "All of it—the combat skills, the composure under pressure—it's my military training."

She stared at him blankly. "What military training? You never said anything about being in the military."

"I was a Navy SEAL, Chloe."

She laughed maniacally. "A Navy SEAL? Are you seriously going with that? And you want me to believe *that's* a coincidence? That I just happened across the only Navy SEAL on all of St. Gideon?"

"No." His flat answer surprised her, and her expression showed it. "I know it seems too coincidental to be true. But that doesn't mean I'm lying. Maybe there's just a bigger plan going on here—"

"The only plan going on here is yours and Sampson's!" She held up the passport. "Normal people don't use aliases, Jack!"

"They do if they're hiding from someone," he shot back, then held his hands up, begging her off. "Just bear with me for a minute, okay? Hear me out."

She raised an eyebrow and with one hand gestured impatiently for him to continue.

"I told you that I came here right after my divorce as a sort of . . . escape from it. But what you have to understand is that it wasn't your typical divorce." He hesitated briefly, then plunged in. "Chloe, have you ever seen a movie called *Battlezone Zero*? Or heard about it at least?"

She stared at him blankly. He tried again. "Have you seen it?"

"What does that have to do with anything?"

"Chloe, did you see it or not?"

"Yeah, I saw it. The one with that Scottish actor."

He nodded. "That was my team."

"*Your* team?" she asked. "The one stranded in . . . what, Afghanistan?" Chloe's eyes widened disbelievingly. "You're asking me to believe that was *your* SEAL team? As in you were *on* that mission?"

"I know how it sounds, but it's true. After I left the service, a publisher approached me and a buddy of mine—he thought my English background would help—and asked if we'd consider co-writing a book about it. It took some convincing, but, eventually, we did it. The book did well, and when they ended up making it into a

155

movie, I was the consultant on it. It's easy to check, if you don't believe me. Anyway, I made connections with some people in the industry, and it sort of turned into a regular thing—consulting on movies, books even, when there's a military angle—just behind the scenes, really—"

"What exactly are you saying?"

He sighed. "I really am an English professor. I finished my master's degree while in the service and got my doctorate right after leaving. But the thing is, well," he paused, looking embarrassed, "it just *sounds* so boring. So, back before Lila, I used the Hollywood thing to be, well, more interesting. You know, when I'd . . . meet women and . . . it was stupid, I know. And when I met Lila, she was working to be an actress, so being a 'consultant' on movies and knowing a few people really got her attention. It didn't hurt when she realized I was worth a little bit, too."

When Chloe looked confused, he clarified, a sad mix of embarrassment and distaste glossing his face. "Family money. Anyway I guess between the two she figured it was a good idea to marry me. Unfortunately, when my connections didn't pan out, she got tired of me and moved on."

He searched Chloe's face, as if looking for some sign that she believed him, then continued. "But she didn't want to move on from the money. For the last two years, I've had one sleazy private investigator or another constantly following me. *Everywhere*. Some places you wouldn't even believe. And this woman that I loved—that I thought loved me *for me*—did it so she could bleed me for all I'm worth, trying to dig up something she could use to blackmail me into a bigger settlement."

He rubbed his eyes, as if disgusted by his own story. "In the end Lila got her settlement, but it wasn't anything like what she was hoping for. She threatened to keep the heat on me, and I just couldn't take it anymore. So I left and came down here. I holed up in a hotel and just tried to forget.

"I hadn't been there a week, when I met this girl at one of the fishing piers—you know, the ones downtown near the wharf? Anyway, she seemed nice enough, and we sort of hung out that afternoon. She gave me her number and even though there weren't any fireworks, I figured, why not, can't hurt to make a few friends down here, right? But when she shows up at dinner the next night, she's got this weird glow about her. Almost buzzing. That's when she tells me she's Googled me. Knows all about me. Can't believe her luck."

Jack snorted and shook his head. "I'm not even sure I said anything to her. I just remember getting up and walking out. Cleared out of my hotel that night and by the next day was living on a rented boat, walking around as Jack Collings."

He paused, letting all of it sink in for a few moments. "There were just too many strings attached to being me. I didn't want Lila to find me, and I didn't want anyone else to want to be around me for the reasons she had. And the only way to be sure that didn't happen was to *not* be me."

"So why didn't you tell me?"

"And when would I have done that, Chloe? When we first met? That would've been a charming opening. 'Hi, my name's Jack Collings, only that's not my real name. It's an alias I'm using to hide from my ex-wife while I escape from my life for a while.' And then all this started happening. You were already suspicious and scared. I was afraid if I told you the truth you'd think I was in on it. Or at the very least not trust me."

For several moments she held her quivering stance, judging his story, weighing his alibis. Finally, she rendered her verdict. "I don't believe you," she insisted stubbornly, her visibly trembling hand still poised to shoot.

"Chloe," he urged gently, "come on. Do you really think that if I was going to lie to you *this* is the explanation I'd come up with?"

Wet drops pooled in the corners of her eyes. "I don't know what to think," she mumbled distrustfully.

"Well, I don't know what else to say to convince you. I just—" He cut himself off, his expression brightening. "I can prove it. You can check—" he said, stepping towards her.

"Hey!" Chloe shouted, jabbing the gun at him.

He froze, holding up his hands again. "I just—look, grab one of the phones Manny got for us. Mine's right over there," he said, nodding his head towards another built-in shelf. "Just Google me. You can see for yourself that I'm telling the truth."

He wasn't lying. It only took a second for her to use the boat's Wi-Fi to pull up a handful of sites referencing Michael J. "Jack" Bartholomew, the former Navy SEAL, now a published N.Y.U. English professor and, sometimes, behind-the-scenes movie consultant. There were photos, too, and though they showed someone a little heavier and much paler, and most with that ridiculous hair and goatee, it was clearly Jack. A short but vitriolic post from some low-grade online gossip rag outlined the terms of the ugly ending of his divorce. It was just as he'd said.

"Why didn't you tell me?" Her voice was noticeably unsteady.

"I told you why," he said gently, and crossed to her. As he neared, she lowered the gun and he took it from her, tossing it onto the bed. He stood there waiting for what seemed like an eternity, their eyes searching one another out, until finally she gave in, letting him gather her up amidst her fierce sobs.

* * * * *

Once she managed to calm down, she slept. He held her tightly, promising safety, if only the little bit that was within his arms reach. For both of them, consciousness came and went with the lullaby-like rhythm of the ocean as the night spent itself. As dawn approached, her mind began spinning again.

"Tell me something, Jack," she whispered, the feeble light of morning slipping through the porthole, painting the room a pinkish-gray.

"Mmmm?" he mumbled drowsily.

"Why English?"

Jack twisted towards her. "What?"

"English. The English thing? Just—why English?"

He sniffed and stretched his neck, giving the impression he was working on waking up. "I just, always liked it. Ever since I was a kid, I'd read anything I could get my hands on. When we had to settle on a major it just seemed like a natural fit."

"It just seems an odd choice for somebody with your—skills."

He pulled a face, and with an air of the dramatic, recited, "*Oh, to be all that I am and to not be forsaken. To be held high, a banner of my own, in splendor and grace and to not be judged, and the words—oh the words—that they would be light and airy and full of promise—*"

"Okay, you need to stop now."

"I'm just saying," he quipped. "Know who wrote it?"

"Umm . . . that poet that starts with an 'S'—oh, what's his name—"

"Okay, now you stop," he sighed, pretending disgust. "Not even the right century. You really weren't kidding about being bad in that class."

She punched him lightly in the arm and rolled flat on her back. "Can I ask you something else?"

"'Course."

She inhaled deeply through her nose as if gathering courage. After a second, she plunged ahead. "All that . . . God stuff. So that was for real?"

He eyed her carefully, warmth emanating from his words. "Yeah. That was all for real."

"And what you said awhile ago about a bigger plan—about us meeting, I mean—you mean 'bigger' as in some kind of divine intervention or something?"

He sniffed again. "Something like that."

She stared at the ceiling, not really seeing the mildewy shapes anymore, preoccupied solely with digesting his answer. Then she pressed on.

"Well," she sighed exasperatedly, "if there is a God, and He has a plan for me, why does it have to be this one? I mean, I'm a good person. I don't cause any trouble. I don't cheat or steal. I stay away from bad people. Well, except when I'm being transported by drug smugglers—"

An amused smile spread across Jack's sleepy face.

"But that was out of our control. So then why is all this happening to me? If this is part of a plan, it doesn't seem like a very fair one."

"You're asking the 'why do bad things happen to good people' question?"

"I guess."

He pressed a hand to his eyes, rubbing away the drowsiness. "Well, when you ask Him about it, what does He say?"

"Uhh," she stalled, "I can't say I've ever asked Him."

"Well, maybe it'd be a good place to start. See where that gets you."

"I told you. Prayer never did me any good. My dad still left. My mom still died. After that there didn't seem to be much point."

He gave her a warm squeeze. "I can understand that. But it couldn't hurt to try."

She let out a long, thoughtful exhale. "*You* still haven't answered my question."

"I'm not sure I can, Chloe," he admitted, his words starkly

honest. "This world can be a bad place. Bad things happen to good people all the time. Sometimes there's no apparent explanation—you just have to trust that God has a reason for allowing it. And that can be really tough. Sometimes God allows the bad thing because He knows that in the end it'll work out for the greater good, the eternal good, and even that person's own good, although we can't always see that good or understand it. Sometimes it's testing, to show you who you really are. Sometimes, if the person is involved in something they shouldn't be, it's God's way of disciplining His kids, the way we do ours. Other times, he allows it in order to grow us." He paused, eyeing her meaningfully. "And then there are those times when He uses it to get our attention."

"You think He's trying to get my attention?" she asked perceptively.

He shrugged. "Just something to think about. I mean, when was the last time you gave God much thought?"

"Positive thoughts? Probably before Mom's diagnosis."

"And yet here you are, years later, finally talking about Him, but only after an insane round of nastiness has been injected into your life."

"You'd think He could've gotten my attention another, less potentially fatal way," she complained tersely.

"Maybe He tried that already."

She chewed on that awhile. "I still didn't deserve this."

"No, you didn't."

"But none of that matters. It's like in the end, I don't really matter."

"Of course, you matter. You matter enough to die for."

"That's ridiculous, Jack. You don't have to die for me."

"I'm not talking about me," he replied.

His meaning took a few moments to register. "Oh," she sighed, staring at nothing in particular on the opposite wall. "You're talking about the whole Christ dying for me thing."

"Uh-hmm," he mumbled.

She turned to face him, exhaling heavily. "You know I've heard that a million times. Jesus dying for me." Her words hung over them, daring a response from Jack, but getting none. "Never really meant anything to me, you know? Just some nice idea put out there by nice people who already had nice lives. Besides, even if it were true, I don't see how I would deserve that, either."

"You don't. None of us do." He brushed a short strand of hair away from her face. "But I'm pretty sure that when it comes to God, nothing is about getting what we deserve."

"So what is it about?"

"Trust. Grace. Giving all the bad stuff in our lives up to Him and leaning on Him to help us through it."

"And what if I can't get through it? What if instead of getting my attention, it breaks me?"

"He hasn't let you break yet."

She thought about that for a minute, then rolled over to face the wall. He turned after her, gathering her up again. She relished the sense of his warm cheek on back of her head.

"I wish I could believe it, Jack," she said, closing her eyes and fighting for sleep again. "I really do."

THIRTY

The sun was hot and the wind whipped through the open windows as they motored down the freeway towards the business district in which Rohrstadt's building was located. Something distinctly Miami was playing over the radio, and neither of them had bothered to change it. It was cheerful, the heavy beat of the music and the glowing rays, and as Chloe stared out the window towards the soaring skyscrapers that made up downtown Miami, she could almost pretend they were just a couple out for a mid-afternoon cruise around town. Almost.

Unbelievably, everything over the last two days had gone off without a hitch. They'd had no problems with customs and immigration in either San Juan or Orlando. Jack said that meant that Sampson hadn't put out any alerts to the States, which was good for them. They had spent the night in San Juan and flown into Orlando that morning. They'd both slept for the entire three hour flight, which was great because as soon as they landed, they'd rented a car and driven another three hours towards Miami—though not before meeting up with some "guys" Manny had arranged to rearm them, since they'd had to leave their weapons on the boat. The little midnight special felt wrong in her waistband, especially now that they were home and she had no permit. "That'll be the least of your worries if we get ambushed by Sampson's people," Jack had told her when she'd confessed this.

They considered going straight to the Feds once they landed in Orlando. And if they'd had any evidence at all, it's probably exactly what they would have done. But now, without the flash drive, it was their word against Sampson's. On paper, they were fugitives from St. Gideon, evading interrogation relating to Ruby's murder—the murder of a U.S. citizen. Maybe the Feds would hold them in the States, but maybe they'd send them back. And that would be the end of it. So instead, they stuck with their original plan to try to contact Herb Rohrstadt, hoping he had kept a copy of the file on the flash drive.

"How much farther till that turn?" Jack asked.

Chloe checked her smartphone. "Two more exits."

Once they exited onto the downtown streets, they turned left and right a few times, until finally they reached it: 1919 Westwood Avenue. It was an office complex dubbed "The Grove," that consisted of three, ten-story buildings arranged in a semi-circle around a paved courtyard. At the center was a sizable decorative fountain surrounded by a thick carpet of well-manicured grass.

"Let's keep going," Jack suggested, rolling past the buildings. "We'll stop a block up just to give ourselves a little room." He found a spot near a meter, fed it, and then set off down the street, Chloe at his side.

From what she could tell, they were in an area somewhere just north of the business district she had seen from the freeway. Most of the buildings were new, rising five to ten stories on average, flanked on all sides by dozens of assorted palms and mound after mound of brilliantly colored bougainvillea. They were arranged neatly, clearly planned rather than evolving over time. *Maybe the result of a hurricane that passed through*, she thought. Sandwiched amongst the larger buildings were smaller, stand-alone businesses. Directly across the street from Rohrstadt's office was a row of shops encased in stucco painted every shade of pink known to man.

"Let's cross here, before we get too close," Jack whispered, nudging her as he checked the traffic. At the first opening, he hopped off the curb and dashed across four busy lanes. Chloe followed right behind. Once safely across, they continued on, now on the side of the street opposite The Grove.

Chloe fought the urge to look around her for anything or anyone out of place. She glanced at Jack and, although his head faced directly forward, she suspected his eyes were darting back and forth behind his dark, aviator sunglasses.

"See anyone?" she asked quietly.

"Not that I can tell," he answered. "But we've got to assume they're watching the area. They had to know we might come here."

"Only if they know where the flash drive came from."

"If we know, we have to assume they know."

They kept walking until they were directly across the street from The Grove's courtyard fountain, then stepped casually into the shadows of a green, logo-emblazoned awning above the entrance to a trendy coffee shop. Jack scanned the mirrored glass reaching several stories high on each of The Grove's three buildings. "Somebody could be watching from any one of those and we'd never know it. This thing could be over before it starts."

"It's not like we have a choice," Chloe said. Even knowing that Rohrstadt's phone might be tapped, they had still tried to call his office. But every attempt to reach him had failed. No one had answered the phone, replied to their messages or responded to the emails they'd sent him requesting an appointment under a fake name.

Jack opened the door to the coffee shop and ushered her through, placing his hand on the small of her back and guiding her inside. Wooden tables and chairs filled the seating area and lined the large windows fronting the street. Half were occupied. A long counter with glass cases displaying sandwiches, salads, and muffins sat at the back of the room. There was a register at its end, and behind it, a clerk ringing up a sale.

"Sit down over there for a minute," he told her, nodding towards a table against the wall furthest from the windows. "I'll be right back."

"You gonna tell me what you're planning?"

"In a minute," he said and strode away towards the counter. The clerk, a pimply-faced kid that looked to be in his early twenties, was busy cleaning one of the espresso machines. Chloe watched as Jack got his attention, then chatted quietly with him. The kid nodded responsively a couple of times, then moved to the swinging gate that separated the counter from the dining area. He waved Jack behind it, then took him through a door leading into the back of the store.

They weren't gone long. When Jack emerged, he had on a blue apron and a baseball cap, both emblazoned with the shop's logo. He came back through the swinging gate to the front of the counter and waited while the kid fixed three oversized coffees, then pressed them into a cardboard tray. The kid grabbed a couple of sandwiches out of the glass display case, tossed them in a paper bag also imprinted with the shop's logo, and handed them to Jack. Jack paid him and returned to Chloe's table.

"I gave the guy a twenty," he said, sliding into the chair next to her. "Told him I was playing a joke on a friend. What do you think?"

"You really expect that to work?" she asked, raising her eyebrows skeptically.

"You have a better idea?"

"No. But I should be the one to go. It's not right."

"Uh-uh. You're the one they really want. Chances are they'll be watching the females more closely than the males. Besides, if something does happen, I'll have a much better chance of fighting them off than you would."

"I'd do okay. I handled you pretty well on the boat," she argued. This little plan did not sit well with her. Sending him off alone into potential danger seemed wrong. At the very least she should be with him. It didn't fix it, but at least she was sharing the risk.

"Yeah, well," he started, "*they* won't be asleep."

She sighed. "Just be careful."

He handed one of the cups to her. "I got you something. I'll be back as soon as I can." He started to turn, then stopped. "Tell you what, if it's safe for you to come up, I'll call you and ask for," he glanced at her shorn, ink-black hair, "Ms. Minnelli."

Chloe glared at him good-naturedly. "Thanks."

"Otherwise, stay put. Unless you haven't heard from me in an hour. Then I want you go straight to the Feds."

"I can't do that. We've talked about this."

"If something happens to me the safest thing for you will be to turn yourself in."

She seemed to think about that and frowned. "How do we know that they don't have a connection with the Miami police like they did on St. Gideon?"

"That's why it has to be the Feds. Promise me."

"How 'bout you just come back."

He groaned and gave up. "See you in a few. Maybe say a prayer for me."

She smiled thinly. "How about I just think really good thoughts, instead," she called after him, as he walked out the front door looking every bit the part of a delivery boy. He darted across the busy traffic, leaping onto the sidewalk just in time to avoid being run over by a bunch of college kids whooping it up in a red convertible. Chloe watched as he started over the terracotta-colored stones that paved the courtyard of the complex. Fortunately there was a fairly steady flow of people in and out, so he wasn't particularly noticeable. Add to that his altered appearance and the getup, and he had a decent chance of pulling it off, even if someone was watching. Maybe.

Chloe's nerves tingled as her eyes followed him past the fountain, down a wide path nestled between bush-like palms. Building three was on the far right. She watched him enter its swiveling glass doors right behind a woman dressed in a pastel suit and a UPS guy. Chloe swallowed the lump in her throat, and settled back to wait.

* * * * *

Inside the brightly painted lobby, Jack waited in a group for one of two elevators. No one seemed to be watching the area, or interested in anything more than staring at their shoes or the elevator doors. The car on the right finally arrived and, after it emptied, he was the first one on. According to the marquee, Rohrstadt's suite, J, was on the sixth floor. The others filed off on the lower floors, and by the time the elevator reached Rohrstadt's floor, Jack was alone.

He stepped out onto a cream tiled hallway lined with potted ferns and bold, art deco prints. Three black lacquer doors, each marked with a brass placard bearing the suite letter and name of the tenant, were spaced along the length of the hall. Suite J was all the way down to his left. Like the elevator, the hallway was empty. Jack strode quickly to Suite J and read the doorplate. *Law Offices of Herbert K. Rohrstadt, Esquire.*

The doorknob was locked. He tried again, just to make sure, but it didn't budge. He knocked. No answer. His gaze flicked to the doors of the neighboring suites, and he wondered if he should inquire about Rohrstadt's hours. But showing his face around could be dangerous.

No choice but to try again later, he decided as he walked back to the elevator and pressed the call button. When the elevator car arrived a few minutes later, he was thankful to find it empty. Just as the doors began to slide shut, the elevator beside his began to open. Instinctively, Jack stepped swiftly to the right, obscuring himself behind the button panel. The doors shut completely before he could see two sharply dressed men step off the opposite elevator and stride purposefully towards Suite J.

* * * * *

"So what now?" Chloe asked after Jack finished telling her what had happened.

"I don't know. I could go back and ask around, but if they've put my photo out and I start asking questions . . . Then again, we may not have a choice."

"Well, this is ridiculous. We can't just sit here and wait." She glanced at her watch. "It's nearly four-fifteen now. We're losing time. It's Friday. Inverse Financial closes at 5:00 and won't open back up again till Monday. I'm barely going to have time to get there as it is."

"What about trying to find Rohrstadt's house again—"

"I'm telling you, I've tried every search I could think of. He's unlisted and not very anxious to be found by the public."

"Great." Jack fumbled with the ball cap that now lay next to the apron on the table. "Maybe I'll just head back over there. I could try another floor and ask around. It's unlikely they'd be watching all the floors."

"I think we should split up," she suggested. His eyes shot to her, denouncing the idea. She pressed on. "You stay here, try those other offices—"

"No way we're splitting up like that, Chloe. It's one thing for me to go across the street, but—"

"If I don't go now, we won't be able to make any headway all weekend. This is only going to work if we move faster than Sampson does."

"No. I *do not* like the idea of you going alone. Look, it probably wasn't much of a stretch for Sampson, or whoever he's working for, to guess that we might head to Miami, since everything seems to point here. Don't you think he's watching Inverse? Your only links to this place are Rohrstadt and Inverse. Don't you think he's smart enough to figure you'll go back there to retrace Tate's steps? We stay here, *together*, until we find Rohrstadt. Inverse is a long shot anyway."

"The fact that it's a long shot is why they won't expect me to go there. Besides, they aren't going to snatch me up in broad daylight in a place where people know me."

"That doesn't stop them from snatching you when you walk out."

"I'll be careful. I can wait inside. They know me. I'll be fine."

Jack sat there stonily, not agreeing, but not arguing anymore.

"If they still have any of Tate's calendar records, or other notes, or *anything*, there might be something pointing us to whoever he met with at WorldCore, or whatever those other banks were that he hacked. It's our only other shot at getting anywhere."

He bit his lip contemplatively. "When you're done you'll stay in the lobby till I come and get you?"

Chloe nodded. "Absolutely."

"And if they close before I get there—"

"There's a Starbucks across the street. I'll *literally* run over there and park it till you get there."

"You've got it on you?" he asked, nodding towards the ankle boots Marta had given her before leaving St. Gideon. She nodded. "And your gun?" he asked.

She sighed. "Yes, of course I do. Jack, I've gotta go."

"I'm coming straight there after I nose around here a little more."

She nodded and rose.

Jack exhaled deeply, his face full of worry. He slid the keys across the table. "I still don't like it. I wouldn't let you go if we had any other choice."

"I know," she told him, reaching out to take the keys, and squeezing his clenched fist where it rested. "I'll be careful."

He stood, leaning in to kiss her forehead. "You'd better be."

"Just find Rohrstadt," she said.

"Seriously, be careful," he called after her as she pushed open the door. She turned back to him, nodded, and walked out. He moved to the window, eyeing her nervously as she headed towards their rental. "Watch over her," he murmured softly as she got inside, then drove off.

Because Jack had dumped the coffees and delivery sack into a trashcan on Building Three's second floor in order to avoid looking suspicious by carrying them *out* of the offices, he'd need a new supply before heading back in. He trudged back up to the counter and ordered another two coffees and a sandwich from the pimply-faced clerk.

The clerk eyed him suspiciously. "Uh, what happened to your prank?"

"Not there. I, uh, gave the stuff away. Was getting cold. I'm gonna try back in a minute."

"Whatever," the clerk mumbled as he turned toward the coffee machine to fill the order.

Jack drummed his fingers on the counter. This whole thing with Rohrstadt was growing more ominous by the minute. Lawyers just didn't shut down contact like that. "Come on, Rohrstadt," he muttered to himself. "What kind of lawyer closes up shop like that?"

"A dead one," the clerk answered matter-of-factly, as he turned around and set Jack's coffees down in front of him. He had just turned for the sandwich case when Jack grabbed his arm.

"What did you say?"

"Uh, dude, my arm?"

"Sorry," Jack said, letting go. "But what was that about a dead lawyer?"

"You said Rohrstadt, right?" The clerk cocked his head, putting something together. "Is that the guy you were playing the prank on?" He snorted. "Looks like the joke's on you."

Jack rubbed his face in frustration, grimacing tightly as he kept his voice calm. "You know something about him?"

The clerk paused, eyeing Jack. He shrugged. "Maybe."

Jack groaned, then slipped the clerk a twenty from his pocket.

"Yep. Rohrstadt," the clerked nodded. "I just know what his secretary said. She used to come in here to get coffee and lunch stuff for him. Came in here bawling weeks ago. It was kinda sad. Apologized for it and everything. Said Rohrstadt had died."

"Are you sure it was Rohrstadt? Herbert Rohrstadt?"

"Yeah, I'm sure. Like I said, she picked stuff up all the time, and her name or his name was always on it. Not much of a loss, if you ask me. He was a jerk whenever he stopped in here. Killer car, though. But real nasty attitude. Kept asking when his coffee'd be ready. Didn't care how many people we were dealing with." Another man stepped up to the counter beside Jack. "You mind, man?" the clerk asked, gesturing for Jack to step aside.

"Uh, no. Sorry." Jack stepped to the side and turned towards the windows. Building three loomed in the distance.

"How did he die?" he asked the clerk.

The clerk shrugged. "She said something about a heart attack."

With Rohrstadt dead, Chloe was right. Inverse was their only shot. If he hurried, he might catch her before she went in.

"His secretary was pretty cool, though."

"What?" Jack replied distractedly, checking his watch.

"Rohrstadt's secretary. She was really nice. A little off—big poufy hair, kinda bleached blond—like yours," he said nodding towards Jack, who frowned. "But always waited patiently, you know? Never 'how much longer,' and stuff."

"You wouldn't remember her name by any chance, would you?"

He paused, as if thinking about holding out for another twenty, but after seeing the look on Jack's face, seemed to decide against it. "Elena. Grabney. Been writing one or the other on bags for the last two years straight. Haven't seen her since her boss bought it though."

"Grabney? You're sure?" Jack asked.

"Positive."

"Thanks," Jack said breathlessly.

"What about your coffee?" the clerk said, gesturing to the cups Jack had left on the counter. But Jack was already halfway through the door, its bell jangling in his wake.

THIRTY-ONE

The building was exactly as she remembered. Fifteen stories of steel with large glass windows covering the entire structure. To the far left of the front entrance was the ramp leading up from the subterranean parking garage. Huge, coconut-dotted palms lined the entrance into a small short-term parking lot. Chloe turned in, passing the substantial island dividing the lanes in and out of the property and the hefty rectangular pillar inscribed with "Inverse Financial Holdings, Ltd.," and the company's emblem—a capital "I" encircled by two rings— erected in the island's center. Her stomach flipped. The last time she'd seen the pillar, she'd been there with Tate.

She parked in a visitor's spot and walked under a vine-covered canopy to the glass front doors. Inside the lobby, minimalist ebony chairs upholstered in searing red fabric dotted with gold curlicues lined the way to the receptionist's desk on the far side of the room. Behind her, about halfway up the charcoal-colored wall, a marquee gave the names of the other tenants in the Inverse building. Beside it hung an oversized pewter replica of the company's emblem.

Her boots padded silently across the marble tile as she made her way to the desk. She passed the stone goldfish pool in the center of the room and cut her eyes at hundreds of coins resting on the bottom. She smiled wistfully, remembering how she and Tate had thrown a penny in for luck. *A lot of good that did.*

The twenty-something receptionist wore her blond hair in a tight bun at the base of her neck, and her understated makeup was so calculated it could have been professionally done. She smiled politely.

"May I help you?"

"My name is Chloe McConnaughey. My brother, Tate, used to work here."

"Wait, I'm sorry. You're—Tate's sister?"

"Um, yes."

"Oh," she said, her aloofness dissolving. "I am *so* sorry. Tate was a really nice guy, or—at least he seemed like he would be, you know? He um, was always so busy, running around . . . he didn't really talk much. But he didn't complain either," she quickly offered, as if just realizing she may have said the wrong thing. She cleared her throat and blinked her false lashes. "Just kind of kept to himself. Always focused on his mission, you know?"

Chloe eyes softened. "Yeah. I do," she replied. "Thanks. I was hoping to see Mr. DiMeico. I know it's short notice with me just showing up like this, but it couldn't be helped. If he's not here, maybe his assistant?"

"Let me check." The receptionist held up a French-manicured index finger. "Just give me one second."

Chloe turned towards the pool while the receptionist babbled into her headset. She knew the chances that Renaldi DiMeico, Inverse's CEO, would be available were slim, but what was the alternative?

Memories flooded back of the last and only time she had been here. She had come at Tate's urging, insisting that she get a look at the life he was going to have once he finally got the job. DiMeico had even put them up at his own mansion on Star Island, one of the most expensive and exclusive locations in all of Miami. She had once written a piece on the city that addressed Star Island briefly, but she had never finagled an overnight stay at any of the estates. The grandeur of DiMeico's thirty-room mansion, with its own tennis court, pool complete with waterfall, home theater, and yacht parked at the dock at the rear of the property, had dazzled her. He had pampered them for three days, treating them to the finest of everything, from the choicest wines to the choicest company. The guest list for their Saturday night dinner on the terrace had included a state senator, a primo fashion designer, and a pop star that, as she put it, also had a "little place" on the island.

Tate was enamored with the world DiMeico had built for himself and assured Chloe more than once that he would make the same thing happen for himself. And for her. She wondered how long it had taken him to decide that Inverse wasn't making that happen soon enough, driving him to consider something more illicit—

"Ms. McConnaughey?"

Chloe turned and looked at the woman expectantly.

"Mr. DiMeico's assistant said he would be delighted to see you. He's in a meeting right now, but he should be out in a few minutes if you can wait."

"I absolutely can wait."

"Well, then, Mr. DiMeico's office is on the fifteenth floor," she said, gesturing to the elevator which had just opened. "Mrs. Falco is Mr. DiMeico's assistant. She'll take care of you."

"Thank you," Chloe said as she passed in front of the desk, then stepped onto the elevator and disappeared behind the sliding doors.

* * * * *

Elena Grabney turned out to be much easier to find than Herb Rohrstadt. Her neighborhood was located in an older section of Miami Springs, just twenty minutes from Rohrstadt's office. The homes were all one-story, siding-clad structures painted a multitude of pastels and varying shades of white. The landscaping was nothing fancy, but was generally well trimmed, whether solid green or bloom-kissed, creating modest but pretty yards. As Jack's cab navigated the streets, he passed more than one white-haired person strolling along the sidewalks, enjoying a late afternoon walk in the winter sunshine. The majority of cars parked in the concrete driveways were large American sedans. In one yard, a man leaning on a cane rolled an inflated ball to a toddler; a few houses away, an elderly woman in a flowered house dress beat a jute rug against her front steps. The area abounded with senior citizens; Jack hoped desperately that Elena Grabney was one of them.

When they finally turned onto Thirty-Fourth Street, he began counting house numbers. Halfway down the block, he spotted number 8248—light pink with black shutters—easily fitting in with the rest on the block. A short, stocky woman with poufy, blond hair was stooped over on the porch, repotting red begonias in a rust-colored plastic planter.

Jack asked the cabbie to let him out in front of the house. "And would you just wait here? I'm not sure how long it'll be."

The driver shrugged. "It's your dime."

The woman continued working as Jack exited the cab, hovering intently over her pot as he approached.

"Ms. Grabney?"

It wasn't clear whether she was hard of hearing or ignoring him. He stopped a few feet behind where she crouched.

"Elena?"

She spun around, clutched her chest and swore. "You always sneak up on people like that?" she exclaimed, looking him up and down as she drew in deep, rapid breaths. She squinted, narrowing her gaze to his face. "Do I know you?"

"Are you Elena Grabney?"

"Who wants to know?" she asked suspiciously, rising to her feet and noticeably tightening her grip on the spade in her hand.

"My name is Jack Collings. I know this is strange, but I'm a friend of one of Mr. Rohrstadt's clients—"

"Herb's dead," she interrupted, taking a step backwards towards the front door.

"I know, I heard. I'm sorry. We were just at his office."

"We? We who?"

"The client and I."

Grabney's expression turned stony. "Why are you here?"

"Look, I'm not here to cause you any trouble. I just want to talk to you for a minute. My friend, Mr. Rohrstadt's client—well, actually it was her brother that was the client—he passed away a little while ago. Apparently he left instructions with Mr. Rohrstadt to mail a package to my friend—which she got—but then she lost it. We were hoping to talk to Mr. Rohrstadt about it, but when we got to his office we found out what happened. Someone mentioned you were his secretary—"

"Assistant."

"Sorry. Assistant. Ms. Grabney, I'm just here to ask a few questions. That's it. I thought you might be able to help. Remember something. Anything."

"Where's Ms. McConnaughey?"

Grabney's unexpected use of Chloe's last name threw him for a second. "You—you know about her?"

"Where is she?" Grabney insisted.

"She had . . . another appointment." Jack let a moment pass, sizing up his options, then plunged ahead. "I heard Mr. Rohrstadt died of a heart attack."

Her eyebrows rose slightly. "Why does that matter?"

"Because I don't think it happened how you think it happened."

Ms. Grabney stood quietly, fingering the longest of several gaudy, gold chains that hung around her neck. She took a long look at the cab, then stood. "Come on," she growled, marching up the porch steps and slamming the screen door behind her, leaving Jack on the lawn. He lingered for the briefest of moments, then paid the cabbie and followed her inside.

The first thing he noticed was the black-and-white photographs plastered over nearly every inch of the living room walls. Had the pictures been of family or friends, it might not have seemed so peculiar. But Jack recognized every one of them. They were entertainers. Of the Las Vegas breed. Wayne Newton, Elvis, and Frank Sinatra smiled down at him from behind framed glass. And where there weren't photographs, there were posters, colorful and gaudy, hawking acts like Siegfried and Roy, or movies like *Vegas Vacation* and *Viva Las Vegas*.

"Well, come on in here if you're coming," she ordered from behind the corner of the next room. "I don't have all day."

He followed her into the dining room where she plopped down behind an oval-shaped Queen Anne-style table. It took up most of the space, leaving only enough area for the china cabinet behind her, which, instead of china, displayed hundreds of shot glasses emblazoned with the logos of Las Vegas casinos, restaurants, and hotels.

"So your friend is Chloe McConnaughey, right?"

Jack nodded.

She folded a knobby, aged hand around a glass resting on the table in front of her and the other on the bottle of Smirnoff beside it. "What's your angle?" she asked, taking a stout swig of vodka.

Jack shook his head. "No angle. I'm just here to help Chloe— Ms. McConnaughey. She's in a bit of trouble now and needs what was in that package. We were hoping there's a copy somewhere. If you could help us—"

"Know why I let you in here?" she asked, staring Jack down.

Jack shook his head.

"Because I've known all along Herb didn't die of a heart attack. From day one that's what the cops told me, but I didn't buy it for a minute."

"Why not?"

She pulled a pack of cigarettes off the table and lit one. "Because he had his ticker checked out two weeks prior. Completely. Even had a scope done. The doc found nothing. Healthy as a horse. Even offered to trade hearts with him. If he had a heart attack, it's because somebody gave him one."

"Look," Jack started, treading carefully, "I'm glad—more than you know—that you're talking to me, but I have to ask—why? How do you know I'm not that somebody?"

A knowing grin twitched at the corner of her mouth, pulling the cigarette up. "Because they've already come to see me."

"What?"

"Two days after the cops talked to me two more guys showed up on my lawn—just like you did. Only they're dressed in suits, flash a couple of badges, and tell me they're following up on the investigation. But I know right off they're not. I know that these guys are with whoever McConnaughey ticked off."

"How? And wait . . . what exactly do you know about Tate?"

"I knew they weren't cops because of their shoes. And the suits. But mostly the shoes. Too nice. Armani, I think. Not something your average detective wears on the job. And because I'm a very good people reader. I can tell when people are lying. Have to do it all the time in Vegas. Have to take care of myself.

"Well these guys reiterated the heart attack story, but said that they just had to ask a few procedural questions to close the case— that the final medical workup wasn't back, and they wanted to cover all their bases since Herb was found parked on a side street like he was. They asked me all kinds of questions about what Herb had been doing, did I know of any odd cases, anybody with a grudge? I was smart enough to play dumb. Told them no, no issues other than the odd angry husband of a client. After that song and dance they got around to asking about McConnaughey specifically, along with a couple other clients. Said standard procedure had turned up the names. I said I thought maybe I'd heard the name, McConnaughey, but couldn't remember where. I asked who he was, gave the impression I didn't know anything, hadn't done any work for him. It was obvious they wanted to see if I knew anything. Probably would've killed me if they thought I did."

"So what happened?"

"They left. Satisfied, I guess. Haven't heard from them since. I'm betting they don't want the exposure of getting rid of me unless they know I'm a threat. They probably realize the cops would get suspicious, start looking more closely, if all the sudden I kicked it, too. And because I don't want them re-thinking that strategy, I'm not telling the cops anything either."

"So why talk to me?"

"Like I said, I'm a good people reader. Knew right off you weren't with them."

"What if I had been?"

She shook her head. "Hit men don't usually take cabs. Plus," she continued after another sip, "I'm a bit of a gambler. I decided maybe you had something to offer here and it was worth the risk. And," she said, rolling the word out slowly as if there was a difficult admission coming, "I guess, because Herb was good to me. Not the best husband or father, mind, but a good boss. Paid me well. Gave me paid vacations and sick leave. Flowers on Secretary's Day. Sent me to Vegas once a year for a conference. He didn't deserve this. I'm not brave enough to go to the cops, but if you're working with McConnaughey's sister, then at least you're causing them trouble somehow."

"Do you know what was in the package?"

She looked at him like he was crazy. "Course I did."

"So, you know there was a flash drive in there."

She nodded.

"Do you know if he made a copy?"

"Sorry. Not one I know of anyway."

"Oh," Jack remarked, deflating.

"Why do you need it anyway?"

He pursed his lips before answering, as if gauging how much to say. "There's a video on it. But we didn't get to watch it all. We need it to get out of the mess we're in."

"I thought this was Ms. McConnaughey's mess," she said, smirking.

"Can you help us or not?"

"Like I said, there's no copy. But," she said, pausing dramatically, "I could tell you about the video if you want."

"You saw it?"

She nodded. "Watched the whole thing. Wasn't supposed to, of course, but it gets boring in there sometimes."

"Ms. Grabney—again, I'm glad you're talking to me, but everybody else that's touched that flash drive is dead. You need to be more careful."

She shook her head, chastising him. "I'm careful enough. Besides, nobody suspected I'd ever seen the thing. Herb kept McConnaughey's file locked up in his private safe, and he mailed the package himself. He never even knew that I knew it was there. He sure didn't know I'd made a copy of the safe key years ago." She smiled mischievously. "That's where Herb keeps all his," she drew quotation marks in the air, "*top secret stuff*. The McConnaughey file was just sitting in there with all the others."

Jack shook his head. "Others?"

She took a wheezy breath and continued. "P.I. videos, you know? From divorce cases. Mr. Right cheating with Miss Wrong? Better than soap operas sometimes. I'd watch them when I'd get bored. One day I saw the McConnaughey file in there, but I didn't have time to check it out. So I just left it for another day."

She took a deep breath, which seemed like hard work, and continued with her story.

"So, anyway, Herb had to go to Italy for a few weeks, and that's when he told me about this client named McConnaughey that was supposed to check in every week. Herb didn't say why, he just said that I was supposed to let him know right away if McConnaughey didn't call the office while he was gone.

"Well, of course, that got my curiosity going. The minute he left I got my copy of the safe key, pulled out the McConnaughey file, and took a peek. There it all was, scratched on some notes Herb'd made—all of Tate McConnaughey's instructions, with the flash drive tucked inside. Tate was supposed to check in with Herb every week, his way of letting Herb know he was still around. If he didn't call, then Herb was supposed to forward the package to his sister.

"I popped the flash drive in my computer. I'm just biting into my tuna on whole wheat, when this Tate kid pops on the screen and starts telling his sister how he's got seventeen million of somebody else's money, he's probably dead—"

"Seventeen million?" Jack interrupted.

Grabney nodded and kept going, "and she needs to get a hold of it right away. Says people are going to come after her and try to kill her. Well, you can imagine what that did to me. I locked the thing back up, but I couldn't stop thinking about it. Kept me up at night. Nightmares."

Jack nodded his understanding.

"Three days later, Tate didn't call when he was supposed to. But I was too scared to tell Herb. I was afraid of what would happen if he mailed that thing off and got mixed up in that mess, or worse, had me do it. I hoped the kid was just late and would call eventually. When he missed the call the week after that, too, I started thinking that whoever he'd stolen that money from must have finally caught up with him. So, I decided the best thing I could do was keep my mouth shut and pretend I didn't know a thing."

"So who mailed the package to Chloe?"

"Herb. When he got back from Europe and Tate missed that week's call, Herb quizzed me about it. I acted like I'd forgotten all about it. He laid into me, but he bought it. He didn't have any contact info for Tate, so he couldn't check on him. He got on the Internet and finally found mention of Tate's accident online. That's when he mailed it."

"The morning the cops came in to tell me they'd found Herb—I don't know—a light bulb went off in my head. I went to Herb's private safe to check on the McConnaughey file, you know, just out of curiosity." She shook her head. "It was gone."

"What was on the video? We only got a couple minutes into it. How much do you remember?"

Grabney adopted a sly expression, exposing yellowed teeth. "I've been a card counter for years. I remember every jot and tittle of that boy's words."

"Okay . . . well, great. Tell me."

"Like I said, I'm a gambler Mr. Collings."

"Yeah, I got that."

"And I'm gambling you'd be willing to pay me to hear what was on that video."

Jack's face grew stony. "You've got to be kidding."

"That information's worth millions, Collings, and now I'm out of a job. I am *not* kidding."

"That seventeen million is blood money. People have *died* over it. Doesn't that matter to you?"

She glared at him again. "Of course it matters. I loved Herb in my way. And I want to help you if it means stabbing his killers in the back. But I gotta take care of myself. Nobody else is gonna."

"How much?"

"I'm not asking for anything crazy." She eyeballed him. "Let's say twenty thousand."

Jack's eyebrows shot up. "Well, we have a problem, then, because I don't have twenty grand on me."

"Looks to me like you and your lady friend don't have much of a choice. So I suggest you figure something out."

He could call his financial advisor. *He wouldn't have to know anything's wrong. I could have him move it to Grabney's account. If they are watching her, it might get noticed, but what choice did he have?* He took a gravelly breath. "I'll give you ten. Take it or leave it."

The ticking of the grandfather clock in the living room echoed in the aftermath of his offer. She extended a veiny, mottled hand. "Deal."

Jack didn't reach out to shake it.

THIRTY-TWO

Renaldi DiMeico was the founder, President, and CEO of Inverse Financial Holdings, Ltd. He had started the investment firm nearly ten years ago from scratch, and now its client list included companies and individuals from all over the world, each with millions that needed managing. But to this day, Renny insisted on being heavily involved in the day-to-day operations, handpicking most of its employees. That was how it happened with Tate. More than that, Renny had been personally involved in courting Tate before he accepted, wooing him with the very best that Inverse and Miami had to offer.

Chloe was convinced that Renny himself was part of the reason Tate had ultimately taken the job. She had to admit that the man did have a certain magnetic charm that made it impossible not to like him. And then, there was the way that Renny had taken Tate under his wing. By the time she came down for her first and only visit, right before Tate accepted the job, the mentor/mentee relationship was already solidified.

Tate's death had seemed hard on DiMeico. He was one of the first to call Chloe after the crash, completely beside himself as he tried to convey his sympathies. He even came up for the funeral, something that surprised her. At the gravesite he discreetly approached her, expressing his condolences again and pleading with her to call him if there was ever anything he could do for her. She had never thought she would need to take him up on the offer. Here was someone who actually had the resources to do something to help them, but the last thing she wanted was to drag him into it. She'd just find out what, if anything, they still had of Tate's, and then go.

The double doors to the conference room swung open. DiMeico, a big bear of a man, strode over to Chloe and swept her up into his Hugo Boss suit.

"Chloe, my dear Chloe!" he exclaimed, hugging her tightly. "I am so very glad to see you. It has been far too long." His mild Italian accent was as charming as ever, and, as always, he was dressed impeccably, right down to the tasteful gold cufflinks. Chloe squeezed back warmly.

"You're right, Renny. It has been too long. It's really good to see you."

He pulled back and looked at her appraisingly. "You look much different than the last time I saw you." His eyes settled on her hair. "Quite a bit, I think."

"I needed a change. How are you?"

"I should be asking you that question, should I not?" he replied, still grasping her upper arms. "But I am well. And you?"

Chloe cleared her throat. "I'm managing. It's still hard."

Renny nodded. "He is missed."

"Thank you, Renny."

"But enough of that depressing talk. To what to do I owe this unexpected pleasure?"

"Actually—" She cut herself off when she noticed Renny's secretary seated behind a desk just yards outside the conference room door and a few others milling around in the waiting room. She nodded towards them. "Do you think we could go somewhere and talk privately?"

He turned his head in the direction of her gaze and understood immediately. "Absolutely, darling. Absolutely," he acquiesced, ushering her out of the room. "Besides," he said, flashing a smile, "I'd rather not share you."

Chloe shook her head. "Ever the charmer, Renny."

He shrugged unapologetically. "I am what I am. Margaret, we will be on the roof," he announced as they walked past the secretary's desk, then added, "I would prefer to not be interrupted."

"Yes, sir."

"And have some drinks brought up." He turned to Chloe. "Still Tom Collins, no?"

"Good memory," she replied.

"If you will take care of it," he said, nodding at Margaret.

"Yes, sir. Right away."

A short trip on the elevator landed them on the roof, sixteen stories above downtown Miami. She had been up there only once before, for drinks late on a Saturday night. The view was as spectacular as she remembered, relatively unhindered, as the building was one of the taller ones in the area. In the distance, stretches of ocean were visible between breaks in the cityscape.

The wind ruffled her shortened hair as she stepped onto the first of several hundred squares of exquisite Mexican tile that bordered raised gardens generously edging the patio, each overflowing with a rainbow of vegetative color and lush greenery. In addition to several potted palms, towering willows swayed gently in the breeze, their feathery branches sweeping the floor in small strokes. A strong gust shook loose a frond that floated gracefully into the sparkling lap pool at the roof's center, initiating an infinity of tiny ripples.

"I hope this is all right," Renny asked with obligatory humility, as they sat down at one of the tables near the water.

"It's perfect, Renny. And still gorgeous."

"Not unlike yourself."

Chloe cocked her head and gave him a wry smile. "Really, Renny. You're too much."

"As I said, dear, I am what I am. So," he said fingering the edge of the table, "what is it? I can tell that something is bothering you."

Chloe sighed. "Is it that obvious?" He smiled sympathetically. Chloe took a deep breath, then dove in. "The thing is, well, I have some questions. About Tate. About what he was doing before he died."

Renny's brow furrowed. "I'm not sure I understand. You know he worked to keep our computers secure and operational. And he developed software and such."

"No, I don't mean at Inverse. I need to know what else he was doing—on the side."

"If Tate was moonlighting, I was not aware of it. I strictly prohibit that sort of thing. I want my employees to stay focused."

Chloe swallowed hard. "I'm not sure he was moonlighting, exactly. But I do need to try to put together how and with whom he was spending his time."

"Why? If I may ask?"

She sighed. "It's just . . . important to me. That's all."

The elevator door slid open and an attendant stepped out carrying a tray of drinks. He walked directly to their table and set it down beside Renny. "Anything else, sir?"

"Not at the moment. Thank you, George."

"Yes, sir," the graying attendant replied, then exited the way he came.

"You were saying?" Renny asked, taking one of the glasses off the tray and handing it to Chloe. She took it from him and sipped.

"I came to you in the hope that maybe Tate kept something here, anything, that might shed some light on his time here in Miami."

"But we sent you his things."

"His personal things, but not his business records. Not his calendar or his date book. I didn't ask for that stuff. I know it's been a little while and if you've gotten rid of it—"

Renny held up a hand to stop her. "No, no. I think we should still have everything."

Chloe's face lit up. "Really? Because I thought it was a long shot. I mean, I know it still is—there's no guarantee any of it will help me. But if I could just look through it tonight, I swear I'll be out of your hair tomorrow."

"Chloe, you are not 'in my hair.' And, of course, you can see whatever we have. But, first, quell an old man's curiosity. I am worried about you. You seem . . . unsettled. Is there nothing more I can do?" he asked, fingering the beverage napkin bearing the Inverse emblem upon which his martini now rested.

"Look," she started again, "I don't want to involve you any more than I already have, so I don't think I should say anything else. I wouldn't have come at all, except I think this is my last hope. I'm sorry I can't say more."

"Pshh," he said dismissing her concern, "do not be foolish. I want to help you in any way I can. I am glad you came."

"Well, I promise, once I get a look at those records, I'll be out of here."

She hoped that he would sense her urgency and quickly summon someone to assist her in locating the records straightaway. But, instead, he sat there idly rubbing the same beverage napkin, now worn thin at the edges. His fingers moved to the lip of his glass, which he traced in slow circles. A singular bead of condensation trickled down its side, slipping onto the napkin, where it was absorbed into the dark blue emblem imprinted on the paper.

That dark blue emblem. The double encircled letter "I." The one on the pillar in the parking lot. The one etched into the glass doors of the lobby. The one . . .

A shiver shot violently down Chloe's spine as she gazed at the emblem, completely transfixed. She had seen it dozens of times while Tate worked for the company and at least a dozen since she had arrived that afternoon. But it wasn't until she was sitting there on the roof with Renny, watching the sweat on his glass drip onto the napkin, that she remembered the last time she saw it before coming to Miami.

THIRTY-THREE

Chloe's stomach swirled as she watched another bead of water follow the last onto the napkin, further soaking the already drenched paper. She became aware of Renny staring at her, and forced herself to breathe.

"Are you all right?" he asked.

"I'm . . . I'm fine."

"Because you do not look fine, darling. Not at all."

"No, I'll—I'll be okay. I'm just really tired."

"I would imagine so. After all you've been through."

Chloe eyes rocketed up to meet his. "What?"

"Chloe, darling, you really don't have any idea what's going on, do you?" he asked, lifting his perspiring glass to his lips, then lowering it onto the napkin. Onto the emblem.

And there it was again. That memory, that recollection that only seconds ago had thrown her into the tailspin she was still fighting her way out of. Her cottage on St. Gideon. The dark front room. A sliver of moonlight through the front drapes and . . . a stranger. The intruder. Slamming into her, throwing her to the floor. The loud crash of porcelain striking tile. He raised a fist, and she turned away to protect her face . . . and she reached up and tore something. His keys fell out, landing on the floor just feet away. She had glimpsed them only briefly, and somehow lost the memory in the aftermath. This was the runaway memory she had been chasing that morning in the hospital.

A set of keys with a key fob on the ring. The kind that you use to electronically unlock a door. Silver with a single, simple marking on its face. A blue, capital letter "I" encircled by a double ring.

Renny snapped his fingers in Chloe's face. "Chloe, are you still here?"

Chloe's gaze rolled back to him.

"Where did you go, darling? Seemed like I lost you for a moment." His eyes were narrow, burning into hers.

Chloe rose smoothly out of her chair and began slowly backing away towards the elevator.

Renny sighed tiredly. "What are you doing?"

She pulled her gun from her waistband and pointed it at him as she continued stepping backwards. "I'm leaving, Renny."

"Chloe. Be sensible. Do you really think I am just going to let you walk out of here after I have been looking for you all over the Caribbean?" He tsk-tsked. "After the ingenuity you have displayed recently, I would have expected much more. Of course, I had also expected you to keep as far away from me as possible, and yet," he said, gesturing widely, "here you are."

As if on cue, the elevator door slid open and Korrigan and Vargas, both armed, strode over to her, taking up positions on her right and left. "You've been rather elusive, you and your friend—Jack?"

Chloe pressed her lips together and tightened her grip on the gun, still leveled at his chest. "Darling, surely you realize there is no way off this roof for you, except, of course, as I see fit. So I suggest you hand that weapon over and *sit back down.*" His last words were cold and forceful, leaving no room for doubt that, one way or another, she would be returning to the chair.

In that moment she knew that it was over. She wanted to run, wanted to try something, anything to get away, but it was obvious she wouldn't succeed. She felt like such a fool. She had risked her life, and Jack's, to evade the very people she had ultimately come to for help. She had walked right into their hands. Voluntarily. Everything, all of it, had been for nothing. And that was simply more than she could bear. Defeated and drained of will, Chloe lowered the gun, dropped it at Vargas's feet, and returned to her chair.

* * * * *

Jack's cab sat mired in the late afternoon traffic as he pressed the disconnect icon on his cell again. Ever since Grabney had finally explained things, Jack had been trying to get Chloe on her cell. But she wasn't answering. Worse, the "Find Your Cell" app they'd installed showed her phone as offline. Her GPS tracker, though, showed that she was still at Inverse.

The trackers had been Manny's idea. *We've got them on hand for our . . . shipments. Just to make sure we know where they are. If you get separated without phones you'll need a way to find each other.* The little GPS trackers were medallions about the size of a quarter, about half an inch thick. Manny had insisted they wear hiking boots—not normal footwear for Miami, but easy to hide the tracker in. He'd cut out enough of the rubber soles to accommodate the unit, completely hiding the thing under the shoe liner. They'd had to keep them in their pockets for their air travel, but after arriving in Orlando, they went right back in.

Manny had switched the trackers over to a separate account and showed Jack how to access the app through two old smartphones he'd given them to replace the cheap flip ones Jack had bought. Now Jack watched Chloe's dot on a fifteen second update loop on his phone. Another fifteen seconds passed. Her dot remained at the Inverse offices.

"Can't you go any faster?" Jack barked at the cab driver.

"Are you lookin' at the same road I am, man?" the driver said. "No, I cannot go any faster. There's probably som' accident up ahead or somethin'. It's bumper to bumper for sure all the way to Highland."

Jack slammed a hand hard into the back seat and grunted loudly. She was there. At Inverse. "Come on!" he yelled indiscriminately at the traffic.

"Hey, man, there's nothin' I can do about it, so you might as well relax. Chill."

"Why don't you just focus on moving us out of here," an incensed Jack snapped, then peered out the window, feeling helpless. *What's going on, Chloe?* he wondered, and tried her cell again. She still didn't answer.

"At this rate it'll be an hour until we get there!" Jack complained, banging on the front seat again in frustration.

"Lay off the car!" the driver shouted. "If you're that hot to get there, maybe you should just get out an' run."

Jack looked up the block. "How far is it?"

"I don't know. Eight, nine, blocks—"

The thump of the rear door slamming interrupted the driver, and he whipped his head to see Jack sprinting down the sidewalk towards the next intersection.

"Hey, man! Hey!" he yelled, sticking his head out his window. "What about my fare!"

* * * * *

Chloe was done. It was over. Lost. As soon as she'd sat down again, Renny had asked for her cell, then removed the battery. Now the two thugs that'd stepped off the elevator stood guard just feet away. She was not walking out of here and had no way to let Jack know what was happening.

"I am glad you made it here in one piece. I was concerned you might end up getting yourself killed."

"I thought that was the whole idea."

Renny shook his head. "Hardly. You are no good to me dead."

She glared at him from under her eyelashes. "And just what good am I to you alive? What do you want from me?"

Renny drummed his fingers on the table, watching her expression as if waiting for something. Finally he leaned in. "I want my twenty million back."

Chloe choked. "Twenty million? Renny, I . . . I don't have your money," she stammered. "I didn't even know," she muttered under her breath.

"Oh, but you do. You do."

"Renny—"

"Where's your friend?"

Chloe's body stiffened. "I don't know."

Renny slammed his fist on the table, causing her to jump. "Do not lie to me, girl!" he spat angrily through clenched teeth, his eyes wicked, all traces of his charming personality gone.

"I'm not lying!" Chloe yelled back, aggressively leaning forward in her chair. "I don't know where he is. He left me when we got here. I haven't seen him since. He said I slowed him down, made bad decisions. Kept telling me his chances were better without me. Looks like he was right."

Renny eyeballed her. "You are lying," he said as he reached into his jacket and pulled out a cigar. One flick of a gold lighter ignited it, and he took several long puffs. "But, it doesn't matter. We will find him eventually." He watched her over the end of the cigar, waiting for a reaction. When he didn't get one, he changed subjects. "So," he asked, tapping ashes into a tray, "how *did* you get here?"

Chloe bit her lip, determined not to give him any information that might lead him to Jack. Renny looked away coolly and blew out a stream of thick smoke. "You know, Chloe, you can tell me now or you can tell me later, but now would be much less . . . *stressful* for you."

Despite his not-so-veiled threat, she remained mute. In the face of her silence he changed subjects again. "So you have seen the video. No?"

"No."

His eyebrows arched. "Really."

"Why would I lie?"

"Why would you not?"

"I don't know, Renny, you tell me."

He smiled. "Actually, I believe you. Tate made it very clear that the person he stole from was *me*. I am quite sure that if you had seen that, you would not have come to see me. No?"

"No."

"So I can only assume that you were unable to view the video, at least not in its entirety, before you lost it at the hotel."

Chloe's jaw dropped. "How did you—"

"We found it. Quite a stroke of luck for us."

"So then, if you've got it, why do you need me?"

"Well, that is the rub, now isn't it?"

Chloe looked at him blankly, still not understanding. Renny sighed. "When I first met Tate, I could tell that he was, well, something of a prodigy. What that young man could do with a computer—the Da Vinci of the information highway."

"You don't have to tell me," she retorted bitterly.

He cast a patronizing look in her direction. "Are you sure about that? It does not seem you knew him as well as you thought." He took another toke on his cigar while he let the comment sink in.

"He had a certain drive, an ambition that, combined with his other talents, set him apart. From the beginning he made things— some very profitable things—happen for us. Changed the way we do, well, *business*. He was innovative, determined . . . reminded me of myself at that age. I suppose that is why I took to him so," he said, swiveling his gaze towards the horizon. "Perhaps even against my better judgment. But at the time . . ." He shifted his stare back to Chloe. "Well, hindsight is twenty-twenty."

"What happened, Renny?"

"Very simply—Tate stole from my clients. *From me.*" A reddish hue blossomed at the base of his neck and began to spread. His words were sharp and angry. "I do not suffer betrayal. Not by anyone. Especially not by those I have brought in close. Do you know I was actually considering promoting him?" He shook his head. "Never before have I been such a poor judge of character."

"Why kill him, Renny? If you didn't know where the money was, why get rid of the only person who did?"

"That was not my fault. Tate crashed into that divider as we were trying to intercept him. I wanted to catch him, not kill him."

"At least not until after you got your money back."

He nodded at her, a non-verbal *touché.*

"Why are you telling me all this?"

"Because, to be blunt, in the long run your knowing will not present any risk to me. It is not the way I want it, Chloe, but sometimes we do not get what we want. Even me. I like you. I did from the first time we met, here on this roof. And I do not blame you for any of this. So, I see no reason why you should spend the rest of your time wondering why all this has been visited upon you. Perhaps telling you will make it easier for you to accept the inevitable." His eyes glazed with warped warmth. "If I had any other choice . . ." His voice trailed off, leaving her to fill in the blank.

"But why pursue me in the first place? I had no idea what was going on."

"I do not doubt that now. But you were the only lead we had. There were two possibilities. Either you were involved in this with him—"

"But I wasn't—"

"Or," he said, drowning her out, "you knew nothing about it. After Tate's death we watched for some sign that you knew what was going on, some clue to where he'd squirreled away the money. It didn't take long to figure out you were not working with Tate, but still, you remained our only lead to the money. So we followed you to the island. Then we noticed an entry on his calendar—you were right about that by the way. We missed it the first time, but, upon re-evaluation, two lunches with an 'H. Rohrstadt' drew our attention."

Chloe gasped involuntarily, making the terrible connection that explained why Rohrstadt's office was closed.

"Yes," he said, confirming her unspoken, but obvious conclusion. "Well, the only information Mr. Rohrstadt had to share was that Tate had arranged for a flash drive to be sent to you upon his death. One that Rohrstadt *vehemently* insisted he had not perused. At any rate, there was no copy. So we set about recovering the one that had been sent to you."

"So you killed him?" she asked boldly.

"We eliminated a potential threat," he said callously, then extinguished the cigar in the ashtray and took another swig of his martini. "Speaking of threats, you have been very lucky, with this . . . this partner of yours. Jack."

"He's not my partner. I told you, he left me."

He ignored her protestations. "Did he tell you he was ex-military? Special forces?"

Chloe worked to keep her expression even, to not give anything away. Inside, however, her hopes for Jack plummeted. *They know who you are.*

"Did it occur to you that if he lied to you once about who he was, perhaps he is lying still? It would not surprise me to learn that he had an agenda in this. After all, it is quite possible that I am not the only one after the funds."

"What are you suggesting? That he's working for one of your clients?"

Renny laughed. "My clients? No, dear, no. My clients have no idea that their investments have been tampered with, and I have every intention of keeping it that way. I have myself replaced their stolen monies with my own, leaving them none the wiser. No, I am thinking more along the lines of someone who knew exactly what Tate was up to. Maybe a partner. Maybe someone he became loose-lipped with. There are any number of possibilities."

He left the thought hanging there, egging her to come to Jack's defense. When his provocation had no effect, he exhaled heavily. "In any event, I believe that is enough storytelling for now. I have told you more than I should, even under the circumstances." He pushed his chair back and stood.

"We need you to do something for us," he said matter-of-factly. "Korrigan will explain it to you shortly. Be cooperative and . . . well, we'll see how things go. In the meantime, please do not hesitate to ask for anything you might need." He took several steps towards the elevator, then turned back to her. "Chloe, I wish that things had turned out differently. But unfortunately, your brother saw to that. Now, if you will excuse me, I have some things to attend to."

He started to turn.

"You're a monster." She spat the words at him and he stopped momentarily.

Then, seeming to absorb the insult without effect, he turned his back on her and walked to the elevator, his Gucci loafers softly slapping the floor as he went. "I told you, my dear," he said dispassionately as the doors began to slide shut. "I am what I am."

THIRTY-FOUR

Jack scrunched down in the back seat of the cab, just high enough to keep an eye on the Inverse building directly across the street. He had arrived on foot, but wanting to have an escape ready, he had hailed another cab and instructed its driver to park and wait. Nearly ten minutes had passed since then, and he had spent every one of them internally debating what to do.

Should he stay in the car and gamble that she would come out, either on her own or under Inverse's control, and grab her then? Or should he charge the building and take his chances? Based on what Grabney had told him, he knew they needed her alive, but for how long? Every second that passed was one less chance to get her out of there safely.

But he also knew that going inside was akin to suicide. *And I can't help her if I'm dead.* Prudence dictated a wait-and-see strategy, but he didn't have that kind of time. He had nearly decided that it was time to call in the Feds, get her out of there, and just take their chances with the authorities—when he noticed that the dot representing Chloe had moved on the app's map. He looked toward Inverse's garage, where, after a few seconds, the nose of a long, black SUV materialized at the entrance.

Jack slunk further towards the floorboards.

"Hey, what's the deal, man?" the cabbie asked, unsettled by Jack's behavior. "I ain't tolerating nothing illegal in here."

"No, no, it's just—I think my girlfriend may be in there," Jack said. The driver rolled his eyes and grabbed his paper again. The SUV pulled out of Inverse's garage then turned right, coming towards the taxi. Jack checked the dot. It had moved down the street too. As the SUV drew close, Jack squinted, trying to see into it, fighting the urge to rise up for a better look. But it was several lanes away, and the windows were tinted. He glanced down at the dot. It had moved in keeping with the SUV.

"That SUV that just pulled out—follow it. But don't let them know you're following it."

"You're the boss," the driver said calmly, shifting gears with no real urgency.

"Go, go, go!" Jack shouted, waving a hand in the direction of the SUV.

The sluggish cabbie did a U-turn and pulled into the far right lane heading north, four cars behind the one that held Chloe.

"Just so's you know," the cabbie mumbled as he changed lanes to keep up, "running red lights'll cost you extra."

Jack tossed a fifty over the seat. "Just drive the car."

Stepping hard on the gas, the driver sped right past the SUV.

"What're you doing? I said follow it, not lose it!"

"Relax, man. Relax. You think I haven't done this before? You're not the first guy who tried to catch his girlfriend in the act. I know what I'm doing. There's no side streets on this stretch. They aren't going anywhere. And they sure won't get suspicious if we're ahead of them, now will they?"

"Just make sure you get behind them before they can turn."

"Like I said, man. Relax."

They drove for twenty minutes, the cab darting from lane to lane, alternating positions in front of and behind the SUV so as to avoid raising suspicion. It led them out of the commercial district, towards the bay, and finally onto MacArthur Causeway, the bridge linking Miami to the City of Miami Beach.

Palm Island Park, one of the posh residential islands between Miami and Miami Beach, rolled by on their left; on their right, the Port of Miami. A mammoth cruise ship sparkled, thousands of white lights strung on its massive decks, beckoning passengers to embark as dusk began to fall. Jack focused on a different set of lights—the glowing red taillights of the SUV three cars ahead.

As they neared the bridge to the next residential island, the SUV veered into the far left lane. It slowed, then pulled into the palm dotted median. Jack's taxi sped by just as the SUV completed its left turn and headed across the bridge that separated the exclusive island from the not-so-privileged masses.

"Can't you follow them in there?" Jack asked, whipping around to watch through the rear window as the SUV pulled up to the gate at the island's entrance.

"No," the cabbie said, shaking his head. "We'd never get past the gate."

Jack turned towards the cabbie. "So which one is that?" he asked nodding towards the island.

"Star Island."

"Tell me everything you know about it."

As they sped over the remainder of the causeway, the driver gave a spotty lecture on Star Island, which consisted primarily of naming off the famous people who owned houses there. When the causeway deposited them on Miami Beach, Jack had the driver turn around and head west, back over the causeway and past Star Island again. As they passed by, Jack scrutinized it for as long as he could make it out, taking in everything he could at fifty miles an hour. When he couldn't get a visual anymore, he flipped around and considered his limited options.

Chloe had mentioned once that the owner of Inverse Financial had invited her and Tate to stay at his house on Star Island when he was trying to persuade Tate to take his job offer. If that was where she was headed, getting her out of there would be more than difficult. There would likely be guards. A security system. Maybe even dogs. Not to mention the neighborhood's own private security that likely patrolled regularly. At present, his entire armory consisted of a .45 caliber semi-automatic and one and a half clips of ammunition. Even with the edge his training provided, he didn't have a rat's chance of getting in there. Not to mention getting out with her.

Was going to the Feds really his only option? And if he did that, would they take him at his word? Would they storm the place or make phone calls first, alerting DiMeico's people, giving them time to move her, or worse, get rid of her? She still had the tracker on her, but how long could he count on that? What if they checked her for devices? What if they made her change clothes? *I know where she is now*, he thought, eyeing the dot that had indeed stopped on a little spot on the backside of Star Island, *but what about ten minutes from now?*

He squeezed his eyes tight in frustration. *Lord, please help me figure this out. I can't believe you've brought us this far to have it end like this. Tell me what to do. Help me save her.*

A back-numbing jolt from a particularly large pothole jerked Jack from his prayer, his eyes flying open. He was about to spout off when he noticed a billboard of a marine in full dress plugging for new recruits. A memory flashed in Jack's mind, and he snapped forward, his eyes darting around as he engaged in mental somersaults. *He'd be perfect . . . but that was years ago. Were the rumors he'd moved away from Miami true?*

Try anyway. The phrase scrolled through his mind, and Jack felt an unexpected surge of optimism as he pulled up the white pages on his cell.

THIRTY-FIVE

Chloe sat wordlessly in the spare study of DiMeico's mansion—at least that's how he had referred to the room when he'd given her a tour of his estate months ago, when she'd come down for Tate. Long velvety drapes hung in deep folds, covering a solitary floor-to-ceiling window. The walls were paneled in wide sheets of some rich wood stained a reddish hue. Chloe sat in a thin leather chair positioned behind a glass table furnished with a banker's lamp and leather blotter set. On her previous visit, the small room had seemed cozy; now it possessed a palpable chill that scuttled across her skin, making her draw her arms in close.

On the opposite wall, the man others called "Vargas" stood in front of an inset entertainment curio. He slipped a disc into the DVD player, then stepped away from a large, flat-panel television affixed to the wall. As he moved to stand obstructively in front of the study door, the silver DVD player whirred and the blizzard of black and white static on the screen flashed to solid bright blue. Then the picture flashed again, and suddenly, there was Tate, just as she had last seen him on the computer screen at the LeClaire.

Chloe stared numbly at her twin brother's face as he began telling his story for the second time. It only took a few minutes to get to the part they'd been watching when Sampson had shown up:

"I guess I should start at the beginning. I'd been in Miami about six weeks when I met this guy in a bar in Bayside. I never caught his name, but he worked for WorldCore Bank's Miami office in some kind of management position. Anyway, he tosses back one too many and gets loose-lipped. We get to talking

about our jobs, and when he finds out I'm in tech security, he launches into this story about how he's in for a conference on system security, and isn't that a coincidence. Tells me how they could really use a guy like me because so far they haven't been able to come up with a reliable gatekeeping system. How they're constantly crashing, getting invaded, hackers playing havoc with accounts. And apparently WorldCore's not the only one with the problem. He even names names for me. He's practically on the verge of tears because he had something to do with buying their current firewall program and his job's on the line. Well, eventually, he wanders off, and starts blubbering to somebody else. But I can't stop thinking about it, and suddenly, I realize that the universe has dropped the perfect opportunity into my lap.

"So, I started checking out some of the banks he'd talked about. It's me, so, you know, it wasn't even really that hard to hack in and cover my tracks. But it didn't take long to figure out that I would need someone else, someone on the inside—"

Chloe's ears perked imperceptibly, as she recognized this as the spot where they'd had to leave off back at the resort.

"—someone on the inside to help with the paperwork and transferring the money if I really wanted it to look good, and that was going to take time. And there were other problems, too. Banks are heavily regulated. They're audited all the time. And of course, over time, people would notice the money missing from their accounts, even in minute amounts. Once the bank figured out that money was being siphoned off, the Feds would have gotten involved. Which would mean trouble.

"So, I started to give up on the idea, figuring the risks were too high. I got pretty depressed about it. But a week later, right in the middle of my pity party, it hit me." He paused dramatically for a moment, as if he expected Chloe to guess what it was that had dawned on him, then continued. *"Inverse."*

Tate paused briefly, as if he wanted to allow time for the genius of his idea to sink in, before continuing.

"When it finally came to me, my first reaction was to kick myself for not coming up with it sooner. It was a perfect plan, with none of the kinks of the bank job. First of all, I was already on the inside. Second, I had total, unmonitored access to the financial records of the clients. What they deposited with us, what they invested, what the stocks sold for, their share of the net proceeds . . . With the right keystrokes I could skim a little here, a little there—and adjust the records to make it all jive. Third, I've got no outside regulation and audit hassles because, well, the operations I'm involved in aren't exactly above board. Once a client's money comes in, it's combined with funds from legitimate clients, then

invested corporately but tracked with my software—long story short, no one else on the outside ever sees the books I'm playing with. And fourth, even if DiMeico figured out something was going on, there's no way he'd drag the cops in because the whole operation is illegal to start with." Tate's eyes were bright with confidence, as if he were certain he had thought of everything.

"Which leads me to this. Chloe, Inverse isn't what you think it is. I mean, it is an investment firm—but it's so much more. It's basically a high-end money-laundering outfit with wealth management services tacked on. You always said DiMeico sought me because he wanted the best. But that was only part of it. He also needed someone who understood the benefits of breaking the rules in order to achieve results more quickly. When he asked some pointed questions about how far I was willing to go to see my dreams realized, I told him I was tired of being cheated. If by the world's rules I had to bend the rules to get what I deserved, then so be it. That answer was the real reason he hired me. That and the fact that I can hack into anything running off electricity.

"My job really has very little to do with standard tech security work. A more accurate title would be professional hacker. The whole thing is brilliant, actually. But, it all boils down to the oldest trick in the book." Again he paused for a guess that wasn't coming. *"Inside information,"* he said with a smirk, letting the phrase roll of his tongue. *"You always wanted to know what I do all day. Well, the truth is I spend most of my time hacking into hundreds of networks—Fortune 500 companies, law firms, accounting firms, investment banks—you name it, I break into it. Spreadsheets, e-mails, letters, draft press releases, internal reports. I read anything and everything that might tell us things the rest of the world doesn't know yet. Things that are going to make a company's stock go up—or down. Soon to be reported earnings, buyouts, scandals, bankruptcies. Our clients' recently laundered money is easily doubled, sometimes even tripled, in very short periods of time, and Inverse is able to take a hefty percentage on each transaction.*

"Well, everybody was happy with what I was doing. Especially DiMeico. He was making it hand over dirty fist. Since I was the key to the hacking, I had the run of the place—the accounts, data entry, the division of the profits. That was his big mistake—"

"He trusted you," Chloe mumbled.

"—he trusted me." Tate finished. *"Over the last few months I've managed to skim nearly seventeen million, and it's growing daily. It could have been more but I was afraid I wouldn't be able to hide it well. I haven't heard a word so far. Not so much as an awkward glance from DiMeico. I'm positive he doesn't know."*

"Stupid," Chloe muttered.

"When I hit twenty-five I'm calling it quits. I figure that with this kind of money we can both make the life for ourselves we always wanted. The kind of lives we deserve. I'm working on a story for DiMeico. Family ties and all that. Something to get me out without drawing attention. I figure we'll have to lay low for six months or so, but after that, we ought to be good.

"But, just in case, I thought I should leave you with this. So you would know how to get the money." His expression turned regretful. *"It didn't really occur to me at first—I didn't consider that, well, if they ever found out what I was doing, they might not stop at me. That they might come after you, too, on the off chance you knew about it. On the chance that you were involved. I, um, hope you can forgive me for that. But,"* he covered quickly, *"that's not going to happen. I figure it's worth the risk. We'll never get a chance like this again."*

"You already have everything you need to get the money. You just have to think about it. Go to Miami and just think about it. The money's just waiting for you, but you and I are the only ones who can get it and, I can't stress this enough, you'll have to do it in person. This way, even if DiMeico gets his hands on this video, he'll still need you to get the money. At least then you have something to bargain with."

"This video tells you everything you need, Chloe. You just have to think like me. Which shouldn't be hard for you. We've got that twin-brain thing going for us, and it's always worked like a charm. Get this one right, and you'll be celebrating our next birthday in high style. I love you, Chloe. And I'll be there for you. Always."

Tate promptly rose from his chair and walked towards the camera, his body increasingly filling the screen until the only thing visible was a close-up of the threads that crisscrossed to make up his powder blue, button-down Polo. After a few seconds, the screen reverted to solid electric blue.

From his spot at the door, Vargas raised the remote and started the video again. The furnishings of Tate's apartment appeared on screen once more, followed by Tate himself.

Chloe's stomach seized as she wondered how many times she'd have to watch Tate's message before she figured out what he was talking about. Even more worrisome was the thought of what would happen to her once she did.

THIRTY-SIX

Aaron Riley opened the refrigerator door and pulled out his third beer of the night. He was generally cautious about his drinking, determined not to end up like his father. As he popped the tab and waited for the head to diminish, he glanced at the clock. It was just seven-thirty, and he had already reached his limit for the night. Still clad in his dingy, auto-shop jeans and the graying white tee he wore under his work shirt, Riley retreated into his den and sank into his chocolate leather Lay-Z-Boy parked conveniently in front of his wide screen television. On the schedule for tonight: a beer, a buzz, and basketball.

It was not the life he had imagined for himself. He owed that to an irresistible onyx-haired, onyx-eyed Cuban girl he met six years ago on Daytona Beach. After a tornado of a romance that spanned just one week, they spontaneously eloped on the steps of the Volusia County Courthouse—to the great shock and skepticism of all who knew him. Riley had no doubts whatsoever about his nuptials, wholeheartedly convinced that heaven itself had landed in his lap. But the bubble burst quickly when Rosie insisted on staying in Miami near her family. She gave him an ultimatum: either leave your beloved Philadelphia or this is over. Next thing Riley knew, he was a bona fide Dade County resident.

They bought a modest house west of the city, complete with a pool and fenced backyard for his beagle, Charlie. He opened his own auto repair shop, specializing in American cars, which finally turned a profit heading into the second year. But as business got better, things with Rosie got worse. He could never make enough money to satisfy her shopping habits. And money wasn't their only problem. Riley was bored. Critically, bordering-on-comatose bored.

It wasn't Rosie's fault. The problem had existed long before she came into the picture. He was an addict. A full-fledged junkie for the spine-popping adrenalin rush he experienced every day during the military career that ended so abruptly eight years ago after his diving accident. Like everything else he tried, she failed to fill the void. One day, when she was through being a token distraction, she left without so much as a note on the pillow.

And so Riley was a born-again bachelor, living in a two-bedroom house in Miami Springs with Charlie, his best take in the split, and, once again tonight, his only companion. Charlie leaned against the recliner, letting Riley absentmindedly stroke his ear. After half a minute of this, the dog lazily reached his tongue over and licked the top of the can clutched in Riley's hand.

"Hey!" Riley scolded, jerking the can out of the dog's reach. "That's not good for you. I've told you that about a hundred times."

Charlie whimpered in protest and implored Riley with his soulful eyes. "No way, Charlie," Riley answered adamantly, shaking his head as he rose from the recliner, walked into the kitchen and poured a sip or two of beer from the can into a plastic blue bowl on the floor. "You gotta drink it out of there, remember?"

Happily, Charlie trotted over to the bowl and starting lapping.

"You better slow down," Riley warned, "'cause you know that's all you're getting." The dog ignored him, quickly finishing his treat. Riley shrugged. "Well, don't come complaining to me in the morning when you have a hangover," he said over his shoulder as he walked back into the den.

The Heat were winning by a landslide and the game had gotten stale. Riley repetitively mashed the remote control buttons, watching dozens of satellite channels blink by one by one. The television landscape was a wasteland of reality shows, game shows, or those stupid 'Lifetime for Women' movies where somebody always gets some horrible disease. He was just about to give up and stick in his *Black Hawk Down* DVD when a flash of military uniforms caught his attention. It was a re-run of a show about lawyers in the JAG Corps, investigating the murder of a Navy pilot. He had followed the storyline for several minutes when there was a rapid knock on the front door.

With a groan, Riley pushed his forty-one-year-old body out of the chair and made the short walk to the door. Charlie was standing on his hind legs, front paws against the door, clawing at it as he barked. "Good boy, Charlie," Riley told him, patting his head. "Good boy. Now down." When a still-barking Charlie refused to back off, Riley tugged him down by his collar, then shoved him gently aside to look through the peephole.

"I don't believe it!" Riley bellowed loudly as he flung the door open and gathered the caller into a smothering bear hug. "Jack Bartholomew!" He walloped Jack hard on the back, nearly knocking the air out of him.

"Hey, Riley," Jack gasped as he looked up at his friend. Even at six-two, he felt puny in the shadow of Riley's six-foot-six frame.

Riley released him, taking a giant step backwards to get a better look at the man he had served four years of duty with. A wide smile flashed across his stubbly face, the flush of enthusiasm blossoming beneath his ebony skin. "What are you doin' here man? What's it been? Five years?"

"Six," Jack corrected. "You mind if I come in and talk for a minute?"

"Yeah, of course! Wow," Riley replied enthusiastically, and stepped aside to make room. "Jack Bartholomew. I can't believe it."

Jack turned towards the curb, waved his cab off, and moved past Riley into the house.

"So, this is Charlie," Riley said, introducing the dog as he followed Jack inside. Jack reached down to vigorously rub behind the dog's ears.

"I was sorry to hear about Rosie."

"Me too."

"I thought you moved back to Philly."

"Did for a couple months," he said, sauntering over to the recliner, "then I got sober again and realized I wasn't gonna make any money sittin' there feeling sorry for myself. And it is *ridiculously* cold up there in the winter, man." He slapped the back of the chair as an invitation to Jack to sit down in it. "You want a beer?"

"Sure," Jack replied, taking a seat in the Lay-Z-Boy.

"Be right back." Riley disappeared into the kitchen. Charlie sat down in the doorway, staring intently at Jack. He did not move an inch until Riley came back, then followed him to the navy-and-green plaid couch where he sidled up to him protectively. Riley handed one of the beers to Jack and popped open the other for himself.

"Thanks," Jack said, opening the can and taking a swig.

Riley nodded. "No problem, man." He looked at Jack appraisingly, turned his own can up, and swallowed. "So I gotta say, I'm pretty surprised to see you sittin' over there."

"I'm pretty surprised myself."

"So what's up? People you haven't seen in half a decade don't usually just show up on your doorstep. At least not without calling first."

His eyes flicked down to Riley's right arm, then back up. "I heard about your arm, too, Riley. Had to be hard. I know how much the job meant to you."

"Navy's loss, right?" He smiled thinly. "Truth is, I miss it so much it nearly kills me sometimes." He leaned back, crossed his arms and wrinkled his eyebrows, taking in the serious look on Jack's face. "But I get the feeling you didn't come here to hear me tell sad stories," he said.

Jack nodded and inhaled anxiously. "I've got a favor to ask."

It took Jack the better part of an hour to bring Riley up to speed. Even as the story came out of his mouth, it sounded so far-fetched that Jack began to wonder whether Riley would even believe him. Riley listened, sitting on the couch, shifting his weight every now and again, crossing and uncrossing his arms. Jack kept waiting for him to call bull, but he never did. When Jack was finally done, Riley's face was set in a steady expression that masked any thoughts he might have.

"So, that's it," Jack finished, running a hand through his hair. "Her GPS signal disappeared right before I got here, but the last place it showed up was DiMeico's. I've got to get her out of there, and I can't do it on my own."

Riley blew out a deep breath and leaned back into the couch. "So," he said, crossing his arms again, "naturally, you thought of Aaron Riley."

Jack sighed. "I've got my reservations about getting you involved, and wouldn't even ask if I had any other choice. But I don't, so here I am. This thing is going to be dangerous, I know, and I realize I'm asking a lot. So if you don't want to come along, I'll totally understand. But I need to know right now, because I've got to do this before they do something drastic."

A broad grin erupted on Riley's face. "So what are we waiting for?"

* * * * *

Riley shoved his shoulder into the door of his detached garage twice before it opened with the nauseating sound of metal scraping metal. "Sticks, sometimes," he explained, reaching his hand inside to tug on the string that would turn on the light. He stepped inside, Jack and Charlie following behind.

There was no car inside, likely because it was already completely full. In the middle, a grimy push mower flanked a wheelbarrow holding sundry garden tools. On one wall, a long pegboard stored an array of disorganized screwdrivers, saws, wrenches, and such. A tall, rusted, tool cabinet stood in the corner, its drawers haphazardly open and crammed with all manner of do-it-yourself materials.

"Tell me again why we're out here?" Jack asked, stepping over an edger.

Riley nodded towards a cluttered shelf at the back. "Help me with this." He stepped to the right of the shelf and took hold. Jack did the same on the left. With Jack pulling and Riley pushing, they moved it aside a few feet, revealing another door. After fishing a small key from his pocket and unlocking the padlock that secured the door, Riley pushed it open.

"After you, man," Riley said, seeming very pleased with himself.

Jack shot him a curious look, then took a tentative step inside.

"I spend a little cash at the army surplus from time to time," Riley explained as Jack speechlessly surveyed what was nothing short of a miniature arsenal lining the narrow corridor. Rifles, pistols, and shotguns hung in locked glass cases pushed against the walls. A standing multi-drawer toolbox held, not tools, but ammunition for the weapons, each labeled appropriately. Boxes on a shelf on the opposite end held grenades, knives, binoculars, and other military paraphernalia. A couple sets of night vision goggles hung from hooks protruding from pegboards, along with commercial diving gear including tanks, masks, wet suits, and flippers.

Jack walked up to the gun cases and took stock. "Two Berettas, a Sig, a .45 . . . a *CAR-15 and a MP-5*?" he said in disbelief as he eyed the submachine guns that were favorites among SEALS. "What did you do, take a walk through the armory before discharge?"

Riley shrugged. "I guess I've got a little obsession."

"*Little?*"

"What can I say? They called out to me. Never actually used any of the stuff, though. I just come out here when I'm feeling a little outta place." His face brightened. "Hey, I've even got a boat. I'm telling you, I've got your back."

"Did Rosie know about this?"

"Not till after we got married. Said it freaked her out."

Jack snorted. "Imagine that." He took another look at the boxes. "Where did you get grenades? And that CAR-15? Anything with a launcher on it can't be easy to come by."

Riley's face turned down. "Probably better if you don't ask."

"Okaaay," Jack drawled, turning around to a workbench that had several knives laid neatly on its surface. He ran a hand along the handle of one he knew as a K-Bar, standard equipment for any member of a SEAL team.

"Seems maybe I'm not the only one who misses it," Riley said, his arms folded in front of him.

Jack looked up and smiled. "Different life, Riley. Different life. I'm only interested in getting her back."

"Well, then," Riley said, sauntering over to him and picking up the knife. "We'd better get started."

Back in the house, they spent an hour on the Internet downloading everything they could find on Star Island. Eventually their scouring turned up an obscure article about a charity event that gave DiMeico's otherwise unlisted address. They found the estate on a map, got directions off Yahoo, and even downloaded an aerial shot of the island that included DiMeico's place. They spent the next forty-five minutes planning the snatch and another half hour choosing and packing gear. Around eleven they finally pulled out in Riley's Bronco, headed for a little boat launch in Coral Gables.

THIRTY-SEVEN

"I make out two tangos," Riley whispered, referencing the guards moving around the rear of DiMeico's property as he lowered his binoculars. He propped his elbows against the side of the small inflatable boat and turned to Jack. "They're moving in opposite directions around the house, meeting up at center of the backside. Every other rotation they walk the perimeter," he reported.

Jack shifted uncomfortably in his prone position beside Riley and reached for the binoculars to inspect the situation for himself. "What about her?" he mumbled, as he scanned the property.

Riley shook his head. "Nothing. A lot of the drapes are closed so I'm not sure we're gonna have much luck."

The two were floating about seventy-five yards off the northeastern tip of Star Island, facing the rear of DiMeico's estate. The moon was small, and with them huddled down in the black rubber boat while clad in wetsuits of the same color, even someone in the water would have had to float by within feet in order to see them. From land they were positively invisible.

Just after midnight they had put in at the launch in Coral Gables, about thirteen miles southwest of their present position. They piloted up the coast, past Key Biscayne, Fisher Island, and finally under the MacArthur Causeway to Star Island. From an inconspicuous distance, they made their way up the eastern side and around the northern tip of the island to the spot where they were now, which gave them a perfect view of the rear of DiMeico's estate. They waited and watched, hoping to get a feel for the resistance they would face once they stormed the place. And, if they were lucky, maybe visually confirm that Chloe was there before they headed in. Their first fifteen minutes had offered no sign of her.

"Anything?" Riley asked Jack, whose eyes were still glued to the binoculars.

Jack shook his head. "Negative. Wait. Tango One just entered the house through a set of doors on the patio overlooking the pool. Looks like he slid a card to gain entry."

"Well, at least we know how to get in—"

"There she is!" Jack interrupted excitedly.

"Where?" Riley asked, scanning the back of the house.

"Third floor, third window from the right. Sheers over it. I think I saw a woman—yeah," he said, smiling, "that's her."

"You sure?" Riley asked, straining to catch a glimpse of the form Jack was talking about. Jack stared hard at the female figure standing behind the thin veils covering the window, a small, but warm glow from what was likely a lamp outlining her silhouette. She faced out, her arms crossed. He couldn't make out her hair color, but he could tell that it was short and choppy. "Affirmative. Hold on. Tango One is exiting the house. He's . . . going back around the west side."

Riley checked his watch. "Let's wait one more cycle. Make sure we've got their timing down."

"Yeah. Okay," Jack reluctantly agreed, knowing it was the wise thing to do despite his growing urge to barrel in there and get her.

The night was as perfect as they come in Miami. The water was calm. The air had a soft breeze with a hint of salty coolness to it. Quiet surrounded them, the vibrant sounds of the city and South Beach miles away. They floated comfortably for another thirteen minutes before the guards came around to the back and met up on the patio again. When they did, Riley turned towards Jack expectantly.

"So what now? We good to go?"

As he considered the question, Jack lifted the binoculars again and gazed at Chloe's now empty window. She had moved away ten minutes ago and hadn't returned. "Yeah," he agreed, "let's move."

With the motor quietly churning, Riley piloted the boat back down the island's eastern side, away from DiMeico's. Once out of sight of his estate, they started looking for a suitable place to stash the boat. A Mediterranean-style home a few properties down was completely dark, either empty or shut down for the night. Thick, bushy landscaping hugged the property's rear. Still fifty yards out into the water, they cut the engine and paddled the boat in. After anchoring the boat, they strapped on their backpack-like mini scuba systems and unceremoniously flipped into the water.

After a hundred-plus yard swim to DiMeico's estate, they surfaced together along a stone wall that ran along the property's back edge, its top even with the land and its bottom dropping into the water. Tight rubber hoods resembling ski masks covered their heads. The little bit of exposed skin around the eyes, nose, and mouth was caked with black shoe polish. They bobbed in place, indistinct from the dark water.

Jack signaled to Riley, who nodded back. In nearly synchronized motions they removed night vision goggles from pouches in their utility belts and slipped them on. Then each pulled a semi-automatic with a silencer from their belts. When they had assembled themselves, Jack nodded to Riley and pointed up with his index finger. Riley nodded and hiked himself up onto the wall, holding himself in place with his elbows.

The backyard was about forty yards wide and thirty deep. Every inch was neatly and deliberately landscaped. Stone paths meandered through the blooming vegetation, all leading to the kidney-shaped pool, replete with waterfalls, centered at the back of the house. A cloak of darkness shrouded the far rear of the property, untouched by the generous lighting closer to the house, including pool lamps and underwater lights and a lantern-dotted slate patio, bordered by delicate primrose bushes on every side. The structure itself, harkening from the 1960s, had lights shining upward from its base and floodlights spaced along the roofline. Clearly, once they got near the house, it would be an all-or-nothing proposition.

None of the guards were in sight. Based on their routine, it was likely they were in the process of working their way around the property. Dropping his hand below the wall, Riley signaled as much to Jack. For a couple of minutes Riley watched from his position on the wall, then lowered himself beside Jack to rest his arms. Jack took Riley's place for a bit, then swapped with Riley again. Riley had been watching for less than a minute when the first guard reappeared, followed shortly by the second. The two made their way to the center of the patio, where, just as before, they spoke briefly. If they stuck to their previous passes, the two would soon part, then return to the front yard by going around either side of the house. Riley waited in position, ready to give Jack the signal to move as soon as that happened.

But instead of parting, the two guards turned together, walked down the patio steps and into the backyard, headed straight for their position. Every step they took deeper into the gardens brought them closer to the spot where Riley and Jack waited. Riley's upper body remained still, but he dropped one hand below the wall and rapidly flexed his fingers through a series of signals, warning Jack that the guards were approaching.

Jack wrapped his forefinger more firmly around his trigger, keeping his eyes trained on his partner's right hand. It was tensely splayed out in a hold signal, like a conductor preparing to cue an orchestral percussionist to strike. Then, Riley's hand suddenly relaxed. Five yards from the wall, the guards had unexpectedly fanned left and right. They walked in wide arcs back to the house, ultimately returning to the patio. After another brief discussion, they parted once again, proceeding in opposite directions around the house and disappearing on either side.

Riley kicked into gear the second they moved out of view.

"Go, go!" he whispered forcefully, his voice carried to Jack's ear by the tiny microphone embedded in the band wrapped around his throat. Jack reacted instantly, pulling himself up and over the wall then dropping flat onto the well-manicured lawn on the other side. Riley went next, landing noiselessly beside him. Staying low, they crept along, hidden behind a long row of hydrangeas. They kept moving through the yard, darting behind bushes, benches, and any other available cover until they reached a white, wooden gazebo at the edge of the darkness. It sat less than ten yards away from the two-tiered, raised slate patio extending from the back of the house. An enormous semi-circular thing, the patio resembled half of a two-tiered wedding cake, with the flat side backed up against the house where glass doors lined the wall.

Riley shifted, readying to move from the gazebo to the patio's first tier, when he detected a flicker of movement at the back of the patio. Instinctively, he shrank back into a narrow space between two bushes planted at the gazebo's base. Jack, positioned right behind him, did the same. A quick flick of Riley's fingers and wrist told Jack that someone was moving, and to stay down. Cautiously, Riley craned around the bush.

Another guard, one they hadn't seen before, stood on the patio's second tier. "Tango Three," Riley whispered to Jack. They watched as Tango Three pulled a cigarette from his jacket pocket. He popped it in his mouth, then from the same pocket extracted a lighter and raked his thumb across it. As he brought it up to the dangling cigarette, a voice called out from somewhere to their right.

"Hey, Mick!"

Tango Three's head snapped up and he pivoted hard, his eyes boring into the darkness to the west of the house. "What?"

Tango Two emerged from the shadows, walked around the pool, then tromped up the patio to where Tango Three stood. Their hushed conversation apparently involved a request for a cigarette, because Tango Three reached back into his jacket, pulled one out and handed it to Two. He struck another flame, and Tango Two leaned into it before pulling back to inhale the bitter smoke deeply.

The former SEALS remained motionless as the guards held onto their cigarettes, puffing them lackadaisically until they were used up to their last embers. Only then did they toss them into nearby flower beds, where they disappeared beneath mounds of fiery red begonias. With apparently no other excuse to keep them, Tango Two finally headed back around the west side of the house, while Tango Three returned to the patio doors, slid a keycard through the security slot and entered the house.

"Clear," Riley muttered into his microphone.

"Not completely," Jack cautioned and nodded towards the house. "Second floor. Seventh window to the left."

Riley looked up, counting windows until he came to the seventh. Through his goggles, he made out the shape of a man standing behind the sheers. After a few seconds he disappeared from view.

"That's at least four," Riley whispered.

"At least."

Jack's eyes drifted up one floor and over to Chloe's window. Still nothing.

"Time to move," Riley nudged.

Jack nodded.

They crossed the open space between the gazebo and the first tier quickly. But because the first tier rose only a foot off the ground, providing little to obscure them, they couldn't stay long.

"I'll take the east side," Riley whispered.

Jack nodded. "I'm west."

Without another word, the two split, Riley taking one side of the mansion, Jack sprinting around the other. Within minutes, both men had returned to the rear patio.

"Tango One disabled, out cold. Got his keycard," reported Riley. They'd agreed to disable only, if possible, as this wasn't exactly legal and any deaths might cause a lot of problems for them down the road.

"Ditto for Two," said Jack.

Together they moved to the patio doors. Jack slid a keycard through the groove on the access box and its glowing red light was replaced by a tiny green one. Jack depressed the door latch and pushed it open. No alarm.

They stepped into a massive sunroom and quietly pulled the door shut behind them. Soaring windows stretched fifteen feet high along the outside wall. Wicker furniture, plush chaise lounges, and potted plants filled the space. Expensive looking vases and other breakables resided between hard-covered books lined up on built-in shelves. White French doors marked the center of the wall in front of them. A single lamp cast a dim light around the room.

They flipped their night vision goggles up as droplets of water fell from their bodies onto the milky marble tile. Jack nodded, took a position to the left of the double doors, and raised his gun protectively. Riley pressed his ear expectantly against the right door. He signaled all quiet, then opened it slowly.

A wide hallway led away from the sunroom, its bisque colored walls lined with gold-framed paintings. The remaining decor consisted of one ornately-carved teak table crowned with a Waterford vase crammed to the hilt with fresh flowers. The minimal furnishings offered no cover. If this went bad, they'd be sitting ducks. Fully committed sitting ducks.

Their rubber-soled boots padded silently down the left side of the hallway. The first door they came to opened into an exercise room, occupied only by a stair machine, weights, and treadmill. Crossing to the opposite side of the hallway, they slid along until reaching an arched opening leading into the adjacent room. After signaling his intentions to Jack, Riley poked his head inside.

The cavernous kitchen easily equaled half the size of Riley's entire house. Coffee-colored stone floors complemented striking black granite counter tops. Custom cabinets sandwiched two refrigerators, a full freezer, and a commercial stove. Polished copper pots and pans dangled above a butcher block island. And beyond that, in front of a bay window in the far corner, sat a guard drinking something from a bottle at the banquet sized oblong table.

Tango Three dead ahead, Riley signaled.

Take him? Jack signaled back.

Negative. Too far away. Might get a warning out. Keep moving.

Crouching as low as they could without crawling, the two scooted by the entrance unseen and continued down the hallway past the study. Then the music room. Each time they passed a doorway, Jack tensed for a firefight. But other than the kitchen, the rooms were unoccupied. *Maybe we can pull this off,* Jack thought, finally stepping into the front foyer at the end of the hall. He signaled to Riley he was proceeding, then started up a set of winding mahogany stairs to the upper floors where, hopefully, he would find Chloe.

That was when he heard the footstep on the marble. The clunky, fearless footstep of someone who belonged there. Jack whirled around, his eyes meeting those of a startled guard just entering the foyer from the front dining room. Jack dropped, preparing to fire, but Riley beat him to it, nailing the armed man twice in the shoulder. The guard flew backwards onto the hard floor, the impact loosening his gun from his grip and sending it clattering away.

"Cat's out of the bag," Riley commented calmly as he stepped swiftly to the guard and knocked him out with the butt of his weapon. He bent down as he whipped out cable ties and secured the man's hands and feet. "This does *not* make this easier!" Riley growled as Jack bounded past him.

"Cover me," Jack grunted, continuing up the stairs that curved towards the center of the two-story foyer and ended on a landing that overlooked Riley below. Jack swiveled left and right, but saw no one coming from either end of the hallway that extended along the second floor of the house. He grabbed the railing of the next flight of steps and, taking them two at a time, stormed to the third floor where he had seen Chloe's silhouette from the water.

THIRTY-EIGHT

Chloe angrily rubbed the wetness from her cheek and swore that this tear was the last. Her eyes stung from crying off and on for the better part of the last two hours, and she hated herself for it. She wanted to be stronger than this. She'd promised herself that she wouldn't let them see her cry, and they hadn't. But the minute they'd locked her up in this room, she'd fallen apart.

Now, curled up in the corner made by the headboard of the sleigh bed and the wall, she leaned against the down pillows, hugging her knees tightly. They'd made her watch that video more than a dozen times before sticking her up here. She was exhausted. Physically. Mentally. Emotionally. But she was too afraid to fall asleep, though she knew at some point she'd end up giving in, whether she wanted to or not. Her eyelids felt like fifty-pound weights. And then, there was the hunger. Two bites into the turkey sandwich they'd brought her earlier, it had occurred to her that it might be drugged. She'd spit it out and forced herself to gag up the rest. Her stomach ached. Her head hurt. And she was all out of hope.

They'd taken all her belongings from her at Inverse and made her change her clothes once she'd arrived at the mansion. She had no idea whether they'd found the GPS tracker, but without it or her cell, she had no idea how Jack would ever find her. How *anybody* would ever find her. She thought she remembered telling Jack about DiMeico's house when she'd told him the story about Tate bringing her to Miami, but would he remember that? And even if he did, Jack wouldn't be looking at DiMeico unless he first figured out that

DiMeico was behind everything. And how would he figure that out? If he had gone to Inverse looking for her, either it would've been closed by the time he got there, or worse, maybe he managed to get inside and now DiMeico had him, too. That terrified her the most. Because, unlike her, DiMeico had no reason to keep Jack alive.

She choked back a threatening sob. *No. I won't think about that. I can't.* Because if Jack was dead, it was her fault. She clung desperately to the logic that if DiMeico had captured or eliminated Jack, he would have wasted no time telling her about it, stamping out any lingering hope she might have.

But there really wasn't anything left to stamp out. She was alone. In what amounted to a fortress. She'd counted at least four men with weapons, and she suspected from the occasional noises outside her door that one was parked right in front of her room. In all likelihood, no one was coming for her, and there was no way she could get out of there on her own.

Her palms had grown slick with the cold sweat of panic. Death wasn't just a possibility anymore. Not even a probability. It was a certainty. All this time, during all the running, another way out had always shown itself right in the nick of time. There had always been another chance for them to get away. But now there were no more chances. No way out and no one to help her. And tomorrow or the next day, or the next, she was going to die.

The only thing she could do to make a difference was to find a way to stall for time. Which was why she hadn't told them that she had finally deciphered Tate's clues. It had happened during her fourth viewing of the video, when finally, something just clicked and it all came together. She had done her best to disguise the moment the lightning struck, trying to keep them from realizing she was on to something. Apparently it had worked because they seemed none the wiser. She had to keep it from them as long as possible, because the moment they got the answer they were looking for, they would use her to get the money, then kill her. And there was nothing she could do about it.

Cold blades of reality stabbed her insides. *I'm not ready to die!* she wanted to scream, and did in her head. *I'm not ready to be done yet!* Terrifying images of graveyards and freshly dug holes flashed in her mind. Cold stone tablets marking lives gone; one inscribed with her name. *And what then?* She trembled, truth radiating in feverish waves throughout her body as she clutched the pillows ever tighter.

Nothingness. Eternal blackness. Like she never even was. Or . . . worse?

Jack thought differently, she knew. Jack believed there was more. So much more. He would have been praying now. He would have still held out hope. But she didn't even know how to begin to pray. It had been so long. She selfishly wished he was here now to show her. To help her. He had tried before, but she wasn't willing to listen.

Her own thoughts struck her as familiar, and then she remembered. Jack had said that very thing about her and God. Maybe He was trying to get her attention. Maybe He'd tried a hundred different ways, but anger and loss had left her unwilling to listen. Until now. Until there wasn't anything else to try. When death was coming and there was nowhere to run. *What if . . . what if Jack had been right?*

The frantic stabbing slicing her insides slowed to a warmish buzz. Her stomach settled. Her head seemed to clear. She considered the notion again, really pondering it. *What if God has been trying to get through to me? What if there is more?*

But God wasn't foolish. If she came to Him now, He would know that she'd only done it when she had nowhere else to go. Why would He listen to her pleas now? Why would He take her back when He was only her last resort?

The prodigal son. The words came to her without even trying, and she gasped. She had no idea where they had come from. She knew the cultural reference, even recognized it as the title of a story from the Bible. One she'd heard in vacation Bible school maybe, as a child when her mom had used church after church as summer daycare. Or maybe somewhere else. But wherever she'd first heard it, she hadn't thought of it since. But she clung to it now, latching onto it like a life preserver. Because the little she could recall of the story—one that Jesus himself had told—was that a son who had turned his back on his father finally returned home as a last resort. And the father had welcomed him home with open arms. Not only that, but the father had run to him.

Oh God, forgive me, Chloe wailed inside. *Please let me come home. I don't know what to say or how to say it, but I'm sorry. So sorry. I'm ready now, God. I'm ready to believe you. To be yours. Please help me. Please, Jesus.*

Her prayers echoed in her head, and she drifted to sleep that way, talking to God in her heart, laying out her fears and daring to hope.

* * * * *

Chloe had no idea how long she'd been out, but she woke in the dark to someone yelling frantically outside her door. She shot up in the bed as muffled pops sounded from somewhere down the hall, followed by more gunfire, louder but still muffled, right in front of her room. She heard someone scream, then there was a loud thump, and footsteps running in her direction. Terrified and confused, Chloe sat frozen as someone pounded fiercely on the door.

"Chloe! Chloe, are you in there?"

Shock radiated through her. "Jack?" she cried incredulously. "Jack!"

"Get back right now! Clear away from the door! I have to shoot the lock!" he shouted.

"I'm clear, I'm clear!" she screamed back.

The door splintered near the knob as bullets tore through it. A bizarre figure clad in a dark wetsuit and strange, thick-lensed goggles charged through the door.

"Jack?" she asked with uncertainty.

"Yeah! Come on!"

Chloe pushed off the bed and threw her arms around his neck. She let go nearly as soon as she grabbed him. "I never thought—" she whispered, searching the dark lenses for some glint of his emerald eyes.

"We've got to move. Now."

Chloe nodded and followed him to the doorway. Her guard lay face up on the hallway floor, eyes closed.

"Wounded and knocked out," Jack explained, as he pulled a gun from his belt and handed it to her. "Try not to shoot me or the other guy dressed like me."

She eyed his suit. "The other guy?"

"Not now. Come on."

Jack stuck his head out of the doorway. It was still clear in both directions.

"Head for the stairs," he ordered, pushing her along. "Snatch made," he said into his microphone, mid-run. "Headed to your position." There was no answer. "Do you copy? Snatch completed. Over." Again, there was no answer.

They reached the stairs and Jack's voice exploded as they

charged downward. "R, do you copy!"

"Copy, J, copy!" Riley barked back. "Been busy. All clear now."

Jack passed Chloe, grabbed her by the hand and practically dragged her down the remaining flight of stairs to where Riley waited in a small sitting room to the foyer's right.

"You okay?" Jack asked him.

Riley nodded. "This 'wounding only' plan is really complicating things," he said, breathing heavily. "Dude came to again. He's gonna have one massive headache, but he'll live." He appraised Chloe. "She okay?"

Jack nodded. "She's good to move. Let's go."

"You just stay behind me," Riley told Chloe, who nodded.

The trio moved back through the house following the same path Jack and Riley had taken into the foyer. When they reached the kitchen doorway, Riley peered inside. No one. He started to step past it, when a flicker of movement triggered his reflexes.

"Down!" he yelled, spinning towards Chloe, who had been following him and was now standing in front of the doorway. With Riley yanking on her calf, she dropped to the floor just as Jack, behind them, jumped backwards. As Riley pulled Chloe down, a man popped up over the huge island and took a shot, nailing Riley in his left thigh. Riley howled, and the guard disappeared again just as Riley's leg collapsed beneath him and he fell to the floor.

Jack swung into the doorway, firing at the island to cover them.

"Go, go!" Jack urged, shoving Chloe forward and getting off a few more shots. The guard behind the counter stayed put. As Jack bent down to help Riley up, Chloe fired a shot over the island.

"What are you doing?" yelled Jack.

"Helping! Get him, go!"

"I can't believe he got a shot into me," Riley complained, throwing an arm around Jack's neck as Chloe shot twice more over the island when the guard started to raise his gun above the counter.

"Let's move!" Jack ordered, sending three more shots over the island before all three ran through the sunroom and out the back door, headed for the water. Chloe turned, ready to fire if need be, but no one was following them. Either the guard had been injured, or he had decided it was too risky to run after them in the open.

"Here," Jack said, pulling an emergency scuba canister from the backpack he wore and handing it to Chloe, along with a set of goggles. She took them, eyeing the canister's rubber mouthpiece.

"Use it like regular gear," he said. "Depress here," he told her, pointing to the button on the top, "to clear it—just blow. Then breathe. You'll have more than enough to get where we're going. Just breathe slowly."

"Got it," she said and inserted the mouthpiece. As she secured the goggles on her face, Riley slid into the water and disappeared.

"Ready?" Jack asked, offering her his hand.

She nodded, clenching her fingers around his.

"Just whatever you do, don't let go."

Unable to speak, she just nodded again. He inserted his own mouthpiece and with an iron grip on her, pulled her into the deep, black water.

THIRTY-NINE

Korrigan's expression was rigid, his eyes hard as he moved through the first level of DiMeico's house. As he examined the evidence of the firefight, his anger intensified like the temperature in a renegade reactor. Finally, he marched out through the sunroom to the patio overlooking the pool. He wasn't alone for long.

"I got here right before you did," Vargas reported, stepping briskly behind Korrigan. "Four injured, no one dead. Drake got shot in the shoulder, but he'll pull through. They shot to wound, not kill. Used cable ties to restrain most of them once they were out. The two outside said somebody snuck up on them, then used a sleeper hold to put them out. Woke up with the cable ties on. I've got the security video cued up for you. They look like special ops, like—"

"SEALS?" Korrigan interrupted coldly through gritted teeth, still staring at the pool water and the counterfeit lily pads floating atop it.

Vargas nodded. "Looks like they got here by water. Only they never saw a boat. Must've swum a good ways."

"Who's they?"

Vargas shook his head. "No idea, yet."

Korrigan passed through the lawn to the stone wall at the rear of the property. He leaned over it, peering down, then straightened, scanning the water in the distance. Vargas stood silently beside him.

"I told those idiots he was military," he muttered in between slightly labored breaths. "I told them to prepare accordingly."

"Drake said there were maybe three of them," Vargas offered

by way of excuse. "At least."

Korrigan inhaled, nostrils flaring. "You've been in the house. You believe him?"

Vargas shrugged. "Maybe. I only see two on the video. But the cameras could've missed one."

"And DiMeico?"

"We found him in his panic room. Says he heard the commotion and locked himself in there."

Korrigan turned back to the water. Vargas remained still and quiet, waiting for orders. Suddenly, Korrigan turned towards the patio again, Vargas striding to keep up. When they reached the steps, Korrigan began bellowing as if Vargas were half the yard away, instead of nipping at his heels.

"Vargas!"

"Yes, sir."

Korrigan spun around to face his subordinate. "I'm going upstairs to tell *Mr.* DiMeico why he can no longer afford to dictate to me how this crisis will be handled." His eyes darkened like storms brewing, and if it was possible, his voice grew colder. "If he hadn't put his privacy over security we'd have seen them coming on live cameras, but no—" He broke off, pausing in an apparent attempt to regain control of himself, which seemed to be requiring a great deal of effort. In a deliberate, steely voice, he continued. "Call everyone in. Meet up at the office. We are going to use every contact we have to scour this city."

"Yes, sir."

"And Vargas?"

"Yes, sir?"

"This is on you. You were in charge of security here tonight. If they get away, it will be your head that rolls."

With an iron gaze that matched Korrigan's, Vargas replied evenly, "Yes, sir."

FORTY

"It was the pendant," Chloe finished, pulling a forest-green blanket tighter around her as she concluded her account of Tate's entire recorded message. "It was the pendant all along."

They sped down I-95, all three packed into the front seat of Riley's pickup, headed back towards his house. Jack's arm was draped protectively around Chloe, water dripping steadily off them onto the floorboards.

"He kept talking about celebrating our birthday together . . . and he ended by saying, 'Always.' It finally just clicked for me—the pendant he gave me for my birthday last year. The engraving on the back—"

"Always," Jack interjected.

Chloe nodded. "Always." She shivered and Jack squeezed her.

"Here," Riley offered, "let me turn the heat on," he said, reaching over to turn a dial.

"Thanks," Chloe said, tossing him a faint smile. They'd barely had time for a lightning-fast introduction as they'd moved from the boat to the truck, speeding away from the water as quickly as possible.

"So what about the pendant?" Jack pressed. "How does it figure in?"

"There's a series of numbers engraved on the back, very small, right below the 'Always.' I just thought it was a serial number, or model number or something. But now . . ."

"What are they? Let me look," Jack asked, extending his hand towards her.

"I don't have it," Chloe replied flatly.

"What?"

"They took everything. When we got to DiMeico's they made me change into other clothes and took my jewelry, too."

"So we're back to having nothing."

"No, I can find out what was on it," Chloe said, a hopeful note in her voice. "Before I take a trip, every time, I take a photo of my jewelry, cameras, you know, just in case they get lost or stolen. For insurance. I thought they were serial numbers so I took a shot of the back."

"But how—"

Chloe smiled. "The cloud. All my phone photos go directly to the cloud. Get me access to a computer and I can pull it up."

"Well," Riley chimed in, turning off an exit, "once again, it looks like it's Riley to the rescue."

* * * * *

"This brother of yours seems like a real winner," Riley said, handing Jack a beer and opening his own as they sat in chairs around Chloe, who was parked in front of his computer waiting for it to boot up.

"Riley, not now. Okay?" Jack rebuked, putting a hand on Chloe's arm.

"Sorry, it's just . . . well, for somebody you say was brilliant, he sure comes off like . . . well, like a little bit of an idiot to me."

"He's right," Chloe conceded, before Jack could admonish Riley again. "I mean, I knew Tate would go to any length to get what he wanted, but this . . ." Her voice trailed off sadly.

"He might as well have painted a bulls-eye on your butt," Riley chimed in.

Jack flashed him an impatient look. "Nice."

Riley glanced at Chloe sheepishly. "Sorry. Not much of a filter here," he said, pointing at his mouth.

"It's fine. It's nothing I haven't said." She paused, seeming to struggle with her thoughts as she rubbed her forehead. "He's done so much damage. All these people, dead. Ruby, Rohrstadt—Tate himself even—and those are just the ones we know about." She spun around to face Riley. "And you, Riley. I don't know what Jack was thinking dragging you into this. I'm so sorry."

Riley shrugged. "Are you kidding? This is the most fun I've had in a long time." He tilted his head towards the computer. "It's up finally."

Chloe turned back towards the screen, her fingers pecking at the keyboard. Riley and Jack moved to hover closer, and in under a minute the screen was displaying her cloud storage photos. It didn't take long to find the one of the pendant.

"There it is!" she exclaimed, clicking on it. The photo expanded, revealing a clear shot of the pendant's backside.

"Here," Riley said, handing her a pen and a piece of junk mail to write on. She took it, scribbling away.

"Okay," she said, whirling around to face them and holding out the paper. "What is it?"

There were ten numbers, then a dash, then another seven. They stared at it for several seconds before anyone said anything.

"It's a phone number," Riley said. "The first three," he pointed at the paper, "7-8-6, that's a Miami area code." They all looked at each other, then Riley and Jack both pulled out their cell phones.

"No wait," Jack said, placing a hand on Riley's arm. "There doesn't need to be any record of you in this. Let me."

Jack dialed the ten numbers and pressed the speaker button. All three waited, nearly holding their breath.

"You have reached Bio-Tite, your biometric storage solution. We are open seven days a week, ten to eight. Please call back during business hours or leave a message—"

Jack hung up. "Bio-Tite?"

Riley shrugged. "No idea."

A quick search on the computer revealed that Bio-Tite, Inc., operated biometric safe deposit box facilities up and down the east coast. Similar to a traditional safe deposit box, these biometric boxes differed in that no keys were necessary. Instead, fingerprints were used to verify the identity of the box owner and a special code granted access to the box.

"Tate would've loved the idea. One way to insure that either he or I would have to be there to get into it," Chloe commented dryly.

"The question is, what's in the box?"

Chloe shrugged. "Something that proves what's going on, I hope."

Jack sighed. "From what you say about Tate's video, it sounds like it'll be directions about how to actually lay hands on the money."

"Whatever it is, it's more than you've got now," Riley said, slapping Jack on the back. "I'd say we'd better get planning."

* * * * *

Chloe leaned back and let the hot Caribbean sun drip over her. She was back on St. Gideon, in the swing on the porch of her perfect little beach cottage. She could see Ruby waving to her from the other side of the fence. She had a date that night. With this guy she had met on the beach that morning. Maybe they'd go to that seafood restaurant—

A creak from inside the cottage startled her. Frantically she dashed inside, where a strong arm grabbed her—

Chloe's eyes flew open as she bolted up in the little twin bed inside Riley's second bedroom. Jack stood in the doorway, looking very guilty.

"I'm sorry," he said. "I just wanted to check on you."

It took a moment for her to reorient. "I was having a nightmare."

"You okay?"

"I'll let you know after my first cup of coffee." She cast around the room for a clock, but didn't see one. "What time is it?"

"Six."

"Where's Riley?"

"Messing around in his garage." Jack stepped inside the sparsely decorated room and sat down beside her on the worn navy comforter. A knotty pine dresser topped with a rectangular mirror occupied the wall opposite the bed. The plastic blinds were drawn, but the Miami sun bore through the slight gaps, reflecting off a cheaply framed poster of a famous painting hung over the headboard.

Jack regarded her with a gaze so affectionate that he might as well have told her that he thought she was beautiful. Even now. Even with that crunchy black hair and the matching dark circles under her eyes. Even as a paler, terribly exhausted, disillusioned version of the woman he had accosted on the beach on St. Gideon. It made her feel warm and self-conscious at the same time.

"So how's the planning going?" she asked, neutralizing the moment.

He sighed. "We'll leave soon. They open at ten but we plan on getting there early. It's only thirty minutes away—less with light traffic." He leaned forward, elbows resting on his knees, his hands clasped. "So, this nightmare. What was it?"

"More of the same."

Jack nodded, as if he knew exactly what she meant.

A few moments passed. She looked at him, a need building within her to tell him what she had realized at DiMeico's before he'd come to get her. She wanted to share it with somebody, someone who would understand. Someone who wouldn't laugh. And he was responsible for it after all. But still . . . her nerves flared at the prospect of traveling the road she was about to go down.

"I need to ask you something," she started.

Jack's eyebrows arched, his expression nudging her to continue.

"When I was at DiMeico's I started doing a lot of thinking, about death and dying and what that means."

Jack looked down, took one hand from her lap and held it. Her heart fluttered as he just stared at it. "Okay," he said, inviting her to keep talking.

She continued. "The thing is . . . I prayed, Jack."

Though he continued staring at her hand, Jack's lip curled with a hint of delighted surprise. "Really? You did?"

Chloe nodded, her face pink from embarrassment. She fought it back and kept going.

"I think you were right. I think God may have been trying to get my attention. I've got this big, empty space in my soul. It's never been filled. And through all this craziness, it's just grown and grown and . . ." She sniffed and Jack squeezed her hand.

"I don't know . . . while I was up in that room I just suddenly had this rush of . . . knowing, I guess, and realizing that I didn't want to be that way anymore."

She stopped talking then, and bit her lip anxiously. The quiet of the house surrounded them, insulating them from the noise and the urgency of the world outside. There was just his breath, her pounding heart, and air charged with expectation. Then timid words spilled from her lips, testing Jack's reaction even as they came. "I told God I believed Him. About Jesus. About everything. That I was sorry. I asked Him if I could come home."

When Jack failed to instantly voice his approval, Chloe averted her eyes to her lap. "I sound like an idiot, I know."

Jack shook his head, his expression empathetic. "Don't be ridiculous." He put his arm around her and drew her to his side. "No. What I was thinking was that I've never heard anyone put it better in my whole life."

They stayed that way for a while, wrapped up in the fragile solace of each other, warding off whatever was to come. Nestled in his shoulder, Chloe breathed in deeply, soaking up the scent of fresh soap on his skin and the brief moments of comfort she knew would end all too soon.

"I could never thank you enough, Jack," she whispered.

He reached a hand up and stroked her hair in response.

"For everything," she continued. "For sticking it out with me."

He let a thin smile slip. "Really wasn't another option."

"Sure there was. You could have disappeared. You could have gone to the cops. You were never DiMeico's real target anyway. They would have lost interest in you once some time had passed."

"Doubtful," he said, reaching out to run a tentative finger across her cheek. "Besides, by then it was too late for me."

"Too late for what?"

He turned towards her, his gaze narrowing to meet hers, the space between them dissolving. "You know what I mean, Chloe. You know *exactly* what I mean."

He leaned in then, and as their lips finally met, her heart gave an almighty lurch, and the breath rushed out of her body. She pressed into him, her only conscious thought being that she had never felt anything so wonderful in her whole life. And then, lost in a swirl of ardent color and heat and light, she couldn't think about anything at all.

"Um, excuse me," Riley said, clearing his throat uncomfortably at the doorway. "Sorry to interrupt, but, uh, the door was open . . ."

Jack pulled away slowly, squeezing his eyes shut in exasperation, before regarding Riley with a forced smile. A blushing Chloe looked sideways.

"Don't worry about it," Jack said, not sounding the least bit convincing.

"Well, I've gotten most of the gear together." Riley continued, plodding into the room with Charlie in tow. He wore faded jeans and a faded charcoal gray tee shirt that cuffed his biceps. "Charlie's hungry, so I thought I'd make us some breakfast if you're up for it." He reached down to scratch the dog's ear.

"Yeah," Chloe nodded. "I could eat."

"Good, because you'll need your strength if we're gonna pull this off today."

"Wait," said Chloe, concern clouding her face. "We?"

"Yeah, we," replied Riley confidently.

"Um, no. There's no *we*. I can't let you."

Riley bent down to rub the dog's ear more vigorously, Charlie's head craning toward him. "Look, somebody's got to keep an eye out, make sure no one's waiting for you at this place or jumps you when you come out."

"I don't think they'll know where to look." Chloe's gaze flashed from Riley to Jack. "I didn't tell them I'd figured it out."

"Even so, the smart thing would be to assume they'll be waiting for you," Riley said. "Jack needs to go in with you to keep an eye on things from the inside. That means you need me."

"He wants to, Chloe. He'll be fine. He can take care of himself," Jack protested.

"Clearly," she said doubtfully, eyeing his wounded leg.

"This?" Riley asked, gesturing at his leg. "This is nothing."

"No. You've done enough. It's not safe."

"Safe, schmafe."

"This isn't your problem," Chloe said. "I don't want anyone else getting killed because of me."

"Well, we're all set then, because I don't plan on getting killed. So you can stop worrying and just concentrate on thanking me for saving your target-painted butt last night."

When Charlie barked in agreement, even Chloe had to smile.

FORTY-ONE

Bio-Tite, Inc., was located in the heart of the Brickell area, a stand-alone structure tucked between two longer strip-mall buildings that, altogether, took up the whole block. The strip-malls were tall and cream-colored, housing various small businesses, including a nail salon, office supply store, and a copy/mail box store, among others. The squatty plain building that housed Bio-Tite resembled a safe deposit box itself. There were no windows, very few doors, and the outside looked to be made of some kind of concrete block painted a drab gray. Both Jack and Riley assumed that extra precautions must have been taken to shore up the space with the level of impenetrability that would be expected for a business of this nature, probably including doubled concrete walls and a great deal of extra security. Its minimalist sign—a polished silver plaque with "BIO-TITE, INC." engraved on it—drew little attention and gave no indication of its purpose, which was most likely intentional for security reasons.

Jack, Chloe, and Riley sat in Riley's pickup, parked in the lot of a Burger King situated catty-corner across the street. They'd arrived shortly before eight just to keep an eye on the place. Now, five minutes till it opened at ten, it was time to move.

"You ready?" Jack asked.

Chloe nodded. "Ready to be done with this." She heaved a sigh. "Just . . . done."

Riley patted her shoulder. "Piece of cake. Just walk in, do your thing, and come right back out. I'll be watching the whole time. If anything goes wrong—"

"Just say 'cold,'" Jack interrupted. "Like—it's cold in here—"

"Cold," Chloe echoed. "Got it. Cold."

"If Riley hears that, he'll come in after us."

Chloe nodded again. Though she was trying to seem confident, the slight tremor in her hand suggested otherwise. Jack took it.

"Come on. Let's go."

The two exited the truck, while Riley started it up and repositioned it in a space that had opened up almost directly across from Bio-Tite's front door.

As they crossed at the light and turned left towards the storage facility, Chloe could almost feel Riley's eyes on them. *Was he using the binoculars he'd brought?* she wondered. *Probably not. Too conspicuous.*

The parking lot that stretched in front of Bio-Tite and the adjacent strip malls was sparsely filled with cars. Though she couldn't see him doing it, she was sure Jack was once again scanning the area from behind his sunglasses.

"Everything okay?" she asked.

Jack nodded. "So far so good." He stopped to listen to the Bluetooth earpiece around his left ear. "Riley says you're doing great, stop worrying."

"Thanks, Riley," she said, elevating her voice to be sure he could hear her.

"He says stop yelling at him."

Chloe smiled.

A bell jingled delicately as they opened Bio-Tite's steel front door, in striking contrast to how thick and heavy it was to move. The lobby was quite wide, but only about eight feet deep. A counter took up the whole of the left side, behind which stood a thirty-something, red-haired man in a suit he'd probably outgrown several hamburgers ago. To the right was a waiting area consisting of two groupings of several leather-padded chairs spaced around free-form, shiny metal coffee tables. It had an antiseptic feel to it, with stark white walls and floors and no artwork to add color. Two large plastic bubbles, likely concealing video cameras, faced each other from opposite ends of the ceiling. A security guard, dressed in a black uniform resembling a police officer's, stood watch in a far corner opposite the desk.

"Good morning," the clerk said, placing his hands on the counter and interlocking his fingers. Though he was pleasant-looking, well-groomed, and not the least bit scary, Chloe's nerves began elevating by the second.

"Morning," Jack replied. Chloe cleared her throat anxiously.

"Hi, um," she said, and cleared her throat again, "I need to access my box, please."

The clerk nodded. "Certainly," he answered, with a supercilious precision that obviously wasn't natural. He waited, as if expecting a follow-up from her. When nothing happened, he fidgeted. "Do you need assistance?"

She nodded. "Please."

Jack put his hand on Chloe's arm. "We haven't been here before. Someone else set this up for her to safeguard some items. So we'd appreciate a tutorial, if you don't mind."

"Not at all," he answered with a smile that did not quite hide the slight annoyance he apparently felt at having to leave his spot behind the counter. Exiting through a narrow swinging divider, he pointed Chloe and Jack to another steel door on the back wall, directly opposite the front door.

"You enter through this booth," he said, pointing at the door. "It's the only way in and out of the vault. Once you enter, the door will lock from the inside. You can come back through, but no one else can enter. There's a terminal inside. Place your right hand flat on the glass so it can scan your prints. Once it matches them, it will ask for your passcode. Enter it into the terminal. Once accepted, it will buzz you through to the vault. Your box will be the one with the green light activated. Retrieve it and choose any of the three privacy rooms on the right of the vault to conduct your business. The privacy room door will lock behind you. When you are finished, press the return button inside the privacy room. If someone else has entered the vault in the meantime, I'll buzz you back into the vault as soon as they've left it. Once you're back in the vault, replace your deposit box, then exit through the booth. Questions?"

"No, I think we've got it," Chloe replied.

The clerk nodded. "Well, just buzz me if you have any problems. There are intercoms inside each location."

Chloe nodded as Jack opened the booth door, and said, "After you."

They stepped inside the booth, which was maybe double the size of a standard phone booth. The terminal to the left reminded Chloe of a self-scanner register at a grocery store. Instructions flashed on the mini-screen above it. Following them, she placed her right hand flat on the scanner and waited.

"I don't know, Riley," Jack said spontaneously, then, after listening for a bit, asked Chloe, "Riley wants to know how Tate got your prints to set this up?"

Chloe snorted. "Seriously? That would've been easy. He probably just took something from the house the last time he was there. A glass maybe? Who knows. It wouldn't be hard." The instructions asked her to place her right thumb on the scanner and she complied.

"But all five from one hand?"

The terminal pinged and a colored diagram of a right hand with the forefinger and thumb highlighted appeared on the screen.

"Guess he didn't need all five," Chloe noted. A grid containing digits zero through nine replaced the hand diagram, and the screen instructed her to enter her passcode. "Okay, then, here we go," she said.

"She's putting in the code," Jack muttered for Riley's benefit.

With her hand slightly shaking from nerves, Chloe entered the code they'd taken from the pendant.

* * * * *

The truck's cab grew stuffy as the mid-morning sun rose higher in the sky, prompting Riley to roll down the driver's side window. Traffic rolled steadily by, the sounds louder now with the open window. A light breeze fluttered through the truck as he remained laser-focused on Bio-Tite.

"Still all quiet out here," Riley reported. A steady number of vehicles streamed through Bio-Tite's lot, but all of them headed to businesses in the strip malls. None had shown any interest in Bio-Tite.

"We're through," Jack relayed, relief and excitement evident in his voice.

"Well, all right," Riley said. "Keep it up and—" He stopped mid-sentence. A red Civic had pulled into one of the spots directly in front of Bio-Tite.

"You've got company, I think," he said, retrieving the miniature binoculars from the seat beside him. "Two people. A guy and—I think, yeah—a girl driving. A blonde. She's staying in the car. Red Civic. There's a dog in the back. The guy is getting out. He's going in."

"Should we be worried?"

Riley shook his head, "Well, never say never, but this looks pretty harmless."

Jack didn't bother to ask if Riley could see what was happening inside the lobby, since it had no windows.

"Just keep an eye on it," Jack muttered to Riley.

"10-4."

* * * * *

Upon accepting the code, the door on the backside of the booth unlocked automatically. They went through into the vault, which turned out to be a large room with three entire walls lined with hundreds of deposit boxes. Rows of more boxes filled the interior. To their right, three doors were marked Privacy Room #1, #2, and #3, respectively.

The faces of the deposit boxes lacked the traditional two keyholes and numbers. Instead, each one was unmarked, with the exception of a small round, unlit indicator about the size of a pencil eraser. Jack and Chloe each turned on their spots, quickly scanning the plates for the one green light that would signify Chloe's box. When she moved past the first row, she saw it.

"There!" Chloe gasped, pointing to a narrow box on the left side, about two-thirds of the way up the inside of the first row. Its indicator light was glowing a bright, neon green. Jack reached up and pulled it out by its handle, nodding Chloe through to the first privacy room.

"We've got the box," he told Riley. "Should be just a couple more minutes. What's going on out there?"

"Nothing new," Riley replied. "Blonde's still waiting."

They hustled inside, and Jack closed the door behind them. A soft click told them they'd been locked out of the vault. On the wall was a panel with a button labeled, "VAULT RETURN." The room was empty except for a bar height steel table, its center covered by a padded, carpet-like material. Chloe dropped the box onto it with a thud, flipped the latch, and opened it. Crushed black velvet lined the interior, and on it lay a single business card for "Fourth Bank of Grand Cayman." It contained no employee name, just the bank's contact information. She flipped it over.

"It's an account number," declared Jack, eyeing the first string of handwritten numbers as he pulled out his cell and snapped a photo of the back of the card.

"And the amount," Chloe said, referring to the figure, "17,244,292.00," scrawled beneath the account number. A date was jotted beside it, presumably indicating when that balance had been accurate. "And it's grown since then. Renny said twenty million." Their eyes flicked to the card again, neither one able to voice the rest of what was written there.

You finally have it all. Love you, Tate.

Jack flipped the card back over, took a photo of the front, then handed it to Chloe, who put it in her pocket. "Okay," Jack said, "now the envelope."

From another pocket, Chloe pulled a small, white envelope. Although they hadn't known exactly what they'd find inside the box, they assumed it would be some sort of instructions on how to proceed. So, they'd faked a letter from Tate telling Chloe he'd wired the money to a Swiss bank and that further instructions awaited her at a hotel in Zurich.

"I still say that sounds ridiculous," Chloe opined as Jack tossed the envelope inside the box and slapped its lid shut.

"This whole thing is ridiculous," he shot back, snatching up the box and depressing the vault return button. "But leaving something in here might buy us a little time if they do find it." After a few seconds the door unlatched and they went through. "You get all that, Riley?" Jack asked.

"Copied most. You headed out?"

Jack replaced the box and the light turned green before blinking out completely. "Almost," he said, taking Chloe's hand and pulling her back towards the booth.

* * * * *

Riley was starting to sweat. Drops beaded on his forehead, and he wiped them away with a napkin leftover from one of his late night taco runs.

"We've got it," Jack buzzed in his ear. "Coming out now."

"Roger," confirmed Riley.

"Things all clear?"

"No change. The guy inside is still—" Riley stopped suddenly as the taillight on the Civic flicked on. "Hold on—"

"Riley . . . what?"

"There's movement out here." Sure enough, the red car backed out in such a hurry that it nearly took out a pedestrian carrying a box from the copy store located one storefront over.

"Riley," Jack repeated urgently, as he pushed through the steel door leading back into the lobby, "what kind of mov—"

"The girl in the car—she left. Without the guy. And in a hurry. I don't like—"

* * * * *

Jack pulled Chloe into the lobby close behind him. He knew something was wrong as soon as the door closed after them.

"—don't like it," Riley was bellowing in his ear.

The guard was gone. And the clerk—

A masked man, standing where the clerk should have been, raised a semi-automatic pistol and fired.

FORTY-TWO

"Jack!" Chloe screamed as he went down simultaneously with the muffled *pffft* from the barrel of the silenced 9mm. Before she could react, the clerk strode around the counter, threw her away from Jack and stomped on Jack's right hand. Jack roared, red beginning to spread from his right thigh onto the pearl-white tile floor.

Chloe's mind spun frantically, unable to formulate a coherent thought for the shock.

"He's bleeding out fast," said the shooter, now standing over Jack with the barrel pointed at his head. "Looks like I may have nicked an artery. You come with me without a struggle, and I leave him to his chances. You don't, and I pop him in the head right now and take you anyway."

"No!" Jack yelled and reached for the shooter's ankle, the only thing within reach.

He kicked Jack's hand away, then kicked him in the head. Hard. The earpiece flew off to the side, and Jack stopped yelling. He was out.

"No—No!" Chloe cried. "Stop! I'll go, I'll go!" Was that Riley's muffled voice she heard yelling out of Jack's earpiece? Where was he! Did he understand what was happening?

"Who's got whatever was in the box—him or you?" the shooter barked.

"What?" she cried, shell-shocked and uncomprehending until he jabbed the gun at Jack again and clarity struck. "Wait—yes! Yes! I've got it."

"Toss your weapon—I know you've got one somewhere—and your cell on the floor."

As she complied, a bang sounded as the front door shuddered. It was locked and bolted shut.

"Jack!" Riley shouted frantically, his voice muted by the thick steel.

"Not a word!" the shooter growled. "Out the back," he ordered, gesturing toward the door behind the counter. "Go!"

With a final glance towards Jack, unconscious, his life pouring out of him second by second, Chloe obeyed.

* * * * *

"Chloe! Jack!" Riley yelled, banging on the front door over and over. It was drawing attention, but he didn't know what else to do. This development wasn't something they had anticipated. They'd figured that DiMeico might make a discreet attempt to catch them on the way out, or enlist a quiet tail to ambush them down some side street—but an all-out assault on the building? In broad daylight?

Why didn't I see it? That dog completely threw me . . .

He shook off the thoughts. None of that mattered now. All that mattered was getting to them.

Jack wouldn't respond over the Bluetooth. He'd said nothing that Riley could make out since the screaming started. It wasn't a good sign. And where was Chloe? He pulled out his gun, to try, well, he didn't know what, when the lock clicked and, after the sound of a bolt sliding, the door opened.

Riley tumbled through the door and spotted his friend on the floor. "Jack! Aww, no!"

"Are you the police?" the red-haired clerk, now very sweaty and disheveled, asked in a panic. "I called as soon as they left—Abe's been shot, but I think he'll be okay. That man made me lock him up in the back. Kept me out here behind the counter, told me he'd kill me if I made a sound. Said he needed me to operate—"

Riley was barely listening. "Jack!" he said, flopping down beside him. "Jack!"

He spun to face the clerk. "What happened!" His head snapped side to side, searching. "Where's Chloe! The girl! Where's the girl!"

"They left—the guy made her leave with him. Through the back. Said he'd kill him," he nodded towards Jack, "if she didn't."

Riley felt for a pulse. It was weak. Slipping off his belt, he wrapped it around Jack's thigh and tightened it as much as he could to staunch the flow of blood. In the distance, sirens sounded.

"Stay with him," he ordered the clerk. "Press here." He indicated the belt.

"I can't with this on," he said, holding up his hands, bound together with a cable tie. "Can you—" Before he could finish, Riley had whipped out a blade and sliced deftly throughout the tie.

"Do it," Riley barked, and ran for the back door.

FORTY-THREE

Jack. Chloe whispered his name into the darkness of the trunk the shooter had forced her into. *Please, God, not Jack. Please save him.*

The shooter was ready for us. Somehow, he had known. And he had planned his escape well. After he had ushered her out of Bio-Tite through the employee's entrance at the rear, he'd made her climb into the trunk of a car parked in the alleyway behind one of the strip-malls. Riley had checked there this morning for anything suspicious before heading to the fast food parking lot. She even remembered seeing this car as they had navigated through the alley. But, like the other vehicles parked back there, it had been empty and not the least bit suspicious. So there hadn't been a lot of concern.

And what could they have done anyway? There was only so much they could do with just the three of them. They'd known it was a risky move, going in there at all, but they hadn't had any choice. And now—now it was over. Riley would never catch up in time, if he even found her at all.

Her mind raced through the possibilities of what the driver was planning. It seemed like they'd been traveling for at least half an hour already. *Where were they going?* Most likely, they were headed right back to DiMeico's. More panic erupted in her belly. *What would DiMeico do with her?* That one seemed obvious, because, unlike before, now she had no bargaining chip. She knew where the money was, and they knew she knew it. Which meant DiMeico would soon know, and then he wouldn't need her anymore.

He drove for another ten minutes then slowed. She wondered if she should yell for help, but reconsidered. She didn't want some bystander getting hurt because of her. Not ever again. Eventually the car came to a stop. The trunk latch clicked and light spilled inside. He was standing over her, a cell phone to his ear. His mask was gone. She immediately recognized him as the man from DiMeico's called "Vargas," who had played and replayed Tate's video for her.

"It's Vargas," he was saying into the phone, clearly annoyed. "Where were you? . . . Well I had to handle it myself . . . Yeah. No, it's done. Hold on." He turned his attention to her.

"Whatever was in the box, hand it over."

Chloe hesitated. He groaned darkly. "Now, or I'll just shoot you and search for it myself."

Chloe pulled the business card from her pocket and gave her last hope away. She choked back a sob. *Jack. Jack, I'm so sorry.*

The man looked it over, and flipped it to the reverse. A thin smile stretched through his lips.

"Korrigan? I've got it. All of it . . . No, Grand Cayman, Fourth Bank of. You ready?" he asked, and then rattled off the account number. He paused, apparently listening. "No that's it. You should be able to—" he paused again. "Why your place? I can just head to the office and we can talk there—" Cut short, he waited, listening, and Chloe had the horrible thought that maybe he was receiving instructions on exactly how to dispose of her.

"Fine. Your place in," he glanced at his watch, "twenty minutes." He shoved the phone in his pocket and stared at Chloe, eyeing her with obvious indecision. Stepping back from the car, he paced for about a minute, clearly mulling something over. Then he turned towards her again.

"Well, you may have lucked out. I think I might need you, so that means you get a reprieve. For now."

"What are you—"

"Shut up and listen. Chances are I'm wrong and nothing's screwy and I'll be back here to get you in under an hour. Which would be too bad for you. But, if I'm right, and Korrigan's gone off on his own with this thing to take the cash for himself—I might not make it back here if things go *really* wrong. If that happens, someone else will be back to collect you. When they do, remember that name—'Korrigan.' If I don't get back, he's the reason why. I'm not sure it'll buy you much favor with DiMeico, but who knows?"

She laid there, at a loss for how she was supposed to respond to that.

"Got it?" Vargas barked, and she jumped a little where she lay.

"Yeah! Yeah, I've got it."

He sighed, taking in a deep breath. "Good." He slammed the trunk, ushering in the darkness again. Through the lid, she heard him.

"And you better hope he kills me. Because somebody's got to die today. And if it isn't me, it's most definitely going to be you."

FORTY-FOUR

Chloe had tried screaming, pounding, and even kicking out the taillights—all to no effect. With all that and still no response from anyone outside, it was obvious Vargas must've taken her somewhere remote. When he had opened the trunk, she could see she was parked under something, and that there was some tall vegetation, maybe a tree or two, nearby. But other than that she had no idea where they had ended up after all that driving.

Was Jack dead? Alive? Where was Riley? Was he staying with Jack, trying to keep him alive? That would be okay, even if he never made it to her in time. Better than okay. Jack had to make it. But there had been so much blood. So much.

Vargas would be back soon. And then it would be over. *She* would be over. Her newfound faith might be giving her a little more courage, but she certainly wasn't ready to go yet. Not when she and Jack were so close to being done. Not when she was so close to maybe, finally, having something real.

She screamed again and pounded harder, the skin on her fist aching with each blow, her bones already bruised and skin raw. *Please God, let someone—*

"Chloe! Chloe!"

Riley's glorious voice was muffled but strong.

"Riley! Riley! In here! In the trunk!" She resumed pounding and Riley answered, slapping his hand down hard on the lid's outside. "I'm here, I'm here! Hold on!"

She heard the sound of glass breaking and the latch popped as he released it from the car's interior. She pushed herself out, blinking as she took in the light, Riley burying her in an enormous hug.

FORTY-FIVE

Korrigan walked out of the elevator and purposefully strode down the hall. It was late. Other than the two idiots flanking him on either side, everyone was gone. He passed the unoccupied secretary's desk outside DiMeico's office and without slowing threw open the right double door.

The neon lights of Miami brazenly dotted the view through the large windows that were the walls of DiMeico's corner office. The man sat in a large camel-colored leather chair behind the extravagant black mahogany desk that was the centerpiece of the room. He sucked heavily on a cigar, smoke curling in no particular pattern above his head, contributing to the dusky haze surrounding him. The room was low lit, with only a porcelain lamp on a credenza behind DiMeico turned on. Shadows draped everything.

"Explain," Korrigan growled, planting himself in an aggressive stance in front of the desk.

"Funny. I was going to say the same to you."

Korrigan breathed menacingly. "It's after eleven. They've been holding me for hours in the basement. Why?" It was more a challenge than an actual question.

DiMeico puffed heavily on the cigar. "Sit down," he said gruffly, nodding at the oversized black-and-grey striped armchairs arranged in front of his desk. Korrigan seemed to consider refusing, but after a few moments, sat down, still tense, anger seeping from every pore.

"Well?" DiMeico asked between puffs.

"Well, what?"

"What have you been doing, Korrigan?"

"What—what have I been doing! I was doing my job. Then I get back from checking out a lead up north and these two," he barked, jabbing a thumb behind him, "usher me downstairs without so much as an explanation."

"Why were you up north, Korrigan?"

"I told you. I was following a lead. Vargas put me on to it."

"That is not what Vargas says," answered DiMeico, his face deadpan.

"What are you talking about? Where is he? He was supposed to meet me and never showed."

Slowly and intentionally, DiMeico slid a piece of paper across his desk towards Korrigan. "This arrived in my private email around six this evening."

Korrigan snatched up the paper and read.

To: R. DiMeico
From: A. Vargas
Re: Korrigan

Mr. DiMeico, if you are receiving this, chances are I'm dead. I'm guessing that Korrigan has silenced me in an effort to make off with your money—the $18 mil McConnaughey stole. I set this email on a delayed send, just in case I'm wrong about this. If Korrigan isn't trying to steal from you, it wouldn't be good for my health to say anything. But if he is, and I'm not back to delete it before 6, it'll go out and you'll finally know what's been going on.

Something hasn't been right with this whole operation. Korrigan's a professional—he doesn't make mistakes. But this whole thing, from McConnaughey's death to us losing his sister, has been one disaster after another. It just isn't the way Korrigan runs things. Unless he's running it that way on purpose.

Right after they stormed your house last night, I went back and reviewed the recordings we made of Chloe McConnaughey watching Tate's video. After several run-throughs, I saw it. She kept reaching for her neck—where a pendant we took from her would have been hanging—while Tate was going on about how to find the money. I pulled the pendant out and took a second look. Sure enough, on the back there are two numbers. One turned out to be the phone number for a private biometric deposit box company downtown. I figured the other was a passcode.

I called Korrigan, told him about it, and suggested we get someone down there right away to watch the place and be ready to move in case McConnaughey showed up the next day. He told me to keep it quiet. That he suspected a mole in our security team and that until we knew more, we should handle it ourselves. He said to be prepared to move on McConnaughey if she showed and that he'd provide support himself. Between the two of us, we figured we could handle it. What he said made sense, and the thing about the mole explained why everything had been going so badly.

I followed his instructions. And McConnaughey did show as soon as the place opened. I'd been keeping watch since before 5 from the roof of an office building across the street. But Korrigan never showed, and when I called, he just said he'd gotten tied up and would get there as soon as he could. He told me to handle it. So I did. After they'd retrieved the contents of the box, I shot Collings, but had to leave him behind. I took the girl.

I drove to a remote spot to put some distance between me and the deposit box location, and to get someplace where I could deal with her more privately. I figured I'd get whatever they'd found in the box, pass the information to Korrigan as soon as possible, then bring her in to you. She gave me a card with an account number, which I called in to Korrigan. He told me to dispose of the girl and meet him at his apartment to discuss what to do next to try to flush out the mole.

That makes no sense to me. I understand keeping it quiet until we actually had the money in hand—but after? And why kill her now? Didn't you want to see her first? The only reason to not tell you we'd finally gotten the money back is if Korrigan has no intention of giving it back.

So right now I'm sitting outside his apartment, finishing this email. I'm not stupid enough to move on this without some proof, so I'm going to try to get some. I don't know what he's planning—maybe to offer to cut me in, maybe to pin it on me, maybe to kill me. Anyway, if I'm wrong, you'll never see this. But if I'm right and something does happen to me, I want you to nail him. I've been loyal to you DiMeico—even now Chloe McConnaughey's sitting in the trunk of a car parked in the location contained in the attached map link, just waiting for you. And Korrigan has your cash. Make him pay.

At the bottom was a map link showing Chloe's location and photos of the front and back of the contact card for the bank in

Grand Cayman.

Korrigan broke the smoky silence hovering in the room. "This is not right," he fumed indignantly, his iron stare rising to meet DiMeico's gaze. "This did not happen. This," he said waving the paper, "is an absolute lie. Vargas never came to my apartment. I never said any of these things. Vargas called *me* a little before eleven. He told *me* that he'd found a lead in Port St. Lucie; somebody Tate had dealings with, but that *he* suspected a mole and that he would meet me there personally. Said he couldn't trust anyone else. Get him in here!" Korrigan barked, gesturing around the office. "Ask him!"

"We don't know where he is," DiMeico said. "But I think you do."

"What, you think I did something to him? That he's, what, dead? I'm telling you he's lying!"

"There is more," DiMeico said darkly. "While you were downstairs, we checked on your apartment."

"And?" Korrigan hissed, his eyebrows raised as if daring DiMeico to make further accusations.

DiMeico tapped a laptop set on the right side of his desk. "Tucked away in a spare closet. It took us a bit of time to hack it, but we managed in the end. There are some interesting emails. A confirmation from an overseas bank of a twenty million dollar deposit. Then a subsequent electronic withdrawal, deposited again who-knows-where. And then there is the confirmation of multiple one-way plane tickets purchased today: Miami to Berlin set three days from now; Miami to London in one week. Looks like you were covering all your bases, no?"

"I've never seen that laptop in my life," Korrigan said, an uncharacteristic anxious tone underscoring his words. "You think I'd be so stupid as to leave that thing *in my closet* if it were mine?"

"I think that men in a hurry often do things they would otherwise not do."

"I wasn't in a hurry. I wasn't doing anything but following Vargas's lead. He's the one that's behind all this. I just . . ." Korrigan trailed off, as if realizing something, then announced with a hard certainty to his voice, "He's framing me."

When DiMeico just continued staring at him, Korrigan repeated, "Vargas is framing me. Don't you get it!"

"Funny, he said you might try to blame him."

"I'm blaming him because it *is* him!" Korrigan said, shooting out of the chair. "Listen to me—"

"No!" DiMeico said ferociously. "You listen." His pupils were perfect black beads, trained intently on Korrigan. "It has always bothered me how Tate was able to pull this off alone. It bothered me how everything went wrong on St. Gideon. None of the explanations and excuses ever truly satisfied me. Before now, I shrugged off these nagging doubts, believing I was overthinking everything after Tate's betrayal. But in light of this new information, I believe I was right to wonder."

"Find Vargas. *Ask* Vargas."

"Vargas is dead." He made the flat pronouncement as if declaring an end to the matter. "In addition to the laptop, we discovered where you *attempted* to quickly clean up an enormous amount of blood from the carpet. Even moved a chair to hide what you could not clean. So much blood, Korrigan. More than someone would be able to survive losing. What did you do? Slit his throat when he was not looking?"

Korrigan did not answer.

"As I am told, the trip to Port St. Lucie would be a nice, two-hour drive up the coast. It would provide multiple locations to dump a body where it would not be found. Swamps, backwoods, rivers . . . endless possibilities. Convenient, no? Maybe you did take a drive up there, but it was not to meet Vargas, was it?"

There was shuffling behind Korrigan, as the two men moved to stand behind his armchair.

"We have checked everything, Korrigan. Your cell. Your car's GPS. Everything supports Vargas's email. I am so very disappointed in you. So very disappointed."

* * * * *

Korrigan's head was roaring. Everything was disintegrating. He barely heard DiMeico as his boss demanded that he return the cash immediately. *Where was it?* DiMeico was saying. *Which bank? What time zone? Was it open already? If not, they'd stay there until it was and then Korrigan would transfer the money back to Inverse, or else.*

Or else. But Korrigan knew this was not a matter of choosing between walking out or being killed. DiMeico was talking about the difference between being killed quickly, or being made to wish you had been.

"Are you listening to me, Korrigan?" DiMeico fussed. "Say something." When Korrigan remained mute, DiMeico rolled his eyes in frustration and said to the men behind Korrigan, "Take him back downstairs. Work him over. Bring him back when he's ready to talk."

This was it, Korrigan knew. It was either now or, truly, never. They'd taken his weapons when they'd grabbed him in the parking deck earlier, so he'd have to improvise. His chances weren't good. But they were a lot better than they would be once they got downstairs.

When Korrigan didn't move, the beefier man on his right came around the chair and grabbed his arm. With his other hand holding a gun to Korrigan, he directed Korrigan back around the chair towards the door. At first Korrigan made like he was going to comply, but once around the chair he pulled hard against the man's hold. When the man redoubled his pull on Korrigan, Korrigan reversed his momentum and used the man's force against him, driving a stunning head butt into the man's chin.

In a matter of seconds, everything came apart. Dazed, Korrigan's captor stumbled just long enough for Korrigan to snatch his weapon from him, shove him backwards, and fire randomly at him as a bullet, fired by the second man, tore through Korrigan's shoulder. Korrigan spun, firing on the second man, dropping him to the ground with a bullet through his center mass.

And then a hot white flash burned though Korrigan's core, and he dropped to his knees. A small red dot appeared on the belly of his crisp white shirt. His breath grew labored as he sank back against DiMeico's desk.

DiMeico grunted in disgust as he moved to the side of the desk, keeping it between him and Korrigan as a shield. He tilted his head, taking Korrigan in. Korrigan's head drooped limply as he grabbed at his abdominal wound with his left hand. His trembling right hand still held the gun, and he attempted to raise it. But the shot to the shoulder had apparently done too much damage. Only inches above the floor, his hand spasmed and dropped uselessly to the ground, the gun resting impotently in his open palm.

Sensing Korrigan's incapacitation, DiMeico slowly stepped out from behind the desk, his gun aimed at Korrigan's chest. "It will not end like this. You do not get to dictate this to me. I will get that money back if you have to stay in the basement for the next month. I'll keep you alive until you tell me what I need to know. But just barely."

With his focus still on Korrigan, DiMeico pulled his cell from his pocket and pressed the voice activation button. "Call Metzger—"

And in that one-second distraction, when DiMeico's eyes flicked to the phone out of habit, Korrigan directed every last bit of strength into his right hand, tilted his gun up and fired.

Another bullet from DiMeico's gun ripped through Korrigan, but it made no difference. Korrigan had been dying anyway. But he had done what he'd wanted to do. Though Korrigan couldn't see DiMeico's face, he could see the dark hole beneath the man's chin bleeding onto the Persian rug where his boss lay in a crumpled heap.

Korrigan choked, struggling for air that just wouldn't come as he slipped further down the desk. As the edges of his vision darkened, he gleaned a twisted satisfaction from the knowledge that, wherever he was going, he had taken DiMeico with him.

FORTY-SIX

It was her turn to watch over him now.

He looked smaller somehow in the bed with the IV and monitor attached. But he was out of the woods. Still weak, still sleeping a lot, but out of the woods.

The bullet *had* nicked an artery. Not only had it nearly killed Jack, but it had slowed Riley down, too. Thankfully, that morning before they'd left for Bio-Tite, Jack had convinced Chloe to take his GPS tracker. With that, Riley had been able to find her where Vargas had left her—parked under a shed on some remote property west of Doral, not too far from the Everglades. Riley had driven her straight to the U.S. Attorney's Office, because, come what may, she was done with running.

It had been a struggle to get anyone there to take them seriously at first. But when the name DiMeico came up, they'd been shuffled onto a higher floor and then into an interview room. She spent the next two hours telling their story to a riveted audience, but not before demanding protection for Jack, who'd been taken to the closest hospital by paramedics called to the scene at Bio-Tite. That hadn't been a problem, and, after assuring her that the hospital reported Jack was in stable condition, Chloe had told them everything. By the end, she was sapped of every last bit of energy she had. But she was done. Done with running. Done with lying. Done with carrying this burden and endangering people she cared about. If this meant extradition to St. Gideon or jail, she didn't care anymore. All that mattered was that she—and Jack—were done hiding. That they were free. And if this was what she had to do to get there, then so be it.

They'd wanted to put her up in a hotel, under a protection detail, but she'd insisted on going to the hospital, where she'd stayed at Jack's bedside for nearly eight hours, waiting for him to wake up. Once he did, they had explained as much as they could about what had happened before he drifted off again.

That had been at ten o'clock last night. She'd stayed over, as had Riley, who slept in a chair in the corner of the little room. He'd refused to leave, insisting he watch over them both. She knew he felt guilty about losing her and how everything had gone south—he'd apologized over and over—but she assured him it wasn't his fault. It was no one's fault. Well, no one except Tate.

She sighed and wondered how long it would be before she could really, truly forgive him. Or if she ever would. She liked to think that maybe, someday . . .

Jack stirred. For a moment, she wasn't sure it had been him. But then he shifted, groaning softly, and she bent over him, her ear close to his face.

"Jack?" she asked hopefully.

He rolled his head towards her and opened his eyes. "Hey you," he croaked.

"Hey you," she whispered back and dropped her forehead to his cheek.

"Miss me?" he said softly, still weak.

She lifted her head and smiled. "Just a little. It's good to see you up again."

"You okay?"

She nodded.

"What time is it?" he asked.

"Just after noon."

Jack's eyes flicked to the corner where Riley sat. "I see he's still here."

Their voices had apparently roused Riley, because he twisted in the chair and stretched. "Hey brother," he said. "How you feeling?"

"Like somebody tried to kill me."

"Yeah, well," Riley said, prodding Jack's good leg, "Pretty sad, really. Seem to remember that I got shot in the leg a couple nights ago. As I recall I just got up and walked away."

"Grazed," Jack emphasized. "Grazed a couple nights ago."

"To-may-to, to-mah-to," Riley grinned. "Look, I'm going to get some coffee—give you guys a minute. I'll be right outside if you need me, annoying that U.S. Marshall on your door."

"Thanks, Riley," Chloe offered.

"No problem. I'll let 'em know you're up, too," he said, nodding at Jack.

"He's really worried about you, you know. Won't leave," Chloe said, as the door closed behind Riley.

"It's not his fault."

"It's his fault you're still alive. Slipping that belt around your leg? It kept you from bleeding out."

"It also almost kept him from getting to you."

Chloe shook her head, no. "I told you. I was only in that trunk about twenty minutes before your tracker led Riley to me." She heaved a grateful sigh. "Thank God for Manny and his toys."

"Thank God you finally took mine, like I told you to."

Chloe rolled her eyes playfully. "Yeah, yeah. You were right. *Again.*"

Jack grinned. "So, have you heard anything new from the Feds?"

"No," Chloe replied, dissatisfaction in her voice. "Still nothing since yesterday. They said they'd know more today. Someone is actually supposed to stop by sometime soon." As she spoke, the lunch tray that food services had brought in earlier caught her eye. "You hungry?" Chloe asked, motioning to the food.

He said he was, so she set the tray out for him and helped him raise the bed to sit up. They talked while he ate, and by the time he was done, they had just about covered everything that had happened at the U.S. Attorney's Office.

"But you gave them proof—you actually *had* something," Jack said, just before taking the last bite of his dessert brownie.

"Sort of."

"That account number, even if the account was empty, is still something. Maybe they can trace the cash."

"Good thing they found your phone on you. Without those photos—"

A knock on the door silenced her.

"Mr. Bartholomew? Ms. McConnaughey?" a tentative female voice asked as the door opened a crack. "It's Assistant U.S. Attorney Christa Langley. You met me yesterday."

Chloe nodded at Jack, who called, "Come in."

The woman, in her early forties, was sharply dressed in a charcoal-on-black pinstriped pants suit. She extended a hand to Chloe.

"Nice to see you again."

"You too," Chloe replied, glad it was someone she recognized. They had promised not to send anyone Chloe hadn't personally met at their offices the day before.

Langley eyed Jack. "And you're up. That's good."

Jack nodded. "I'll be fine."

"Glad to hear it."

"So what's happening?" Jack asked.

"Sorry about that," she said, setting down her shoulder carryall and crossing her arms. "We've been busy the last twenty-four hours. You gave us a lot to wade through."

"And?" Chloe asked, her eyebrows raised.

"We looked into the St. Gideon murder investigation. There's been no extradition request, and we don't think there will be." She eyed them, gauging their reaction. "Pete Sampson is missing. They haven't seen him since shortly after you left the island. After he disappeared, his office started raising questions about the Kreinberg murder investigation—seems he'd made some pretty odd decisions about how to run it."

"Like what?" Jack asked.

"For one, he kept the entire department out of the details. Second, he explicitly ordered what passes for a Crime Scene Unit there to conduct no DNA testing on evidence found on the corpse or in her house, no fingerprint matching—other than the murder weapon, which was apparently a knife from your house. And he told his people not to contact the States to alert us to Kreinberg's murder, or to your suspected involvement, which is usually done as a matter of courtesy when Americans are murdered on foreign soil. Then there's the cash—when Sampson went AWOL, his department tried to find him, and took a look at his finances. He'd received more than $50,000 over the last few months from untraceable sources."

"DiMeico," Chloe muttered.

"That's what we're thinking," agreed Langley.

"So then maybe they'll find Sampson washed up on shore next," Chloe proposed.

Langley shook her head, the tight, brunette bun at the base of her neck not budging. "Doubt it. If it was DiMeico, and he wanted Sampson gone, that body'll stay gone."

"But they found Ruby," Chloe said.

"Ruby they wanted found," Jack countered, receiving a nod of agreement from Langley. "To frame us."

"It definitely looks that way. From what we can tell, the only concrete thing linking you to Ruby's murder is that knife from Chloe's house. But when you consider the whole story, the whole conspiracy, it's easy to explain how that could happen—why they'd use your knife and how they'd get it. And then there's the matter of the missing motive. You just don't have one. And none of the stolen items are traceable to you. The jewelry never turned up and as for the money, there was a deposit of around $1,000 made into one of Sampson's accounts the day after Ruby was found—"

"The cash stolen from her house?"

"Maybe. And then there's Sampson's suspicious activity, which even his own department admits is against standard procedure. We're communicating with their police about the whole conspiracy angle. I don't think it'll be long before you're dismissed from the investigation. You might have to have a phone conversation with their police, but that should be it. And you can do that from our offices. Their governor is mortified. This whole thing is terrible for their U.S. tourist business. I think it'll go away fairly quickly."

"What about the account? Tate's account?"

Langley nodded and ran a hand over her still perfectly pinned hair. "The money's gone. Bounced to another account we could trace, and then on to ones we couldn't. The first account was linked to the name 'Korrigan.'"

"The man Vargas was concerned about," Chloe offered.

"Exactly."

"So where is Korrigan?" Jack asked.

"There's been a development on that front, too. This morning DiMeico and Korrigan were found dead, apparently shot by each other, in DiMeico's private office. His secretary found him. Looks like somebody else was injured, too, but there's no sign of him. There's all kinds of evidence there proving Korrigan was trying to make off with money from the account, including a laptop that apparently belonged to Korrigan containing some pretty incriminating emails. Looks like he'd been planning this for a while. Maybe even with Tate. It's consistent with everything you told us about Vargas's phone call to Korrigan while he had you in the trunk. It appears Vargas just got in Korrigan's way.

"We also checked out Korrigan's apartment. There's enough blood—seems Korrigan tried to clean it up quickly, but not well enough to hide it from our lights—to suggest someone was killed there very recently. We're testing it against Vargas's DNA now. And, thanks to that double homicide, now we've got access to the records at Inverse. We're mining their computer files now, but they're encrypted—"

"I'll bet they are," Chloe said regretfully. "Probably Tate's doing."

"Could be," Langley offered with a sympathetic smile. "But we'll get there. Even the unencrypted stuff will be enough to do what we've been trying to do for years. Not just with Inverse, but maybe with some of its nastier clients, too. This could potentially put a lot of bad people out of business, or at least make it harder for them for a while. The good news for you is that with DiMeico and Korrigan dead, and Inverse telling on itself—"

"You're safe," Jack declared, and Chloe looked down to see his eyes fixed on hers. "There's no one left to come after you, and no reason for them to try."

"He's right," Langley confirmed. "Anything you might know will be superseded by the records there. We even found a copy of Tate's video in DiMeico's desk. And you don't have any information on the clients of Inverse, so you can't help us there. They won't consider you a threat if we don't need you two to testify."

"But the clients don't know that. What if they think we could hurt them—or that we have their money?"

"We're planning on giving a press conference this morning highlighting just enough to get you in the clear, but not enough to compromise the investigation. They'll know you don't have any damaging information on Inverse's business to share, that you don't have the cash, and that you won't be on any witness list if and when we make a case."

"Do you have to give our names?"

"We don't have to, but, unfortunately, we can't guarantee that your names won't eventually be leaked. And, if we don't say something now, it looks like we're keeping you secret because we still need you. DiMeico's death forced the investigation into the open much earlier than we would have liked. You should know that apparently someone leaked Tate's name to the press. About half an hour ago CNN covered the story—what they know of it anyway—and released his name. You weren't mentioned, of course, but still . . . Given the way this is coming out, a finely tuned statement from our office is the best way to take care of you both."

"So that's it?" Chloe asked, disbelief edging her voice.

Langley smiled. "A few more days and you'll be free to head back to your life. We'll keep in touch, despite what we've said publicly, just to make sure you're okay. But you're done running. Nobody is targeting you anymore."

For the first time in a long time, Chloe's entire body relaxed. It was over. Jack laced his fingers through hers and squeezed.

"I'm headed back to the office," Langley said, bending down for her bag before stepping to the door. "We'll leave the marshal outside for as long as you're here, Jack, and probably assign one to you, too, Chloe, until we tie everything up on our end. I'll be in touch," she promised and slipped through the door, closing it behind her.

"So," Jack said. "Now what?"

"I don't know. I guess, well, first thing I need to do is call Izzie as soon as we leave here. And Jonah—oh, that poor dog. I need to get him . . ." She drifted off, then said thoughtfully, "Do you really think it's over?"

He shrugged. "I don't know. Did you notice she didn't say anything about how we got you out of DiMeico's? I thought for sure we'd have trouble over that."

Chloe looked guilty. "I, um, didn't really tell them everything about *how* I got away. I just said I was able to run off when they got distracted. I didn't mention what was distracting them."

"Seriously?"

"Well, yeah, I mean, what difference does it make? Anyway, apparently no one's complaining. What are they going to do? Say that after they kidnapped me you didn't play fair?"

He snorted in amusement, nodding his agreement. "True. And they've got bigger concerns now. At least I'm hoping." They sat quietly for a minute or two against the sound of cool air blowing in from the air conditioning vents.

"So you're, uh, headed home, then?" he asked, breaking the silence.

She shook her head. "Not till we get you better. Then . . . yeah, I think it's time for home. What about you, Jack?" Her nerves tightened as she put the question out there, but this time not out of fear, but rather, out of hope. "You've got a life back in New York."

"Mmm," he mumbled thoughtfully. "I don't know. I don't think I'm done running yet. But maybe somewhere a little less exotic this time. Maybe somewhere like . . . Atlanta—"

And with a rush of relief, she bent over him, hugging him awkwardly around the shoulders, kissing him as she squeezed him more tightly.

"Um, ow," he mumbled.

"Oh! Sorry!" she said sheepishly, pulling back.

"Not complaining," he said, that grin riveting her, "just, well . . . ow."

That same rush of possibility she'd felt that night with Jack on the deck at Mendoza's engulfed her, and for the first time, maybe ever in her life, she didn't try to squelch it.

Then the door opened again and Langley's voice called out, "Um, excuse me, again?"

"Sure," Jack said, his own questioning glance matched by Chloe's. Langley's head peeked inside the door. It was obvious from her expression that something was off.

"What . . . what is it?" Chloe asked worriedly.

Chloe's concern must've been evident to Langley, because she quickly clarified, "No, no, everything's fine. You're fine. It's just . . . I've had a call come through from the office. Someone who says they saw the CNN piece and called us." She paused and held out her cell to Chloe.

"He says he's your father."

EPILOGUE

The barren cotton fields of Arkansas rolled by the windows of the rented SUV, one boring mile after another. *Boring, but safe.* Much safer than flying out of any airport in the U.S. Every mile was another little victory, another assurance that, not only would they never find him, they would never even suspect he was still alive.

It had all happened so fast, almost too fast, once he'd put Tate's video clues together. But because he and Tate had been planning something like this for so long before Tate turned on him, he'd been able to make a go of it at the last minute. And the pieces just all fell into place. Almost like providence.

Stupid kid, Vargas thought. It had been such a good plan. Tate had the access to the money; Vargas had the access to Korrigan. It was perfect: siphon off the money little by little, pin it on Korrigan, then disappear. Pinning it on Korrigan was an element Vargas found particularly appealing since he hated the self-important, egotistical little—

Vargas took a breath, calming himself. *Stop. He doesn't matter anymore. He's just a corpse on a slab somewhere now. He got what was coming to him, pushing me around for years like some idiot lackey without a brain.*

It really couldn't have gone any better. Vargas had known that all the evidence he'd planted would eventually make it into DiMeico's hands, and that, eventually, he'd take Korrigan out. He just didn't expect it to happen the same day he'd sent the email. And then, DiMeico dead too? It was almost too good to be true. Somebody up there must really like him.

According to the U.S. Attorney's press release he'd heard on the satellite news channel, they were all over Inverse now. So that meant they likely had his email to DiMeico. And once they found that blood, or what was left of it after he'd made it look like Korrigan tried to clean it up, they'd believe him to be dead. He'd drawn more than enough from his own veins over the last months to make it look like he'd bled out too much to survive. Cleaning it up had been risky, and had taken more time than he'd planned, but it was necessary to paint the right picture. Fortunately, Korrigan had bought into the story about Port St. Lucie. The drive had kept him away more than long enough for Vargas to do what he needed to do, including planting that laptop.

With all that, there was a strong likelihood that nobody—not the U.S. Attorney, Inverse, or any of its clients—would suspect him as anything more than another casualty of Korrigan's plan.

And Chloe McConnaughey had done her part. He hadn't expected her to be found so quickly. He'd actually considered that he might have to place an anonymous call to make that happen. *She must've had an extra cell on her,* he thought.

Still, it had played out all right. From the sound of it she'd gone straight to the Feds and spilled everything. If she'd bought the fake call he'd pretended to make to Korrigan in front of her, which she seemed to, they'd probably heard all about his "suspicions" of Korrigan from her by now.

It was strange how easy it had been to frame Korrigan. Even now as he retraced his steps, it was hard to believe. From where he'd left McConnaughey, he'd only had to walk a few blocks to meet the cab he'd called for on his throwaway phone. After the cab dropped him near his stashed car, he'd driven to Korrigan's apartment building and parked just down the street where he could keep an eye on the front entryway. Then he made the call to Korrigan about Port St. Lucie and waited for him to leave.

It was like Korrigan was following a script he didn't even know existed. Once Korrigan had left, it had been so easy to call to Tate's bank and transfer the money into the account he and Tate had set up to frame Korrigan. After a couple dozen keystrokes, the program Tate had shown him moved the money again and again until it ended up in an untraceable European account awaiting Vargas's arrival next week, where he would start over. A new continent, a new life.

And it was all thanks to Tate McConnaughey, and that greedy, great big brain of his. And his sister and her pendant. He nearly missed it on the video, watched it a dozen times before he'd noticed her reach for the absent pendant and the simultaneous flash of realization that had crossed her face. He'd pulled the pendant from her things and after seeing the back of it, figured that the numbers on the back might be a phone number. After one call, he'd known exactly how he'd be able to find them—because they'd have to bring her to open the box.

Granted, he'd had to scramble to make the Bio-Tite thing work. Without knowing exactly when they might show or how many they might show up with after the ambush at DiMeico's, he'd had to improvise. He'd been right, though. They'd moved on it the first chance they got. And the girl he'd used as a decoy—a junkie prostitute—was a brilliant diversion, if he did say so himself. He looked a lot less suspicious with her around, and especially with her dog in the car, though he hadn't planned that. He'd tied up that loose end, too, after leaving Korrigan's. They'd never find her or the car. Not now anyway. He hoped the dog would get taken in by her neighbors, though. Animals he liked. People, not so much.

He switched the radio from CNN. "*Don't You*," the '80s original, not the remake, blared through the speakers, the lead singer for *Simple Minds* pleading with someone not to forget about him. Vargas laughed and turned it up. *Ironic*, he thought, and laughed harder. Soon they'd all forget about him.

And that's exactly how he wanted it.

TO THE READERS

Thank you for reading UNINTENDED TARGET and taking a chance on a new author. If you liked the book, and I truly hope you did, please consider leaving a positive review on Amazon, Goodreads.com, and the like. Good reviews are essential to getting a book out there, and I would be very grateful for yours. If you do choose to leave one, let me thank you in advance for taking the time to submit it. There is nothing like word of mouth.

I enjoy hearing from readers and invite you to email me by visiting my website, **dlwoodonline.com**. You can also check out my CleanCaptivatingFiction™ Booklist—my recommendations of books by other authors that are not only engaging, but clean as well.

While you're there, don't forget to join my email list to stay posted on all new releases, so you'll know when you can grab the next installment in the Unintended Series.

Speaking of which . . .

COMING SPRING 2016

UNINTENDED WITNESS
Book Two of the Unintended Series

In the aftermath of Chloe's harrowing experiences with Inverse Financial, she finally decides it's time to meet her estranged father in the charming Tennessee town where he's settled down, while Jack tends to his own business out in LA. Unfortunately, Chloe's meeting doesn't go as planned, and, unable to face the mounting tide of secrets that have been kept from her, she decides to abandon the attempt. But when a murder investigation entangles her newfound relations, Chloe can't bring herself to walk away. Partnering with a young private investigator in her father's office who seems to have more than surveillance on his mind, Chloe works to solve the crime before it destroys the only family she has left and drives a wedge between her and Jack that is impossible to overcome.

Want a reminder?
Join my email list at my website: **dlwoodonline.com**.

And, one last thing . . .

IF YOU ARE LOOKING FOR HOPE . . .

My goal was to write this book in such a way that anyone who picked it up would enjoy it as a good story and a great thrill-ride, whether that person is a follower of Jesus or not. I hope that was the case for you. I also hope that if you, like Chloe, are feeling hope*less*, and you have never considered the grace offered by Christ, that you would consider it now. Though Chloe is a fictional character, the truth she realized when things were at their darkest in her story is real.

YOU are loved by the God that created you. So much so, that He chose to send His son, Jesus Christ, to be born and to die an undeserved death, rather than be separated from YOU because of your sin. But Jesus did not remain dead. He rose on the third day, defeating death and, in doing so, defeated it for YOU. How? Because now, by accepting this gift of grace from God, death can no longer hold you separated from God. Instead, one day, death will just be the gateway for you to an eternity of peace in the presence of the God that made you. Not only that, but when you accept Christ as your Savior from the consequences of sin, He will be with you here. Now. And you will build a relationship with Him during your time on earth that will offer more hope, peace and purpose, even in the most difficult of times, than you could find anywhere else. This has been true for me and it can be true for you. No matter what you've done, where you've been, or how far you've fallen, God still holds this grace out to YOU.

Please check out these scriptures that do a much better job of explaining this than I ever could: Romans 3:23; Romans 3:10; Romans 6:23; Romans 5:8; Romans 10:9-10; Romans 10:13; Romans 5:1; Romans 8:1; and Romans 8:38-39.

For more information, check out the "Find HOPE" link at dlwoodonline.com. If you are looking for hope, trust God. Confess your sins. Accept Christ as your Lord and Savior. Your life will never be the same.

53777073R00163

Made in the USA
Lexington, KY
18 July 2016